ALEX VEGA
and the
ORACLE OF THE
MAYANS

Book One

ALEX VEGA

and the

ORACLE OF THE MAYANS

BOOK ONE

D. J. Burchell

with M.A. Burchell

South Bay Publishing LLC

Printed in USA

Cover Illustration- Adobestock/Victor Habbick
Moon – 123rf/Constantin Sutyagin
Kids, Dog – 123rf Syntika82
Spheres – Adobe-Angela Harburn
World Map by 123rf-nezezon Vertes Edmond Mihai
Chichen Itza map by 123rf – Lesniewski
Cover Design & Underwater Map by ServicesForWriters.com
Glyphs by 123rf – Mila Gigoric
Z-con illustration by Pip Cherio

South Bay Publishing, LLC

ISBN 978-1-941952-10-8
Library of Congress Control Number 2017917413

3 4 5 6 7 8 9 10
Printed in the United States of America

iv

Dedicated to all dogs,
especially Buttons, Hey-U,
Casey and Samantha.

Z-con

THE WORLD

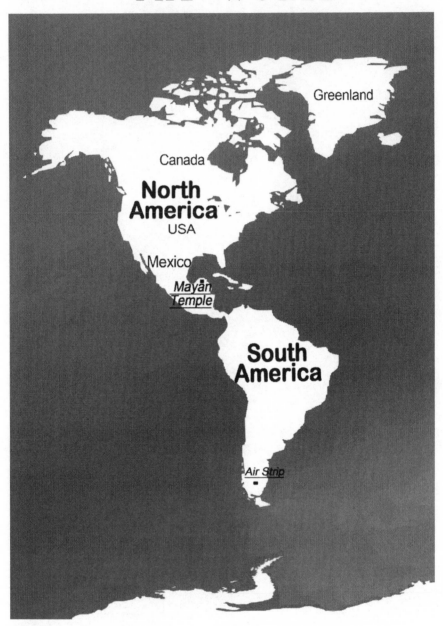

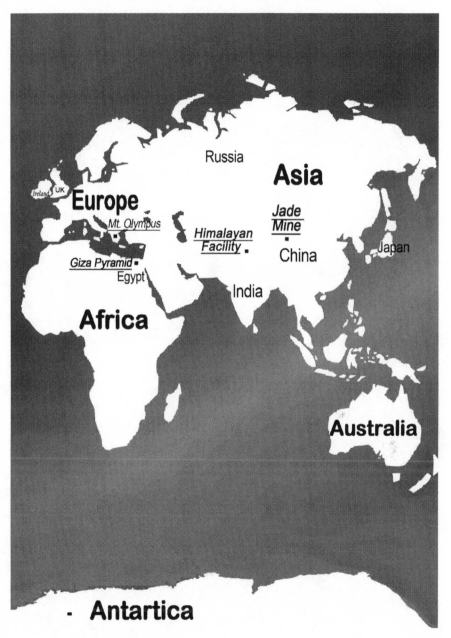

Training Facility

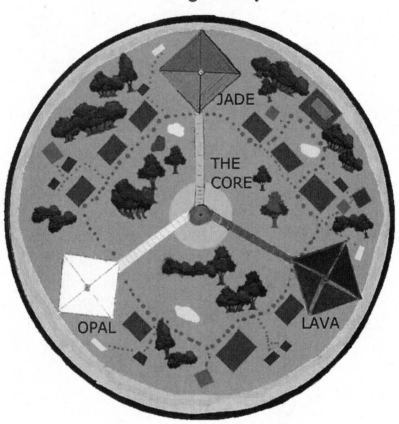

Mayan Glyph Numbers 1-9

| 1 | 2 | 3 | 4 | 5 | 6 | 7 | 8 | 9 |

Map of Mayan Temple

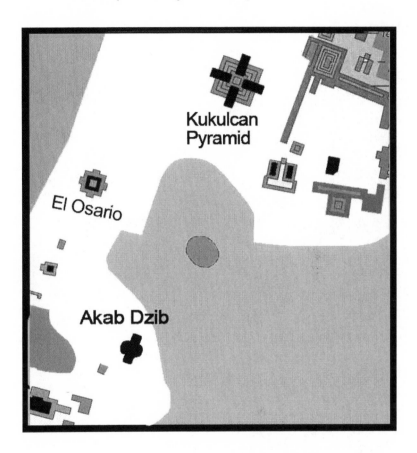

Mayan Glyph Numbers 10-18

10   11   12   13   14   15   16   17   18

PROLOGUE

B y the start of the twenty-first century, The Praefectus had served 4,712 years of duty.

Hundreds of generations of dedicated agents filled all the posts throughout those years– many serving their entire life without much hint of danger or adventure.

But their leader, Zeusra, knew from experience that every 100 years or so there was always some disturbance that would arise. With such a huge organization, and over so many centuries, one would have to expect it. And throughout the centuries, when the troubles came, Zeusra handled them.

It had been over seventy years since the last calamity – that one was for the salvation of The Praefectus. In the days since then, Zeusra had gladly updated The Praefectus history log with little of interest to report.

He had just started to make his latest entry into the log – this one was far more troubling.

A tall, young man burst into his office.

"Confirmation, sir. They're headed right at them."

Z leaned away from the book.

"Inform Lava Division," he said. He moved back to his log entry. "Tell them to use Bellon."

ONE

A few minutes past midnight, a man known as Carl Bellon popped out of a small hole that sat in the middle of a vacant lot. He flew up as if shot from a cannon and landed with a soft thump just a couple of feet away from the opening. His four-foot, six-inch frame absorbed the blow easily.

Both Bellon's ears perked when they detected the sound of a huge dog charging up to him from behind. He turned just in time to brace himself against the two large paws that came crashing down on his shoulders. After a few seconds of stumbling around with the full weight of the dog upon him, Bellon managed to steady himself. The huge, black and beige German Shepherd was almost as tall as Bellon and just as wide.

Bellon laughed and enthusiastically scratched both sides of the dog's big neck.

"Mercure! You old fella. How ya doing?"

Of course, like most dogs, Mercure loved having his neck scratched.

Unlike most dogs, Mercure understood everything that was said to him.

"Have you seen any sign of them?" Bellon asked.

Mercure tilted his head and shook it from side to side.

The crisp sound of a foot stepping onto a pebble pile came in from the roadway.

Both Bellon and Mercure snapped their heads around.

Alex Vega stepped further out into the lot. The light from the street corner illuminated him.

"I haven't seen anything either," he said to Bellon.

"Alex!" Bellon shouted. "Young, Alex. It's a pleasure to see you again. Why, the last time I saw you, I don't think you were much more than three or four."

"Alex, this is Bellon," Mercure said. *"A good friend of mine, and of your father."*

Mercure didn't actually say any words. Alex could just tell what Mercure was thinking. All the members of the Vega family could.

"I figured you were up to something," Alex said while approaching Mercure. "Every time you sneak out of the house, something happens."

"And you just had to find out for yourself. Is that it?" Mercure replied.

Alex nodded as he kept his eyes focused on Bellon.

Bellon stiffened his back.

"We must go to your father's house and get the family away from here immediately," Bellon said. "No time to lose!" He was already trotting away as he finished speaking.

Alex and Mercure easily caught up to him, and they all ran together through the cold, dark neighborhood.

Alex leaned down to Mercure and whispered, "We've got to leave just because this guy says so?"

2

"Trust him, Alex," Mercure said. *"He's never let me down in all the years I've known him. If he says, leave, we leave!"*

After two minutes, they reached the driveway of Alex's home. Bellon stopped and bent over, taking in several deep breaths. Except for Bellon's wheezing, things were as quiet here as they were in the empty lot they had just left.

"Go get'em," Bellon ordered between gasps.

Alex and Mercure bolted through the front door of the house and ran down the long hallway leading to his parent's bedroom, with Mercure leading the way and Alex right behind him. The bedroom door wasn't completely closed, and Mercure pushed right through it without slowing down. Mercure trotted up to the near side of the bed where Alex's father, Miguel, lay.

Miguel had one arm hanging off the side of the bed, and a part of his head hung off too, making it easy for Mercure to stretch up and touch his nose to Miguel's forehead, waking him almost instantly.

Alex banged into a small table before arriving at the side of the bed. Unfortunately, Alex's eyesight was not quite as excellent as Mercure's and ever since he turned thirteen, just three months ago, he was growing bigger and stronger than his balance could keep up.

"Something's going on, Dad," Alex said, reaching down to rub his right foot while jumping up and down on the left one. "A guy named Bellon is here. He said we've got to go."

Mercure added, *"We have to get to the portal as fast as we can. Everybody needs to leave, now!"*

Miguel sat up and turned on the lamp sitting on his nightstand. He reached over and softly tapped his wife on the head.

"Janet!" he said. "Wake up, honey. Listen to Mercure." Miguel slid back to his side of the bed and in one swift motion jumped up.

"What's going on, Dad?" Alex said. "Do you know why we're leaving?"

"Don't worry about the reason now, son," Miguel said. "Go get your little sister and bring her to the front door."

Alex turned around and headed away, limping slightly. Mercure followed him down the short hallway to Aura's room. Alex reached the bed in the far corner and tapped his little sister on the shoulder.

"Aura!" he said. "Wake up. We have to leave. You need to pay attention." Alex helped her to sit up.

"Why?" Aura whispered as she rubbed her eyes. "Are we going fishing again?"

"No, it's more important than that. We have to get out of the house right now! Come on."

Aura picked up a small doll that she slept with and stood up from the bed grabbing Mercure by his thick, brown collar. Alex and Mercure led her down the hallway to the front door where Janet came running up to them from behind.

As soon as Janet reached Aura, she picked her up into her arms, hugged her tightly, and turned to Alex.

"Why are we doing this?" she demanded.

"I really don't know, Mom," he said. "I'm not sure what's happening."

Miguel rushed up to Alex and stopped next to him. In his right hand, Miguel had a flashlight. In his left hand, he held a small flat tablet made of highly polished black stone. Miguel had always referred to it as a Z-Con. It was about half an inch thick and three inches wide by five inches long—about the size of a large cell phone. It had a small stone handle that folded down from its back surface.

"Everybody stick together," Miguel ordered. He bent down in front of Alex. "Son—don't let your mother out of your sight."

"I'll try," Alex told him.

Miguel turned to the front door where Bellon stood guard—Bellon had been watching the entrance the entire time.

Bellon cracked the door open and peered outside.

"Let's go," he whispered.

Mercure took off down the street ahead of everyone, his head darting from side to side.

Alex quickly forgot what his father had just told him, and he ran out past his mother, up the street, towards Mercure. As he gained on him, Mercure slowed down, allowing Alex to catch up. Mercure had protected Alex for so long that by now it was practically instinct to keep him by his side. The two of them ran down the middle of the roadway, leading the way for everyone else.

Then Alex sensed a change. A pressure closed in on him from all sides. Something was coming. He wasn't sure how he knew, but he felt certain of it.

Mercure was the only other one who seemed to sense the trouble approaching—Alex could see it in his eyes.

Mercure turned toward Alex and told him, *"It's going to be okay. Go back and tell your mother to hurry up."*

"What's going on?" Alex demanded.

"Just go tell her to hurry."

Alex ran back to his mother, passing Miguel and Bellon. They were running side by side, looking out for danger—one watching the left side of the street, the other the right.

Four shining green spheres appeared behind everyone, flying high on the horizon, and speeding in faster than a jet. They headed directly for Alex's home.

Alex slowed down, looking back toward the spheres. Mercure ran back and placed his mouth over Alex's hand, trying to pull him forward, toward the portal in the vacant lot. Alex ignored him.

The spheres reached the house and surrounded it on all four sides. They floated almost twenty feet above it, hardly moving at all. Alex stopped in his tracks to watch, and naturally, Mercure stopped too.

"Run, now!" Mercure told Alex, but Alex insisted on ignoring him.

The four spheres glowed brighter and brighter. They all let a small blue ball drop away from their centers. The balls didn't fall as fast as you would expect, rather they just drifted down to the four corners of the house—all landing at the same instant.

As they touched down, the entire house exploded into flames.

The flames reached fifty feet high—even higher than the spheres themselves, but they didn't seem to be affected by it at all. The explosion shook the entire road.

Alex looked down at Mercure and then turned to run.

"Let's get out of here!" he shouted back to Mercure over the sound of the roaring fire.

Mercure caught up with Alex and dashed past him. After a few seconds, Alex caught back up. Alex was running faster than he had ever run before.

The two of them approached the rest of the family, and Alex took a quick look back. All four spheres were moving again—right in their direction! The spheres would be upon the group before they reached the portal.

"Dad! Look!" Alex shouted ahead.

Miguel turned around, and as soon as he saw the spheres, he stopped and flung his arms around Janet and Aura. He raised his Z-Con into the air above everyone's head.

Alex and Mercure reached Miguel and threw themselves into the middle of the group—with Bellon ducking in behind them.

The flat top of Miguel's Z-Con began glowing orange. Janet reached up and grabbed the Z-Con's handle right below Miguel's hand—the Z-Con glowed slightly brighter.

The four spheres reached directly overhead and slowed to a stop. One of them let go a small blue ball.

Janet turned toward Miguel.

"Deflect, or destroy?" she asked.

"Deflect!" yelled Miguel.

Janet closed her eyes as if she was concentrating on something.

The blue ball fell within five feet of their heads when a small ray of white light screamed out of the top of the Z-Con. The thin beam struck the ball and sent it flying off to the side. It landed about a hundred feet away and exploded into flames—the enormous blast knocking everyone to the ground. Miguel landed hard, hitting his head on a small rock on the side of the road, stunning him into silence. Alex struggled to his feet and staggered over to him. Alex's legs were shaking slightly, and he shook his head from side to side, trying to get his mind clear. The rest of the group picked themselves up and reformed around Miguel.

Janet held the Z-Con by herself now, and its glow was much softer. She turned to Bellon and screamed, "Help me!"

Bellon grabbed the Z-Con with Janet. They both raised it above the group—the orange glow on the top surface just barely noticeable.

Over the roar of the nearby fire, Janet yelled to Bellon, "Will it work?"

Bellon hesitated a few seconds before answering. In a low voice, he said, "Maybe."

Another blue ball drifted down.

"One's coming," Alex shouted. Everyone lowered their heads.

The ball fell to within a few inches of the Z-Con before being flung off to the side, less than half the distance as before. A split-second before the ball exploded, Alex shouted out, "Duck!" Everyone turned their heads away.

The blast knocked everyone over again. Since the explosion was so close this time, they all felt the terrible heat. Alex picked his head up and saw everyone still tightly bunched together.

The explosion shook Janet, and she dropped her hand from the Z-Con. Bellon held the Z-Con by himself now, but no color came from it at all.

Mercure turned toward Alex and told him, "*Grab the Z-Con.*"

Alex, still laying on the ground, moaned, "Me? Are you crazy? My dad hasn't taught me anything about that thing!"

Mercure told him, "*Hold the Z-Con as high as you can and say the word 'omega' over and over in your head. Think about wanting to get rid of those orbs and those bombs! Picture it! Concentrate! Do it now!*"

Alex stared at Mercure for a couple of seconds. The events of the last few minutes flashed through his head. Alex knew he wasn't prepared in any way for this. But something took over. He wasn't sure what. He just took a deep breath and grabbed onto the top of Bellon's shoulders with both hands, pulling himself up off the ground, just as another blue ball began drifting down. He reached over Bellon's back and grabbed the lower part of Z-Con's handle. The top of the Z-Con instantly glowed bright red, and Bellon yanked his hand away from it as if the handle had turned to fire!

Alex turned to Mercure.

"Will it work without Bellon?" he shouted.

Mercure rushed over to him.

"*Don't worry about that! Just raise it as high as you can! Right now!*"

Alex raised his hand over the top of Bellon. Alex didn't have the strength to get completely to his feet, but since no one else was standing, he managed to raise the Z-Con above everyone's head. He said 'omega' over and over in his mind, picturing the ball disappearing.

As soon as Alex's hand stopped moving, a brilliant beam of red light shot out from the top of the Z-Con and slammed into the ball, burning it into a glowing white vapor. There was no sound at all.

Alex felt devastated by the effort. He relaxed his arms and let the Z-Con drop to his side.

Mercure stepped closer to Alex. *"It's not over! Keep concentrating!"*

Alex looked up toward the four green spheres still floating above him. One more time he raised the Z-Con high over his head. After concentrating again, four blue beams shot out the top of it—one beam for each sphere.

The blue beams pushed the spheres away, each one in a different direction. The spheres moved faster and faster away from the Z-Con until they were going faster than Alex could follow. Within seconds, the spheres flew out of sight, over the horizon. The beams shooting out of the Z-Con stopped.

Alex slumped over and sat down, letting the Z-Con drop. Feeling shaky, he placed his hand on the ground to help steady himself.

Mercure limped over and laid down next to him. Alex grabbed Mercure's back for support.

Mercure lifted his head and placed it on Alex's lap.

"Good job," Mercure told him. After a few seconds, he added, *"I wish I could tell you it's over."*

TWO

Alex had gone to bed the night before with very few problems on his mind. Just another unremarkable Thursday night—one that would surely lead to another typical Friday at school the next day. Nothing much to worry about.

Now, and only ten short minutes after Mercure and Bellon had warned the family, Alex looked back and watched his home burning to the ground. He sat motionless and confused, all the time feeling the enormous heat coming from the two large fires still raging a hundred feet away. And to add to his confusion, a constant buzzing rang throughout his head. He couldn't figure out what that buzzing was. Alex never felt anything like it before.

He looked around and saw his father Miguel lying against the street curb, surrounded by Aura and Janet. Slowly the fog in Alex's mind began clearing, and he realized that the buzzing, now much sharper, was his sister Aura. She was standing over their father, crying.

Alex finally mustered the energy to stand—giving his head a few shakes as he did. He exhaled hard, several times, trying to get the burning smell of the nearby fire out of his nostrils. He still felt the effects of using the Z-Con—every muscle, every bone in his body vibrated slightly. It was similar to the tingling he felt whenever the funny bone in his elbow got hit, but he now had that same sensation in every one of his muscles.

Looking around it occurred to Alex that even with his house exploded and a running battle between four green spheres and his entire family, not a single person in the neighborhood had emerged from their homes to see what was going on.

After a couple of last shakes of his head, he bent down and helped Mercure up onto his paws. Mercure's mouth was open, with just a few of his front teeth showing. It seemed to Alex that Mercure was trying to smile at him. A poor looking smile for sure but with Mercure being a dog, Alex thought it was a good effort. Even though Mercure was the entire family's dog, Alex had always been closer to him than the rest. It seemed all animals were attracted to Alex, although he never could figure out why.

Alex turned around sharply when he heard his mother call to him.

"Alex! Help me with Dad!" Janet yelled. She had her hands under Miguel's arm, struggling to lift him off the ground. Groaning, she said, "Help me get him up."

Miguel was recovering quickly from his head injury. The blood from the wound on his head had stopped flowing, and the wound itself was rapidly healing. Everyone in Alex's family seemed to recover from injuries quickly, so he wasn't surprised to see his father already on his feet.

Alex's heart raced while he slid past his sister to the other side of Janet and reached for Miguel. He lifted his father's arm as much as he could, but since Alex was more than a foot shorter than him, he was only helping a little. After several seconds of struggling, Janet had a good hold on Miguel.

Alex watched Mercure rocket by him, running toward Bellon. Bellon was on his hands and knees attempting to shake off the effect of the last explosion, and not looking like he was succeeding at it.

Alex felt that his father was now steady enough to stand on his own, so he slowly let go of him and ran to catch up to Mercure.

When Alex reached Bellon, he knelt down and touched his arm. Amazingly, Bellon bounced right up to his feet. Alex had seen this effect before on some of his friends when they sprained an ankle or had some other small injury. He would simply touch the area, and they always felt much better. But Alex had never seen anyone react as strongly to his touch as Bellon did.

"Okay," Bellon sighed. He steadied himself and put his hand on Alex's shoulder. "Grand now, Alex. Grand now. Thanks."

"What were those things?" Alex asked, releasing his hold on him.

"Never mind about that now," Bellon said, "You'll learn all about it soon enough. Let's get going before there's more trouble."

Miguel appeared behind them and placed his hand on Alex's other shoulder.

"Right," Miguel said. "Let's get everyone together and start moving." Miguel seemed to have completely recovered from his head wound. He glanced at Alex and almost in shock, shouted out, "Where's the Z-Con?" Miguel scanned the whole area in a panic. "Son? Where is it?"

Alex rapidly looked around and panicked when he realized he no longer had the Z-Con. He sprang up and desperately ran to the spot where he remembered holding it last, followed closely by Miguel. Alex dropped to his knees and started to reach for the Z-Con, but Miguel held him back.

"Hold on, Alex—I'll get it," Miguel said. He picked up the Z-Con and studied it carefully. After looking over every part of it, he knelt next to Alex and said, "It would be best if you didn't touch this anymore. Not until you learn how it really works. Okay?"

Alex nodded his head and said, "Sure." He stood up with Miguel, "But what is that?"

Miguel studied his Z-Con for a second and then looked back to Alex.

"Z-Con stands for Zero Point Field Condenser," Miguel explained. "It allows humans to manipulate certain fundamental forces of nature. Some people are better at using it than others. But you must be taught more about it before you begin working with it, okay?"

"Okay, Dad."

Bellon clapped his hands and said, "We have to get going." He turned in the direction of the portal. "Everyone, this way," he said, walking off with quick, purposeful steps.

Each member of the Vega family lined up—first Miguel, holding his arm around Janet, then Aura followed closely by

Alex. Mercure brought up the rear, keeping pace, but turning around after every few steps watching to see if anything was behind them.

Alex also kept looking back to see if there was anything else following them. Fear crept into his thoughts, and that was unusual for Alex. But this night he found himself having to work somewhat hard to keep himself calm. Every so often he felt that he might be losing that battle.

Far off, he heard the wailing sound of fire trucks approaching. Apparently, someone in the neighborhood had noticed the commotion after all.

Finally, Bellon reached the portal and stopped alongside it. Alex walked right up and peered down along with him. The portal looked like nothing more than a small hole in the ground that a raccoon could have used as a home.

"Ready, Miguel?" Bellon asked.

Miguel came over and plunged his Z-Con through the top of the hole. Its dirt sides instantly turned into highly polished metal, pulsating in color from silver to black. Miguel moved away, and Bellon bent down to inspect the opening.

With his head buried inside the hole, Bellon said, "Looks good!" He stood up. "Follow me, everyone."

Alex moved aside, and Bellon stepped forward. Bellon jumped slightly and fell right through the hole. The hole glowed red and grew wider for an instant—wide enough to let Bellon's body fall through without touching the sides. Totally surprised, Alex took a few steps back when he saw that happen.

Alex had seen many unusual things take place around his house while growing up, and whenever he asked his parents about it, he'd get, "You'll learn all about these things when you're older." But this, this disappearing through a hole in the ground—events were getting stranger by the minute. Alex stood looking down and shaking his head.

Miguel moved up behind Alex and took charge.

"Janet, you go through next," he ordered. "Take Aura with you."

Janet bent down, picked up Aura and walked right over the hole. In a flash, she disappeared.

Miguel turned back to Alex and Mercure.

"Okay, Alex. I'll go next," Miguel said. "Then it's your turn. Remember to step out of the way after you land." He tucked the Z-Con and his flashlight up near his chest. "Mercure, you follow him through."

Alex snapped his head up to Miguel.

"I can't go through that thing!" Alex shouted. He turned toward Mercure and then back to his dad. He slowly took another step back.

"It's okay, Alex," Miguel reassured him.

Miguel stepped over to Mercure and bent down to scratch the top of his head.

"We've done this many times over the years, haven't we old boy?" Miguel said to the dog. Mercure barked.

He stood back up and said, "Really, you'll be fine, Alex. Do you trust me?"

It took a few seconds, but Alex straightened up a bit and nodded his head.

"Of course, I trust you, Dad. I can do it."

Miguel patted Alex on the back. He walked over to the hole and disappeared through the portal.

Now that Alex was alone with Mercure, he desperately needed to ask him questions about what just happened.

"I don't understand any of this," Alex said. "What's a portal? What were those things? Where's everybody going?"

Mercure hesitated. Alex wasn't sure if he was going to get an answer, but after a few more seconds of thinking Mercure relented.

He looked directly at Alex and told him, *"A portal is what we use to get from one point to another. And as far as those orbs are concerned, well, those are very bad objects. Ones so bad, we thought all of them had been destroyed a long time ago. It looks like a few of them survived. You're going to learn more about them later. But right now, we have to get to safety. Now go on."*

The answer didn't satisfy Alex much. But at this point, he figured that there wasn't much to be gained by arguing with a dog, so he didn't press it. This was just one more time in his life he had to leave his home for another one. Too bad he thought—he was just getting used to this place. He walked over to the portal and stood over it, looking down.

The cold, dark hole gave no hint of where it led. But Alex had to jump. He drew in a long deep breath, closed his eyes tight, and took a big step forward.

Nothing happened for what seemed like an eternity to Alex, but in fact, only lasted about thirty seconds. He had no sense of falling, but then again, he had no sense of floating. He felt like he was standing as normal, but without a floor under him to push against. There was no sound at all, except his breathing—which sounded far more intense than normal due to the fact that he was breathing in and out just about as fast as a person could.

Finally, Alex shot up, head first, through the hole at the other end of the portal—softly landing a couple of feet to the side of it. He opened his eyes and found himself standing in the middle of a little room with a small amount of soft light streaming in from a doorway a few feet in front of him. His chest immediately tightened up, and he tried to force himself to calm down.

Then, in a flash, Mercure landed right next to him. Mercure moved forward a few steps and looked back at Alex.

"Let's go," Mercure said. He continued to the door, turned, and waited. But Alex still didn't move an inch.

Finally, Alex started making small steps forward. As he got closer to the door, it dawned on him that it was not exactly a door but more of a hatch—just big enough for an adult to step through without hitting their head. Alex worked up some courage and placed one foot at a time through the opening, with Mercure following right behind him.

Alex found himself in a gigantic circular room, brightly lit from high above, but from no obvious light source—the entire ceiling just glowed light blue. The room had light gray walls and a white floor. In front of him stood his father, mother, and sister, holding each other's hand. They were looking away, toward the middle of the room. Bellon walked ahead of them toward a large, round, white table in the center. The table had a huge base, and its top was so big that you could easily fit twenty or thirty people around it. It was the only furniture there was—not even a chair.

Alex gazed around. The walls were lined with several dozen hatches, side by side, and each one had a small unique

18

symbol above it. On the left side of the room, a large opening led down a long bright corridor.

Alex moved forward, and when he reached his father, he grabbed his arm.

"This is freaking me out, Dad," Alex looked around. "What is this? What are we doing here?"

Miguel gripped Alex's hand.

"Nothing to worry about, Alex, just stay close for now." He took a step forward. "Let's go over here."

Miguel started following Bellon toward the table in the center of the room with Alex remaining closely alongside him. Janet and Aura followed right behind. They all reached the table and stood around, waiting.

Alex suddenly realized that Mercure was not standing with them. He looked behind and saw Mercure sitting in front of the hatch that everyone had just come through. Alex signaled Mercure to come over to the table, but Mercure just shook his head and stared straight ahead. Alex called over to him, "Come on!" But Mercure remained perfectly still, not showing the slightest response.

A rather tall man came in from the corridor. He wore a white jacket that had no buttons, a white shirt, and spotlessly white trousers. The suit was extremely white, almost glowing. His weathered faced implied his old age, but the brightness of his shocking blue eyes implied a youthful spirit. His skin was dark, with a slight reddish tinge to it. Combined with his completely bald head, he presented a rather distinguished looking figure.

Alex studied the man from head to foot. He paused a little when he realized that the man wasn't wearing any shoes or sandals. Then it dawned on Alex that none of his family had shoes on. They had left the house in such a hurry that nobody had bothered to put on any shoes. He had his on since he had gone out looking for Mercure. Although he was amazed that his feet weren't cold at all. Even when they were running through the freezing streets to the portal, his feet felt fine.

The man glided to the section of the table directly across from Alex. In his hand he held a larger version of a Z-Con. It looked like the one that Alex's dad had, but this one had a slight amount of purplish gas oozing out from all four of its sides. He placed the Z-Con on the table, and the entire tabletop instantly turned colors—first black, then brown, and then finally a pleasant green. The top of his Z-Con slowly turned the same color, and it started pulsating slightly. The man bowed slightly to everyone and turned his attention to Bellon.

"Hello, Bellon. I hear from my sources..." he turned toward Mercure, nodded slightly to him, and then back to Bellon, "...that you had a small slice of trouble."

"Well, just a small chip of it, sir," Bellon said to the man. Bellon stood up a bit straighter. "But we're all safe now, ready to get on. Sorry to say the four of them are still flying around out there."

"I'm afraid you'll be going back to set that straight, won't you, Mr. Vega?" he said.

Alex looked at his father. Miguel's face was serious.

"Of course, sir," Miguel said. "We'll finish it."

As far back as Alex could remember his father always stressed to Alex that he should finish what he started. Now Alex saw that commitment in his father's eyes again. If those orbs were his father's responsibility, there was no doubt in Alex's mind that he was going to handle them.

Alex heard a commotion behind him. Another group of people came out one of the portals, several hatches down from the one he had just popped out. The people came through the hatch one at a time, a couple of seconds apart. It was a family of four, with a dog. Alex didn't recognize the breed of the dog, but it was a large one, almost as large as Mercure.

The family followed closely behind a man who was leading them. He looked remarkably like Bellon – right down to the pointed tips on his ears.

The group looked to be in fine shape, each member wearing a coat and shoes. There was a father, mother, and two twin girls about the same age as Alex.

The family stood silently at the portal entrance, studying the room. Their dog walked off to the right, toward Mercure. When he reached him, the two of them sniffed noses, and the dog sat down facing the table.

Everyone in the group removed their coats and placed them on the floor alongside the portal opening. They all bent down, took off their shoes and socks, and placed them next to their coats. Alex figured that the family must also have been awakened in the middle of the night, as each one was wearing pajamas. One of the girl's pajamas was lightly colored in a blue and yellow camouflage pattern. The other girl's pajamas had pictures of various colored soccer balls printed all over it. The girls were almost his height and looked to be around his age too. One had shoulder length brown hair and the girl with the camouflage pattern pajamas had very long brown hair. Both girls looked around the room with wonder and delight.

The group moved toward the table, and Bellon ran out to greet his look-alike.

"Hello, Tallon!" he yelled. "So glad to see you!"

The two of them hugged, and Tallon said, "Me too, me too." He slapped Bellon on the back a couple of times. "Considering the situation that is."

"Any trouble?" Bellon asked.

"No, not a bit of it," Tallon said. "In and out of Egypt quick as a wink."

They separated, and Bellon walked back to the table alongside Tallon, Bellon's face beaming with delight. When Bellon passed Alex, he patted him on the shoulder.

The newly arrived Egyptian family reached the table and they all clustered around each other. They seemed so familiar with the surroundings that Alex thought perhaps they had been here before. He wondered if many families had visited this place, and if so, why would his parents keep it secret from him? After all, there was a direct connection from his neighborhood to here. What would have been wrong with telling him all about it before now?

Bellon turned and addressed the tall man standing across the table.

"Well, that's that," Bellon said. "Everyone's safe and well as you requested, sir." He looked at his twin and turned back to face the group. "We'll be off now. Goodbye ladies and gentlemen."

Alex jogged over in front of Bellon and stopped him.

"Thanks for all of that tonight," he said.

"You're quite welcome, young Alex," Bellon replied. "Of course, I should be thanking you too, shouldn't I?"

He held out his hand, and Alex shook it for a couple of seconds. Then Bellon and Tallon headed away through the large corridor and disappeared down its length, chatting and laughing the entire way. Alex watched them leaving as he made his way back to his father's side.

The man standing across the table again spoke to the group. "I'll take the children and dogs with me to the Great Hall. I believe the rest of you desire to be briefed."

Alex looked at his dad. Miguel nodded his approval.

"Best be going with him, Alex," Miguel said. "Your sister will stay with us. Behave yourself now." When Alex didn't move, he continued, "It's all right, we'll be along in a few minutes. Go on."

With his home having been just destroyed, Alex wondered if this were to be the next place he would be living. It seemed to him that he had been moving his entire life. From him being born on a boat in the middle of the Pacific Ocean, to his sister being born in Mexico City, and then throughout all the cities of the world he had lived in after that, Alex was constantly on the move. He had never arrived in a place that he felt he belonged. Everyplace always seemed so temporary. Now it looked like he would once again have to adapt to a new home.

Alex stepped around the table and headed over to the tall man, joining the two young girls who were already on their way. As he walked, he looked back at his parents. The two dogs stood up in unison and sprinted toward the exit quickly catching up to Alex.

23

The tall man walked off toward the long corridor and headed out of the room. Over his shoulder, he said, "Please come with me, everyone."

Everyone followed right behind as ordered, with Alex finally turning forward when he no longer could see his parents in the room behind him.

Along the corridor walls, six statutes stood embedded in enormous cubby holes. Three large female statutes on the right, and three large males on the left. The statues were immense. Alex figured that with such large statues dedicated to them, these had to be people of some rather great importance.

Alex broke out from the middle of the pack and sprinted up to the man.

"Excuse me, sir, but who are these people?" he asked.

The man stopped and pointed to the left. "Well, the three on this side are my two brothers and me," he said. He turned to the right. "The ones on this side are the three women who helped form our organization those many years ago."

Alex looked at the twin girls, and when it was clear from the look on their faces that they didn't know anything about it, he asked, "Excuse me, sir, but who are you?"

"My name is Zeusra. Although people in the past have called me other names." He abruptly swung around with a stern look about him. "Some Egyptians called me Ra—some Greeks called me Zeus."

"But those weren't real people," Alex said skeptically. "They're made-up gods."

"Oh no! I was not made-up, I was real!" the man said. A second later a warm smile reappeared on his face. "A real human being, in fact. Not a god. And by the way, none of

24

the people along these walls ever claimed to be a god. Others made that up about us because they couldn't understand what they saw us doing." He signaled for the group to form around him. "Zeusra lived many centuries ago, and he did many amazing things. Great things. After that, like all things, he died."

Alex frowned for a second. He stepped forward again.

"How can you be here if Zeusra is dead?" Alex asked.

"I was created by Zeusra, using a very complicated..." He stopped himself for a second before continuing. "I'm a projected image of who, and what Zeusra was. I am in fact, everything that made Zeusra the unique individual he was."

Alex looked around trying to spot a projector. There was nothing to see but the smooth corridor walls and the statues.

"Projected from what?" Alex asked.

"Projected from the Zero Point Field," the man said. "And by the way, you can call me Z—everybody else does."

One of the girls spoke up.

"What's the Zero Point Field? Where is it, sir? I mean Mr. Z."

"You'll learn all about that soon enough when you get to the training community," Z said. He bent down and put his hand lightly on top of the little girl's shoulder. He smiled more broadly. "It would be best if you all just call me Z," he said. "Just Z."

He stood up, turned, and started heading down the hallway again. Alex walked right up beside him.

"What is this place?" Alex asked. "I mean, where are we?"

Z stopped, pondered for a short moment, and then stepped forward to address them again.

25

"We are in the interior of a mountain in the north section of the Himalayan Mountain chain. We carved out this facility so that we could have a place where all our people could come and interact with each other. They come here from all the countries of the world."

He took a second to gaze around.

"We had originally made the facility in the center of Mount Olympus in Greece with another base in Egypt. That's where we ran into too many people thinking we were some kind of gods. But we don't run into any people walking around these mountains, that's for sure. No more chances for misunderstandings."

Z turned and continued down the hallway. No one said anything for a few seconds, so one more time Alex felt the need to step forward.

"Where's the training community?" he asked.

"I'll let others tell you all about that," Z said. He reached a large open door at the end of the corridor and stepped to the side, motioning for everyone to continue through.

"For now, let's go in here and take a rest from all this excitement. You may move about freely but stay together and do not touch anything until I instruct you on how things work."

Alex went through first. When he looked out, he was astonished.

The room was larger than the baseball field at Alex's school—as a matter of fact, you could play four baseball games in it. On the far wall was a huge waterfall that started over a hundred feet in the air and fell all the way down into a large pool of water that had a few dozen people swimming around in it. The water fell right out of the ceiling—a bright, sky-blue ceiling that had what seemed to be small clouds slowly floating around it. The wall on the left side was translucent—not exactly glass, and not exactly solid. Through it, Alex could see a valley far below winding around a snow-covered mountainside—a mountainside that the room was located inside of. In the distance, Alex could see several people walking in and out of the room right through the translucent wall.

In the middle of the room were a number of distinct gathering areas filled with dozens of people. Most of the areas had perfectly manicured grass for floors, and several of the areas had immense statues at their centers—statues like the ones Alex had seen in the corridor. There were several large, open areas that people used to play a game, although from a distance Alex could not figure out what the game was. Many people sat in groups lounging about, eating, talking, and enjoying each other's company.

The right side of the room had other areas where small clusters of people sat around in circles participating in energetic discussions. There was also a large door that opened off to another long corridor.

Alex heard a single bark from a dog coming up from behind him. An instant later, he watched Mercure and the other dog race past him, heading toward the middle of the hall. They quickly joined up with several other dogs, all of them playing together. The entire group of dogs began frantically running around in circles, enormously delighted in meeting up with each other.

Z moved forward and stood in front of the children.

"Would you like some food?" he asked.

"What can we have?" both girls asked together.

"Well, actually anything you want. Do you have something in mind?"

"Cookies!" one girl said, followed immediately by "Pancakes!" from the other.

Alex was not particularly hungry, so to tease the girls, he thought of the least appetizing thing he would want to eat right now and said, "Cabbage!"

Z headed toward a table a few feet away.

"Well, let's go over here and get you all three then," he said.

Z sat down at the far side of the table. The girls sat together on a wide sofa directly across from him, and Alex sat down on a chair to their side.

A moment later, Z rested his Z-Con on the table and immediately three small slots opened in the middle of it. Three plates came up—one with cookies, one with pancakes, and one with a large serving of steamed cabbage. Z slid the plate of cabbage over to Alex.

"All for you," Z said, sitting back to watch. "Help yourself."

Both girls sat with their hands over their mouths, giggling.

Alex decided to go on with the joke, and he picked up a silver fork that rested on the side of the plate. He started eating quick, large mouthfuls, saying "Hmmm," repeatedly. The girls giggled louder and louder until they, and Z, were in full out laughter.

Alex's parents came strolling up to the table and sat down next to him, looking somewhat puzzled.

"Well, I see you've been well fed," Miguel said. "All getting acquainted, are you?"

Alex put down the fork and forced a last swallow before answering.

"We just got here, Dad. Come to think of it—I don't know everybody's name yet."

At that moment, the two other parents came up from behind Alex and sat down next to their young girls.

"Let's get some introductions going then," their father said, sliding over to his daughter, and putting his arm around her. "This is Maia." Maia moved in tighter against him.

Their mother moved toward the other daughter and sat down. She wrapped her arm around the girl's waist.

"And this one is Elecktra," she said. "But we call her Elka."

"It's a pleasure to meet you both," Miguel said.

"Pleasure to meet you both," Alex said. After a couple of seconds of hesitation, he added, "I'm Alex."

Both girls said, "Hello, nice to meet you."

Miguel tapped Alex on the arm.

"We need to talk to you for a minute. Come on with us son." Miguel stood up and addressed the rest of the group. "Be back in a few minutes."

Miguel, Janet, and Alex walked over to a small triangular table a couple of dozen feet away, and they all sat down across from each other.

"We have to go back and take care of those green orbs," Miguel said calmly. He added, "We'll have to be away from you for a little while."

Nobody spoke for several seconds. All the delight that Alex had been feeling ceased. His shoulders slowly fell, and his gaze switched between his father and his mother. He stood up and moved next to Miguel.

29

"What were those things, Dad?" he asked.

Alex's mother moved over and held his hand. His father put his hand on top of both of theirs.

"It's a little too much to explain all to you now son. Before tonight happened, we thought we'd have a lot more time to discuss things with you. But tomorrow you'll be heading off to a school that's going to teach you all about it. You'll be learning all about our people and what we do."

Alex looked at his mother, and back to his father.

"But how long? I mean, how long will I be gone?"

"About three months," Miguel said. "Then you'll be back to your mother and me for at least a month. After that, you can go back and learn some more."

"When are you going?"

"Unfortunately, we have to leave right away."

It stung Alex. He slowly moved back to his seat on the other side of the table and sat down in a daze. What in the world was going on? How could his parents leave him in this place? A place he didn't know anything about and, until a few minutes ago, didn't know anybody in it.

"Those things destroyed our house—all our stuff!" Alex shouted. He thought for another second before saying what was really on his mind. "They almost killed us, Dad! They'll kill you!"

Miguel rose and moved over to Janet. He stood behind her and took hold of her upheld hand.

"We know all about them now, Alex," he said. "That means we can handle them. You don't need to be concerned about it."

A new thought dawned on Alex.

"What about Aura?" he said to his mother.

30

"Well, you're over thirteen now so you can stay here, but Aura is still too young for all this," Janet said. "We'll take her to my sister in Puerto Rico, or maybe to Aunt Rosa's house in Mexico City – we'll figure it out." When she saw the look on Alex's face, she continued, "She'll be safe, Alex. We'll all be safe."

Alex's attention went back to his father.

"I don't want to go, Dad." He looked at his mother, "I don't think I can do it." When she didn't say anything, he turned back to his father and pleaded, "Please don't make me!"

Panic welled up in Alex that he never felt before.

"You have to go, Alex," Miguel said gently. He sat down next to Janet. "You'll meet lots of new people, and you'll make a lot of new friends. You always do, don't you? You'll take Mercure with you. He'll keep you safe."

Alex leaned back and dropped his head.

"Let me go with you, Dad. You know I can help. I helped us get away from those orbs, didn't I?"

"You did, Alex, and it was amazing what you did." Miguel leaned across the table and placed his hand on Alex's shoulder. "No one could have expected that from you." After a few seconds of contemplating, Miguel moved back to Janet. "But you have a more important job now. I wish I could tell you how much you need to learn, how much the future depends on young people like you learning everything they can about what we do."

After some more thought, Alex started to concede that it was going to happen and there was nothing he could do about it. They were leaving, no matter what he said.

31

His parents stood up, and they each reached for one of Alex's hands. Alex gripped them, and they all slowly walked back toward Z.

"You don't need to be concerned about us, Alex," Miguel said. "I wish we could tell you more about what's going on, but there's just no time right now." After a couple of more steps, they all stopped. Miguel bent down on one knee and held Alex's shoulders. "While you're gone I want you to learn everything you can. Help everyone you can." He hugged Alex for a second and stood back up, holding Alex's hand again.

They all continued walking, and just before they reached Z's table, Alex's mother bent down and hugged him for a long time. Alex loved her hugs—they were so tight and warm. Then she stood up and held hands with Miguel.

"We'll see you soon, Alex," she said smiling broadly. "I don't want you to worry. We'll be fine."

"Goodbye, son," Miguel said. "We're very proud of you. I'm sorry this had to happen so quickly."

It was hard for Alex to speak. "Goodbye," is all he could manage.

His parents walked away toward the corridor on the right. It looked like his mother was now crying. She stared back at Alex the entire time.

A moment later, his parents disappeared down the long length of the corridor.

Alex wondered what would happen to him next. In less than an hour, his whole life had changed. It just didn't seem possible.

After a few minutes, Z walked up to Alex and placed his hand on his shoulder.

"It's time for a rest," Z said. "Wouldn't you say, Alex?"

Alex didn't look away from the corridor. He just said, "Yes."

Alex looked around for Maia and Elka. He couldn't see them anywhere.

"Where is everybody?" he asked.

Z pointed to a table toward the middle of the big room where the two girls and their parents sat across from each other.

"They're having a talk," Z said. "I imagine they're discussing the same subject your parents just did."

After the two of them stared for a minute at the conversation happening at the other table, Alex turned toward Z.

"Where are we going?" Alex demanded.

Z thought for a moment. He looked down at Alex and then back up.

"Someplace wonderful."

THREE

Maia and Elka stood at the table quietly holding hands while they watched their parents walk away toward the exit. When the girls could no longer see them, they turned to each other and hugged.

Z gave Alex a small shove in his back, toward the girls. Alex slowly walked over to them and, still standing a couple of feet away, in a low voice said, "I'm sorry." It was easy to tell from the waver in his voice how much he meant it. Alex still felt the ache from watching his parents leave, and he knew what the twins were going through.

The two girls broke their embrace, held hands, and turned toward Alex.

After a few seconds of silence, Maia said, "Do you know where we're going?"

Alex turned back toward Z, and then to the girls again. Happy to be able to say something that would cheer them up, he smiled.

"Someplace wonderful!" he said.

Z walked up.

"Let's start now," he said. When he had everyone's attention, he turned and headed out the corridor on the right. "Everyone, come along, we'll have a rest. And in the morning, you'll start."

Maia and Elka fell in behind Z, followed by Alex. As they approached the corridor, two dogs came running up from behind. It was Mercure and the dog that arrived through the portal with Maia and Elka.

Alex leaned a little closer to Maia and asked, "What's your dog's name?"

Maia let go of Elka's hand and bent down to pat the dog's neck.

"Her name is Pandareos, but we call her Panda for short. She's a Bernese Mountain Dog," she said. When she noticed Mercure trailing behind Alex, she asked, "What's his name?"

"Mercure," Alex said. After thinking for a second, he said, "We don't call him anything for short. Just Mercure."

Alex wasn't sure if it was proper to ask someone about their dog's capabilities, but he just had to know.

"Can you hear Panda talk to you?" he asked Maia.

"Sure," she said. After a couple of seconds of hesitation, she looked up at Alex and asked, "Can you hear Mercure?"

"All the time!" Alex said. It was quite a relief for Alex to be able to talk to someone else about Mercure—someone outside the family that is.

Maia smiled, gave Panda one last scratch, then straightened back up. She looked at Alex's pajamas for a second.

"It looks like they woke you up too," she said to him.

As soon as she said it, the entire event flashed through Alex's mind again. He felt a little queasy.

"Yeah," he answered flatly. He looked off into the corner for few seconds before gathering himself enough to continue. "It was pretty rough," he said. He looked back to Maia. "Where were you when they got you up?"

"In Cairo. We just moved there last month. We've been moving all around Egypt for the last few years."

"I was just getting used to Cairo," Elka lamented, staring at Maia while she did.

Then Maia and Elka went back to holding hands, and everyone continued following behind Z.

The corridor they followed was long and high, perhaps thirty feet high, and had many incredibly tall doors along its length, none of which were open.

After a few minutes, Alex saw a large opening in the distance, near the corridor's end. As they approached it, the ceiling of the corridor sloped down to about ten feet. The group had arrived in front of the entrance to a long street, filled with storefronts of all different types. Clothing stores, food stores, furniture stores, in fact, every type of store Alex could imagine.

Alex could not understand the writing on the store signs, but he could figure out what each shop sold by looking at the incredibly intricate and beautifully designed window displays that adorned them. The closest store to them was an ice cream shop of some type.

When Alex and the girls stopped and gazed at the wondrous concoctions displayed in front of it, Z said, "Perhaps the three of you could use something nice. Would you like to go in?"

Without saying a word, Alex darted in through the doorway, followed closely by Elka and Maia. Right in front of them were several groups of monitors, each display made up of three screens. There was enough room in front of each display for one person to stand. Alex walked forward and stood in front of the first one, and Z gently moved each of the girls over to displays of their own.

As soon as the girls lined up, all the screens began flashing scenes of many kinds of interesting events. Cross-country skiing, bands playing in concert, people hang gliding, and on and on. Each scene flashed on the screen for only a few seconds before changing to something else.

While Alex watched them, he felt somewhat familiar with each scene he saw. Desperate for some instruction, he looked at Z.

"When something strikes your fancy just touch it," Z said to all of them.

A picture of a high-diver jumping off a cliff into the ocean appeared on the screen just to Alex's right. He quickly stabbed his finger at it, and the picture froze with the diver halfway into to the water.

Then Maia touched on a scene of horses running wild through a green meadow, flanked on two sides by enormous, snow-covered mountains.

Elka selected a video of cars racing around a huge oval track on a beautiful summer afternoon.

The moment they finished their selections, a round-faced young lady popped out from behind a long counter on their right side. She was dressed in a multicolor suit, wearing a hat decorated with several varieties of fruit—some of which Alex had never seen before. Her blonde hair was tied back.

"All ready then?" she asked, tying a short white apron around her waist. Near her left shoulder was a name tag that said 'KHARIS.'

Z stepped up to the long counter, peered through its glass front and said, "What are we waiting for? Time to choose a flavor!"

He looked back at the young lady.

"Hello, Kharis. First time for them. Perhaps you could help them decide."

"Well, it would be my honor," Kharis said. In her right hand, she held what looked to be several extremely thin sheets of highly polished stone. "Why don't you all just follow me down the line and pick something that amuses your tastes."

Alex jumped forward and looked at the counter. There were rows of small cups, many dozens of them, each one filled with colored ice cream.

"How do we know what they are?" Alex asked as he slowly strolled past the samples.

Kharis handed Alex one of the stone sheets.

"Place your palm on this and concentrate on the ice cream you're looking at," she said. Smiling, she offered a sheet to each one of the girls. "I think you'll like the effect."

Alex took the stone sheet with his left hand and gingerly placed his right palm in the middle of it. Nothing happened at first—not until he gazed back at one of the samples again. As soon as he did, his mouth burst into a concentrated sensation of cherry flavor, more powerful than Alex had ever experienced before in his life.

He looked at the next cup, the green one to the right. The sensation instantly turned to mint, with a hint of banana.

His head snapped toward Maia and Elka, and he shouted, "You've got to try this!"

The girls ran forward and started a long, slow walk down the counter, following right behind Alex—all of them smiling, with the girls periodically giggling to each other.

When they reached the end, Kharis, who was following right behind them, asked, "Have you all decided?"

"I can't make up my mind," Elka said. "There are so many good ones!"

Alex and Maia immediately agreed with her.

"Well, that's okay dears," Kharis said brightly. "I've been noting your reactions. I think I'll be able to get you something you'll like."

Kharis gathered the sheets from each of them and walked around the counter. Alex stood on the other side of the display case watching as Kharis stopped in front of a dispensing machine. She only worked it for a few seconds before she turned around with three large cups, each one filled with a different color ice cream. She handed Alex a blue one.

"Sky with Blueberry," she announced to him. She handed Elka hers. "Mint with Cherry." And lastly, she turned to Maia. "That leaves the Red Roses and Coffee for you."

Alex picked up the spoon embedded in his cup and scooped up a small sample. He looked at Z, wondering if any advice would be offered before he ate it. Z just smiled.

Alex put the ice cream in his mouth and, as anticipated, the flavor was magnificent. But as soon as the flavor washed over his tongue, an incredibly vivid picture of a man diving into the ocean popped into his head—the exact scene Alex

39

had just chosen on the monitor. Incredibly, Alex felt like he was the one diving! In his mind, he deeply saw and felt the entire event—the jump, the fall, the splash, even coming up for air at the end.

Between the flavor and the feeling, this was the most incredible thing Alex had ever eaten! He could not imagine that he would ever eat anything else more spectacular.

He looked over at the girls to see if they had started. Their faces could barely contain their astonishment. Their eyes seemed to sparkle! After a few seconds, they both yelled out.

"I'm racing!" Elka shouted. "I'm racing around a track!"

"I'm riding a horse!" Maia yelled back. "Look at them!"

Nobody spoke again. Everyone kept eating mouthful after mouthful.

It didn't take long for Alex to realize that the bigger the mouthful he took, the more intense the feeling he had of diving. He finished his entire cup in just a couple of minutes, slightly ahead of Elka and Maia.

When Elka finished her last spoonful, Z said, "Well, that looked enjoyable. We must get going now. Let's continue."

They all handed their empty cups to Kharis, and she exclaimed, "Everyone come back soon! Lots more to try!"

Z headed out of the shop, and Alex reluctantly followed behind him. Elka and Maia joined in—all looking a little sadder for leaving.

When Alex caught up to Z, it dawned on him that nobody had paid for the ice cream. He ran out in front of Z and turned around.

"We forgot to pay!" he said.

Z kept walking.

"There is no payment," he said. "Not here."

Elka jogged forward to Z.

"Why not?" she asked him.

"We use the Zero Point Field to make all the things we need. There's no cost."

Maia moved up next to Z.

"When are we going to learn about the Zero Point Field?" she asked. "Why the big mystery?"

"I'm afraid it's too complicated to go into right now," Z said. "Trust me—you will all be learning about these things soon. Any questions you have will be answered." Z moved in between the two girls on and put his hands lightly on top of their shoulders. He moved them forward. "Do you believe me?" he asked.

They nodded together.

Alex looked around for the dogs. Mercure and Panda were several stores behind, intently looking into a shop that appeared to be a travel agency.

"Not to worry, Alex," Z said without looking. "The dogs will be along."

Soon they passed the rest of the stores with Alex and the girls periodically stopping to gaze in the windows—and Z having to hurry them along each time.

They reached the intersection at the end of the street when Z turned around and held up his hand.

"Now everyone pay attention," he said slowly. "From this point on you will have to remain very quiet until I tell you. Understand?" He looked at each one of them until he received a nod.

Z continued with the children following closely behind, all three of them looking a little more anxious. They walked past several small rooms on their right, all having walls made of glass.

Alex observed two people in each room. One person in the center of the room wore a single piece suit that covered most of their body. The other person stood next to them holding up a stick, pointing it right at the suit. It all looked very formal and precise—whatever it was they were doing.

They quickly passed the rooms, and Z stopped in front of a door that led to a big office. The office had one desk and chair up against the far wall. Only a small lamp on the corner of the desk provided the light for the entire room, making it very dark. A large man sat behind the desk, and he sprung to his feet when Z entered with Alex and the girls right behind him.

The man wore a matching set of red pants and shirt. The shirt fitted snuggly around his large chest and shoulders. Alex read the name tag on it aloud.

"Joeks Burlm, Head Fitter"

"Hello, Z," the man said. "New recruits?"

Z reached behind him and nudged Alex and the girls forward.

"I know it's a bit late in the season, Mr. Burlm, but I've got three more that need to be outfitted for training," he said.

"Training outfits?" Mr. Burlm said. "I thought I was through with that for this period." He hurried around the desk and stopped just in front of Z. "But not to mind, we'll get them all sorted. I'm sure I'll be able to find enough material to get them through."

Mr. Burlm spun around, reached out, and shook Alex's hand. He stared for a few seconds, contemplating something, and then headed away towing Alex along with him. He marched to a round white dot painted on the floor near the right side of the room. Alex felt stunned. Things seemed to be happening so quickly.

When Alex reached the white dot, Mr. Burlm let go, and a beam of white light slammed down on Alex from the ceiling. He felt a slight pressure on every square inch of his body—even on his eyes. It came in from all sides—the same kind of pressure Alex felt when he dove underwater in a pool.

Within a few seconds, the light disappeared. Mr. Burlm motioned with his hand, signaling the girls to come over to him. He nudged Alex to the side and motioned for Elka to replace him on the dot. While the beam surrounded Elka, he lined up Maia to go next.

While this was going on, Alex looked around the room. Posters lined the walls, each one showing a person covered in different kinds of colored cloth. In each picture, the person held a different kind of helmet and goggles. Some of the people had large bulky belts around their middles. There was a title under each poster in a language the Alex didn't recognize but, as before, somehow felt familiar.

Ever since he arrived, Alex had that same feeling—everything he saw was familiar, but not familiar enough that Alex could completely understand. Like the rest of the surroundings he encountered so far, it was just not enough to be useful.

Mr. Burlm finished both girls and trotted back to his desk. Sitting down, he looked at a screen embedded into the center of the tabletop.

43

"All's well, Z. Measurements complete!" he said, studying the screen. "I should have them ready tomorrow morning. Stop by then, and we'll get everyone suited up."

"Thank you, Mr. Burlm," Z said. "Come along everybody."

Alex, Maia, and Elka fell in line and followed Z out the door, all of them jogging for a few seconds to catch up. Alex moved up alongside Elka.

"Did you see the pictures on the wall back there?" he asked.

Maia contemplated for a moment.

"Yes. Very strange, wouldn't you say?"

"Could you read the writing?" Alex asked.

"No. Not at all." Maia stopped and gave a quizzical look at Alex. "Could you?"

Alex kept walking, as not to display his confusion about the whole thing.

"No," he said. "I was just wondering if anybody could."

Z came to a stop at the doorway of another room that turned out to be a bunk room. Bunk beds lined the left side of the room, and small doors lined the right side—one door directly across from each bunk. The small rooms behind the doors contained a bench, sink, and several places to lay out clothes and things.

The bunk room looked like it could hold fifty or sixty people, although empty now. The lighting in the room was very soft until Z walked in, at which point several bright lights quickly turned on overhead. Alex looked around and jumped back a few inches when he saw a rather odd-looking man lurking in the corner.

The man slowly slid off the perch he was standing on and moved toward Z. Alex thought his walk seemed abnormal. And his body seemed abnormal. As far as Alex could tell, there didn't appear to be anything normal about him. Everything was a little off.

As the man stood stationary in front of Z, Alex realized he was not completely solid. It greatly startled Alex when the man began speaking to Z.

"Everything all right, sir?" the man asked.

"Yes," said Z. He pointed to the group. "We have these three students going through for training, and another one will be coming in shortly. Get them situated, and I'll be back in the morning to collect them."

The man, saying nothing, just gave Z a bit of a bow.

Z motioned for the children to come together in front of him.

"This is the room attendant. You can call him Qen. All the room attendants are called Qen. They're robot-like projections created from the Zero Point Field." He looked over at the man, "We specifically constructed this one to take care of all the students that come through here on their way to the training facilities. He'll get you settled in. Anything you need, any questions you have, you can go to him."

"Who else did you say was coming?" Alex asked.

"Another student. He's coming in from China. He couldn't go through with the group of students he was with the last time, but he's ready now. He'll be along in a few minutes, and he'll be going through with you three tomorrow."

Z put one of his hands gingerly on each of the girl's shoulders and then moved his other hand over to the top of Alex's head.

"You all have a good sleep now. You're facing a full day tomorrow."

Z smiled and headed to the door. As he walked out of the room, the two dogs came trotting in.

Panda sprinted up to the girls, nuzzling her snout into Elka's hand. Mercure zigzagged around them and made his way over to Alex and jumped up on his shoulders.

"Very exciting to be here wouldn't you say?" he said.

Alex stood as still as he could, trying to show Mercure how he didn't have to struggle under the load.

"Did you know about this place?"

Mercure nodded.

"How? How long?"

"Ever since I was very young! I grew up in here."

He dropped down off Alex's shoulders and started sniffing around the beds.

"Always wonderful to be back here. Just wonderful!" Mercure said.

Alex watched Mercure wander around for awhile and then gazed over at the twins scratching Panda's belly. After a few minutes, he sat down on one of the lower bunk beds and tried to think.

He knew nothing about this place! His parents had told him absolutely nothing. Even Mercure seemed to have been purposefully hiding it from him. All these years! His father would go away sometimes, and when he did Alex's mother always worried beyond what Alex thought was normal. Now he was getting a sense of what all the worrying was about.

His father must have been coming here—and then going off on some mission like the one he was sent out on tonight. No wonder his mother was so upset when it happened. And he remembered even more—like the time he was very young, maybe six or seven, and his mother went away for over a month. He now remembered how upsetting it was to his father, and how happy everyone was when his mother finally returned. Was she sent through here on a mission; was she in danger the whole time?

Elka and Maia came over to Alex and sat down on the bed directly across from him. Maia started brushing her shoulder length, brown hair into a pony tail.

Alex looked over.

"Did your parents ever tell you about this place?" he asked them.

"Sure!" Elka said. "Of course, seeing it now, I mean for real, it's more than I thought it would be. They never really talked about how everything worked and all. They did tell us that we had some capabilities that we didn't know about yet, and that in a few months we would be heading here to go to school to learn about it. And now, well, it's all happening sooner than they thought."

Maia chimed in, "And they told us about how sometimes part of their job was to go out and protect people, and how they came to this place to find out what they needed to do and all. They never went into much detail." She looked at Elka and then back to Alex. "I guess they didn't want to worry us." She stood up and turned away. "Until now, of course." She turned back. "I'm plenty worried now."

Elka nodded at her, and then at Alex.

At that moment, a boy came striding into the room. He had rather broad shoulders for his age—giving the impression of being in extremely good shape. He had slicked back, dark hair with a one-inch wide section of it that was completely white. That section ran from the front of the right side of his head all the way to the back. He carried a very large duffel bag slung over his right shoulder.

"Hello. I'm Dion," he said with what sounded like an Australian accent. He threw the duffel bag onto the bunk bed nearest the door. "Dion Yang," he said. "Been waiting long?"

Alex stood up.

"We just got here a little while ago. This is Elka, Maia, and I'm Alex."

Dion nodded to the girls.

"Well, again, hello," he said smiling. He turned to Alex. "Alex? I heard a few people talking about a guy named Alex. Wouldn't be you, would it? Something about fending off some orbs with a Z-Con. They all seemed very impressed with the whole thing."

Alex sat back down. Elka and Maia stared at him, interested in his response.

"I guess they meant me," said Alex sheepishly. "But it wasn't all that impressive really. To tell you the truth I didn't even know what I was doing. Until Mercure told me what to do."

"Who's Mercure?" Dion asked.

"That's my dog. Over there." Alex pointed toward the opposite wall. Dion looked at them and nodded.

Mercure and Panda had settled in across from the bunk beds. Both were curled up on the floor, with their backs lined up against each other.

Alex turned back to Dion.

"Z said that you were coming in from China, but you sound Australian," he said.

"Yeah, I was born in China, but I spent the last eight years in Australia. All over it really. My family lives there most of the time, you know for business and all. We traveled around a lot."

"What do your parents do?" Alex asked.

"They investigate things," Dion said. "Mostly research." He walked closer to Alex. "So, who's got what bunk?"

Elka jumped up on top of the bunk Maia was sitting on.

"I guess we'll take this one," she said.

"I'll take this," Alex said.

Dion moved over to the same bunk that Alex sat on and leaned against it.

"Then I'll take the top."

Qen came sliding over to the group. He held three bags in his hands.

"Here you are." Qen handed the bags to Alex, Maia, and Elka.

Alex opened his bag and took out its contents. A set of blue pajamas, and slippers.

"I assume you still have your equipment?" Qen asked Dion.

Dion walked over to the bed that held his duffel bag and picked it up.

"I've got everything."

Qen slid over to the small room directly across from Alex's bed and motioned for everyone to follow.

"Please change in these rooms. Leave your old clothes on the bench. If you would like a shower, stand over there." He pointed to a large white dot painted on the floor near the corner of the room. "You can clean your teeth by standing in front of the dot on the mirror. Any questions?"

Alex had a ton of them, but before he could speak Dion stepped forward.

"I'll show 'em around," Dion said.

"Very well," Qen said, pointing to the far corner. "I'll be over there if you need anything." He slid back to his perch in the corner, turned around and stared out, frozen.

"The whole thing couldn't be easier," Dion said. "The shower works only on your skin and hair." He moved toward the corner. "It ignores everything else, so you don't even need to take off your clothes. Watch."

Dion stopped on the white dot, and a light blue light came down from the ceiling. After a few seconds, he said, "It's best to push your hair around a bit to get it clean." He shoved his fingers into his hair. "That's about it."

He stepped away from the corner, and the blue light disappeared.

Then Dion stepped over to the mirror and aligned himself in front of a white dot painted on the right side of it. He leaned down a bit so that his mouth was on the same level.

"Best to open your lips as wide as you can." He smiled, and another beam of blue light shot out, illuminated his teeth for a few seconds, and turned off. He turned around. Still smiling, he said, "There you go, clean as could be."

50

Maia and Elka left and went into the next room on the right, shutting the door behind them. Dion retrieved his duffel bag and went into the room on the left, leaving Alex by himself.

Alex put on his new pajamas, took a shower, cleaned his teeth, and left the room. He walked over to his bed and sat down. Dion was already on the top bunk, leaning on his side with his head propped up by his hand.

"Everything work okay?" Dion asked.

"Yep," Alex said. He stretched out on the bed, ran his fingers through his dark hair, took a deep breath, and exhaled. "This is happening kinda fast."

Maia and Elka came over to the bed across from Alex. Maia very carefully smoothed out the blanket before they sat down. Elka started to put her long, brown hair into a ponytail.

"I wonder what will happen tomorrow," Maia said. She looked up at Dion. "Do you know?"

"I know a bit," Dion said. "I kind of had a head start. I was supposed to go with a big group several weeks ago, but I couldn't make it through. My parents did tell me a few things though. You know, what to expect and all."

Alex popped up, intently interested.

"What did they say?" he asked.

"Well, they started speaking to me about it a couple of months ago. They said I'd learn all the details when I got here. All they would tell me was a little history." He stopped for a moment as if trying to remember. "They said it all started about four or five thousand years ago. A group of people were taken from Earth and brought up to space, into

51

a ship, or something. Anyway, after a few years, they all came back down to Earth to straighten out some mess."

"Who took them up to the..." Alex searched for the word. "Spaceship?"

"They didn't give me all the details," Dion said. "They just said I'd learn all about it after I got here. Anyway, by the time they left the ship and came back down to Earth they had all learned about the Zero Point Field and how to use it."

"Did they tell you what the Zero Point Field was?" Alex asked.

"Only that it's a fundamental force that exists everywhere. And that if you had a device to access it, and you knew how to use it, you could make it do all sorts of things."

"Did they tell you how to use it?"

"No. Only that the Z-Con they had helped them to control it. Something about being made out of special stone, and that the stone helped concentrate the Zero Point Field."

"Why were those people taken up into the ship?" Alex asked.

"Well, they said because they needed help on the ship, and in return for the help they were treated to all sorts of things—you know, like learning how to use the Zero Point Field."

"Sounds like slave labor to me," Maia said.

"That's what I said!" Dion replied. "But my father said that they were all told what was going on, and they were given a choice to either stay on the ship and do the work or go back down to the ground. It seemed like a good deal to them, so most stayed."

After sitting up, Dion continued. "Then at the end, they all came back down to Earth and started straightening out the mess. It took all of them and their descendants a couple of hundred years to do it."

"What was the mess?" Alex asked.

"They didn't tell me. Just that when everything was cleaned up, they concentrated on another mission." Dion jumped down off the bed and stood with his back against the wall, leaning in slightly toward the group.

"It turns out there's plenty of nasty people out there in space just trying to find planets like Earth that they can come to and take over. You know—by force. So, everybody who knew how to use the Zero Point Field came together and decided to make a group that would dedicate their lives to protecting the Earth from invasion—if it ever came to that. My dad said they call themselves the Praefectus." Dion stood back up and continued. "So far, they haven't had many problems with alien invaders, but every generation has to be ready." After a few seconds, he said, "We're going to a place that's going to teach us how to do that."

"Why us?" demanded Alex.

"Well, we're the ones who have the aptitude. You see, anybody can use a Z-Con to influence the Zero Point Field, but the people in charge know which kids can influence it better than everyone else. They get those kids from all over the world and train them. It takes a few years to get trained. When they grow up, it's their job to be always ready."

Alex turned to Maia and Elka. "Did you know any of this?" he asked.

"Not all of it," Maia said, "Just the part about the people being taken up to the ship and coming back down later."

"I think our parents were trying to tell us the story slowly," Elka said. "So as not to scare us. I guess they thought they were going to have more time. Everything changed sort of suddenly."

"Why did they bring you here?" Alex asked. "Were you attacked?"

"No, but our parents woke us up and told us we were in danger and had to leave the house right away. Next thing we knew we were all jumping through a hole in the backyard."

"I never even noticed that hole before," Maia said shaking her head. "And I notice everything."

She looked up at Alex. "How did you get here?"

"Same thing," Alex said. "Only there were these green orbs that dropped bombs on us while we were trying to get away."

At that moment, they all noticed the room Qen standing silently at the end of the beds. The Qen didn't speak until everyone had turned their full attention to him.

"Time to sleep," he said. "I am turning down the lights. I will wake you when it is time to rise."

"Do you know anything about the Zero Point Field?" Alex asked.

"Time to sleep," Qen responded. "I will wake you when it is time to rise."

The lights in the room dimmed to almost nothing.

Dion jumped back up to the top bunk and rolled over.

"You'll have to tell me more about those orbs sometime," he said to Alex.

Maia reached over and pulled a loose thread off Elka's shirt before climbing up to the top bunk and lying down.

Alex lay very still on his side, looking out through the long rows of empty bunk beds. He didn't feel sleepy at all. How could he be? As hard as he tried, he couldn't ignore the questions that were bouncing around his head. In the last few hours he had lost his home, his family, and now he wasn't even sure where he would end up tomorrow. The last hour had been a fine distraction, but now in the quiet of the bunk room, the events of the day caught up with him. His thoughts jumped from one event to the other and back again—and every one of the thoughts scared him. With the way that he felt, he knew he wasn't going to be able to sleep at all.

At that moment, Qen took a small blue box out of his right pocket. He started to slide quietly from one end of the hall to the other, and then all the way back to his corner. By the time he returned to his perch, Alex and the other training recruits were deeply asleep. Qen returned the box to his pocket, and his lips curled into a slight smile before he froze.

FOUR

Alex cracked his eyes open to a bright, quiet room. Scanning around, he noticed Qen standing in the middle of it. He threw off the bed covers and jumped up.

The bunk above him was empty, but since one of the changing rooms against the other wall had its door closed, Alex assumed Dion was in there getting dressed. Mercure and Panda stood in the far corner, head to head, eating breakfast out of large bowls on the floor. Maia and Elka sat on the edge of their bunk, whispering to each other.

Qen came over to the bunks carrying three large duffel bags, exactly like the kind Dion had. Each one had a name tag on it.

"Change into these clothes and place your other things back into the bag," Qen said. "Please be quick."

He handed a bag to each of the girls and tossed Alex's bag across the bed to him.

Alex followed the girls across the room and continued to the same changing room that he used the night before.

Within a couple of minutes, he quickly changed into the new set of clothing the bag contained and then headed back to the bunks where Dion, Maia, and Elka stood around, waiting. Everyone at this point was dressed exactly alike—black sneakers, black pants, and maroon t-shirts.

"Any pointers for today?" Alex asked Dion.

"There's not much I can tell you from here on out," Dion said. "I imagine they'll be fitting your training suits next. I already got mine" Dion picked up his bulky duffel bag, shaking it a bit. He put it down and said. "It's a bit of a procedure, but don't worry. Everyone gets through it."

Qen glided over to them and pointed to the far corner of the room.

"If you would like, you can get something to eat over there," he said. "Please be quick."

Dion led the group over to the corner where a stack of thin stone plates sat in the middle of a long table. He picked up a handful of the plates, turned to everyone and asked, "I guess you know how these work, right?"

"Kinda," Elka said. "We had ice cream last night."

"Isn't that the best!" Dion exclaimed, handing out a plate to everyone. "Just place your palm on it and try to think of a picture of your breakfast." He placed his palm on his plate. "It all works by how well you can picture it in your head." He closed his eyes for a second and then put the plate down on a large white dot in the far corner of the table. A few seconds later a slot opened up in the wall. He reached into it and pulled out a tray containing orange juice and a bowl of some cereal that Alex didn't recognize.

Alex placed his hand on his plate and tried to think of the exact same breakfast he saw on Dion's tray. He put his plate down on top of Dion's, and when the slot opened, he pulled out his tray. The orange juice was there, but the bowl had just milk in it—no cereal.

"What gives?" he said to Dion. "I was thinking of an exact picture of your tray!"

Dion started to laugh. "Do you even know what kind of cereal this is?"

"No," Alex replied sheepishly.

"Well, give it a break man! You have to know at least what you're asking for!"

Everyone laughed, except for Alex.

He quickly placed his palm back on the stone, and when he put it down, a small plate of scrambled eggs came sliding out of the slot.

Maia and Elka made their breakfast next, and the four of them headed back to the beds to eat. They finished quickly, and Dion rounded up all the plates. He went over to the same slot that had dispensed them and pushed the pile through.

At that moment, Z came through the door.

"Good morning, everyone," he said. "Gather around now. Bring your bags with you."

Alex threw his half-empty duffel bag over his shoulder.

"You look well-rested, Alex," Z said. "How do you feel?"

Alex felt like he just had the best sleep of his life, but he still felt the same apprehension he wrestled with last night—before he inexplicably fell asleep that is.

"Fine, Z," he said. "Ready to go."

The dogs came trotting up to the group and received a few seconds of scratching from everyone.

"Splendid," Z said. "Let's get going." He turned toward the door. On the way out, he gave a slight nod to the Qen, who remained on his perch, stiff as a pillar.

Everyone once again traveled as a group down the corridor, back to the office of Joeks Burlm, Head Fitter.

This time, Alex saw a table in the middle of the Head Fitter's room. Three neatly stacked piles of uniforms sat on top of it—each one with a name tag. The clothes were the same type that Alex had observed being run through some testing the night before.

"All ready for you, Z," Mr. Burlm said. "Just have everyone take their stack to one of the first three rooms on the right."

Z motioned for Alex, Maia, and Elka to retrieve their pile. Alex picked up the one with his name on it. He was amazed at how light it was—practically weightless. He stuffed the entire pile into his duffel bag and slung it over his shoulder.

The two girls returned from the table, and the group once again headed back down the corridor. Z stopped in front of the first room they came across.

"While the three of you get situated, Dion and the dogs will stay with me," he said. "Elka, you take your equipment into this one." Z pointed to the next door over. "Maia, you go into that one."

Z walked on with Alex, and when they came to the next room, he turned and said, "You take this one. Good luck."

Good luck? Alex felt a small shudder go through him when he heard Z say it. Was this going to be hard?

Alex tentatively stepped into the dark, quiet room, and waited for a moment before putting his bag down. A bright light shot down from the high ceiling, hitting the floor, and illuminated the whole room. A man came out from the corner. Alex recognized him immediately.

"Qen?"

The man floated over to Alex with his hands folded in front of him. "Yes, I am Qen for this room," he said. "Please go into the changing room in the corner and take off your outer garments. Then put on your GEM suit. Please do it quickly."

"GEM suit?" Alex asked.

"Gravity-Energy Manipulator," responded Qen.

Alex took his duffel bag into the corner room and set it down on a small table that lined the wall. He rummaged through the bag's contents, searching for 'the GEM suit.' First, he found a pair of dark socks, a dark hood, and a pair of dark gloves.

It was obvious when he found what he was looking for. A GEM suit turned out to be a one-piece body length garment that was put on by stepping into the legs, inserting both arms into the long sleeves, and then closing the whole thing up in front. Alex took off his shirt and pants, put them into his bag, and stepped into the suit. When he brought the two sides of the front together, they merged almost by themselves into one piece. He could barely tell there was a seam there.

The suit was so lightweight that once Alex had it on, he could not feel it against his skin. It felt like it wasn't there at all.

He turned around and stepped out a couple of few feet from the dressing room. Qen came over to him, tugging here and there on the GEM suit. After a few moments, he seemed satisfied that there were no problems with the fit. Qen went into the corner room, retrieved Alex's bag, and moved it to a table in the center of the room. "Please put on the other items," Qen said. "Please do it quickly."

Alex went to the table and put on his new socks, gloves, and hood. The socks and gloves went on easy enough, but the hood was a very snug fit. It had only one wide hole in it, for his eyes—and that was just big enough for him to see out. Even though the hood covered his nose and mouth, it didn't affect his breathing at all—even in the slightest.

It seemed to be the same feeling as the GEM suit. It was hard for Alex to feel that he had any of it on him.

Alex turned back to Qen, and three beams of intense light appeared from the ceiling, hitting the floor a few feet away from the table. The first beam formed a two-foot wide circle, the next a triangle, and the third one a star.

Qen stepped over to the circle. Alex followed right along, feeling excited, wondering what the lights would do.

As soon as he stepped into the circle, he found out.

The white light from above turned into dark blue, and the GEM suit started slowly squeezing in on him. It got tighter and tighter. After a minute of the intense squeezing, Alex felt he couldn't stand much more. He darted his eyes over to Qen, and Qen lifted his right arm slightly.

Instantly, the light turned a different shade of blue, and the squeezing came to a stop. The entire GEM suit started changing color—first to dark brown, then to white, and then pulsing back and forth between the two. Less than a minute later, with a great flash of white light from above, the pulsing stopped, and the suit color turned into an exact match of Alex's skin—imperfections and all. Unless you looked very, very closely, you could hardly tell Alex was wearing it.

Qen moved over to the next symbol on the floor, the bright triangle. "Please step here," he said.

Alex was not sure he was going to do that. After all, what would be next? What if Qen made a mistake and hadn't stopped the squeezing in time, would Alex just be a puddle of goo on the ground right now? What if Qen made a mistake on this next procedure? Why should Alex trust him?

Alex didn't move. He just stared at Qen.

Qen looked back toward Alex and smiled slightly. He moved a couple of steps over and gently held onto Alex's right elbow.

"This reaction is not unusual, Alex," he said. "But the fact is, you must have some trust, or you will not continue onward. Are you willing to have that trust, or shall I call Z back in?"

Alex took a few deep breaths and gathered himself. He walked past Qen, over to the triangle.

"Let's keep going," he said. Alex reached the triangle, paused for an instant, and stepped into the beam. The GEM suit immediately turned rock hard. Alex couldn't move a single muscle.

Qen went over to another table on the other side of the room and picked up two objects. He returned to Alex with a long, heavy, metal rod in one hand and a short metal tube in his other. As soon as he reached Alex, he swung the metal rod as hard as he could into Alex's stomach. As the club came at him, all Alex could do was wince in anticipation of the blow. But nothing bad happened. He hardly felt it. When the metal slammed into the GEM suit, it absorbed the entire blow.

Qen put the small tube against Alex's stomach and took a reading. He then proceeded to hit Alex again, hard! He hit him over and over, on various parts of his body—each time taking a reading with the tube.

Alex felt almost nothing.

The beam of light disappeared, and the GEM suit once again turned soft. Qen moved over to the third beam and calmly said, "Please step onto the star." He looked back at Alex. "Please be quick."

Alex was just as concerned as the last move, but he wasn't going to show it again. He walked over to the star and stepped in. Qen moved up next to him.

"I will be hitting the suit again," he said. "I will have to ask you not to move. Can you do that?"

Alex still wasn't going to show him any sign of his intense apprehension. He looked straight ahead.

"Of course," Alex said fearlessly

Qen started hitting him, hard, in several places. Each time the metal rod impacted the GEM suit, it instantly turned rock solid, absorbed the blow, and immediately turned soft again. Alex remained perfectly still the entire time. Qen hit him once on each foot, once on each kneecap, once on each shoulder, and once on the top of the head. Alex's suit, gloves, socks, and hood absorbed every bit of it.

Qen went back to his table, put the rods down and picked up a heavy, metal board. He returned to Alex.

"Please punch this as hard as you can," he said.

Alex quickly swung his right arm forward and hit the board. His glove absorbed the blow. He realized that he could have hit it much harder and still would not have felt anything.

Qen lowered the board.

"One last test," Qen said. "Do not be concerned."

At that moment, the light Alex stood in started pulsing, and Alex began floating upwards. A hole in the ceiling opened, revealing a tube about ten feet wide. Alex drifted right up into it, continuing higher and higher into darkness. All he could see below him was the brightly lit star on the floor, with Qen standing right beside it. They were both getting smaller and smaller. Before long, Alex reached fifty feet in the air, where he abruptly stopped.

"Do not be concerned," Qen shouted up.

A split-second later Alex dropped. He accelerated downwards as if he had just jumped off a building. He closed his eyes and brought his hands up to his head, anticipating the crash. It took a couple of seconds before his feet slammed into the ground.

When they did, the entire GEM suit once again instantly turned solid. Alex felt the force of the impact flow around him, and then, as before, the suit immediately turned flexible. Alex stood there, straight up, and completely fine.

He slowly brought his hands down to his side, and it dawned on him what this was all about. The GEM suit would protect him during training. No matter what mistakes he made, no matter how dangerous the situation would become, his suit would ensure that Alex survived it. Under his hood, Alex couldn't be smiling any wider.

Qen headed away, toward the table that held Alex's bag.

"You can now take off your gloves and hood," he said. "Please keep your GEM suit and socks on and put your other clothing back on over them."

Alex walked confidently toward Qen—proud of his success with the suit. When he reached the table, Qen handed him a large bottle that contained a yellowish lotion. "Rub some of this on your hands every morning," Qen said. "It will protect them during the day, almost as well as the gloves. The technical name for it is Energy Tension Dispensing Solution." He turned back to the table and said, "But I believe the students refer to it as 'Yellow Goop.'"

Alex started putting his clothes on over the GEM suit. Qen turned to him and held out his hand.

"This is a pair of goggles that will fit over your hood when eye protection is needed. They are called Zeps." He put the Zeps down near Alex's bag. "When you wear them, everything you see will get recorded. You can retrieve those recordings anytime you want by using your Z-Con."

Qen turned to Alex and folded his hands in front of him.

"Wear your GEM suit and socks every day. You'll only use your hood and gloves when your instructors tell you to."

Alex packed up his equipment and turned back to Qen. Qen stood there staring. Alex thought about it for a second and then gave Qen a slight nod. He turned and started moving toward the door.

"One last thing," Qen said. "The suit cannot protect you from everything. Under extreme conditions, it cannot always keep you on this side of it."

Alex turned back.

"On this side of what?" he asked.

"Death."

FIVE

Z walked into Alex's testing room with Elka, Maia, and Dion following along behind him. Everyone had their GEM suits on under their other clothes. Elka was still wearing her gloves, and when Alex saw her, he put his right glove back on. He walked over to give her a fist pump. When Dion saw what was about to happen, he lunged at them.

"No!" he yelled, reaching out.

But he was too late. Alex and Elka swung their fists at each other, but when their two fists hit each other, it hurt! Alex was stunned. He had just done things that should have killed him, so why did banging his fist up against Elka's fist hurt so much?

"What do you think you're doing, fools!" Dion yelled.

Elka was shaking her hand when she looked over to Dion.

"What's your problem?" she said back at him. "Calm down. It didn't hurt that much."

Dion started to answer, but he stopped and walked away instead.

Z headed over to Elka and Alex.

"I think that's enough of that," he said.

"Why did that hurt?" Alex demanded.

Z gave him a puzzling look.

"I mean, why did that hurt so much, Z?" Alex asked, with much less intensity this time.

"GEM suit material does not protect well against other GEM suit material. Please remember that. Now, we must be going. Grab your bag, Alex. Everyone, follow me."

After a couple of more seconds of hand rubbing, Alex's hand felt fine again. He went back to retrieve his bag and noticed that Qen had returned to his pedestal in the corner.

On the way out, Z gave a slight nod to Qen who, like the Qen in the bunk room, remained perfectly still on his perch.

Alex stepped over to Qen and gave him another slight nod to see if there would be any reaction—but there was no response at all. It was unnerving to Alex the way the Qens turned on and off so quickly. They seemed very real when they were on, except for the fact that they were a little transparent of course.

Alex joined in behind everyone else and followed Z back down the long corridor. They passed the bunk room and then passed another room that looked something like a gymnasium. A couple of dozen people were occupied in it, exercising on various types of machines that were so complicated that he couldn't tell exactly how they worked. He stopped for a minute to watch, trying to figure it out. Dion stopped alongside him.

"I guess they'll have us doing that kind of stuff pretty soon," Dion said, as they both looked on. Alex shook his head.

"I used to run a lot, but I never exercised much," he said. "Do you think it's a big part of the training?"

"I think so. My parents were always getting me out to exercise. They said that I'd need to be in shape to succeed. I guess I know what they were talking about now."

Now Alex felt even more his parents should have told him about all this. Maybe he could have gotten a head start on getting into shape, as Dion did.

Z was soon far ahead of them.

"Please move on you two," he said softly—but both boys heard it as if Z was whispering it directly into their ears. They both looked at each other, startled. They hitched up their duffel bags and trotted ahead toward Z. Alex overheard Elka whispering to Maia.

"They're both rather inquisitive, aren't they?" she said.

"You'd think they never saw a stamina room before," Maia replied.

They reached a set of doors that were over ten feet tall, and when Z waved his hand, they opened almost instantly, revealing an enormous room inside. Z walked into the center and motioned for Alex and the rest to join him.

Alex led the way, but there was something disturbing about the room. There was nothing in it except for Z. No windows, no furniture, and just one small light in the center of the ceiling that barely lit the interior. The walls were dark, the floor was dark, the ceiling was dark, and the room cold—very cold. It smelled old.

The sense of foreboding that Alex felt when he entered the room was intense. He couldn't figure out why, but he saw that the room was affecting everyone else too. He worked up the nerve to keep placing one foot in front of the other until he reached Z. The girls, Dion, and the dogs followed. Everyone stepped warily as they approached Z. Even the dogs moved slowly.

Z increased his hand gesturing.

"Let's go, no dawdling," he ordered.

The group eventually formed a circle around Z with Alex looking straight on at him. Z dropped his arm to his side, and the doors slammed shut. He looked around the group and, with a humorous grin on his face, asked, "Well children, shall we drop fast or slow?" Dion spoke right up.

"Fast!"

Z immediately waved both his arms and the entire room dropped out from under all of them—faster than Alex thought was even possible. He felt his stomach rising in his chest, and his feet getting lighter against the floor. If it weren't for the fear he felt about what was going to happen when they stopped, it would have been a most thrilling ride.

"Woooooo!" Maya yelled.

"Cool, isn't it?" Dion shot back.

Alex's stomach caught up with the rest of his body and settled back into place, providing a small sense of normalcy. He looked over at Dion who was smiling. Obviously, he had done this before. If Dion had survived it, Alex figured he could.

A couple of seconds later the elevator slammed to a sudden stop. When Alex's feet hit the floor, his GEM suit hardened, and once again he felt the energy of the collision flow right through him. The second his suit relaxed Alex shouted out.

"Yeah!"

Then everyone shouted!

Alex laughed, stomped his feet, and clapped his hands as hard as he could. He looked over to the side and saw the two dogs floating slowly down to the floor.

When they touched down, he asked Mercure, "How in the world did you do that?"

Mercure first looked toward Panda and then at Alex, *"We've done this before."*

"You know, you could have told me!"

"Some things you should discover for yourself. More exciting that way, isn't it?"

Alex scratched Mercure's back and looked around for Z.

Z had not moved a muscle during the fall. He walked nonchalantly to the door and when he reached it, waved his arm again. The door instantly opened into another room— just as dark, just as dingy, just as smelly. Only much smaller. There were three holes in the floor; The first two had plaques embedded in the floor near the top of them. The plaques displayed the same strange characters that Alex had been noticing throughout his visit. The third hole looked like its plaque had been taken up and removed.

Standing at the apex of the three holes was a man wearing a long brown robe that draped all the way to the floor. He had reddish hair and dark blue eyes that seemed to glow from the soft light beaming down from the ceiling. His skin was a unique combination of brown and gold, and it also had a subtle glow to it in the pale light. He stood there with his hands crossed behind his back, slightly bobbing up and down on the balls of his feet.

"Hello Z!" he said. "Looking good! But why, of course, should that change, right?" He stepped forward and extended his hand. Z grabbed it and firmly pumped up it and down. Z turned to the group.

"Everyone, this is one of your master connectors, Master Kattan."

Master Kattan bowed deeply.

"Good morning, everyone," he said. "I hope you're all ready to travel." He remained bent over. Nobody was exactly sure what to do in response. Alex decided to bow, and everyone else followed along. Master Kattan straightened back up, and so did the group.

"Well then, I now leave you with Master Kattan," Z said. One by one he touched Maia, Elka, and Dion on the shoulder. "I'll be watching," he said. "Trust yourselves and all your new friends." He turned to Alex and motioned for him to follow along as he headed back toward the elevator. When they were out of hearing range of everyone else, Z crossed his arms in front of him. "If you need me, just ask," he said. "You'll soon learn how."

Z then grabbed both of Alex's shoulders. "Good luck, Alex. I hope you do well."

He turned and entered the elevator, waved his arms and the door shut behind him.

Alex felt a small shudder run through him again. Why was Z so concerned about him? Was there a problem with him being here that Z was hiding?

"Time to leave," Master Kattan said. He turned toward Alex. "That is, everyone."

Alex took the hint and headed back to the group. Master Kattan motioned for everyone to gather around.

"We'll be taking one of the original portals. They still work very well, but they are much less forgiving than our newer ones. I wouldn't let anyone of you go through one of these if you didn't have your GEM suits on. Our destination is about three thousand miles away. It should take you less than a minute to get there."

Master Kattan walked to the center hole in the floor and intently peered into it for a couple of seconds. Alex couldn't tell what he was checking for, but when Master Kattan picked his head back up, he displayed a wide grin and seemed pleased.

He continued, "A couple of rules to follow. First, keep your hands crossed in front of your chest the entire time. Second, breathe normally. Third, don't panic. If you start scraping against the walls or start tumbling, your suit will protect you. When you get to the end, move quickly out of the way so that the next person has a place to set down."

He strolled around the group, in and out, and even over them—he was after all a shade over six and a half feet tall. He checked that everyone had on their suits and gloves and that their duffel bags were secured over their shoulders.

Master Kattan moved to the front of the group and gave everyone one last look. He took hold of them, one by one, and lined them up in front of the central portal, with Maia in the front and Alex at the back. The dogs joined the line in front of Alex.

"Any questions before we go?" Master Kattan asked.

Everyone indicated that they had none, but Alex had several. He wasn't exactly sure how concerned he should be about going through an 'original portal,' especially the part about 'tumbling.' But he figured it would be best to remain quiet about it and follow along with everyone else.

"No questions?" Master Kattan asked again. "No? Then go ahead."

Maia jumped, soon followed by Elka. Dion paused a few seconds before jumping. Both dogs followed along—Mercure followed by Panda.

Alex moved forward, ready to go, but Master Kattan's hand darted in front of him, holding him back.

"Wait with me for a moment, Alex," Master Kattan said. "I have a question for you." Master Kattan swung his body between Alex and the portal. "How did you know how to repel the orbs that attacked you?"

Alex was unprepared for the question. He paused a couple of seconds before answering.

"Well…I didn't actually know what to do." He shrugged his shoulders. "My dog just told me to raise the Z-Con and think of saying the sound 'omega' in my head, you know like a chant or something. Everything else just happened by itself. I didn't know what was really going on."

Master Kattan pondered for a minute and stepped out of Alex's way.

"Go ahead," he said. "I'll be right behind you."

Alex stepped forward and jumped into the portal. It was the same, but somehow different than the first time he had done it. He was amazed how much light came in from the sides of the tube, and how the patterns of light formed. He laughed to himself about not paying too much attention to the light show the first time he traveled through a portal. He was just too scared to pay much attention then.

In what seemed like just a handful of seconds he landed on a stone floor—a section of the floor that was raised up a few inches above the surrounding area. Remembering the instructions from Master Kattan, he quickly moved aside. A few seconds later Master Kattan popped out of the portal and landed near the spot Alex had vacated.

The room was another cold dark square that stank with age. Three large, neatly piled stacks of cut stones sat against the wall on Alex's right. One stack was white, one was green, and one was black. The stones were the same rectangular shape and size as the stone that made up the top of his dad's Z-Con.

Master Kattan stepped over to the pile and picked up one stone of each color.

"We have these stones here to keep them energized. You must now all choose a stone that you will use during training. The white ones are Opal with fire-red streaking, the green ones are Jade, and the black ones are Lava rocks that have gold flakes embedded in them."

Alex pondered how he would choose. He couldn't think of a good reason to pick any one color over the others. Perhaps he should choose the black one—after all, his dad used a black Z-Con. Maybe that mattered. He wondered what would happen if he chose wrong—there certainly wasn't much to go on. Was it an important choice, or should he choose the color he liked?

Dion walked over to the pile of green stones. Alex, Elka, and Maia followed closely behind. Dion thought about it for few seconds and picked up one of the green stones from the top of the pile. He tossed it up and down in his hands a few times, contemplating.

"Yep, definitely Jade for me," he said.

"That was quick," Alex remarked. "Why Jade? I mean, you seem so sure of it."

"Well, my brother has

Lava, and he and I don't get along right now," Dion said. "I don't think I should be grouped with him when I get to training." He pointed over to the white Opal stones. "When I went through the first time, I had a bit of a problem with a bunch of people who used Opal, so I think I'll just stay away from them for the time being." He turned back away from the stones. "I just don't want to be causing any more problems."

Alex took a quick look at Elka and Maia. It seemed to him that they had the same thought. One by one, the three of them picked out a stone from the Jade pile. Alex turned to Dion, tossing his Jade stone in his hand.

"I think we'll all stick together on this," he said.

Elka and Maia moved in next to Alex, both tossing their Jade stones in their hands with slight grins on their faces.

Master Kattan put back the three stones he was holding and moved over to Dion. He put his arm around Dion's shoulders and turned to face the other three.

"You all have selected wisely," he said.

Everyone stood there for a moment, tossing their Jade stones up and down and smiling.

Master Kattan walked over to a hole in the floor about ten feet to the side of the landing platform.

"Put your stones in your bags and line up here please," he said.

Everyone quickly put their stones away and moved in behind him. Alex moved past everyone, up to the front so that he could peer into the hole. It wasn't a portal! It was just a big five-foot diameter hole in the floor. He couldn't see the bottom.

"We'll all jump down from here," Master Kattan said. "It's about forty feet. Not to worry, you'll be all right with your suits on." He motioned for Alex to jump first, as he was now closest to the hole.

Alex gulped hard and jumped. There sure was a lot of falling associated with all this, he thought to himself. After a second or two, he hit the floor and again the GEM suit did its job. Master Kattan yelled down, "All okay?"

Alex looked around and realized that he was standing in a long dark tunnel.

"Everything's okay," he shouted back up.

"Stand clear—we're coming down!"

Elka, Maia, Dion, and Master Kattan landed in succession, each one moving out of the way for the next person. Then, as before in the elevator, Mercure and Panda came floating down.

"You'll have to teach me that trick some day," Alex said to Mercure. It looked like Maia and Elka were saying something similar to Panda.

Master Kattan arrived, instantly turned, and led the way down the tunnel—holding his Z-Con out in front of him in his outstretched hand. It emitted a soft white light illuminating the path ahead. Alex followed right behind the master, trying not to bump into him in the low light.

"Where are we, sir?" he asked.

"We just landed in the center of the Great Pyramid of Giza, in Egypt. Now we're heading over to the Pyramid of Khafre."

"Why land here?"

"Because our ancestors learned that thick layers of stone intensified the effect of the Zero Point Field. When they came back on Earth, the first thing they did was help the Egyptians build these pyramids just for that purpose. Our ancestors used them as the endpoints of the first portal system they created—the ones we're using now. Of course, the Egyptians built them to bury their kings and queens, so you know, everybody was happy with the arrangement."

"So, they used the energy of the Zero Point Field to help them lift the huge blocks of stone?" Alex asked.

"Well, they certainly used it to make things easier," Master Kattan said. "These pyramids aren't built with as many blocks of stone as you would think. The Egyptians made the very outer walls of their pyramids out of blocks. Much of the inside is filled with rubble left over from the quarry where the blocks came. Now the Mayans, they made many of their pyramids completely out of blocks—no rubble. But, of course, they built them quite a bit smaller than the Egyptians did."

Master Kattan scanned the walls around him with his Z-Con while he continued.

"They couldn't let the Egyptians know about the Zero Point Field, so they came up with clever ways to make the Egyptians think they were lifting the huge blocks by themselves. And then they had to figure out a way to have the Egyptians build that empty chamber that we just came from—without anyone realizing it of course. A chamber that you can't access from the outside would have been puzzling to them."

He circled his Z-Con around in front of him, lighting up the tunnel walls. "Our ancestors created these tunnels without any help from the Egyptians, but that wasn't too hard."

A few minutes later they reach the end of the tunnel. Alex glanced up at the ceiling and saw another large hole. It seemed to be about the same height as the hole they just dropped down.

Master Kattan moved alongside Alex and looked up. "Master Ebo, are you there?" he yelled.

A soft female voice responded from above. "All ready, Master Kattan. Just let me know when."

Master Kattan said to Alex, "You're first. Just stand still, Master Ebo will do all the work."

Master Kattan shouted up, "The first one is ready to go anytime you are."

Alex remained as still as he could. Suddenly his entire body lifted. It felt like the floor was pushing him up, but when he looked down, he realized he was floating. He drifted higher and higher until after a few seconds he reached Master Ebo in another dimly lit room.

Master Ebo was as tall as Master Kattan and had very short blue hair—cut almost down to her scalp. From a small section in the back of her head a long blue ponytail flowed down—so long it almost touched the floor. She had soft, warm eyes that highlighted her pleasant smile.

Master Ebo was pointing her Z-Con straight at Alex's head. A beam of soft orange light emanated from it, and it seemed like the beam was doing the lifting.

She gently pushed Alex off to the side. When he was clear of the hole, the orange glow on her Z-Con disappeared. Alex fell the short couple of inches to the floor.

Master Ebo yelled back down, "Ready for the next one when you are, Master Kattan."

Master Ebo worked on raising the rest of the group, giving Alex the opportunity to tour the room. It looked exactly like the room they first arrived in, in the other pyramid. It also had three holes in the floor, with two of the holes having plaques labeling them. The third hole looked like its plaque had been removed.

Alex tried to piece together in his head what might happen next. This room was another link in the portal system. But what would be the next destination? It felt odd not knowing where they were heading.

One at a time Maia, Elka, and Dion raised up. The two dogs followed next. Master Kattan came up last, and Master Ebo gave him a slight bow when he arrived. Master Kattan bowed back, and the two of them walked directly over to the three holes in the floor.

"Okay, we have another portal jump," Master Kattan said.

Alex liked being first, so he headed over to the portal before anyone else could get there. Master Kattan looked up at him.

"Keep your hands crossed in front," he said, rising. "Jump away."

Alex peered down the portal.

"Where are we heading now?" he asked.

"The Kukulkan Pyramid at Chichen Itza," Master Kattan answered. Alex looked at him and shrugged his shoulders.

"It's in Mexico," Master Kattan said. "Now, off you go." He gave Alex a slight nudge.

Alex jumped, and this time he more closely studied the light patterns on the wall. For some reason, they started to look even more familiar. In reminded him of something in his past, something dangerous. But before he could figure it out, he landed.

This room was not dark and smelly. Bright lights shined in from each one of its four corners, highlighting the multi-colored walls. Blue, red, green, and yellow lines crisscrossed each other in a kind of a random pattern, extending all the way around the room—even covering the floor.

Alex stepped off the raised platform and turned around to watch the others arriving.

But nobody came.

Alex waited, staring at the landing pad. Several minutes passed, and nothing happened. Then every couple of minutes the center of the portal's opening glowed orange, but just for a couple of seconds. It was the same color orange that had come out of Master Ebo's Z-Con when she raised everyone from the hole in the tunnel.

This went on for several minutes with Alex standing there, watching. He stepped closer to the landing pad and leaned over it.

"Hello. Can anybody hear me?"

When no one answered him, Alex took a step back. He turned and started looking around the room. There was not much to see. He turned back to the portal just in time to see that Mercure's head and neck appeared near its opening and then dropped back down just as quickly. One minute later the same thing happened again.

Alex tried to think of something he could do to help, but nothing came to mind. He felt completely helpless.

Then Mercure popped out of the portal and landed hard on the floor. After a couple of seconds of steadying himself, Mercure started rapidly shaking his head from side to side. Alex leaned down and hugged him around the neck.

"I thought no one was coming!" he said. He stood back up. "What happened?"

Mercure licked Alex's hand.

"They couldn't get anyone through. Everyone tried, but as soon as anyone jumped into the portal, they were pushed back out. So, I was asked to try because I'm much smaller than a human. With both Master Kattan and Master Ebo using their Z-Cons together they hoped I might be able to get through."

"Well, I sure have never been happier to see you!" Alex exclaimed, "I saw you trying to come through a couple of times, but you never stayed."

"Every time I came bouncing back to them—the Masters changed the way that they were trying to get me through. I guess that last time worked. I don't think they'll be able to get anyone else through though."

Alex thought about it for a minute. There was another tunnel hole in the floor, off to the side—just like when they landed at the Egyptian Pyramids. But if Alex jumped down it, and there was no one on the other side to raise him back up again, he could be stuck there. He looked around the room again. There was no other way out—no doors, no windows, no markings that would give Alex any hope of finding a way through to the outside. He stood there, trapped in a room made of solid rock. His insides tensed up and turn cold.

Alex knelt down next to Mercure and said, "It doesn't look like there's any way out of here."

"There's always a way out of a situation. Take a deep breath and relax," Mercure told him.

Alex tried to slow himself down from thinking too quick. There had to be something they could do to help.

Mercure strolled around the room. In the far corner, he spotted a small wooden box. It looked hardly noticeable because it was painted in the exact color pattern of the room, making it blend into the wall.

He turned to Alex, barked, and looked back to the corner. Alex rushed over to the box and picked it up.

"Excellent!" he said. He inspected it from all angles. It had no lid or opening that he could detect. "Any ideas what it is?" he asked Mercure. "Ever see one before?"

Mercure studied the box for several seconds and shook his head.

"I wonder how it opens," Alex said.

"Well, I've noticed that if someone kicks something hard enough, it eventually opens," Mercure offered.

Alex shot him a stern look and then went back to examining the box. He tried pushing in on the sides. One side slid in, but just a tiny amount. He tried manipulating the other sides for a few minutes, but with no results.

"Okay...well, I guess maybe you're on to something," he said.

Alex stood up and kicked the box across the room. The side of the box that slid in before moved in a little more. He went over, picked the box up and tried pressing in on the other sides. They barely budged, so he dropped the box back down and kicked it again. A different side slid in a couple of inches.

Since kicking it seemed to be working, he kicked the box again on the third side, as hard as he could. After all, with his GEM socks on it didn't hurt him in the least. The box slammed into the wall, and this time it broke completely apart. Inside he found a white Z-Con. Alex quickly grabbed it and folded down its handle. He looked at Mercure.

"What should I do now?" he asked.

"Same thing you did with it when we were running from the orbs," offered Mercure. *"This time think about getting the others through the portal."*

Alex held the Z-Con by the handle, raised his arm above his head and silently said the sound 'omega' to himself.

Nothing happened.

He held the Z-Con out in front of his waist, and once again said the sound 'omega' to himself.

Again, nothing.

He looked over at the landing pad. The portal hole was glowing orange. Alex went over and pointed the Z-Con at it. He closed his eyes and thought the sound 'omega' again. The entire Z-Con instantly glowed a solid, bright red. Within seconds Master Ebo popped out of the portal and landed on the platform.

Master Ebo stepped next to Alex, and in quick succession, Maia, Elka, Dion, Panda, and Master Kattan arrived—with Alex pointing his glowing Z-Con at the landing pad the entire time.

Master Kattan looked at Alex.

"Tell me what happened!" he demanded.

Alex stopped concentrating and put the Z-Con down to his side. Its glow immediately stopped.

"Mercure found a box in the corner," he said. "It had this Z-Con in it."

Master Kattan took a deep breath and bent down to scratch Mercure's head. "Seems like we can always depend on you," he said and stood back up. "We tried getting through, but something kept bouncing us out," he said to Alex. "Something was taking most of the power away from our Z-Cons. Whatever you did seems to have overwhelmed it."

"But why was there a Z-Con just sitting in a box in the corner?" Alex asked.

"A long time ago, Z-Cons were not very reliable," Master Kattan said. "We always kept extra Z-Cons in the portal systems in case someone needed them. To tell you the truth it's been so long since anybody ever used one I forgot they were even there." He turned away from Alex with his eyes staring straight up.

"But what caused the portal to fail?" Master Kattan said, essentially to himself. "Yes, that's the question!" He headed to the other side of the room and walked around in a small circle, thinking. He contemplated for a couple of minutes, with everyone just looking on. He returned to the group and said, "We should continue. No telling if the problem was back there, or here. If we try going back, we might get stuck." He looked over at Alex. "That is, with no one there to help us out that is."

Alex gave a sheepish smile. He raised the Z-Con he was holding.

"What should I do with this?" he asked.

Master Ebo was already walking up behind Alex. She gently took the Z-Con out of his hand.

"I'll take it, dear," she said, folding down the handle and stuffing inside one of her robe's pockets.

Master Kattan and Master Ebo headed over to the far wall and started speaking to each other in hushed voices. Everyone else gathered around Alex.

"That was pretty amazing, Alex," Maia said.

Elka nodded and said, "We were all very worried about getting out of there."

Dion didn't say anything, but he slapped Alex on the back as he walked away.

Mercure trotted up to Alex. *"You seemed to be pretty good at connecting to the Zero Point Field,"* he said. *"Very unusual for someone as young as you. Good job."*

Alex leaned down and scratched Mercure's ear.

"Well, I guess I had a good teacher," he said.

Mercure let out a low rumble.

Master Kattan broke away from Master Ebo and stepped over to the hole in the floor that Alex had spotted before. He looked down for several minutes, thinking. Finally, he came back to the group.

"Let's go," he said. "Alex, I want you to jump down first and take a look around. If you have any issues, Master Ebo and I can pull you back up together."

Alex adjusted his bag over his shoulder, walked over to the hole, and stopped. He glanced up to Master Kattan for a second and then inched forward to the very edge. He took one last gulp and jumped.

Once again, his suit absorbed the blow as he landed.

He was in another tunnel. Alex steadied himself for a moment and peered down the tunnel's long length. All quiet—nothing seemed unusual.

Then, just a few feet in front of him, the ceiling came crashing down. It hit the floor with an incredibly large blast. Alex instinctively jumped back, trying to keep the rocks from hitting his head—as he wasn't wearing his hood.

It took only a few seconds for the collapse to stop. Alex stepped forward and tried to make out what was in front of him. The collapse was total. Rubble filled the entire path. There was no way to get through and no way to tell how far back the collapse extended.

It took a few seconds for Alex to notice that Master Kattan was shouting down to him. Alex looked up and called back.

"It's all blocked. There's no way through!"

"Hold on, Alex, I'm bringing you up," Master Kattan shouted.

Alex watched Master Kattan point his Z-Con down the hole, and he felt a force trying to raise him up—but he didn't raise a single inch!

Alex tried to help by pushing off with his feet and toes, but it had no effect. After a few seconds, he saw Master Ebo come over to Master Kattan's side and peer down. Master Ebo pointed her Z-Con down the hole, and immediately Alex started rising. He reached the top, and Master Kattan pushed him to the side. He touched down on the edge of the hole.

"What happened?" Alex asked, "Why did it take both of you to get me back?"

The look of concern he saw on Master Kattan's face was frightening. It took Master Kattan a few seconds to answer.

"Something is changing the strength of the Zero Point Field in this area. It's strange. I don't think we've ever encountered this before." He looked toward Master Ebo. "We need to move out of here, fast!"

"How?" Alex asked. "The tunnel's blocked."

Master Ebo looked over to the side of the room.

"We need to go through that wall," she said. She pointed her Z-Con at the wall, and it started vibrating wildly, making a thunderous, shrieking noise.

Maia and Elka held hands and ran to the other side of the room. Alex grabbed Dion by the top of his shoulder, and the two of them sprinted over to the girls.

Master Kattan raised his Z-Con and pointed it at the wall, trying to assist Master Ebo in her efforts. The vibration and the noise level increased. After a few minutes, they both lowered their Z-Cons. The vibration and the noise stopped.

"Perhaps we should have young Alex assist us," Master Ebo said.

Master Kattan looked over to Alex and then back to the wall. He pondered for a minute.

"Well, we have to get out of here somehow," he said. "I suppose we should give it a try." He turned to Alex. "Sorry to have to ask you to do this."

"Absolutely," Alex said. "It's fine. Give me a second to put on my hood and gloves."

Master Kattan turned to the others and said, "Best be putting yours on too. I'm not sure of what the effect of using three Z-Cons is going have on that wall."

While everyone suited up, Master Ebo took out the Z-Con she had in her pocket, folded down the handle, and handed it to Alex.

"Point it at the same place we do," she said. "Concentrate on what you want to happen. Don't try to think of how you want it to be accomplished. Just think of wanting to have an exit created so you can get to the outside of this pyramid. When you have that firmly in your mind, say the word 'omega' in your head again." Master Ebo moved to Alex's side before continuing. "Omega is one of the basic sounds that help a Z-Con tune into to your thought's frequencies, so just use that one for now."

Master Kattan pointed his Z-Con at the wall. "All ready?" he asked the two of them.

Both Master Ebo and Alex raised their Z-Cons and pointed them at the wall. Master Kattan's Z-Con started glowing first, followed by Master Ebo's. The same vibration and horrible noise started again. Alex raised his Z-Con, but it didn't do anything. He concentrated as hard as he could, but nothing happened.

Over the noise, Master Ebo shouted, "Remember, Alex, don't think of how you want it to happen, just that you want an exit! Be mindful of your surroundings and relax."

Alex did his best to relax. He started to think of how relieved he would be when the exit opened, and how joyous everyone else would be. Then he concentrated on the sound of the word 'omega' again.

At that moment, his Z-Con started glowing bright red. Almost immediately, a large hole opened near the center of the wall. A seven-foot square section of stones powerfully ejected outwards into an open space just outside the pyramid.

They all lowered their Z-Cons at the same moment. Master Kattan turned back toward everyone.

"Let's go!" he said. "Quickly! Quickly!"

The hole was big enough for everyone to run through. Alex was amazed at how long the hole was to the outside—almost sixty feet.

Alex reached the end of the tunnel and stepped out to look around. It was the middle of the night in this part of the world, and they were all standing in an enormous empty courtyard. Alex could just barely see other buildings in the distance.

Master Kattan pointed to the pile of huge stones that had just ejected from the pyramid.

"First things first," he said. "We have to get that wall repaired. Ready Master Ebo? Alex?"

While they walked over to the stones, Master Ebo said to Alex, "This time think about repairing the hole and picture it the best you can. Do not think of how you want it done. Just think of the end result. Got it?"

"Got it," Alex said.

They reached Master Kattan, and the three of them raised their Z-Cons. All the Z-Cons started glowing—this time Alex's Z-Con started glowing almost the same instant as the other two.

All the stones rose off the ground, and one by one they shot back into the pyramid. When the last stone flew into place, they all lowered their Z-Cons. Alex ran over to the restored wall to have a look at their work. He inspected it carefully, running his hand all around the area where the hole had been. Alex couldn't see any markings at all! It was impossible to tell that the wall had ever been breached.

Master Kattan turned to Master Ebo and pointed to the large stone structure in the distance.

"The two of us will have to check it out before we bring the kids over to it," he said. "Get Alex's Z-Con and let's get going."

Master Ebo held out her hand, and Alex gave her the Z-Con, but it felt a little painful for him to give it up. The sensation that ran through his body when he used it became more natural to him. It no longer stung as it did before but felt more like the comfort he experienced when wrapped up in a warm, heavy blanket when it was cold outside.

Master Kattan signaled for the group to form around him.

"Master Ebo and I will be back soon," he said. "We're going to make sure the way is safe. I want you all to stay here quietly. Try not to move around too much. Understood?"

Alex didn't want to remain behind, but he supposed it would be best to do what Master Kattan ordered.

"We'll be okay, sir," Alex said, looking at the others.

Master Kattan turned to Mercure and Panda.

"Keep them safe you two," he strongly commanded, but then smiled and winked.

The two dogs stood up together and trotted over to the group. They flanked them on both sides.

"If there's any trouble, everyone head to the other pyramid over there," Master Kattan said. "We'll meet up with you in the middle." Master Kattan and Master Ebo jogged off.

After a minute of silence, Elka asked, "Is anyone else scared?"

"Glad I'm not the only one," Maia said.

The two of them turned to the boys. Dion gave them a small shrug.

"Well, I guess all this has been a bit distressing," Dion said, sitting down at the base of the pyramid. He looked off at Master Kattan and Master Ebo. "You know what gets me is that neither one of them seem like they ever ran into this kind of thing before."

Alex sat down next to Dion.

"For the last day I feel like I've been just going from one fire to another," Alex said. He wondered if the odds were going to catch up to him. At least for the time being it was as peaceful as it gets. A full moon brightly lit up the entire area, the stars shined, a soft wind was blowing, and most importantly they were out from the inside of the huge tomb.

"What do you think caused the tunnel to collapse?" Elka asked Alex. "I mean, you know, what are the odds that it would happen just when you went down there?"

Alex didn't know what to say, so he didn't say anything—he just glanced at her and looked away. He sure knew what she meant though. The orbs chased him down last night, and now something was coming after him again. It couldn't be a coincidence—something was trying to get him. He started feeling rather exposed out in the open. He wished he had a Z-Con in his hand, or at least that the two masters would return.

Dion stood and pointed to the top of the pyramid, about sixty feet up.

"Last one to the top loses!" he yelled.

Both Mercure and Panda loudly growled out their objections to the idea.

Dion ignored them. He grabbed the top of the stone in front of him and started pulling up. But both Maia and Elka were already ahead of him! They moved incredibly fast—as if they've been climbing large rocks their entire life.

Alex stood and jumped up onto the pyramid, trying to catch up. But by this time everyone already had a big lead on him. The stone block he was trying to climb was the tallest one on the bottom row, and his fingers could not quite reach its top edge. He placed his hands on the stone's face and tried to get some traction on his feet, but he kept slipping down.

Alex felt himself growing desperate to catch up with the other three. He didn't like finishing last, especially at something as simple as climbing. He looked up to see Dion, Elka, and Maia already two levels of rocks ahead of him. His desperation grew.

Strangely, the stone under each one of his palms started glowing—pulsating between light red and dark red. His hands turned hot, and they throbbed slightly. Low rumbling sounds vibrated through him. Alex snapped his head upwards, searching for the origins of the sound.

A huge beam of white light shot out of the tip of the pyramid, straight up to the sky. Alex flew upwards, and in an instant, without trying, he was two stones above all the others! Then the beam of light at the top of the pyramid disappeared. When everyone noticed Alex perched above them, they all stopped climbing.

"How did you get there?" Maia stammered. She looked over to Elka, just slightly below her. "Did you see him get past us?"

Elka just looked at Alex, confused.

Alex looked over at Dion. He looked confused too.

Master Kattan and Master Ebo ran up below everyone.

"Get down off there," Master Kattan said sternly.

Everyone started climbing down. Maia and Elka reached the ground first, but Dion hardly moved. He waited for Alex to climb down to his level, and when the two of them were side by side, he gave Alex a small salute and jumped.

He hit the ground with a heavy thud. It dawned on Alex that he had to start thinking like Dion. Normally, at this height, he was much too high to jump and not get hurt. But with his GEM suit on he would be completely safe. Why even hesitate? He let go and slammed down right next to Dion. No problem.

Alex looked up at the spot where he originally placed his palms, but he couldn't see anything unusual– nothing was glowing. He checked his hands. The warm feeling had stopped, and he couldn't detect anything unusual. He contemplated for a few seconds about telling Master Ebo about the event, but just then Master Kattan started motioning for everyone to gather around him and Alex figured he would keep it to himself for the time being.

"Everything looks like it is going to work out," Master Kattan said to everyone. He pointed south. "The pyramid over there is called El Osario. That's where the outgoing portal is. There is another master waiting inside it for us. I want you all to follow us closely. When we reach it, you will go on to a smaller structure that's just past it. Stay there and wait for our signal to come over. There are some trees that we'll be running through, so stick together and don't get lost."

He looked down at Mercure and Panda.

"You'll keep watching them, won't you?" he asked.

Mercure said to Alex, *"It's not playtime, Alex. Pay attention to Master Kattan."*

Alex nodded at him.

Master Kattan reached into his robe, pulled out his Z-Con and ran off toward the south. Master Ebo moved behind the group and stretched out her hands.

"Okay, quickly, let's go," she said.

Once again Alex swiftly ran to the front. Mercure moved alongside him, and the two of them sped up to catch Master Kattan. Everyone else fell in line directly behind.

It didn't take long to reach El Osario. When they did, Master Ebo broke from the group and continued running to the backside of the building. Master Kattan silently motioned for the rest of the group to keep running. He pointed to a structure in the distance.

Alex continued leading the way, and when they reached the square building, he looked around for a place that might provide some cover. He spotted a large indentation built into the face of the nearest wall. It looked like it might have been the entrance to the building. He figured everyone could fit inside the overhang, giving them at least a little bit of protection.

Alex ran into it, with everyone else following right behind. All the walls of the structure looked ancient and had many small symbols carved into them. Some of the symbols looked very similar to the ones Alex had seen on the walls and plaques back inside the Himalayan Mountains. Elka and Maia studied the walls with him.

"This looks very familiar," Maia said. She ran her fingers over the markings.

"I know where I saw this before!" Elka shouted. "Mom and Dad were studying a picture of this wall. Like six or seven months ago.'

"Why were they doing that?" Alex asked. "Did they teach you what this stuff means?"

"No, I never asked," Elka said. "They just called all those little pictures 'glyphs'."

"I remember them looking at it a few times," Maia said. "They were looking for a clue, but I don't think they ever found it."

Alex asked Mercure, "Ever see this before?"

"I saw a big picture of it on the wall in Miguel's office a little while ago," Mercure responded. *"No idea what he did with it."*

Alex studied each of the three walls that made up the enclosure. He tried to remember if he ever saw the glyphs anywhere before, but nothing came to mind. Obviously, his dad had kept this from him too. A few seconds later, Master Ebo appeared outside.

"Okay, we're going to breach the near wall of El Osario now," she said. "When we do, I want you to run in and wait in the center. Stick together."

Everyone stepped out from the building and surrounded Master Ebo. They all watched the nearby pyramid, waiting.

"What's this building called?" Alex whispered to the back of Master Ebo's head.

"Akab Dzib," she answered. Almost as an afterthought, she explained, "In Mayan, it means *The House of Mysterious Writing*."

Alex couldn't stop thinking about all the glyphs in the room behind him. He looked back over his shoulder at the walls inside the entrance, trying his best to see and remember all the markings on them. Alex was never very good at memorizing. But he felt that if his father thought it was important, then he was going to memorize as much about them as he could. Then he remembered his goggles. The Qen had said if he put them on, it would record everything saw!

Alex quickly swung his bag off his shoulder, rummaged around for the goggles, and took them out. He pulled them on over his head and adjusted them over his eyes. A slight sound began ringing in his ear—like the goggles were barely vibrating. He hoped it meant the goggles were on and recorded everything. He turned to the walls and slowly panned his head around, making sure he scanned every inch of the walls.

The nearby pyramid started to rumble. A few seconds later, over the sound of the rumbling, Master Ebo yelled, "Now! Run. Quickly!" She sprinted off toward the pyramid.

Alex snatched the goggles off his head and threw them into his bag. He joined everyone else following Master Ebo in a tight group, with the two dogs again flanking them on both sides. When they got about halfway to El Osario, the noise stopped. By the time they arrived at the pyramid, a tunnel to the interior had been completely formed, and the entire group continued inside without stopping—followed closely behind by Master Kattan.

The long, dark tunnel led them to a brightly painted center room, similar to the room in the pyramid they had arrived in. The same blue, red, green, and yellow lines crisscrossed the walls and floors, and the four corners were also brightly lit. It also had three portal holes in the floor.

There was a robed man in the center of the room, standing with his hands folded in front of him.

"This is Master Puma," Master Kattan said.

The short man gave a quick bow. When he straightened up, he had a stern look about him. His dull eyes and leathered face presented an intense feeling of depression.

"Let's move on," Master Puma said in a distinctly monotone voice. "All of you line up here." He pointed to a spot just in front of the central portal.

Alex fell in line behind Dion, Elka, and Maia, with Mercure and Panda behind him. This time he didn't try to be first, but not because he was afraid of the jump. He just didn't feel like standing too close to Master Puma. An uneasy feeling came over him when he looked at the man, but he couldn't put his finger on exactly why.

Alex watched Master Kattan and Master Ebo move together and raise their Z-Cons, preparing to close the tunnel.

Master Puma stood silently at the front of the line, not offering any instructions. He raised his hand and simply motioned for Dion to jump through the portal. Dion stepped forward and was gone. Master Puma kept motioning, so Elka and Maia followed along.

Alex moved forward, but Master Puma dropped his hands, blocking the way. For what seemed like a long time he stared at Alex.

"Let the dogs go first," he said.

Mercure stepped over the hole and went through. Panda followed directly behind him.

"Give them a moment," Master Puma droned.

Master Puma kept his eyes intently focused on Alex. Alex stared back for a little while—well, for as long as he comfortably could that is. Eventually, he dropped his eyes downward, focusing rather on the portal hole.

The two other masters began their repair of the tunnel, and the noise level grew intense. Master Puma didn't move for a full minute—he just stared at Alex the entire time.

Finally, Master Puma motioned for Alex to continue.

Alex jumped as fast as he could.

SIX

It was the shortest portal jump Alex had taken so far. He barely had time to appreciate the sensation or even take notice of the color patterns this time. It was so quick he was taken by surprise when he landed. He found himself standing alone in the center of a large, sterile room. It immediately reminded Alex of a brightly lit operating room. The four walls were stainless steel, and the floors were pure white tile. Everyone else must have already left through the exit door directly in front of him.

Alex moved forward cautiously. A low hum came from just outside the door, and as Alex took each step, the sound grew louder and louder. When he reached the exit, he peered through before continuing. The door led to another large room that was almost completely dark. He looked to the side and saw the rest of his companions all grouped in the far corner near a large exit. The humming he heard was coming from the other side of that doorway. Alex now recognized the sound to be a large group of people, all talking amongst themselves. Dion turned around and motioned for Alex to come over.

But before Alex could move, Master Puma appeared behind him and touched him on the shoulder. Alex's head snapped around and looked up into his harsh face.

"What are you waiting for? Move on."

"Yes, sir," Alex said, moving backward. He took a few steps, turned, and jogged over to his companions. There was a different teacher standing at the head of them, but from where Alex stood he could only see her back. She appeared to be tall with short, light brown hair. He bent down and scratched Mercure's ear.

"Who's that?" he whispered.

"That's Master Sasa. She led us over here from the other room. She told us not to wait for you any longer. What took you so long?"

"Master Puma. There's something's strange about that guy. I don't know exactly what though."

"You'd be a little strange if you've been through what he has. By the way, Master Sasa had everyone take off their gloves and hoods."

Alex pulled off his right glove.

"So, any idea what's up now?" he asked.

"Sure, but I think it's best if I don't tell you. You should just let it happen."

Alex took off his left glove, grabbed the top of his hood, and yanked it off.

"No more mysteries! Just tell me."

"Okay! It's an induction process. You're all going to be presented to the whole academy, and they'll help activate your Z-Con."

100

"How?" he asked, stuffing his clothes into his bag.

"The key to everything in life is patience," Mercure answered, turning away. *"It won't take very long. Take a deep breath and relax."*

Master Kattan and Master Ebo walked briskly past the group and on through the opening. Master Puma strolled past everyone and turned around.

"The dogs need to go on now," Master Puma said. "They'll join up with you later. Everyone else remain quiet until we lead you in."

Mercure and Panda obediently went through the opening and disappeared.

The humming coming from the opening quieted down, and Alex heard Master Kattan speaking, although he couldn't tell what he was saying.

A few seconds later Master Puma and Master Sasa stepped toward the opening and ordered the group to 'Follow us.' Alex and everyone formed a straight line and trailed in behind the two masters.

Alex went through the opening, and it was overwhelming. The room turned out to be an enormous auditorium, filled with a few hundred students. Three distinct sections divided the crowd. Each section contained students all dressed in the same color jacket and pants. The section on the right wore white jackets, the center section wore green jackets, and the left section wore black. Everyone wore blue pants, but nobody's shirts matched— they were all various types and colors.

Bright lights from above flooded the stage making it hard for Alex to see much, other than Master Kattan and Master Ebo standing near the center of it.

Elka and Maia moved together and tightly held hands, but Dion seemed to be quite at ease with the whole thing. Alex felt his hands starting to tremble. He didn't like being the center of attention—certainly not in front of hundreds of people. He tapped Dion on his back.

"What's all this?" Alex whispered to him.

"I don't have the slightest idea," Dion whispered back. "I never made it this far."

Everyone stopped just to the side of Master Kattan. He motioned for them to drop their duffel bags to the ground. As soon as they did, Master Kattan moved behind them and introduced each one, placing his hands lightly on top of their shoulder as he did.

"This is Elka Rahal. Maia Rahal. Dion Yang. And Alex Vega."

He moved back to the center of the stage and said, "Please welcome them to our facility."

The entire audience rose as one and broke into enormous applause.

The applause went on and on. Alex thought at several points that it would die down, but it just continued—and the longer it did, the more uneasy he became. He wasn't even sure why.

Elka and Maia looked at each other in bewilderment. They turned to Dion and watched him smiling and waving back to the crowd. After a few seconds, they both started waving—and the applause increased substantially. Alex decided the best thing to do was to join in—and the applause grew even louder.

Finally, Master Kattan raised his hand, and the ovation slowed to a stop. All the students sat, and the room fell completely silent. Master Kattan leaned forward to address Alex and the rest of the group.

"Please get your stones out from your bags and give them to me," he said to the four of them.

Everyone bent down and retrieved their Jade stones. Alex now felt like the stone selection might turn out to be significant. Something important was going to happen with them. Alex hoped that choosing the Jade stone was going to work out for him, and everyone else for that matter.

Alex handed his stone to Master Kattan as he walked by to collect them. After they all had handed over their stones, Master Kattan headed over to a table near the back of the stage.

Maia moved closer to Alex.

"I hope we picked the right stones," she whispered.

"Too late now I guess," Alex said, shrugging his shoulders. He turned to his other side and leaned toward Dion.

"I hope you selected 'wisely,'" he said, a little sarcastically. The two of them held back a laugh.

In less than a minute of working, with the entire hall in absolute silence, Master Kattan returned with the four stones in his hands. Each stone now had a folding Jade handle attached to its bottom. He walked down the line, passing Elk, Maia, Alex, and Dion. As he did, he handed each one of them their new Z-Con.

He took Alex's arm and, in one quick motion, moved him up to the front of the line next to Elka. Alex was a little unnerved by it. Both Alex and Elka looked at each other for several seconds, trying to figure out why.

From the front row, center stood a woman flanked by several of the Masters on either side. She gracefully walked up a set of steps, and onto the stage. She wore a white jacket that had no buttons, white shirt, and spotlessly white trousers. She had a weathered face, and her skin was dark, with a very slight reddish tinge to it. Combined with her completely white hair, she presented a rather distinguished figure. She looked quite a bit like Z.

She carried a box in her hands. It was made of solid silver and had many symbols etched into it. Unlike all the other writings that Alex had observed so far, none of these symbols look familiar to him.

The woman presented the box to Master Kattan to hold. He took the box from her, held it in one hand, and opened its lid with the other. The woman reached into it and pulled out a Z-Con. This Z-Con was larger than all the Z-Cons the other masters used, and it wasn't made of stone. It wasn't made of anything that Alex could recognize. The top surface was multicolored and extremely rough. All its surfaces seemed to have a tiny amount of purplish gas slowly seeping out of them. This Z-Con was very similar to the one Z used.

Master Kattan turned around and faced the new arrivals.

"This is our Head Master," he said. "Our Vizier."

The woman stepped forward, and Master Kattan turned away from everyone to face her as she approached. He bowed, straightened up, and turned back around.

"I present to you Vizier Herabata," he said. "She will help you activate your Z-Cons."

Vizier Herabata moved past Master Kattan and stepped in front of Alex. He looked up at her, desperately trying to think of what to do next. Certainly, with all this ceremony there must be something they expected from him. Should he bow? Should he say something? A bit of panic raced through his entire body while he waited for something to happen. But Vizier Herabata just stood in front of him for several seconds, remaining still.

Then she gently reached forward and raised up Alex's right hand—the one holding his Z-Con. She pointed her Z-Con directly at it. Master Ebo, Master Puma, and Master Sasa moved in next to her. They all raised their Z-Cons as well.

The students in the audience rose—but only the ones in the green jackets. Each one held out their Z-Con, and they all pointed them at Alex. All their Z-Cons were made from Jade as well.

Alex's hand started to shake more.

The Vizier's Z-Con began giving off a soft blue glow, quickly followed by all the other Jade Z-Cons. All the Z-Cons emitted the same blue color, but each one glowed at a slightly different brightness.

Alex's Z-Con began glowing the same color as the all rest. It was so faint Alex could hardly detect it at first, but the Z-Con grew brighter and brighter with each second. After just a bit more than thirty seconds, it stopped getting brighter. At that point, the glowing completely stopped. All the Z-Cons stopped glowing at the same precise instant.

The students in the green jackets raised their Z-Cons over their heads and erupted into a cheer. After a few seconds, all the other students started applauding, and it didn't stop until the Vizier raised her hand. When it finally did stop, Alex let out a small sigh of relief and felt his shoulders drop down a couple of inches. All was well. It seemed like he worried for nothing.

Vizier Herabata moved forward and pressed her hand on top of Alex's Z-Con and said, "Welcome to training."

"Thank you," Alex said. After looking at Vizier Herabata for another few seconds, and noticing that she didn't move, he got the impression that the situation required something more. "It's an honor to be here," he said. Vizier Herabata still didn't move. Alex continued, "Thanks again."

Vizier Herabata brought up her other hand and gently took Alex's Z-Con. She turned it over, and after a few seconds of staring at its handle, she looked up into Alex's eyes. She brought the Z-Con up to show Alex what preoccupied her. Her finger pointed to a symbol that had been newly etched into the bottom of the stone. It was a small square with rounded corners, and in its middle was carved an elongated animal face, with spots on it.

In a low voice, Vizier Herabata said to Alex, "Your Z-Con's symbol is the Mayan Jaguar. The character for strength."

After a few more seconds Vizier Herabata released Alex's hand, gave him a warm smile, and then moved over to a nervous Elka. She pointed her Z-Con at Elka's Z-Con and repeated the entire procedure. Again, when the Z-Cons stopped glowing, everyone cheered. Vizier Herabata took a few seconds to discuss with Elka the symbol on her Z-Con, but Alex couldn't hear what she said. After Herabata finished with Elka, she moved onto Maia with the same results. Maia had a smug look on her face the entire time.

Next, she turned to Dion. Again, she performed the procedure, but at the end of it, after he received a cheer from the students in the green jackets, he only received a small applause from the rest of the students—just polite. Certainly, not like the huge cheer the other three had received.

Alex wondered why. He looked at Dion, trying to see if it upset him. But Dion looked indifferent to it. Alex thought that maybe Dion was trying to put on a brave face. It had to affect him. It certainly affected Alex when this sort of thing happened to him—like last year when he tripped during the last section of the cross-country race at the county finals. He had the win; all he had to do was finish. But he fell, and that lost it for him. And even though he came in second, he felt the whole school's disappointment when they presented the second-place trophy to him. He heard the same polite applause that Dion just received and felt the same sort of humiliation. Why would they be doing that to Dion? How did they even know him enough to do that?

Vizier Herabata softly spoke to Dion about his Z-Con and then headed away, toward the center of the stage.

Alex looked at Dion and mouthed "What was that about?"

Dion shook his head slightly and mouthed back, "Later."

Vizier Herabata turned and addressed the entire room.

"Thank you for assisting our new arrivals. As it was when we began, it is now as it continues. These four are now part of our group. Part of the whole and from here on, with our help, better connected to the cosmos. Help them learn. Help them continue our worthy goals."

Master Sasa moved to Maia and led her over to the side of Vizier Herabata. The Vizier turned to her, reached out, and took hold of her right hand. She lifted Maia's hand out in front of her and slid a bracelet over it. The bracelet, made of polished stone, was all black, and the hole was very large—much larger than Maia's wrist.

Vizier Herabata pointed her Z-Con toward Maia.

All the students in the room held up their right arms. They all showed bracelets on their wrists. The bracelets were all different colors; white, yellow, orange, green, blue, purple, brown, red, and black—only a small few of them were black.

Vizier Herabata closed her eyes, and a few seconds later her body began to glow.

The glow started at her head, moved down to her feet, and then out through her arms. When the glow reached her Z-Con, it jumped over to Maia's right hand. The glow slowly crawled from Maia's fingertips, past her palm, and onto her bracelet. As soon as the glow touched it, the bracelet instantly shrunk down to fit Maia's wrist, and it turned from dark black to pure white.

Maia stood there staring at her arm, trying to comprehend the meaning.

Master Sasa led Maia away, toward the side of the stage—with Maia looking at her wrist the entire way. At the same time, Master Ebo moved Elka in front of the Vizier, and she performed the ritual again. After that, she moved to Dion, and then finally Alex.

Alex no longer felt the anxiety he had when he first arrived at the auditorium. After all, he had just seen the Vizier perform the ceremony three times, and everything seemed to be going smoothly—nothing to worry about. It was sure easier going last during these rituals, he thought to himself.

Vizier Herabata took Alex's right hand, slid a bracelet over it, and pointed her Z-Con at his wrist. Once again, a glow started at her head, moved throughout her body to her Z-Con, and jumped over to Alex's hand. But his bracelet didn't immediately turn white—it started pulsating. It turned from black to white, and white to black, over and over.

As Alex looked on, a low murmur started among the students in the audience. The murmuring grew louder and louder as the pulsating continued. Alex's wrist began getting warm. He felt his face turning red. Once again Alex wished he had some idea of what was going on.

Finally, with a brilliant flash of light near Alex's wrist, the pulsating stopped.

Instead of white, his bracelet had turned to a deep yellow color.

The crowd fell silent. Vizier Herabata reached for Alex's hand and studied his bracelet for a few seconds. She looked back up into Alex's eyes.

"Impressive," she said. She gently let go of Alex's hand, and he slowly let it fall to his side.

"Continue the good work, Alex," she said, with a warm smile.

Alex didn't feel like he had done anything worth a comment like that. After all, the bracelet had turned color all by itself.

Master Ebo led Alex over to the others on the right side of the stage. Mercure and Panda trotted up to them from behind. Panda moved in between Elka and Maia. Mercure stopped next to Alex's side.

Alex looked down at Mercure with an expression that left little doubt that he wanted an explanation.

"Yellow means 'more advanced,'" Mercure told him, without looking up.

Alex realized that he was tensing up again. He stood as still as he could, just hoping the ceremony would end.

Alex watched Master Kattan return to Vizier Herabata with the silver box from which she had earlier retrieved her Z-Con.

Vizier Herabata gently laid her Z-Con in the box and closed the lid. Master Puma came over, took the box from Master Kattan, and walked off the stage to the right. When he reached the edge, two other men in blue robes joined him—each one of them holding a Z-Con out in front of them. The three men disappeared out the side exit.

Vizier Herabata, Masters Kattan, Ebo, and Sasa came together in the center of the stage.

Masters Kattan stepped forward and said, "The arrival ceremony has now concluded. Our recruits are six weeks behind. All of you do your best to help them get up to speed. In the meantime, competition number four is only a few days away, so please keep concentrating on your training."

All the students in the auditorium stood as one. They moved out, toward the side exits, quietly talking amongst themselves.

When the hall had completely emptied, Vizier Herabata, Master Ebo, and Master Sasa left the stage, leaving Master Kattan alone with Alex and the other new arrivals. He stepped out in front of the four of them.

110

"Your new Z-Cons are only for use while training. You'll leave them here for safekeeping when you return to your families during breaks. Once you graduate, you will all receive new Z-Cons with more advanced capabilities."

Master Kattan moved to the center of the stage.

"Time to show you our facility," he said.

He pointed his Z-Con at the stage floor. After a slight jolt, the stage broke away and headed upwards. Alex watched the ceiling getting closer and closer. It appeared that they were going to crash right into it! At the last second Alex instinctively crouched down. Just at that moment, the ceiling split apart at the center, swiftly sliding to the sides, leaving a large opening for the stage to pass through.

The stage lifted higher and higher until it passed the ceiling and out into the open air. Alex stared out into the vast open space—it was very still and dark. He looked high above him and realized they were standing in the center of an enormous, clear dome on the ocean floor. The expanse that the dome created was about a mile in diameter, and about a mile high. Even though the ocean water on the other side of the enclosure was very dark, several large schools of fishing were plainly visible swimming past it.

Alex finally brought his eyes back down to the horizon, toward his right side. A huge building, shaped like an enormous pyramid, sat about five hundred feet off in the distance. Its sides were white, and a white road extended from where Alex stood all the way to the pyramid's base. A brilliant beam of light shot down from the ceiling high above and illuminated all the pyramid's walls. The light caused a sparkling of a thousand small flecks of red embedded on its front face.

Alex whirled around to his left.

"Look!" he shouted.

Everyone turned. Another pyramid, about the same distance away as the white one, towered into the air. This one was black, and also had a road extending to it; only that road was entirely black. Another beam of light from above illuminated its front, and small twinkles of gold-colored light reflected off all its black surfaces.

On Alex's left side, Elk, Maia, and Dion silently contemplated the astonishing sight in front of them. Alex looked around for Mercure and found him still sitting next to him, but he was looking the other way.

Master Kattan cleared his throat. Alex and everyone else realized that he too was looking in the opposite direction. The whole group turned around together.

There in front of them was another enormous pyramid covered in green Jade. The pyramid was the same distance away as the other two, and it also had a road leading to it but colored solid green.

The Jade pyramid stood out starkly from the dark waters pushing in on the dome wall directly behind it. An intense white light shining down from above caused the pyramid's green sides to glow brilliantly. Master Kattan turned sideways and faced everyone.

"Welcome to your new home," he said.

SEVEN

Master Kattan led everyone down the long green street, toward the Jade pyramid. Elka and Maia followed behind him with Panda trotting along between the two. Mercure ran out ahead of everyone, periodically waiting for the group to catch up before sprinting ahead again.

"Did your brother ever tell you about all this?" Alex asked.

"Just a little," Dion said. "He was told never to discuss it with anyone who hadn't been here before."

"But what part did he tell you about?" Alex insisted. He was getting somewhat fed up with not knowing what was going on. Any little piece of information might help.

"Well, he did say that three teams competed against each other. I guess he was talking about the three pyramids. He never mentioned the layout around here."

"Did he say anything about what they competed on?"

"Nope. Just that he always seemed to win at everything. The more he said it, the more I doubted it."

They walked on for a few minutes with Alex looking straight ahead, watching in awe as the Jade pyramid grew larger and larger. They finally reached the pyramid's enormous base, and Alex gazed from one side of it to the other, estimating the pyramid to be about three hundred feet wide, and almost as tall. The full length of its base, constructed of twelve steps, leading up to a flat terrace. The terrace was as wide as the whole building, and about a hundred feet deep. Both the steps and terrace looked like they were made from gray slate.

Master Kattan didn't slow down when he reached the pyramid's steps. He just hitched up his robe and jogged up. Elka, Maia, and Dion casually walked up the steps behind him, but Alex kept closely alongside Master Kattan and came to a stop next to him when they reached the terrace. Alex looked around the entire the scene, observing the enormous amount of activity in the area.

On Alex's left, five students played a game that involved a small ball being tossed around by only using Z-Cons. Every once in a while, the game momentarily stopped when four of the players pointed to the remaining one and yelled "Side hit!"

Behind that group, two other students raced each other up an extremely high rocky wall, but they weren't using their hands—just their feet. They both held their Z-Cons pointed directly at the wall face. It looked like they were using their Z-Cons instead of their hands to keep themselves attached to the rock's surface. One of them was having trouble and started tilting away from the wall as he climbed. While he struggled, the other student raced past him to the top.

Elka stopped to watch the climbers and said to Maia, "We should try this." Maia smiled and nodded her head.

Alex closely followed Master Kattan, past several tables on the right and left. Many of the tables had four students sitting around them, discussing things. At most of the tables, the students had their Z-Cons lying on the table top, near the table's outer edge—all of them pointing toward the center. The Z-Cons projected different types of large holograms, taking up the entire table top; various airplanes, boats, cars, and even a small forest that seemed to be on fire.

At one table, a girl sat alone on a chair with her feet propped up. She held a Z-Con out in front of her and talked directly to it. On the Z-Con's surface was a hologram of another girl sitting on a sofa, also talking to her Z-Con.

A few seconds after everyone else had finally caught up, Master Kattan picked up his pace and walked briskly forward. Alex struggled to keep up, distracted by all the activity.

"Can we stop for a minute, Master Kattan?" Alex shouted ahead.

"Plenty of time for that later, Alex," Master Kattan said, without slowing.

Alex caught back up, and they all approached the enormous entrance to the pyramid. It ran the full length of the base, but there were no doors. The entire opening was constructed of a translucent looking material. Students moved right through it as they went in and out of the pyramid. Master Kattan and the two dogs passed through the membrane without slowing down in the least, but everyone else stopped.

"Go ahead," Elka said to her sister.

Maia pursed her lips and shook her head. She turned to Dion. "You want to give it a go?"

Dion didn't seem like he was in any hurry to try, so Alex stepped forward. When he reached the translucent wall, he slowly put his hand into it. He felt absolutely nothing. He closed his eyes, took a big step forward and went completely through. He turned around and exclaimed, "Nothing to it!"

Everyone followed along, each one of them putting their hand through first—just to get the feel of it.

Master Kattan stood on the other side of the membrane with his hands folded in front of him, waiting for everyone to arrive.

"Well, it's great to see you all survived. Ready to move on?" he said.

Alex looked at Mercure a little sheepishly.

"You do realize we're not going to get you killed on the way in, don't you? Mercure said. *"Perhaps a little more trust at this point would be appropriate."*

"Right, got it," Alex said.

Mercure trotted ahead and added, *"Of course, if we do get you killed on your first day, I'm going to feel terrible about it for quite some time."*

"I'd feel bad about it too," Alex said, flicking his finger near Mercure's ear.

The front part of the pyramid was hollow. In its middle, a great Jade wall ran all the way from the floor to the very top, splitting the structure into a front and rear half. The wall had another smaller, translucent membrane at its bottom, allowing entrance to the rear of the building, but Alex couldn't make out exactly what was back there.

Everyone headed toward the center of the structure, with Alex looking straight up the whole way. Directly above him, an entire wall of rooms lined the front face of the pyramid. There were about a dozen levels of floors arranged in a stair step pattern. Each floor jutted out more and more into the inside space of the pyramid as the levels went up. Alex couldn't see any elevators or stairs. He wondered how anyone could reach any of the rooms without at least a staircase.

Master Kattan approached the center of the pyramid where a student stood waiting for him with a clipboard in his hand. Next to the student, on the floor, where another set of four large duffel bags. He gave a bow as Master Kattan approached.

"Hello, Master Kattan," the student said, straightening up. "I see you have our new arrivals with you."

"I leave them in your good hands," Master Kattan replied. He turned to everyone behind him.

"I present to you the head of Jade Division, Kolek Mencher. Kolek has been a student here for six years and, as you can see, has achieved a black band. Please follow all his instructions. I will be back in the morning to give you an orientation tour around our facility. In the meantime, any questions, please direct them to Kolek."

Master Kattan turned back, gave a slight bow to Kolek and walked away, disappearing through the membrane to the rear of the pyramid.

Kolek watched Master Kattan leave. When he was out of sight, he turned back to the new arrivals.

"Everyone listen up please," he said. "Tonight, we'll get you situated in your rooms. I have a bag of uniform clothes for each of you. They have your name tags on the top. I want you to pick up your bag and take out the pair of shoes you'll find in there. Put the shoes on, and we'll get moving."

Alex picked up his bag, opened it, and rummaged around. Among other smaller things, there were a couple of green jackets and a few more blue pants. Near the bottom of the bag, he found a pair of Jade-colored shoes—they were a curious mix of sneaker and dress shoe. He sat on the floor with everyone else and put the left shoe on. It fit perfectly.

"I guess we have Joeks Burlm, Head Fitter to thank for these," Alex said to Elka, continuing with his right shoe.

"He's rather good, isn't he?" she said.

"I wonder how this all arrived here before we did?" Maia asked.

"That's how good he is," Elka responded with a small laugh.

While everyone was finishing, two girls walked up to them. Both girls had braided dark hair and green eyes. They had similar noses, the same shaped mouth, and even their ears looked somewhat the same. Alex had a distinct impression they were sisters. The shorter of the two girls carried a Z-Con in her hand.

"Hello, Kolek, I see you're babysitting our new yellow belt," the shorter girl said.

"Came over to meet him, did you?" Kolek asked.

"Just walking by," the girl replied, intently watching Alex.

Alex jumped up off the floor and stared right back at her. He could tell there was something on her mind, and it felt very menacing.

"Alex, this is Bhedi Haley," Kolek said. "She joined us a few weeks ago. She also arrived as a yellow band."

Bhedi didn't say anything. She just stood there, watching Alex. Alex didn't feel the need to say anything, so he too just remained still. Neither one moved for what felt like a long time. Finally, Bhedi turned to the other girl and pointed at Alex.

"Look what we have here Jordan, our new 'once-a-decade.'" Bhedi said. She stepped forward, so her nose was only an inch away from Alex's. "But I'm the 'once-a-decade' for our class," she said. "So, that means we have an imposter here don't we?"

Bhedi's sister grabbed her by the arm and walked away, pulling Bhedi behind her.

"Let's go," she said as she strained.

Bhedi kept looking back at Alex. When the two girls were a good distance away, Alex turned around to Kolek.

"What was that all about?" he asked.

Kolek shrugged his shoulders a little and contemplated a few seconds before answering.

"A 'once-a-decade' student is someone who arrives here as a yellow band. It only happens about once every ten years or so. I guess she's a little jealous."

Alex was having trouble making sense of what just happened with Bhedi when Kolek swung around to face the rest of the group.

"Okay, everyone ready to go?" he asked.

"Wait, sir," Alex said. "I have another question."

Kolek gave a quick nod to him.

"Where exactly are we? I mean, what is this place?"

"Officially this facility is called the 'Earth Defense Operations School,'" Kolek said. He turned and started walking away. Over his shoulder, he said, "But everyone here just calls it 'The Dome.'"

Alex fell in line behind everyone, feeling kind of numb from all the night's events.

Kolek marched over beneath the wall of rooms lining the front of the pyramid. He stopped when he reached a large white circle on the floor. Printed in the middle of the circle was the number '206' in a dark green color. He stood in the middle of the circle and faced everyone.

"Okay, this is your first lesson on how to use your Z-Cons. You're all in quad two-oh-six." He pointed up with his finger. "The only way to reach it is to launch yourself from this spot, straight up. Give it a try, but I should warn you, it's a little hard to do on your first attempt. It's okay…you'll get it. You wouldn't be here if you couldn't. The shoes that you just put on are designed to react well to the forces you'll be generating with your Z-Cons. Keep in mind that these shoes only work when you are wearing them here, at this facility. When you are out in the field, in your training classes, they won't be of any help. Okay, who's first?"

Before anyone else could say anything, Elka stepped forward. Kolek looked her over for a second and then continued.

"Fine, everyone take out your Z-Cons and listen up."

Everyone rummaged through their duffel bags until they were all holding their Z-Cons by the handle.

"Step into the circle, point your Z-Con at the floor directly below you and, in your head, start saying a vibration word. The easiest one to use while you are starting out is the sound of the word 'omega.' After that, picture yourself standing on the platform directly above us. That platform is the entrance to your quad. It's on the second floor, only twenty feet up, so you're going to get there pretty fast. Go ahead."

Elka looked up and closed her eyes. A few seconds later she shot up about five feet before slowly coming straight back down.

"Very good, but you stopped thinking of 'omega' in your head, didn't you?" Kolek asked.

"I guess I was a little startled," Elka said nervously.

"Try again."

Once again Elka shot up and came back, this time only reaching about six feet off the ground.

"It's important to have the right picture firmly in your mind," Kolek said. He looked over at Alex and pointed. "Okay, yellow band. You show us."

Alex felt like he had been on display all day long, and now he had another task to do in front of everybody. He was looking forward to just getting into his room and out of sight.

He grabbed his bags and stepped forward to replace Elka in the circle. He pointed his Z-Con toward his feet, closed his eyes and thought about standing on the landing pad above him. In an instant, he shot up next to it and slowly drifted over to the platform, gently touching down.

"Like a pro!" Kolek yelled up.

Alex looked down and watched Kolek point back to Elka, saying, "Try again. It helps if you picture what you just saw."

Elka cautiously moved into the circle and closed her eyes. She immediately launched up and touched down next to Alex. She leaned over the side and yelled down, "You're going to love it!"

Within a couple of minutes, Maia and Dion were on the platform, soon followed by Kolek.

Kolek looked down and motioned for the two dogs to join them. Mercure and Panda both lifted off the ground at the same time and slowly rose up. When they reached the same level as the platform, they both pumped their legs as if they were doing the dog paddle in the air. They floated over to the landing platform and touched down.

"You're just full of surprises, aren't you?" Alex whispered to Mercure.

"Like I've said before, this isn't my first time."

"Well done everyone—first lesson complete," Kolek said, making a notation on his clipboard. "Let's get inside."

Alex looked at the doorway to room '206'. It was a light gray color, and it shimmered slightly. Kolek walked right through it—the doorway turned out to be another membrane. Only this one you couldn't see through at all.

After watching Kolek disappear through what looked like a solid wall, everyone acted a little more apprehensive. Once again Alex took the lead, but this time he walked through the membrane in one smooth motion. Elka and Maia gallantly went through the membrane, followed by Dion.

Finally, Alex started feeling somewhat relaxed. The area in front of him was a small living room with four reclining chairs, a large table in the center with four chairs around it, and wooden storage shelves along the left and right walls. Past the chairs, a huge window extended from the floor to

122

the ceiling. It filled the entire length of the front wall, providing a spectacular view of the entire facility, with the Opal and Lava pyramids brilliantly lit in the background.

Kolek moved toward the center of the room.

"You can lock the front door anytime you want by using your Z-con. Just think of it turning solid. Elka and Maia, your room is on the right, Alex and Dion to the left. Both rooms are self-contained with beds, a kitchen, a bathroom, some closets, and more than enough space to lay out your things. Fix them up any way you want. But this is the common room for all four of you. You'll be spending a lot of your time in here, making plans. Everything you do at this facility will be done as a team. You'll be competing together in sets of two and four, and that requires a good deal of coordination between all of you."

He pointed over to the corner.

"That is the pedestal for your room Qen. You can call him anytime you want, as long as you are anywhere near a Z-Con when you do it. He's in control of this quad. He'll help keep you out of trouble and on schedule. Ask him anything you want, or for anything you need. Alex, ask the Qen to appear—same procedure as before."

Alex closed his eyes, and a Qen materialized on the pedestal.

"How can I help you?" the Qen asked.

"Make sure everyone is up and ready at eight o'clock tomorrow morning," Kolek said. "That's all, thank you."

The Qen gave a slight bow and disappeared.

Kolek headed toward the door.

"You can give him a name if you want. For that matter, you can use your Z-Cons to give him a personality, but that's probably a little past your capabilities right now."

He reached the doorway and turned around.

"Your Z-Cons will also allow you to control the lights and temperature. Master Kattan will be here tomorrow morning, so please be dressed and prepared to go. Any questions about the schedule, ask your Qen."

He stood in the doorway for a few seconds without saying anything.

"If I were you I'd have some food, square away your rooms and get some sleep. You'll have another full day tomorrow. Good luck."

He swung around and left.

Alex looked at Dion. Then he looked at Elka and Maia.

After a couple of seconds of everyone standing around grinning at each other, Alex turned to Dion and gave him a high-five. Elka and Maia joined in.

When the celebrating ended, Alex slumped down into one of the recliners. For the first time that day, he felt relaxed. He looked forward to not doing anything more for the rest of it.

Elka and Maia walked over to the Qen's pedestal, looked down on it for a few seconds, and turned around.

They both said, "Let's program this guy!"

EIGHT

Alex woke to bright sunlight streaming in through the large bedroom window. He sat up, looked around, and stared for a while at the Qen standing near the foot of his bed. Alex got his bearings and finally remembered where he was.

"Oh, yeah…" he said, taking a slow look around the entire room. "I forgot." He swung his feet onto the floor. "Hello, Feng. What time is it?"

"As you requested, I have awoken you at seven thirty," Feng the room Qen answered, using a rather dry and proper voice.

Feng glided over to Alex's closet and withdrew his GEM suit, socks, a pair of pants, and a shirt. He neatly laid them at the foot of Alex's bed.

"Best be getting dressed, Alex," he said.

Feng waited a few seconds for an acknowledgment from Alex before gliding over to Dion's side of the room. Dion lay sprawled across his bed, snoring. Feng lifted the covers up from Dion's legs and tickled the bottom of his foot. Dion instantly sat up and blinked several times before finally focusing in on Feng. A few seconds later the puzzled look on Dion's face disappeared.

"Oh, yeah," he said.

"Why were you tickling his feet?" Alex asked, stepping into his GEM suit.

"If you recall, last night Dion instructed me on how to do many of my tasks properly," replied Feng. "This is the method he asked me to use when awakening the two of you."

Alex and Dion stared at Feng for a few seconds before turning away.

"Oh, yeah… I forgot," they both said.

Feng moved over to Dion's closet and retrieved his wardrobe for the day.

"Elka and Maia asked me to wake them with soft music and a new inspirational quote each day," Feng said, laying Dion's clothes on his bed.

He glided back to his perch in the corner and turned around. "A much more practical method of awakening if you ask me," he said, just before freezing with a small grin on his face.

Alex returned to dressing but then turned to face Feng, pondering for a second.

"What was today's quote?" he asked.

Feng immediately became animated again.

"A journey of a thousand miles begins with one step. From the Chinese philosopher, Lao Tzu," Feng said. After Alex and Dion stared at him for several seconds, he added, "In your case, it could mean that to accomplish a very large endeavor it requires that you just simply begin it and then

126

start it with some rather easy tasks." He froze again with the same simple smile.

"Come on, let's get ready," Dion said.

Alex and Dion dressed and ate some breakfast in their small kitchen. They rubbed some 'Yellow Goop' onto their hands and headed out to the common room where they found Elka and Maia sitting at the table, sipping tea and talking. Both dogs lay in the far corner, sleeping—just where everyone had left them the night before.

"I think we have some more programming to do with Feng," Alex said, sitting down across Elka. "It was kind of late last night when we instructed him about our wake-up procedures."

Both girls laughed and nodded their heads. "Boy, that's the truth," Elka said.

The four of them had stayed up several hours the previous night trying to decipher the steps necessary to give their Qen a personality. But the best they could do was give him a name, and explain to him how they liked things done. All of that was a simple matter of just talking to the Qen and telling him how to act under various conditions. No matter how many different ways they used their Z-Cons to try and give him a new personality, they failed. Feng, whom they named after one of Dion's ancestors, remained with his default personality the entire time. Elka and Maia were still working on it when Alex and Dion gave up and went to bed.

"How much longer did you stay up?" Alex asked Maia.

"Only a couple hours more," she nonchalantly replied. "We didn't get much further."

Something suddenly dawned on Alex. There was sunlight coming in through the window! He wondered how there could be any sunlight—after all, they were deep underwater.

He went to the window and stared at an intense glow coming from the far wall of the dome.

"Where's the light coming from?" he asked.

Everyone else moved in behind him.

"I've been watching it for the last half hour," Elka said. "It looks like that shining ball on the horizon must be simulating the sun. It's moved a little higher since the last time I looked."

At that moment, Feng appeared on his pedestal.

"Master Kattan is arriving," he said and disappeared again.

Everyone turned around and faced the door.

Sure enough, a few seconds later, Master Kattan entered the common room.

"Everyone well rested?" he said, cheerfully.

"Master Kattan, how does that light work?" Alex asked, quickly turning back to the window.

"That's a plasma ball we formed using the Zero Point Field," Master Kattan replied. "It starts up in the morning, moves across the sky during the day, and dies out at night."

Feng appeared, slid off his perch, and moved in behind Alex.

"Plasma is highly heated gas," he whispered into Alex's ear.

Alex quickly took a step back and swung around, staring at Feng.

"Don't be concerned about the Qen, Alex," Master Kattan said. "As he gets to know you, he learns from your facial expressions and body language. In this case, he sensed that you didn't quite understand my answer, so he provided you with more information."

"You'll get used to it," Feng added.

"I'm not too sure of that," Alex said, looking annoyed.

Master Kattan slapped his hands together and turned around. "Let's get going," he said. "The dogs can remain here. They've seen it before." Both dogs laid still on the floor, not showing the least bit of interest in getting up.

Everyone else moved to the platform outside the room. Master Kattan checked that everyone had on their Gem Suits, socks, and Jade shoes. And, most importantly, that everyone had their Z-Con's folded safely in their pocket.

"Follow me," Master Kattan ordered and jumped off the platform, dropping to the floor below. Everyone landed behind him with a loud thump—Dion being the loudest as he was the heaviest of the four.

They all headed out of the pyramid, onto the terrace, and into the bright daylight. Alex was a little taken back by the colors overhead. The sky formed by the dome wall was not exactly blue and not exactly white but a pleasant combination of the two. It started from light blue directly overhead, changing more into white the further down the horizon you looked. Small patches of light red and green coloring dotted the false sky, and all the colors shimmered as the water flowed past the clear dome wall behind them. Alex was fascinated and constantly looked upwards at it while he walked. He bumped into Dion's back a couple of times along the way.

Master Kattan jogged down the terrace steps, and when everyone reached the bottom, he turned to face them.

"I'm sure you have many questions," he said. "This morning you'll be shown everything that we have going on here. Ask me any questions you'd like while we're doing it. First, let's go over to the classroom facility for the Jade Division. All your Jade buildings are off to the left side." He pointed off toward the right. "All the buildings over there are used by the Opal and Lava Divisions. Please do not enter them unless you are invited. Keep in mind that much of what we do here results in competitions among the divisions. Each division is rather protective of how they train and how they plan for those competitions."

"I wonder what the penalty is," Elka whispered to Alex.

He gave her a bit of a questioning face and whispered back, "You're not planning on finding out, are you?"

Elka shrugged her shoulders and said, "Maybe no, maybe yes."

Master Kattan started walking away, and everyone followed.

"Competition is the way we measure our success," Master Kattan said. "Under normal circumstances, you should only discuss your competition plans with your fellow division members."

"Lots of secrecy here, don't you think?" Alex said to Dion.

"Yeah, I got that feeling every time I spoke to my brother about it. He never would tell me much. I sort of wished he did."

"I love secrecy," Maia interjected. "This is going to be excellent."

"Secret competitions!" Elka said, bumping into to her sister's side. "What's not to love?" They both laughed like there was an inside joke going on.

Alex and Dion shrugged their shoulders at each other.

Master Kattan arrived at the closest building—a long, one-story structure made from Jade and several types of multicolored bricks. A large green sign over the entrance said 'JD-CF-1'.

"That stands for 'Jade Division, Classroom Facility Number One,'" Master Kattan said. Everyone followed him inside. Near the center of the lobby, a Qen stood guard.

"The Qen keeps out the students from the other divisions," he said, before being asked. "He can tell from the color of the student's shoes. We wear Jade shoes; the other divisions wear opal and lava colors."

They all arrived in front of another Qen standing in front of the entrance to four tunnels. The tunnels extended directly out from the wall behind him. They weren't the square-shaped hallways that Alex expected to see. The tunnels were long, with rounded walls and flat floors. Alex moved forward to see a little further into them. The tunnels started out level, but gradually bent downwards into the ground as they extended away. One went off to the right side of the building, another to the left, and two of them went toward the middle.

"I need a room for initial orientation," Master Kattan said to the Qen. "Four students."

"Take tube one, third room on the right, number one-three-seven," the Qen responded.

Master Kattan led the group down tunnel number one, and into the assigned room. The large room was empty— and nothing on the walls.

Master Kattan stopped in front of a small pedestal near the front right-hand corner of the room. A Qen appeared, standing motionless.

"Please set us up for initial history and orientation," Master Kattan said to him.

The Qen didn't move at all, but the room immediately transformed. Shelves appeared on all the walls, each one holding many objects. Some of the items looked Egyptian, and some looked like the carvings Alex saw near the Mayan temple the previous day. It dawned on Alex that every time he saw these kinds of things he felt more of a connection to them.

Floating near the front left-hand side of the room was a large 3-D hologram of a mountain. Next to it was a hologram of a pyramid, and next to that was a hologram of a large spaceship. The spaceship had the shape of a long tube and had dozens of devices extended out from both ends of it. Again, Alex somehow felt a connection when he looked at them.

Master Kattan stood in front of the mountain hologram and motioned for everyone to move in around him.

"Okay, let's get everyone lined up in front," he said. "Today I'm going walk you through the major events in our history. You'll learn more about the details of these events during your normal history classes. Get out your Z-Cons, and we'll start."

Alex reached into his pocket and pulled out his Z-Con. He folded down the handle and held it out in front of him.

While they were all getting ready, Master Puma entered through the doorway.

"Vizier Herabata asks that you stop by to see her when you are finished with today's orientation," he said to Master Kattan.

"Certainly," Master Kattan responded, giving him a slight bow.

Master Kattan turned his attention back to Alex and the others. "Just picture in your head that you are following me wherever I go," he said. He pointed his Z-Con at the mountain and closed his eyes and said, "Mentally say the sound of 'omega' and... begin."

Alex closed his eyes with a firm picture of him standing alongside Master Kattan. The very next instant, he was standing next to Master Kattan, with Dion and Elka nearby. They all stood in a rocky area at the base of an enormous, snow-covered mountain.

But Maia was missing. Alex could see panic forming on Elka's face.

"It's fine," Alex assured Elka. "Give her a minute."

Within seconds, Maia appeared behind the group. She tapped Elka on the shoulder.

"Sorry," Maia said.

Elka turned around and let out a sigh as she smiled and gave Maia a quick hug.

Alex looked around the area. The mountains formed a deep valley off to the far-right side. Several more very tall mountains stood off to his left. A thin layer of snow covered the ground at his feet, and the snow got deeper and deeper as it extended up the mountainside.

Alex reached down, scraped up some of the snow, and formed a good size ball. The snow didn't feel cold to him at all. He gave a slight whistle, and when Dion turned around, Alex threw it at his chest. The snowball slammed into Dion, but it didn't seem to affect him.

"Didn't you feel that?" Alex asked.

"Not a thing," Dion said, looking all around his front. There was no sign that the snowball had hit him.

Alex turned back to pay attention to Master Kattan.

"You'll notice that you don't feel the extreme cold, or the blowing wind," Master Kattan said to everyone. "You can interact with the environment, but it won't necessarily interact with you."

The cold, intense wind blew around Alex, but he felt perfectly comfortable. It was as if he was standing in the middle of a movie—in this case, an amazingly real movie.

"You are not physically here. This scene is a projection from the Zero Point Field that exists only in your head," Master Kattan said, moving between everyone and the mountain.

"Do any of you know the story of how our ancestors were taught about the Zero Point Field?"

"Dion told us a little bit about it the other night," Alex answered.

"Good. The exact details are not important right now. Over the next year or so all of you will be taking classes that will explain our entire history. For now, you'll need to know that when everyone came back down to Earth after working inside the spaceship, they needed a place to live. Originally, they were in Egypt but then they carved out the interior of Mount Olympus in Greece and used it as their base of operations. But the local population in that area grew too quickly, and our ancestors started to interact with them more and more. Too much really. People started seeing them doing amazing things by using the Zero Point Field. The locals started to worship them as gods. Obviously, the ancestors couldn't stand for that, so they left and took over the interior of this mountain in the Himalayas. The location of this mountain is secret. The only way to get to it is by using our portal system."

"How long ago was the portal system built," Alex asked.

"Four thousand, seven hundred and twelve years ago."

Master Kattan pointed up, toward the center section of the mountain.

"Z gave you all a small tour of this facility the other night when you arrived. At any time in our lives, any one of us can come here and stay, study, or interact with others in our community. We coordinate all our worldwide activity from this facility."

Master Kattan bent down and picked up a stone.

"Early on we learned that being surrounded by rock helped concentrate the ability to use the Zero Point Field. That's why they ended up using the interior of a mountain for their home."

Master Kattan waved his arm slightly, and suddenly they were standing at the base of the pyramid that Alex had seen in the front of the classroom, just before they left.

"After settling into the mountain, the next task they took on was to build a complete portal system that would allow any of them to travel to various places around the Earth almost instantly. Back then they needed to have a large volume of rock surrounding the endpoints of the portal system, so they helped local people all over the world build pyramids for them made from stone. They used the interiors of those pyramids for the portal system. What you see before you is the Great Pyramid of Giza, in Egypt."

He gave everyone a few seconds to ponder the scene before continuing.

"When our ancestors built the original portal system, they sometimes had to have the starting points and ending points separated—otherwise the points might interfere with each other." Master Kattan turned around and pointed to a slightly smaller pyramid a short distance away.

"That's why you had to arrive in this pyramid, and leave out of that one."

"Below us is the tunnel you walked through last night between these pyramids."

Alex looked down, and he could see the tunnel below them as if he had x-ray vision.

"Do you see that?" he exclaimed.

Everyone else looked down.

"Wow! How does that work?" Maia asked, staring.

"I can allow you to see any part of this presentation," Master Kattan replied. "Remember, you are not really standing here. Since this is all happening in your head, you can do things here that would seem to be impossible to do in real life."

Alex looked back up and surveyed the entire scene around him, but he couldn't see into anything else.

"I completely control what you can and cannot do in this presentation," Master Kattan said to Alex. "That's why you can only see through the ground below you and not into the pyramid."

Master Kattan waved his right arm, and instantly Alex could see all the way into the center of the pyramid. He saw the chamber that they had arrived in the previous night. Master Kattan moved his armed again, and Alex could no longer see past the pyramid's walls.

When everyone else looked back up from the ground, and when Master Kattan had their attention again, he continued.

"All your classroom instructions will be given to you this way. You'll be able to learn faster than you have ever done before. And since all the information is being projected directly into your head by The Field, you'll remember absolutely everything that has been presented to you, without having to spend time memorizing it."

When Alex heard him say that, he turned around and grinned at Dion. Dion mouthed the word 'Yes!' back at him. This was the best part yet! Alex had never been any good at just sitting in a classroom, listening to his lessons. For the most part, he did well enough in school, but only if he spent a great deal of his time studying. It looked like all that study time was now behind him.

"The original portal system had its limits," Master Kattan said. "We have since learned how to create a better portal connection between any two points—portals without any of those physical limitations. Z can use his Z-Con to create a portal between where he is and the location of any other Z-Con." He stopped and looked up into the sky. "That's how we were able to create a portal to the moon and establish an observation base on it."

"We have a base on the moon?" Alex said impressively.

"Yes, we secretly placed a Z-Con on the United States space mission that landed on the moon in 1969, Apollo 11. After the astronauts left the moon, we used that Z-Con to create a portal to their landing site and then sent some people up. They established another portal on the far side of the moon, and we used that portal to build an early warning base there."

"Don't we have ships that fly into space?" Dion asked. "Couldn't we have just sent a Z-Con to the moon?"

"We have lots of spacecraft—for all different purposes. But they're all two-person ships. They're built to fly around in the atmosphere and also in Earth orbit. But those ships are designed to fight an invading enemy, not to fly to the moon. Eventually, each one of you will be trained to fly those ships, and to serve some duty on our moon base."

Elka nudged Maia slightly ahead, toward Master Kattan.

"Could we see the spaceship that everyone went up to work in, back in the beginning?" Maia asked.

"Certainly," Master Kattan replied.

With another wave of his arm, the entire group floated in front of a spaceship orbiting the Earth. It looked completely real—much too real for Alex! It seemed like he was going to start falling back to Earth. Alex felt the immediate need to stabilize himself, so he grabbed onto Elka's arm, and Maia grabbed onto his—then Dion grabbed onto hers!

But no one moved a single inch. All four remained completely stationary, just outside of the long tube that made up the spaceship.

"No need to be afraid," Master Kattan assured them. "Remember, the normal rules of space don't necessarily apply. The way that I am creating this presentation allows

you to stand, move around, and breathe out here in space—
everything that you could do as if you were standing on the
ground."

Alex couldn't tell what end of the ship was the front and
what end was the back. The spaceship's walls were
completely smooth and made of highly polished metal.

"Spaceships that use the Zero Point Field to move
through space do not have to be concerned about their shape,
or their age," Master Kattan explained. "This spaceship was
over ten thousand years old when it arrived on Earth all
those years ago."

"Can we see the inside?" Alex asked.

"I suppose the best place to show you is the control
room," Master Kattan said.

He waved his arm, and the entire group drifted forward
together, right through the outer wall of the spaceship. When
they reached the interior, the group headed toward the left,
traveling through the walls, from room to room. Some of the
rooms Alex recognized—bedrooms, bathrooms and such.
But most of them made no sense to him at all.

It didn't take long to reach the control room at the front
of the ship. On the right-hand side, two figures sat
motionless at consoles that lined the wall. All the chairs
along a line of consoles on the left side were empty. In the
center of the room, a huge man sat frozen in an incredibly
large chair. The man was bald on top, and his long and wavy
hair flowed down, almost halfway to the ground. He had
large burly hands with six fingers, and in the center of his
face he had a flat, rectangular nose—it had almost no curve
to it at all. He had one mouth and two eyes, but the eyes
were much further out to the side of his head than you would

expect. The man sat motionless, looking down at the floor in front of him, with what Alex could only interpret to be a gloomy expression.

Master Kattan walked over, reached up slightly, and placed his hand on the man's shoulder.

"This man was called Nedo. He came to Earth to escape the carnage that was happening out in the galaxy. He never fully explained why, but he did tell them that Earth would eventually be involved in it. He said that we needed to prepare to defend ourselves someday."

Master Kattan moved away from the man and addressed the group.

"Before Nedo left Earth, he showed them how to use Z-Cons to manipulate the Zero Point Field. He said that using the Zero Point Field to our advantage was the only way that Earth would be able to survive the coming onslaught. We don't know why he wouldn't tell them exactly what we needed to do. It's possible that he didn't know much about the details himself, but since he didn't tell us about it, we must train as hard as we can to prepare for anything that might come. That's why all of you must learn everything you can over the next few years. Any bit of knowledge, any small skill that you learn could mean the difference between the salvation of Earth or its demise."

Master Kattan turned and started strolling around the room.

"Besides the Z-Cons, this hologram of Nedo's spaceship is the only piece of information that we have about the technology outside of our planet. But Nedo never taught our ancestors anything about this ship. How it moves, how it operates, or what its full capabilities are—we don't know.

We studied this hologram throughout the years, trying to figure it out, but we haven't had much success."

He stopped in front of the group again.

"Perhaps someday one of you will."

Alex moved over to one of the consoles on the left and started to study it.

"Can you see what's behind these panels?" he asked. "I mean, are all the details here?"

"As far as we can tell this is an exact copy of the spaceship," Master Kattan said. "Correct down to the smallest detail. You can zoom in on the panel or even look behind it by just using your hands to magnify the area."

Master Kattan took his Z-Con out of his pocket. While holding onto it, he moved his left arm to the left and his other to the right. The section of console directly in front of Alex immediately jutted forward and grew twice in size.

"Give it a try," he said to Alex.

Alex pulled out his Z-Con and mimicked Master Kattan's arm movements. The console grew again. By moving his head into the hologram of the panel, Alex could see every strange little piece that made up the back of it. He kept zooming in over and over until he had zoomed in so much that he was looking at the atoms that made up the material. Alex became fascinated. He wasn't sure what it all meant, but he couldn't take his eyes off it. Then he heard Master Kattan.

"Alex!"

Instantly, Alex snapped back to the control room, and the console returned to its original size.

"Most yellow bands can't zoom in that far," Master Kattan said to him, with a bit of puzzlement in his voice.

At that moment Dion turned to look at the wall behind them and shouted, "Look!"

There behind them were life-size models of the strangest creatures that Alex had ever seen. Everyone stood and stared at them, fascinated.

There was a mermaid, a gnome, a Minotaur, a leprechaun, and several other creatures that Alex could not identify. One of them floated around in a small circle and looked like some kind of ghost. On the far right side was a Bigfoot.

"So, Bigfoot is real?" Alex exclaimed to Master Kattan.

"None of these creatures were actually ever real," Master Kattan replied. He walked down the wall, looking at each of the creatures in turn. "At some point during his visit to Earth, Nedo created these projections from the Zero Point Field. He scattered a bunch of them all over the Earth."

He reached the end of the wall and turned back to the group. "Most of the creatures that you've heard about in ancient stories existed at one point. Things like unicorns, fairies, dragons—they were all generated from The Field by Nedo. Some people think he was conducting experiments—others think he was just bored and wanted to create some havoc for his amusement. In any case, when our ancestors returned to the Earth's surface, one of the first things they did was to hunt down all these creatures and return their projections to the Zero Point Field. It took them quite a few years to do it, and for the most part, they succeeded. But there are still many of them roaming around. When a report does come in that someone has spotted one, we send out an expedition team to handle it. It doesn't always work out well. Some of these creatures have abilities that make it extremely difficult to catch them. Alex—your Bigfoot for example."

Master Kattan pointed to the entire length of the wall. "As a matter fact, all the creatures along this section are problems. These are what we call 'second generation.' They can pop in and out of the Zero Point Field at any time they want. So, when someone does see one, they can disappear and then reappear somewhere else, usually far away. You have to sneak up on one to capture it, and that's not easy."

Master Kattan clapped his hands and turned back to face everyone.

"That's all the history you need to know for now," he said. "Time to return."

He waved his arm, and Alex found himself back where they started in the classroom, with everyone standing in the same spot where they had left. Master Puma was standing off to the side with his arms folded in front of him.

"Were you waiting the entire time?" Alex asked him.

"You were only gone for a few seconds," Master Puma replied matter-of-factly.

Master Kattan moved over, next to everyone.

"Since we used the Zero Point Field to present this class to you, it only takes a few moments for your minds to absorb it fully. Classes that feel like it took an entire day to experience will just take a couple of minutes of real time to complete. Of course, we always have a Qen in each room standing by—to keep you safe during the short time you're away taking your classes."

Master Puma turned toward the Qen and nodded at him. The Qen slid over to his perch and disappeared.

"Keep in mind that the hard part of your training will not be the classroom work," Master Kattan said. "After you take a class, you'll know everything there is to know about the subject, and you'll remember it forever. No, it's not that—it's the hands-on training where the hard work is. We cannot use the Zero Point Field to give you the exact experience of performing tasks. We can present classes that simulate the feel of doing a task, but it is not anywhere near as good as the true experience. That you'll have to practice in real-life."

Master Kattan turned to the right.

"I'll leave you now in the capable hands of Master Puma," he said abruptly.

Both Master Kattan and Master Puma gave a quick bow to each other, and Master Kattan left the room. Master Puma waited for him to disappear down the hallway before he turned to face everyone.

"Follow me," is all he said, walking away.

Alex moved in between Elka and Maia and pointed to the back of Master Puma.

"What do you think about him?" he whispered.

Elka just made a face and shook her head. Maia shrugged her shoulders and leaned over, near Alex's ear.

"Maybe he's just having a bad week," she said.

"I don't think so," Alex quietly replied. "There's something wrong with him."

Nobody said anything more while they continued following behind Master Puma. A Jade colored path led them to a building directly next to the classroom facility. The layout of the building was almost the same as the one they just left, except that it was four stories high.

They approached it, and Master Puma pointed to the sign over its entrance that read 'JD-MF-2.'

"Jade Division, Maintenance Facility Number Two," he said. He stopped outside the entrance, staring at the building. Everyone else stopped behind him.

"Enter here," Master Puma said, still facing the building. "You'll continue with your orientation inside." He walked away without saying another word.

Everyone stood there, looking a little stunned.

"Not very social, is he?" said Maia.

Alex nodded and then led the way through the entrance membrane, not wanting to give Master Puma too much thought. They all passed the Qen sentry and stopped in the center of the room, waiting.

Standing off to the side, gazing into her Z-Con, was Master Ebo. She wore a dark blue dress and had her long blue hair twirled up into a tall bun that sat on the top of her nearly bald head. Her shoes were blue, and she wore blue gloves. When she finally looked up and noticed everyone standing in the middle of the reception room, she hurried over to them.

"Welcome, everybody!" she shouted. "I hope you're having a great time today!"

"It's the most fun I've ever had at school," Alex said.

"What else will we be doing today?" Maia asked.

"Let's see…" Master Ebo contemplated. "First, I'm going to show you around the maintenance facility, and then we'll head over to the competition ring to show you how that all works. Everybody ready?"

Master Ebo lifted her arm up over her head, spun around, and then dropped her arm down—pointing forward.

"Follow me!" she said, quickly sprinting away.

Alex swung in behind her and started jogging to catch up.

"Let's get up to the top floor so we can get a good view," Master Ebo said.

She stopped when she reached the right-hand wall. Lining the ground were six large white dots that had the word 'Lift Area' printed in the middle of them.

She looked up and said, "All clear! Let's go."

Master Ebo stepped onto one of the large dots, pointed her Z-Con at the ground, and shot up to a landing platform on the fourth floor. Alex moved forward, drew out his Z-Con and followed after her. Within a few seconds, everyone arrived.

Master Ebo moved forward to a walkway running along the entire perimeter wall of the top floor. Looking down from it provided a complete view of the work floor below. Alex moved forward and reached the railing alongside Master Ebo. Below them dozens of students worked, hunching over a large amount of equipment that took up almost the entire floor space. Near the left-hand corner sat a dozen small ultra-light airplanes, with a couple of larger more traditional aircraft next to them. Toward the far wall, Alex watched several students lift an engine out of a go-cart and move it over to a work table alongside them. In the corner on the right side, students tinkered with several small motorcycles, and near the left wall a handful of students washed a matching set of six small sailboats.

Alex looked back up and realized that everyone else had moved on from the railing, so he sprinted over to catch up with them. Master Ebo strolled around the walkway, talking over her shoulder.

"From here you can see students working on the gear that we use in our competitions. Soon all of you will be involved in this activity. It is vitally important that you acquire a great deal of expertise in fixing and maintaining equipment."

She stopped and turned around.

"You never know when it might be important," she said with a sober expression. Then once again, like a switch being thrown, her face beamed with enthusiasm. "So, let's go take a look at our competition arena!"

Everyone moved back to the landing platform and jumped down to the first floor, then walked out of the maintenance facility, Alex noticed a group of five students hanging around near the entrance. All of them were wearing shoes that matched the exact color pattern of the opal pyramid.

"Why are they hanging around?" he asked Dion.

"Don't know," Dion replied a little nervously. But he kept walking as if he wasn't at all interested.

It was too odd for Alex to ignore. Except for that small group, there were only Jade Division students in the area. Alex turned and took a few steps in their direction. As soon as he did, the students moved away, in a hurry. Alex stopped to see what they would do next, but as soon as he did, he heard Master Ebo calling.

"Whatever are you doing, Alex?" she yelled at him. "We must continue. Fall in if you please!"

Alex took one final look back at the students and sprinted back to Master Ebo.

Everyone followed the Jade road toward the center of the training facility, where Master Ebo started her lecture.

"From here you can see the stream of water that meanders around the entire perimeter of the facility, near the dome wall. Over behind the Opal Pyramid is a small forest of trees. Between the Jade Pyramid and the Lava Pyramid, you can see the area for experimental crop growth. Our agriculture classes are growing hybrid corn and wheat in there now. They'll absorb more than ten times the normal amount of carbon dioxide—better for the environment that way."

A couple of groups of small birds flew overhead. Alex started wondering how they got the birds into the facility. For that matter, he wondered how they got everything in it. It must have taken an extremely long time to deliver it all through the portal system.

Eventually, they reached the center of the dome, and Master Ebo continued.

"Here is where we hold all of our major competitions. You'll take training classes in various activities and then eventually prove your skills by competing against your classmates in this arena. We can configure it to hold any type of event we want. There are over two dozen events that we hold periodically. For example…"

She pulled out her Z-Con and pointed it at the center. The ground immediately turned into dark brown dirt, and steep hills popped up all over it. A winding path meandered throughout its interior in a circular course. Surrounding the outside of the dirt ring, three sections of spectator stands shot up from the ground; one with Opal seats, one with

148

Lava, and the other one Jade. Each stand was big enough to hold the entire population of its respective pyramid.

"What you see here is the setup for a standard motocross competition."

"Excellent!" Elka said to Maia, who shook her head enthusiastically.

A short moment later Master Ebo pointed her Z-Con again. The stands slid farther away, the ground turned into concrete, and many strange looking obstacles shot up into the air. Each one of the obstacles sat on top of poles that ranged in height from just a few feet off the ground, up to hundreds of feet high.

"This is one of our ultralight aircraft setups. In this event, students demonstrate their ability to pilot aircraft and show us how well they handle their nerves."

Alex poked Dion in his back to get his attention.

"That's for me," he said.

Dion didn't turn around but gave Alex a thumbs-up.

Master Ebo waited only another moment before she pointed her Z-Con again. The poles withdrew, and the concrete floor dropped down about ten feet to the ground. The hole that it formed instantly filled with water. In its center, waves crashed up against each other, and around the perimeter, smaller waves broke over the wall.

"This is our water pit. During these events, students demonstrate their ability to sailboats and perform tasks underwater by working as a team. Sometimes two students, sometimes four."

She pointed her Z-Con over her head. A large gust of wind sprang up from behind everyone, catching them a little off guard.

"We control the wind speed and direction during all the events to make it more interesting." She motioned for everyone to gather in front of her.

"This area is turned into a gathering hall at night. Everyone eats dinner here together. It helps us remember that even though during the day we compete fiercely against each other, at the end of it all we are one team with one goal."

Master Ebo started circling everyone, looking out at the pyramids in the distance.

"Your typical day will start with a few minutes in the classroom learning your lessons, a couple of hours of assisting in the maintenance facility, and the rest of the day in your various outside classes, learning and practicing your new skills. When you feel comfortable with your abilities, you'll start to participate in competitions." She stopped when she returned in front of everyone again.

"How well you do during those competitions will help you each earn advancement through the various stages of colors on your wristbands."

"What do all the colors mean?" Alex asked.

"Your skill level with The Field is indicated by the color of your wristband. Your goal someday is to become a black-band."

"It seems a little like the colored belts they use in martial arts classes back home," Alex said.

"That they do!" Master Ebo answered energetically. "The concept of colors representing skill levels was—how should I say it, 'borrowed' from us during the early days of the martial arts schools. But we, of course, have been using colored bracelets for over four thousand years."

Master Ebo clapped her hands together.

"Well, that's enough for one day. You'll learn all the details and the rules as you go on. Please return to your pyramid and discuss your training schedule with your division head. He'll assist you in setting up your curriculums. Bye for now!"

She snapped around and sprinted toward the black pyramid.

After everyone standing around looking quizzically at each other, Elka said, "Shall we?"

Alex and Dion walked ahead, toward the Jade pyramid, but close enough to Elka and Maia to overhear their planning. Their hushed discussions all seemed to revolve around riding motorcycles and about how well they were going to do competing in it.

"Were you interested in flying in that ultra-light competition?" Dion asked Alex. "Because I sure am."

"Oh man, I've wanted to learn to fly since I can remember," Alex said. "I think we should sign up for that. Although we'll be flying in separate planes."

When Alex turned to Dion to start discussing plans along those lines, he realized Dion was preoccupied with watching something behind them. Alex turned around to see what was so fascinating. The same group of opal students that Alex had observed at the maintenance faculty, were now on the other side of the water pit, moving fast in their direction.

Dion turned back to Alex and gave him a slight smack on the shoulder. He stopped in his tracks and looked at Elka and Maia.

"Race you back to the terrace?" Dion said.

Everyone nodded. After a split second, Elka said, "Go!"

The four of them ran as fast as they could, but Alex had been running track at school for years and had an advantage over everyone. He reached the pyramid terrace a few seconds before anyone else, and then looked back to see what the other group of students was doing. He watched them running along the same path that he had just followed, but they all stopped the chase when Alex and the others reached the pyramid terrace. The group turned around and headed away in the other direction, periodically looking back.

When Dion passed him, Alex grabbed his arm. Dion swung around.

"What?" Dion asked.

"You know what," Alex said coarsely. "What's up with those kids?"

"I don't know what you're talking about," Dion said, walking away.

Alex remained behind, watching the other students retreating, trying to figure it out. He stayed there, studying the scene until the group was out of sight.

NINE

Division leader Kolek Mencher stood silently in the center of the Jade Pyramid as Elka, Maia, and Dion approached him. He held his electronic clipboard out in front of him, reading it while he waited.

Alex followed far behind the group. Didn't Dion trust him enough to tell him about what was going on? Was Dion trying to keep him out of it for his protection? Maybe Dion didn't know. That was probably the worst case of all—not knowing could be a bigger problem.

Alex jogged up behind Dion and nudged him in the back.

"Sorry bud," Alex said.

Dion turned slightly.

"Forget it."

Alex moved on forward, and everyone assembled around Kolek.

"Master Ebo told us to see you about setting up our schedule," Maia said.

"Yep," Kolek replied, noting something on his clipboard. After a few more seconds of writing, he abruptly turned toward the rear of the building. "This way everyone."

He reached the membrane that separated the front and back halves of the pyramid and, with his head down and still reading from his clipboard, continued through without slowing.

This time nobody in the group slowed down as they went through. Going straight through membranes seemed to be getting to be a rather natural thing for Alex to do.

Kolek headed to the right side of the corridor, and everyone lined up to follow along behind him. He reached the far wall and pointed upwards with his index finger. Everyone stopped and looked straight up at a square-shaped tunnel directly overhead. Alex moved closer to the center of it to get a better look. The tunnel appeared to go straight up to the top of the pyramid. Alex could see several landing platforms jutting out from its right side, each one labeled with a large floor number.

"This is the main connection tunnel to the floors above. Note that nobody is allowed to jump to the top floor. There is no landing platform on it, and it has a solid door that is kept locked. Anyone attempting to get onto that floor without an escort from a Master will be immediately expelled. Do you all understand that?"

Alex and everyone else nodded.

"Good, then let me show you around down here. This floor is the tallest, has the most space, and it has the most rooms."

"Why don't the rooms have signs on them?" Alex asked.

"Because we re-purpose the rooms every once in a while, according to whatever our current needs are. Besides, we don't want students getting too used to labels telling them everything they need to know. You must learn to rely on your memory. Not everything you'll be learning is presented to you by using the Zero Point Field. You will also be in the real world, getting real experience. You have to learn to remember all of it. The more you practice memorizing, the better off you'll be."

Kolek strolled off and stopped in front of the largest doorway in the hallway.

"In here is the movie theater. Some of the classes that students take are in the various arts, including movie production. The movies made in those classes are shown in this room."

Alex peered into the theater but didn't see any movie screen. All he could see was a small stage in front of the hundred or so theater seats, but the stage was just barely big enough to hold a handful of people. He was about to ask about it, but Kolek continued before he could.

"When you're in this room you'll be able to use your Z-Cons to immerse yourself into their movie productions—much the same way that you'll take your classes when they're presented to you using The Field. Many of the movies shown here are designed to go on for extended periods of time. Most of these productions allow you to interact with them and determine what course of action that the movie takes." He pointed to the room across the corridor. It had an equally large entrance way.

"That room is where we assemble as a Division for certain announcements and awards. Throughout the year, on

155

special occasions, we also hold celebrations there. Students can also use their Z-Cons to convert the room for various activities. Soccer, basketball—things like that. If you want to use the room for yourselves, you can have your Qen make a reservation." Kolek turned to face the group. "By the way, did you try programming him?"

"A little," Elka said. "We didn't get very far."

"Try turning off the lights and remaining still while you're doing it." Kolek offered. "If they're busy paying attention to your needs, they won't respond to programming. Ask for 'admin' access when he's standing still."

Elka nodded her head and smiled knowingly at her sister.

"I told you the access would be called 'admin,'" she whispered to Maia. "Sixty percent of the time it's 'admin.'"

Kolek headed off again with everyone following him.

"The other rooms on this floor include a small medical facility, an exercise room, a steam room, and various other utility rooms. Feel free to walk around when you get a chance. You'll notice that there are many students inside here today. That's because everyone gets Saturday and Sunday off to work on whatever projects they want. You probably saw many students working at the maintenance facility. They're working on the equipment that they plan on using during the upcoming competitions. There's no requirement that they do that—they want to do whatever it takes to win. We look for that kind of dedication in our students."

Kolek stopped at the next room they came across.

"This room is important today. We call it the Com Room. Every Sunday morning, we allow students to communicate with their families for ten minutes."

Alex's heart leaped! It was completely unexpected—and wasn't that always the best kind of good news?

"Normally the training facility is completely isolated from the outside world, and no communication is allowed in or out. But during this hour, once a week, we turn on special security protocols that allow you to use your Z-Cons to connect with your parents. In this room, you can sit at any of the open cubicles along the wall and hook your Z-Cons to theirs. This room is only available for one hour, and only at this time on Sunday. There are fifteen minutes left today, so if you would like you can go ahead."

Alex rushed over to the cubicles and jumped into the seat at the nearest one. Elka and Maia took the one next to him, with Dion taking the next one down.

"After you get comfortable, connect your Z-con to your parent's by concentrating on a mental image of them talking into their Z-Con. Start thinking of a vibration word, and you should connect. Don't move around too much."

Alex already had his Z-Con out and instantly started to connect. It only took a few seconds before a perfect 3-D image of his parents projected above the top face of his Z-Con. The two of them sat next to each other behind a desk. His father was ecstatic to see Alex, but there was something wrong with his mother. It was as if the smile on her face was forced.

"Hello, Alex!" Miguel shouted. "It's great to see you son."

"Hi, Dad! Hi, Mom!" Alex responded. "Where are you?"

"We're in Mexico," Miguel said.

"Why Mexico? Where's Aura?"

"Aura's is with your Aunt Rosa in Mexico City. She's going to stay with her while your mother and I finish up our work."

"Are you okay, Mom?"

"Of course, Alex," Janet answered. "I'm just a little tired." She hesitated for a couple of seconds before continuing. "We've been traveling a lot."

"Around Mexico?" Alex said. "I was just at some of the Mayan pyramids in Mexico!"

"Sorry, Alex, but they just cut out most of your last sentence. I think you were trying to tell us where you've been. That's not allowed. The location of the portal sites and the training facility is very secret. It would be best not to mention anything that would point to where they are, okay?"

"Okay, sure Dad."

"Tell us what you've been doing."

Alex told them about all the traveling he had done over the last two days, all about his roommates, and about the tour of the facility he had just finished. He told them how Mercure was doing, and how he was looking forward to learning how to fly. His father asked him many questions, but his mother remained quiet the entire time.

Alex decided not to mention any of the problems he had in the portals, or even how the pyramid had turned red under his palms when he tried to climb it. He didn't want to bother his parents about anything—he got the distinct impression that they were having enough problems of their own to contend with, without having to worry about him too. Besides, he figured the school would have told his parents about anything they needed to know—if they needed to know that is.

"Tell me about the arrival ceremony," Miguel said. "How did that go? You weren't scared, were you?"

"No, everything went fine. I got a yellow bracelet."

"Yellow? Well, excellent!" Miguel exclaimed. Even his mother perked up when she heard that.

Alex noticed the poster of the Mayan hieroglyphs hanging on the wall behind his father—the same one Mercure had spoken of earlier.

"Dad, why are you looking at those pictures? That guy carved into the center of the stone looks familiar."

"It has to do with us handling those orbs that attacked us the other night. But it looks like it's a dead-end. I keep the picture because I like the way it looks."

"I think I saw those same glyphs yesterday."

"Alex, as I said, don't talk too much about the details of where you've been, or they'll start censoring it again."

"Okay, Dad. Mom, are you sure you're okay?"

"Yes, Alex, don't worry about us. We're doing fine. Really. Okay?"

"Okay," Alex said. But he wasn't. It was unsettling to see his mother like this. They had only been apart for a couple of days, and no amount of traveling could make her act this way. But he felt the best thing to do was to ignore it for now, and after a few seconds of awkward silence, he decided to change the subject.

"I guess I should let you know that I took a Jade Z-Con. I know that you have a black one Dad, but it felt right when I chose it."

"That's fine, Alex," Miguel said. "Things like that are often influenced by the Zero Point Field. Many parts of a person's destiny are wrapped up in The Field. If you chose Jade, then there is a good reason for it. Someday you might even find out why."

The picture on top of the Z-Con began flashing red.

"Well that's the end of our time, Alex," Miguel said. "We'll be ready every Sunday when you contact us."

"Promise?" Alex said forcefully.

"Guaranteed son. We'll be ready every Sunday no matter what. Say hello to Mercure for us. Well, we love you, be good, and we'll talk again next week."

The red flashing started getting faster.

"Bye, Dad. Bye, Mom."

"Bye, Alex," Miguel said. Janet removed the Z-Con from Miguel's hand and moved forward, taking up the entire image.

"Bye, Alex, we love …"

The picture on the Z-Con ended abruptly. Alex sat there just looking at his Z-Con. Eventually, he looked up to see Dion walking over to him.

"That was good," Dion said. "I feel a lot better now."

"Were your parents okay?" Alex asked.

"Sure. They seemed happy enough. How'd it go with you?"

"Something's wrong. My dad seemed okay, but my mom was…there was just something wrong."

Elka and Maia turned from their seats to face Alex.

"Something's wrong all right," Elka said.

"They both seemed a little odd," Maia followed. "There's definitely something going on."

160

"Did they tell you what they were doing?" Alex asked. "What they were looking at?"

"No," Elka said.

"Did you see anything?" Alex asked. "I saw some glyphs in the background behind my father."

"We saw a hologram of a pyramid," Maia said. "It was too small to make out very much though."

"Okay, let's get going," Kolek shouted from the corner of the room.

Nobody was in a rush to move, but after a few seconds Alex stood up and slowly headed toward the door. Dion moved in right behind him, but it took Elka and Maia a little while to get up and join in.

Kolek led everyone to a room across the hallway. The room had a normal size door, and the room itself was empty. After he entered, Kolek continued to the far wall and started speaking to the Qen in the corner.

"Give me a scheduling suite. Primary year training. Four students."

Four large screens appeared high on the wall in front of Kolek.

"On these screens, you will see the options available to you for your first session of training," Kolek said. "As you can see on the left screen, everyone will take a full curriculum of class work. Language, math, science, and geography. You'll also have a daily class in The History and Use of Z-Cons. For your practical classes, everyone will take first level training in self-defense. If you have a dog, they will take that class with you—you'll learn to work with them as a team."

Kolek pointed to the other screens.

161

"From these lists, you will pick two electives from the first level practical classes. We always participate as part of a team, so on one of the electives, you'll need to team up with one other person. On the other elective, you'll need to it take as a four-person team."

Kolek turned to the second screen on the left.

"So first pick a two-team class. What's currently available is ultra-light flying, sky-diving, and motocross."

Alex and Dion bumped fists.

"Ultra-lights for us," Alex said.

Elka and Maia spent a few seconds whispering to each other. They answered at the same time.

"Motocross!"

"That leaves the four-team class," Kolek said. "There are only four electives that all four of you can participate in during your first semester—high wire walking, snowmobile racing, sailing, or scuba."

"I've been sailing before," Alex stated. "Anyone else?"

"Well, we've been on boats," Elka replied.

"Okay with me," Dion said.

Kolek pointed to the room Qen and waved his hand. The screens disappeared.

"That's it then—you will all take sailing," he said. "Your Qen will receive your schedules, and he'll make sure you get to your classes on time. Good luck."

Kolek walked out of the room as if he had someplace important to go.

Elka and Maia were positively thrilled. They had their arms around each other's shoulders as they walked toward the door, talking about motocross.

Alex and Dion turned to leave, but after a couple of steps, they stopped. Bhedi Haley and her sister Jordan blocked the doorway, both with their arms folded.

"Sailing, Alex?" Bhedi said with a small laugh. "We're in that class."

Elka, Maia, and Dion stopped in unison, but Alex didn't even slow down.

"Yeah, Bhedi—sailing," he said, continuing toward her. "That a problem?" He kept a smile on his face while he said it. He stopped directly in front of both Bhedi and Jordan.

"It's a bit dangerous," Bhedi said. "I don't mean the sailing part. It's just that when everyone finds out you're not any better at it than anybody else, they're going to realize you're a fraud."

"And what if they find out I'm better at it than you?"

Both girls laughed.

"Why is this so important to you two?" Alex asked.

"Didn't you get the word?" Bhedi said, moving forward to within a few inches of Alex. She was a couple of inches taller than Alex, and she tried to use every bit of it.

"Everything we do around here is important. It's one big competition." Bhedi studied Alex's face for a couple of seconds. "You better start figuring that out right now, or you're going to get run over."

Once again Jordan pulled her away from Alex, but this time Bhedi was having none of it. She pulled back from Jordan and returned to Alex's face.

"It's been all fun and games up to now, hasn't it? But now everyone's going to start keeping score. And when you fall on your face, I'm going to be the one standing over you laughing."

Alex remained calm the entire time. He was almost smiling. He'd been bullied before—this was nothing new.

"If I have problems, can I count on you for some support?" Alex asked.

That was enough for Bhedi. She cocked her arm back, but this time Jordan got a good hold of Bhedi shoulders and pushed her out into the hallway.

Elka, Maia, and Dion came up behind Alex. Elka put her hand on Alex's shoulder as she passed him.

"That's a girl with a problem," she said, and then continued out the doorway with Maia.

Dion remained back, next to Alex. They both stared at the doorway, pondering.

"It's a problem all right," Dion said. "What are you going to do about her? Talk to Kattan?"

"No, she's not so tough," Alex said. "All talk I think."

"Think? Maybe you should find out for sure."

"You're right," Alex said. He turned and faced Dion. "You know…I think I'm going to have another talk with my dog."

TEN

"I thought there would be more dogs here," Alex said to Mercure.

Mercure trotted several feet ahead of Alex, navigating the shoreline of the stream running behind the Jade pyramid. He stopped and waited for Alex to catch up.

"There are usually twenty or thirty dogs here at any one time," Mercure told him. *"Panda and I are kind of rare."*

Alex reached Mercure and kept walking past him. Mercure turned and followed a step or so behind. It was a couple more minutes before Alex spoke again.

"You know for the last couple of days I've been trying to figure out all the things mom and dad hadn't told me about," Alex said. He looked down at Mercure. "You're one of them." After a few seconds, he looked back up. "I mean, I got to admit I knew you were special, and I didn't question it when they always told me not to talk to anyone about you. But the way I see it now…you certainly know a lot more about things than you're telling me."

Alex stopped and took a seat on a bench overlooking the stream and the dome wall. Mercure caught up and sat down in front of him.

"Okay, tell me what you want to know."

"How is it that there are dogs that can speak to their owners."

"They told you about Nedo, right? He used the Zero Point Field to modify a couple of hundred dogs so they could communicate with humans and…"

Mercure stopped for a moment.

"And what?" Alex prodded.

It took a few more seconds of searching for Mercure to figure out how to phrase it.

"And live an extraordinarily long life."

"How long?"

"Not sure yet. Only a few of us have died, and they were all from accidents."

"I guess that means you've been with lots of families over all those years."

Mercure nodded his head.

"As a matter of fact, the last family I was with was your dad's. I was with him since he was born. I imagine when you get older I'll be with one of your kids."

Alex gave Mercure a long, long look.

"Are you a projection from the Zero Point Field?" he blurted out.

"Me? No, I'm not a projection! Nedo just gave us the abilities. Damn Alex! I'm a real dog!"

Alex instantly regretted saying it.

"Okay, sorry buddy," he said. "I just needed to know."

Alex bent over and stroked Mercure's neck.

166

"So, tell me about this place. I mean, how come me? Why did they pick me to come here? And what was all that with those orbs chasing us?"

"First of all, I don't know much about those orbs. As far as I have ever heard, they were created by Nedo, and that they were all tracked down and destroyed a couple of thousand years ago. There's not supposed to be any left. I imagine that's what has Z and your parents all concerned. If they were all destroyed, then where did those four new ones come from?"

"And me? What am I doing here?"

"You belong here. Normally you would have come next semester. By then your parents would have told you all about what you needed to know before they sent you here. It's not their fault you had to come early."

"But that's not true! I could have gone with them. They took my sister with them—they could've taken me too."

"This is the safest place for you."

Alex's back stiffened up.

"Safest? Why? Am I in some kind of danger?"

"No. I mean no one knows for sure why those orbs attacked us. Bellon came to get us that night because Z sent him. Somehow Z figured out that those things were coming after us. He thought they might be after kids that he knew to have superior connections with The Field. That would be you, Elka and Maia."

"How do they know that? I didn't even know that!"

"They can tell. Nobody ever explained it to me, but Z knows."

"Herabata knows too – doesn't she?" Alex said.

"How did you know that?"

167

"She looks so much like Z; I just figured they were related somehow – probably had the same kind of powers."

"Well, I think they're cousins of some sort. Came from the same tribe in Africa."

Alex thought about it for a few seconds. He turned around, surveying the entire training facility.

"Why is this place so competitive?"

"That's how they figure out who goes on to what jobs. The students with the best fighting skills get assigned to the defense forces. Other ones get sent to tasks like planning, research, staffing the facilities we have, things like that. Competition is the best way to see who has what skills. But, if the time comes and we've got to defend Earth, everyone one of us becomes a soldier—no matter what our job is at that moment. We all have to be able to fight at any time."

Mercure waited for a second for Alex to turn back to him before continuing.

"Sure, there's a lot of aggression around here. Many students are driven to succeed. How you handle those kids is going to be noticed. Some kids react to it with aggression on their own. Others let their performance in the competitions do the talking for them. At the end of it, all the instructors try to make sure everybody feels like they're part of one team. But that doesn't mean the competition ever gets any less."

After hearing that, Alex felt unsure. He always avoided confrontation when it happened to him in the past. Now he was supposed to embrace it? Be part of it? That wasn't going to come easily to him. And as if all that wasn't enough, on top of it all, he couldn't stop thinking about how his parents were acting.

"There's something going on with my mom. I saw it on her face when I spoke to her."

"Well if there is, I don't know about it. Sorry."

"It's okay," Alex assured him.

Alex slowly shook his head from side to side. It was a lot to think about. He picked up his head and stood up.

"Let's get going. I want to take a walk around the whole place. If I'm going to be here for a few years, I might as well get familiar with it."

"Very sensible."

Alex and Mercure spent the next hour hiking around the entire length of the stream. It had no beginning and no end. It just flowed around in a giant circle, past the Opal Pyramid and its adjacent forest of tall trees, around the Lava Pyramid—and the stands of crops behind it.

They passed many buildings of maintenance facilities, classrooms, and various other buildings that Alex couldn't identify because all the signs on them were acronyms.

The whole time they walked, Alex thought about the last couple of days and how his entire life was changing before him. Although it still scared him, the more he thought about it, and the more he walked, the more natural it felt. He couldn't figure out exactly why, but the tension inside him slowly left, and he started feeling more like he belonged here. The fact that he was destined to be a part of this school for the next few years was becoming a most thrilling thought. He was going to be part of a small force of people charged with defending the Earth! And it was just last week that he thought the most exciting thing that was going to happen to him this year was making the track team again.

Alex knew he was going to have to start thinking in bigger terms.

Alex and Mercure ended their walk back at the Jade Pyramid, and Alex had become far more relaxed. For the last couple of days everything he saw, touched or even tasted felt somehow familiar. Now the entire school started feeling familiar.

Alex and Mercure made their way up to their quad. They found Elka, Maia, and Dion in the common room, sitting around the center table with two other students. Alex stood in the doorway for a few seconds before taking a step inside. Mercure sat down alongside him.

"Hey, Alex," Elka said. "This is Trish and Brenda. They're from next door."

The two girls stood up, walked over to Alex, and said "Hi." Trish, the taller of the two, moved past him and kneeled next to Mercure and started to scratch his head.

"Good to meet you fella," Trish said. "I take it you're Mercure. Looks like he's the biggest dog in the pyramid, Alex. Not much bigger than Panda though." She looked over at Panda and winked.

"How many other dogs are here?" Alex asked. He had only seen a handful of dogs around the entire area.

"Ten in our pyramid—including Mercure and Panda. They always say dogs bring good luck to the competitions." Trish looked up at Alex. "We sure could use a dose of it."

"Brenda's been telling us about all the competitions they've had so far," Dion interjected. "Jade Division hasn't been doing so good."

"Why not?" Alex asked Trish. "Don't they split the students up evenly?"

170

"It doesn't always work out that way," Trish said, continuing to pet Mercure. "We had a lot of top students graduate last year. It kind of left a hole in the leadership. Kolek is excellent, don't get me wrong. But you've got to have good, aggressive leaders on the competition teams. We've been coming up a little short."

Alex noticed both Trish and Brenda had white bracelets.

"Have you been in the competitions yet?" he asked Trish.

"Not the majors—you know, the ones they hold in the competition ring at the core," Brenda answered. "But when you take the prelim classes, they match you up with other students in the class. Then you compete against them out in the field. That's how you get to the next color."

"Do yellow bracelets compete in the majors?"

"Not really," Brenda answered. "Not that there's any rule against it, but they start the best students in those competitions—yellow bracelets just aren't good enough yet."

"But they rely on all of us to help out though," Trish said proudly. "You know, doing the maintenance, helping during practice, things like that. You learn a lot when you're in the pits. There's a lot of strategies to figure out. You've got to compete within the rules, but you got to push the rules if you want to win. When you're on a crew, you get a chance to learn how much you can get away with. But then again, they change the rules every so often—makes it harder to learn a winning strategy."

Alex was intrigued. "How do you get on a team?"

"They might assign you to one when you start working in the maintenance facility," Brenda replied.

Brenda's Z-Con pulsated blue—Alex could see the top of it sticking out of her front pants pocket. He had noticed that most students kept their Z-Cons in their front pockets, but some of them kept it in the side pouches attached to their belts.

Brenda stared out into space for a second.

"Angie wants to know if we're heading over to the core soon," she said to Trish.

"How did you know that?" Alex asked. "You didn't even look at your Z-Con."

"I have a lens in my left eye," Brenda answered.

"A lens?" Elka said, looking into Brenda's brown eyes.

"Oh...well on the first day of your 'History and Use of the Z-Con class,' they give you a contact lens to put in your eye," Brenda said. "It lets you see instructions and messages from your Z-Con. They show up as floating text, about a foot or two out in front of you."

"Excellent!" Dion said.

At that moment, a short knock came from the doorway frame, and two boys entered the room. The light brown-haired one carried a four-foot long piece of rope that he was playing with. The other boy followed him in, looking concerned that he was interrupting.

"Everyone, these are our quad mates," Trish said. "The guy who can't put the rope down is Jayden. And that's Samuel."

Both boys gave a slight nod to the group.

"This is Elka, Maia, Alex, and Dion."

"Dion?" Samuel said. "From what I hear, there's some Opal students wanting to talk to you."

"Lots of hotheads in Opal," Jayden said. "You should watch yourself."

Alex gave Dion a long look.

"Don't worry about it," Dion said to everyone staring at him. "It's just a little misunderstanding."

Jayden shrugged his shoulders and started straightening out his rope.

"I heard it was more than that," he said. After a couple of seconds, he had his rope under control. "I thought we were heading out to meet Angie and Carol," he said. "They just popped me."

"What's that mean?" Alex asked Brenda.

"Sorry," she said. "I guess this is still all new to you. 'Popped me' is when a message from your Z-Con suddenly shows up in front of your face."

While they were talking, Jayden tied various knots around his arm and his waist.

"What's that all about?" Elka asked him.

"There's a knot tying contest in my sailboating class," Jayden said. "I'm going to set the school speed record." He straightened out the rope in front of him. "For example..."

He held one end of his rope and with a quick flip of his wrist, flung it over his arm. He made a quick, small adjustment with his other hand, tying the rope securely.

"Clove hitch."

He untied the rope, flung it around his waist with his left hand, and with one motion of his right hand, wrapped it around, over, and through itself. The whole thing took less than two seconds.

"Bowline," he said.

He untied himself and started coiling the rope up into a small ball.

"There's over twenty knots you have to tie. I can do them all just as fast. The record's fifty-eight seconds."

Trish stood up from Mercure and headed to the door. All her roommates headed out with her.

"Well, we're going to meet up with some friends at the core, before dinner," Trish said. She reached the door and swung her head back around. "When you come down we'll save you some seats. Pop-ya!"

"What?" Alex said.

"Oh, right... No lens. Well then, see ya!"

As soon as everyone left, Alex sat down next to Dion.

"I think everyone else at the school knows more about your problem than we do," he stated coolly.

"I keep telling you—it's no big deal," Dion said.

"And everyone else seems to think it is!" Alex snapped. "Just tell us!"

Elka and Maia both leaned in, over the table

"All right," Dion relented. "But it just seems so silly. I mean out of nowhere, suddenly I got a whole division of kids mad at me." Dion dropped his head down and ran his right hand through his hair a couple of times. "It wasn't my fault. I just panicked."

"Okay, start from the beginning," Elka said.

"It happened a few weeks ago back in the mountain, when I came through with everyone else, at the start of the semester. All us new kids just got our GEM suits fitted and tested, and we were all feeling pretty invincible. When I came back to the bunk room, I pushed past a couple of guys in Opal. They were both brown bracelets. But you know, at that point I don't even know what the colors stand for and all, and I didn't know that brown was just one step down from the top level. But they both pushed back at me and started in with the whole 'don't be so cocky kid' thing, and like I said I was feeling you know, like Superman. So anyway, I kind of challenged one of them. I swear I was just kidding…But I didn't know how seriously they take that kind of thing around here.

Dion looked up and continued. "At that point what could they do, right? So, one of them says that he'll take me on, one-on-one. Some guy named Jago, if you can believe it. So normally all challenges are between at least a team of two against another team of two. Everything around here happens in teams. But this guy says he knows that I don't have anyone to back me up, so he says that he'll just take me on alone. He asked me what I wanted to do, and he's laughing at me the whole time. Well, I've been boxing since I was a little kid, and one of the challenges we always did back then was to see who could hit the other guy's bare fist the hardest with his bare fist. So, I suggested that. Then Jago holds up his fist, and I swear it looks like a huge rock. I mean like twice as big as mine. So, I'm thinking I just better get this over with, and I swung and hit it. Man, I forgot all about me wearing a GEM glove and all. Well anyway, since he doesn't have a glove on, I ended up shattering his hand."

Nobody spoke for a couple of seconds. Alex put his hand on Dion's shoulder and said, "I can't even…"

"Man, don't I know it," Dion muttered.

"How's the guy?" Maia asked.

"Not good," Dion said after a couple of seconds. "The thing is, around here they can fix just about anything, and they can fix his hand, good as new! But I really pulverized it. He's out for a few months. Anyway, it turns out that he was one of Opal's best team leaders. Now I got an entire division out to get even with me."

He looked up at the ceiling for a few seconds.

"They weren't even sure they were going to let me come back at all. I spent a few weeks waiting for them to decide. I guess they figured with the three of you coming through—it wouldn't be too much of an inconvenience for them to let me tag along. So, they got me up in the middle of the night and said I could go on through if I still wanted. My mom and dad weren't sure they wanted me to, but I said I had to face it. So here I am."

Dion leaned forward and put his arms on the table. Both his shoulders were tightened up, right next to his neck.

"I'm hoping I can get myself squared with them with just one confrontation. I mean like one challenge. That's what my dad said it might come down to."

"What about the instructors?" Elka asked. "Won't they help figure this out between everybody?"

"No. My dad told me that the instructors leave this kind of stuff up to the students. They'll only interfere if it's absolutely necessary."

"I take it you'll need someone to team up with?" Alex asked. "Everything around here happens in teams, right?"

Dion didn't say anything.

"I'm with you," Alex said. After he had looked over to Elka and Maia for confirmation, he said, "We got your back."

Dion slumped back in his seat like every muscle in his body had relaxed.

"Thanks," he said sincerely.

Feng appeared on his pedestal.

"In twenty minutes, you'll be expected for dinner at the core. You should dress in one of your Jade jackets and leave in ten minutes."

Elka and Maia stood, gave a slight smile toward Dion, "We'll see you in a few," Maia said and went to their room, leaving Alex and Dion sitting at the table.

Mercure trotted over to Panda. They gave each other a quick smell, and then both lay down next to each other in the corner.

Alex stood up and said, "Well, let's go see how dinner turns out."

Dion didn't say anything. He just shook his head a little, stood up and went to their room.

A couple of minutes later all four of them came together in the common room and headed out the pyramid.

The artificial sun had turned itself off by this time, but the entire area was still lit up by the reflection of the powerful beams of light streaming down from the ceiling to the top of the three pyramids.

When they arrived at the core, there were already hundreds of students seated around oval tables. The tables had eighteen seats, and a mixture of students from the three different divisions sat at each one of them. The seats at each end of the tables were colored purple. With everyone talking to each other, the noise level was extremely high.

Alex, Elka, Dion, and Maia stood together looking around, trying to figure out what to do next.

Trish came running up from the side, behind Alex.

"Over here everyone!" she yelled before reaching him. "We've saved you some seats."

They all followed Trish to a table where she took a seat next to Brenda, Jayden, and Samuel. There were four empty seats to Trish's right, and everyone sat down on them, with Alex closest to her. Placed in front of each seat was a thin stone tablet. Across from Alex were four students wearing Opal jackets.

"All the divisions sit with each other?" Alex whispered to Trish.

"Yeah," she said. "The core is like neutral ground at dinner time. You can talk and joke around with anyone, from any division. It's all about 'Unit Cohesion.' Every table has to have at least a few students from each division. Nobody eats until that happens."

"Is this where people challenge each other?"

"Challenge? What are you talking about?"

Alex looked over to Dion and then back to Trish. She seemed to know what was going on.

"Oh, you mean that," she said. "No. No grudges allowed. Nobody's going to bother him here. They'll wait for classes tomorrow morning to get that all figured out."

"What do you think is going to happen?"

"They'll either let him off easy or make it sort of a payback kind of thing. It all depends on how they feel about it. Hard to say—I mean they wouldn't discuss that kind of thing with anyone outside their division."

Alex turned to Dion and leaned over.

"Did you hear that?"

"Yep. I guess I got a reprieve till tomorrow."

When four Lava students took up the last seats across from Alex, everyone at the table picked up their stone plates and placed their hand on it.

Trish leaned forward so that Alex and everyone could hear.

"Go ahead and think up a dinner. Then wait for the plates to come around. Put yours on top."

It suddenly struck Alex that he hadn't eaten any lunch. There was just too much else on his mind. He placed his palm on the plate and thought about a big serving of rice and beans with a steak. He didn't want to get too complicated with the selection because this time he was trying to concentrate on the texture and the taste.

The boy sitting in the seat closest to the table's center stood up and passed his stone plate to the left. Everyone passed on the pile of plates, stacking them up until they all arrived back at the starting point. The same boy lifted plates and dropped them into a square hole a couple of feet out in front of him. Within a minute, plates of food started rising from the hole. As each plate came up, the boy grabbed it and passed it to his left. As soon as he did, another plate of food came up to replace it. At the end of it, everyone had their dinner in front of them, and they all started eating.

Alex was impressed. The food tasted exactly like he had imagined—precisely the way his mom had made it at home. At each meal, he was getting better at perfectly imagining what he wanted.

"They sure do feed you good around here," Alex said while slightly nodding his head up and down. He looked around and saw that no one was sitting on any of the purple seats. "What are those seats all about?" he asked Trish.

"The purple seats remind us of the students who didn't make it through training," she told him.

"They failed out?"

"No," she said, putting her fork down. "They died."

Alex stiffened his back and put down his fork.

Trish turned herself toward Alex.

"They've been training students here for many centuries Alex. They try to make it as safe as they can, but accidents happen. Students take quite a few risks over the several years they train here."

"I guess, in a way, I figured that out already," Alex said. "It's just a little weird hearing it out loud though."

"The thing is that no students have died here for over ten years," Trish said. "They get better and better at making it safer. But you know…" She leaned in closer to Alex. "The worst part is that an instructor almost died at the beginning of this semester."

"What happened?"

"A student got into trouble during a sailing competition out at the boating facility. He fell in the water, but he didn't come back up to the surface. The instructor tried to use her Z-Con to pick him out of the water, but it didn't work. So, she dove in after him. As soon as she did, the student popped up, and the rest of the students got him out. He was okay, but the instructor didn't come back up for a long time. Then she floated up, and the students grabbed her and gave her mouth to mouth. She came out of it, but by the time they got her back here, well, she was out of it for a couple of days. She seems all right now, but she can't explain why her Z-Con didn't work, or what happened to her underwater."

"Does that happen often?" Alex asked. "I mean, the Z-Con just failing?"

"No," Trish said. She went back to eating, but after a couple of bites, she looked back at Alex.

"It never happens."

ELEVEN

The next morning Alex and Dion awoke to the sound of soft music. They sat up in their beds and Feng, who was patiently waiting in the middle of the room, began reciting the inspirational quote of the day.

"It does not matter how slowly you go, as long as you do not stop." After a slight pause, Feng glided toward his corner of the room and said, "That was from Confucius." He reached his perch and turned around. "In thirty-five minutes, you must report to 'Classroom Facility Number One.' In today's practical classes you'll start your training on flying. Tomorrow will be devoted to sailing." Feng crossed his arms in front of him. "Ask the Qen at the entrance for directions to your classroom."

Then, as normal, he froze with a small grin on his face before disappearing.

Exactly thirty-five minutes later Alex stood alongside Dion, Elka, and Maia in front of a very tall Qen at 'Jade Division, Classroom Facility Number One.' A line of students filed past on their way to their daily classes, barely taking notice of any of them. After a couple of moments, Alex took a slight step forward and touched the Qen's robe to get his attention. When the Qen didn't move, Alex stepped back. As the room grew more silent, with almost all the other students well on their way to their classrooms, Alex contemplated what to do next. He turned to Elka and Maia as if to ask if they had any ideas.

"You could announce your names!" the Qen shouted abruptly.

Alex jumped back a couple of feet and found himself falling to the floor alongside Dion. The Qen turned his head down toward Alex, and in a soft, normal tone said, "Perhaps then I could help you."

Alex remained seated next to Dion, trying to figure out what the Qen was all about before getting too close again.

"I'm Alex…"

"I know who you are," Qen said. "I'm just messing with you. Everything I need to know about of you is in the Zero Point Field. Can't hide from that, can we?"

"You're acting very odd for a Qen aren't you?" Dion said, helping Alex to his feet. The Qen shuttered slightly. Alex grabbed Dion's arm and pulled him away from the Qen, hoping that he wouldn't agitate him any further. As far as Alex was concerned this Qen was already provoked enough.

"I have tolerated many decades of personality programming from Jade students," the Qen said glumly.

"All of them trying to improve on the choices of the previous generation."

He bent down, staring directly at Dion, giving him a quizzical look.

"Do you like my current version?" he asked.

Dion stood frozen for a moment, so Alex moved in front of him.

"Sure," Alex answered, hoping to get the conversation over so that they could get on with their day.

"Then what can I help you with?" Qen stated, straightening back up.

"We've all been assigned to an eight o'clock class called…"

"Yes, yes. 'History and Use of the Z-Con.' Take tunnel two, all the way to the last classroom on the right. Hurry, you've already wasted two minutes of classroom time—the morning's practically over."

Alex slowly took a few steps toward the right-hand side of the Qen, keeping a close watch on him as he passed.

"We better get a move on," Alex said. As soon as he cleared the Qen, he rushed off toward tunnel number two.

Elka and Maia fell in behind Dion, and all of them cautiously stepped around the Qen. They quickly passed him and sprinted down the tunnel after Alex.

Alex reached the last classroom on the right and ran into it without slowing down, his three quadmates right behind him. He spotted a man standing in the far corner, speaking to the room Qen. Everyone halted abruptly in the middle of the room, and when the man did not turn around, Alex cleared his throat to get his attention.

"We're here for…"

"Of course, you are," the man stated, swinging around toward them. "You're all late. That is not tolerated well at this facility. Please be mindful of that in the future."

Elka turned toward Alex and Dion and shot them a glare.

"I told you we needed to leave sooner," she whispered gruffly at them.

Alex nodded his head to her, but Dion just shrugged his shoulders.

After studying the man for a bit, Alex thought his abrupt voice didn't match his face. He had kind eyes and a pleasant smile. Also, he didn't wear a robe like Alex thought he would. All the other adults Alex had met at The Dome wore robes. This man had on dress pants and a long green jacket that had no collar.

When the man started walking toward him, Alex just barely detected a slight limp. The man passed Alex and reached a countertop stretching the entire length of the wall on the room's right side. Sitting near the center of the counter sat four small metal boxes, each one about two inches square.

"My name is Mr. Serret," he said, lining up the boxes. "I will be instructing you on the history and use of your Z-Cons. But, first things first." He picked up the box nearest to him and looked at the label. "This one is for Alex," he said, holding it out.

Alex stepped over, retrieved it, and looked it over for any clue of what it might hold. As he did, Mr. Serret picked up the other boxes and distributed them.

"Elka...Maia...and Dion."

Mr. Serret dug into one of his jacket's deep pockets and rummaged around for a while before pulling out a pair of wire-rimmed glasses.

"Okay Alex," he said, putting on his glasses. "Step over to the counter, and we'll start working on your projector lens."

Alex wondered if this was the lens that Brenda mentioned yesterday afternoon. He was looking forward to getting it, but he also felt apprehensive about having something floating around his eye.

He moved over next to Mr. Serret and flipped open the box's lid. Dark foam padding lined the inside of the box, forming an indented curve. A small contact lens lay nestled inside the curve, glistening from the light overhead. Alex turned toward Mr. Serret and held the box up to him.

"We heard of these," Alex said. "I thought it would be floating in water or something."

"These lenses never dry out, Alex," Mr. Serret said. "Now keep the box in front of you, still as you can, and I'll place the lens in your left eye."

Alex took a quick look around, trying to locate some type of medical instrument that Mr. Serret was going to use, but he couldn't see anything that looked like it would be useful. The situation was becoming a little too informal for Alex's liking. If something was going to be inserted in his eye, it deserved to be in a more medical looking facility, didn't it? Perhaps a clinic of some type?

But Mr. Serret just used his two fingers to remove the lens from the box and positioned it on the tip of his right index finger. He used his other hand to tilt Alex's head up and moved the lens in toward his left eye. Alex was shaking a bit—he had never had anything in his eye before, except for maybe a small bug that flew into it by accident.

"Try to keep as still as you can," Mr. Serret said, concentrating. He slowly stated, "If I do this right, you won't even feel the lens touch you."

Faster than Alex could think about it, Mr. Serret moved his hand away from his eye.

"All done. Blink a couple of times and tell me how it feels."

Alex blinked, and instinctively rubbed his eye. He looked around the room to see the effect. But absolutely nothing changed. Everything was still perfectly clear.

"I can't even tell it's in there," Alex said, dumbfounded. "Are you sure you didn't drop it?"

"These lenses were built specifically to fit your eye," Mr. Serret said

"Once again, thank you Joeks Burlm, Head Fitter," Elka whispered.

Mr. Serret motioned for Alex to step aside and for Elka to take his place. She held out her opened box, and he went through the procedure once again.

"You'll never feel them," Mr. Serret said while working her lens. "You should keep them in at all times, even while sleeping. And, if for some reason, you ever want to take them out, get an instructor to help you. We don't want to lose them now, do we? They take a good deal of time to make."

When he finished with Elka, she moved away, and Maia took her turn.

187

"As I said, they'll never dry out—they won't affect your eyesight in any way. And germs can't grow on them. You should be able to wear them forever without any trouble."

After he finished working on Maia and Dion, he collected everyone's boxes, headed over to the room Qen, and handed him the boxes. As soon as the Qen received them, he drifted off his pedestal toward the front of the classroom. When he reached it, four school chairs appeared—all of them arranged in a single row. The chairs had built-in desktops that swung in from the side.

"All of you, please take a seat," Mr. Serret said.

Alex sat down in the nearest chair and began blinking his eye. He thought that he would at some point feel the lens floating around in there—but nothing he did cause an issue with it at all. The lens had essentially become part of his eye.

Before continuing, Mr. Serret waited for everyone to get settled into their chairs.

"I want you to place your right arm on the desktop, holding your Z-Con by its handle. Take a few seconds to get comfortable. When I signal you, please visualize yourselves standing in this classroom, exactly where you are all now sitting. Close your eyes, start a vibration word, and then wait for us all to arrive. Ready? Then begin."

As soon as he heard the word 'begin,' Alex closed his eyes and thought of the sound 'omega.' He immediately found himself standing alone in the classroom. Elka and Dion appeared soon after, and a few seconds later Maia appeared.

Mr. Serret appeared in the corner of the room, in the position the Qen normally occupied.

"Hello again, everyone," he said.

Alex turned around to see where they ended up. The room had transformed—one-half of it into a type of gymnasium and the other half into a laboratory. There were mats on the floor to the right, and counters with sinks, burners, and other laboratory equipment to the left. It looked and felt completely real. Alex had to remind himself that it was all happening in his head.

"I understand that yesterday you were given a brief lesson about our history," Mr. Serret said. "That will suffice for now. Today we will be using this projection from the Zero Point Field to demonstrate and practice using our Z-Cons." He removed his Z-Con from an inside pocket of his jacket and displayed it in front of him.

"These are called secondary Z-Cons," Mr. Serret said. "You need a Z-Con Prime to create a secondary Z-Con. Only Vizier Herabata here at this facility and Z at our mountain facility have Z-Con Primes. They are the only two remaining on Earth. There were six Z-Con Primes at the start, but three of them were destroyed on purpose, and one of them was lost by accident a long time ago. In later classes, we will go into those events. The first thing for you to learn is that since all secondary Z-Cons are activated by using a single Z-Con Prime, it links them all together. You can combine the effects of using more than one Z-Con, from more than one person. Also, two people can combine their efforts by holding onto the same Z-Con."

Alex looked at his Z-Con and thought back to the arrival ceremony. Immediately after the ceremony was over, he felt a strong connection to his Z-Con and had assumed the Z-Con was for him only.

"So, anyone can use my Z-Con?" he asked.

"They can," Mr. Serret said. "But the effects will normally be far less than when you are using it yourself. When Vizier Herabata activated yours, it was tuned to the specific vibrational energy of your brain. Your Z-Con's main purpose is to amplify the ability of your brain to interact with the Zero Point Field. Since nobody else's brain vibrates at the exact same frequency as yours, your Z-Con will be less useful to them."

Mr. Serret stepped behind the counters, scanning the contents of the shelves along the walls..

"Everything we see, and everything we can't see, is made up of energy vibrating at different frequencies. You probably know that radio waves are just vibrations traveling through the air at different frequencies. But things like this table top are made up of enormous amounts of very, very small objects called atomic particles. And atomic particles are nothing more than small chunks of energy vibrating at very high frequencies."

He swung around and faced everyone.

"If it vibrates, then your Z-Con knows about it, and can affect it!" He picked a glass up off the countertop and placed it directly in front of him. He pointed his Z-con at it.

"You can make it grow…"

The glass instantly grew to three times its original size.

"You can make it shrink…"

The glass shrunk to the size of a thimble.

"You can make it move…"

The small glass shot down the table, six feet away.

"And you can destroy it…"

The glass immediately disintegrated into small grains. Alex was taken back when it did. He had never seen a Z-Con destroy anything. Even the orbs that had attacked them the other night were only pushed away, not destroyed.

Mr. Serret moved down the length of the table and stopped in front of the small pile of debris that used to be the glass. He pointed his Z-Con at it.

"With advanced training and experience, you can also create things…"

The glass instantly reformed from the debris.

"You don't have to know how it's in fact done," he said, heading back to the front of the classroom. "If you can think it—your Z-Con can make it happen. You and your brain are the only limiting factors. Some people can use Z-Cons to connect extremely well with The Field." He slowly turned around. "And some can't."

Alex looked at the others and then back to Mr. Serret. Alex was sure that he and his roommates would measure up to any standards that the instructors set. After all, he and his friends had so far been able to use their Z-Cons to do whatever was asked of them.

Mr. Serret pointed to each one of the students in succession.

"You are here because your brain can connect with The Field better than most people. In a few years, you'll be able to use this skill, along with all the equipment that our research department has created over the last few centuries, to defend the Earth from any attack—if it ever comes to that."

Alex wondered if he liked the idea of being trained for a job that he probably would never have to perform. After all, there had been many, many centuries of people being trained to defend the Earth and so far, no one had been called on to do it.

"We've seen to it that your Z-Con also has the capability to access all information that has ever been published. Just concentrate on what you need to know, and that information will be projected in front of you by use of your projector lens. Since the information is displayed by your Z-Con projecting it directly onto your lens—no one else will see it. I'm sure you know by now that you can also send messages and pictures to anyone else's projector lens, but I'll leave it up to the other students show you how to do that."

Mr. Serret leaned up against the front wall.

"Today you will practice changing objects with your Z-Cons. You will also practice pulling and pushing objects with them. We're not sure why, but for some reason pushing something with a Z-con is much easier than pulling with it. How well you can pull objects with your Z-Con is a way to measure how good of a connector you're becoming."

"A connector?" Alex asked.

"A connector is someone who interacts on a high level with the Zero Point Field. That is to say—you can 'connect' with it. Every living thing connects with The Field—life would not exist without it. But most living things only connect on a very basic level."

"The Qen outside said that everything he needed to know about us was in the Zero Point Field," Alex said. "Is that true? I mean, everything?" To Alex, it was disturbing to think that the Qens could know absolutely everything about him.

"Not exactly," Mr. Serret replied.

"The Qen outside only knew about who you were and about your schedule because we instructors placed that knowledge into The Field. And since we are the ones who placed it there, we can allow the Qens to access that information. Qens can only access the frequencies that we tell them about—nothing more."

Mr. Serret went to the lab table and picked up the newly repaired glass.

"Your Z-Cons can access all published information, but they also access very detailed information about all objects," He tossed the glass up and down a couple of times. "Not only can they access the information about all objects, but it can be influenced to change that information. That's why I could make this glass grow, move, and break apart. My Z-Con just changed the basic information about the glass that is stored in The Field, and the glass reacted accordingly."

He put the glass down on the table.

"One last thing to know. Your Z-Con cannot harm any living object. It was never explained to us why that is. Perhaps it's a safety measure built into them so that nobody can directly injure people by using them. We assume that there are no other Z-Cons out in the universe that can directly hurt any living beings either. If that is true, then when it comes down to defending Earth, you'll probably have to rely on your skills and knowledge to defeat an enemy rather than relying on your Z-Con to do it. Over the years, we'll try to teach you as many skills and as much knowledge as we can so that you'll be ready."

Mr. Serret placed a glass in front of everyone.

"Now you try it. Everyone, make the glass bigger."

Alex pointed his Z-Con and closed his eyes, picturing the glass growing in size. An instant later the glass took up the same size as Alex had imagined—about three times as large.

A few seconds later Elka and Maia's glasses grew, but only slightly—and an instant later they shrunk back to their original size.

"You have to hold the picture in your head a little while longer if you want them to retain their new shape," Mr. Serret told them. A few seconds later their glasses grew and held onto their new sizes.

Dion's glass grew by a double, but it went back and forth between its normal size and the larger size.

"Try to concentrate on one picture," Mr. Serret advised him.

It took a couple of more cycles, but Dion's glass finally stopped, settling on twice as large.

"Excellent!" Mr. Serret exclaimed. "Now everyone, make it smaller."

They all continued practicing their new skills repeatedly, trying to improve their speed and accuracy—with a stream of helpful suggestions from Mr. Serret.

After a couple of hours, Mr. Serret went around the table and picked up the glasses.

"That's enough for your first class. Next time we'll go into more complicated effects," Mr. Serret said. He placed all the glasses on a shelf under the table. "You must practice these tasks on your own. Since this class is just a projection of the Zero Point Field, it allowed you to learn the procedures, but you'll find that in real life these tasks are somewhat more difficult to perform. Practice outside of this classroom as much as you can."

"Can we see how good we are at pulling with our Z-Cons?" Alex asked.

"Okay. Very well," Mr. Serret said, looking around the classroom. "Let's see how you do with it." He walked over to the other side of the room. "Everyone come here and lay on these mats. Put your legs right up against the wall and your head pointing directly away from it."

Alex went over to the mat closest to the front of the classroom. He laid flat on it and put his feet tightly up against the wall. After everyone else had gotten into position, Mr. Serret moved near the tops of their heads and looked down at them.

"Now try to see how far you can lift yourself off the floor. Point your Z-Con at the wall and try to pull up to it. Picture your body being tilted up toward the wall, pivoting at your feet. The wall will stop your feet from slipping forward as you tilt upward."

Alex pointed his Z-Con and visualized himself tilting all the way up to the wall. A few seconds later his body tilted up just as he visualized it to about forty-five degrees above the ground. He stayed there, perfectly still.

Dion's head moved up about one foot. Elka shot up to about three feet but fell to one foot almost immediately before stabilizing there. Maia managed a couple of inches.

"Well...keep trying," Mr. Serret said. "Over time, you'll see improvement, although I wouldn't take up any challenges from the other students just yet." He briskly walked toward the front of the room. When he passed Alex, he said quietly, "That was excellent, Alex." He continued on and reached the front of the room. "That's it for today," he said.

He waved his hand, and Alex found himself back in his seat in the real classroom, still holding onto his Z-Con. It didn't seem like he had moved a single muscle the entire time. The room Qen stood over him and only moved away to his corner after everyone had arrived back from the class.

"How long were we gone?" Alex shouted over to the Qen.

"Two minutes, eighteen seconds," Qen answered, dryly.

"Everyone stay here for your next class," Mr. Serret said. "From what I can see you all have math, followed by language, and then science. After that Alex and Dion will stay here for a flying class, and Elka and Maia will move one room down for a motocross class."

With that, Mr. Serret left the room. A few seconds later a new instructor came in. She introduced herself as their math instructor, Ms. Mevorah. She was a short woman in a green dress and had dark hair that made her exceptionally light skin stand out. She looked and acted like a considerably strict individual.

"You're way behind all the other students, so we will be taking three-hour classes from here on out until you catch up. Grab your Z-Cons and let's get going. Same procedure as your last class…begin."

With that Alex and everyone else found themselves in a math classroom with Ms. Mevorah standing at the front of it near a whiteboard. She asked everyone about what they had learned in math classes in the outside world and began her lessons from there.

Three hours later they returned from her class and immediately went into a language class with a Mr. Hubner (all about ancient Egyptian writing), and after three hours of that, they had a science class with a Ms. Hartman (basic mechanics and physics).

When Alex returned from the last class, he thought that his head would start aching. It just had to, didn't it? He had just spent eleven hours in a classroom, non-stop! But he felt fine after each one of the classes—even after the last one. When he thought about it for a while, it seemed to make sense. After all, each class only lasted a few minutes in real time. Although he wasn't uncomfortable, Alex stood up and moved around a bit. It just seemed like the natural thing to do. It also seemed to make sense to everyone else, as they all stood up and walked around too.

Finally, the moment had arrived for Alex and Dion. Ms. Hartman led Elka and Maia out of the room to the classroom next door, for their motocross class. As soon as they walked out, a man dress in green overalls walked in and introduced himself.

"Hello, Alex. Hello, Dion. I'm Mr. Bell, and I'll be giving your ground school instruction for your flight training. In ground school, you will learn all about meteorology, air regulations, navigation systems, and medical factors of flight. We will also learn about all the parts of your aircraft. Ready to begin?"

Alex and Dion responded at the same instant.

"Yes, sir!"

"Okay then, sit back down and let's get to the classroom."

This time when Alex popped into the new classroom, it wasn't a classroom at all. He found himself standing on the tarmac of a small airport on a beautiful sunny day. Dion and Mr. Bell were the only other people there.

"Boys, this is the ultralight aircraft that you will be learning to fly on," Mr. Bell said, walking around the plane parked in front of them. "It is a fixed-wing aircraft, made of aluminum tubing, covered with a high-tech plastic film. It has a twenty-eight-foot wingspan and has a fifty-horsepower engine, climbs at nine hundred feet per minute, and cruises at forty-four to fifty-four miles per hour." He stopped and spun around with a wide grin on his face. "It's rated for acrobatics, and it is extremely fun to fly."

Mr. Bell continued around then back to the front of the plane.

"To start with, I am going to show you how to perform a preflight check-out on this aircraft. We call it a walk around. It is essential that you do this every time you fly. To do it properly, you must work from a checklist. When you're flying, you always work from a checklist so that you never forget a critical step. The checklists for all the planes in the world are available to you from the Zero Point Field. Alex, get out your Z-Con and think about getting a preflight checklist for the plane you're looking at."

Alex dug his Z-Con out of his front pants pocket and tried to picture a piece of paper with a 'preflight' checklist on it. With a bit of a flash, the checklist appeared as floating text, about two feet out in front of him. He could see the words, but he could also see right through it, so it didn't obstruct his view of anything else around him.

"Got it!" he exclaimed, looking at Dion in triumph.

Mr. Bell stuck his head in the cockpit.

"Read it out to me, line by line, until I say 'check' or 'set.' Go ahead."

Alex read from the list, waiting each time for a response from Mr. Bell.

"Master Switch—on," Alex said.

"Check," replied Mr. Bell.

As soon as he responded, the line that Alex just read had a checkmark appear next to it. Alex continued.

"Fuel Quantity Gauge—check level."

"Five gallons, check."

"Master Switch—off."

"Check."

"Ignition Switch—off."

"Check."

"Flaps—down."

"Check."

Mr. Bell moved out of the cockpit to the right wing.

"Okay, Alex let's look at the outside. Continue."

Alex read from the card as they all slowly moved around the aircraft. Each time he read an item Mr. Bell made the corresponding response—check or set.

"Flap—*secure and undamaged*...Aileron—*free and correct*...Wing Tip and Light—*undamaged*..." The list went on until they completed checking the right side of the plane.

They all moved to the left wing, and as soon as they did the text that was floating in front of Alex changed to a new list. Even though it surprised him, Alex kept reading from it without the slightest bit of interruption.

After a dozen more items, they finally reached the rear of the plane.

Alex read off the final few items. "Elevators—*free and correct*... Rudder—*free and correct*... Trim Tabs—*secure and undamaged*,... Tie Down —*removed.*" After Mr. Bell's final response, the floating text disappeared.

"Okay, everything looks good," Mr. Bell said, closing the cockpit door. He turned back and addressed both Alex and Dion. "From now on you're going to be doing the preflight walk around yourselves while I watch. We'll do this at the beginning of every class. When you start to do it perfectly, then you'll be on your own."

Mr. Bell motioned for Alex and Dion to step over to him.

"Okay, now follow me to a new classroom," he said right before disappearing.

"This is great!" Dion said to Alex before he also disappeared.

Alex walked over to the plane and touched it one more time, looking it over from nose to tail. He stood there for a minute, and then finally followed Dion to the next classroom, appearing right alongside him.

"What kept you?" Dion asked.

"Nothing," Alex responded cheerfully.

Mr. Bell was already writing on the board in the front of the room.

"Have a seat you two," Mr. Bell said. "The rest of our class today will be spent on learning the procedures for takeoff, cruising, and landing. After that, you will report to Maintenance Facility Number One for a work assignment.

You'll have forty-five minutes for lunch, and then you'll report to the core for flight training."

Alex and Dion sat down behind two desks situated near the front of the room. They both leaned back in their chairs and put their hands behind their heads, smiling.

TWELVE

Alex and Dion left their ground school class and reported to Jade Division, 'Maintenance Facility Number One' to start their mechanical training. It was only nine o'clock in the morning. Today's classes, although extensive in their scope, had only used up a half hour of their day. The next two hours were to be devoted to learning new mechanical skills. But as far Alex was concerned, the best part of today was to be getting assigned to a competition team.

They entered the maintenance facility, and Alex glanced over at the far-left wall. Z and Vizier Herabata stood there, watching all the students enter. He thought it odd that nobody seemed to be paying much attention to them. Perhaps they visited the facilities periodically, and everyone thought it was just normal routine.

As soon as Z saw Alex, he motioned for him to come over. Alex certainly didn't expect to be seeing either one of them on his first day of class, and he wondered if something was wrong. Perhaps he was in trouble, possibly having broken some rule by mistake—certainly not on purpose.

Alex told Dion that he would meet up with him later. He uneasily walked over to where Z and Vizier Herabata stood and gave a short bow as he approached. Vizier Herabata and Z responded with a nod, with Z reaching out to put his hand on Alex's shoulder.

"Hello, Alex," Z said. "I'm glad to see you. I trust all is going well."

"Certainly sir," Alex said. He rubbed the back of his neck with his right hand. "A bit overwhelming, that's all."

Z glanced at Vizier Herabata for a second and turned back to Alex.

"Well, since you have a few moments between classes, would you mind if we asked you about something? We won't keep you long."

"Of course," Alex said.

Vizier Herabata stepped forward and placed her hand on Alex's other shoulder.

"It's related to the trouble you had on the way to our training facility," she said. She looked somewhat intense while saying it. "We wanted to know if you had anything unusual happen to you or your family before you were forced out of your home the other night."

Alex did not respond right away. He thought about it for quite some time, but he couldn't think of anything happening recently that would have been considered unusual.

"Anything at all, no matter how small," Z prodded.

Alex shook his head. He looked at Z and then over to Vizier Herabata.

"I can't think of anything that happened," he said. "You should ask my parents, they might know of something." He switched his stare from Z over to Vizier Herabata and back again.

"Of course," Z said. "But as you know, they're on a mission." Z took his hand off of his shoulder. "It is difficult to get in touch with them right now."

Alex stiffened when he heard that.

"But how can that be?" he said tersely. "With Z-Cons, can't you always get a hold of them?"

"Not necessarily," Vizier Herabata said. She too took her hand off his shoulder. "They might be purposely not communicating with us—for security reasons. Sometimes that's necessary." Her face turned into a warm smile. "Not to worry Alex, I'm sure we'll hear from them soon."

"Best be getting to class now," Z said. "We'll keep in touch. Off you go."

Alex slowly turned and walked away somewhat bewildered. He wondered why they were coming to him with these kinds of questions. Was it because they lost touch with his parents, and now they're concerned? But Z said not to worry, and he wouldn't lie. Alex was sure of it. At least pretty sure.

Alex eventually ended up standing in front of the Maintenance Facility's Qen, while constantly being jostled by the large body of students hurrying past him.

"I'm Alex Vega," he announced loudly to the Qen, hoping he would get a response.

"Yes, of course," Qen said without changing his gaze. "You've been assigned to aircraft competition team J-A-5.

Stay on this level, take the first door on the left, then look for the sign."

Alex followed the crowd going in that general direction into a large maintenance room—an enormous room filled with small planes, boats, motorcycles, and hundreds of spare parts lying out on shelves all around the exterior wall.

Alex stepped to the side and got out of the way of the fast-moving stream of students. He scanned the area to get his bearings. The row he was standing on had a pole planted into the floor every thirty feet or so, and each one had a large sign perched on top of it that started with the letters J-A. The furthest one down the row said J-A-5.

Alex made his way along the row and arrived at his assigned area. Spread out in front of him were four green colored ultralight aircraft, all of them the same kind he had just learned to preflight in Mr. Bell's class. A student dressed in coveralls hunched over one of the plane's engine bays.

Alex tapped the boy on the shoulder, giving him a bit of a startle. When the boy turned around Alex realized that it was Samuel, one of the students that lived next door to him.

"Hi Samuel, good to see you again," Alex said.

"Oh…" Samuel responded after thinking about it for a few seconds. "Alex, right?" He seemed pleased with himself for remembering the name.

"Right," Alex said. "Looks like I'm assigned to your team."

Samuel nodded his head slightly and bent back down to finish what he was doing. A few seconds later, he stood back up and wiped some dirt from his hand. He gave Alex a look of pity.

"Lucky you," he said.

"Don't tell me," Alex responded. "I take it this is one of the Jade teams that haven't been winning much."

"At this point, I'd kill for 'hasn't been winning much.' So far we've come in last place in every competition." Samuel looked around to see if anyone else was near. After a moment, he continued. "And do you know why?"

Alex stared intently at Samuel and answered.

"Poor nutrition?"

Samuel was completely lost by his response.

"Nutrition?" he said.

Alex bumped Samuel's shoulder with his fist.

"Just kidding. Tell me, why haven't you been winning?"

"Oh, okay… I get it," Samuel said, moving a little closer to Alex so he could whisper.

"This team hasn't got the guts that God gave a soap dish." He looked around again to make sure nobody else had heard him. He turned back to Alex. "Nobody's willing to take a chance. You've got to take a risk once in a while if you're going to win these things. Hell, they teach us that in all our classes, but it doesn't seem to sink in with the flyers on this team." He lowered his voice even more. "With the way they act…you'd think they were afraid of flying."

Alex gave him an acknowledging nod and slapped him on the back.

"Well, that gives us a chance to show them how things are done, doesn't it?" Alex said in a cheerful voice.

"We better," Samuel said. "I'm tired of wearing that stupid orange vest every time we lose."

"What vest?"

"Everybody on a team who comes in last in any competition has to wear an orange vest the following Monday—all day. It's a humiliation they make you go through. Nobody makes a big deal of it, but when you end up wearing it every single time…"

"Yeah, sounds like it sucks," Alex said. A second later, a smile ran across his face. "But all we can do at this point is to make sure we win the next time."

Alex turned around and ran his hand over the wing of the plane next to him. He looked back at Samuel.

"Let's get to it. What's first?"

Samuel's head picked up a bit, and he studied Alex for a few seconds.

"Okay!" he said. "Let's go." He bent down over the engine he was working on. "Well, first you could help me check out the throttle connection on this plane. It seems a little…"

"Wrong!" someone said, coming up from behind.

A girl in a green flight suit and a boy in a Jade jacket stopped in front of them. It was the girl who was talking.

Samuel stood up again. When he saw who it was his head dropped a little bit lower into his shoulders. Then he made the introductions.

"Alex, this is two of our team pilots, Joanne and Ken. Alex is our new crew replacement."

"You call me Joey, like everybody else," the girl ordered. She pointed her finger harshly at Samuel. "We've got the competition in five days. I don't want you taking up any of your time teaching a new guy about anything. Let him wash up, run errands, whatever. You spend your time making sure these planes are perfect. Got it?"

Samuel nodded.

Ken walked over to Alex and extended his hand. Alex shook it with a little bit of apprehension.

"I'm the team captain," Ken said. He glanced over to Joey and back. "Although sometimes you wouldn't know it from the way some people here order everyone else around."

He took a step back, next to Joey.

"Glad to have you with us, Alex," he said. "Samuel will get you squared away. C'mon Joey, let's go."

The two of them left, studying something on Joey's Z-Con as they did.

"Don't they help out?" Alex asked, watching them leave.

"They should," Samuel said, once again in a low voice. "All the pilots on the other teams do. Ken's been helping me out once in a while. But now I imagine none of them will be around anymore, now that there's two of us working for them again. They'll just come around to check the work. You know—see if there's anything they can criticize."

Samuel went to the rear of the plane. He picked up a large bucket sitting underneath its tail. The bucket was jam-packed with clean white rags. From the side of it, he retrieved a spray bottle filled with purple liquid and headed back to Alex.

"You're a replacement for our last flunky, Greg. He got transferred to another team when one of their guys quit and went home. Winning teams are allowed to pick their replacements when they're needed. They picked Greg—we got you."

"Do many people quit?" Alex asked.

"Not many. That guy was the first one I heard of this year." Samuel held up his arm, showing his yellow bracelet. "But I haven't been here that long."

He placed the bucket of rags at Alex's feet.

"Well, sorry about this," he said. "Could you just clean off all the surfaces for me?" He held up the purple bottle. "This stuff's specially made for it. It cleans them off— makes them slick."

Alex grabbed the bottle and the bucket.

"Where do you want me to start?"

Samuel had to think about it for a few seconds. Alex got the impression he wasn't used to giving orders.

"Well, start with plane number one over there and work your way back to me, if that's okay."

"You got it," Alex said and went off to his chore.

Alex spent the next two hours going over every square inch of the planes with the rags, taking the time to dig into every small crease and crevasse, cleaning them out completely.

When he finished his shift, he said goodbye to Samuel, left the maintenance facility, and waited out in front of the building for Dion. He spent the time wondering about his encounter with Z and Vizier Herabata. When he added that conversation to the way his mother was acting, Alex grew more apprehensive every minute he thought about it.

Dion came up from behind him, cheerful as could be.

He slapped Alex on the back and said, "How'd it go?"

"Okay, I guess. I got assigned to an aircraft competition team. I had to clean up all the planes."

"I got assigned to a flight team too! The fighting Jay Sevens."

"Jay Sevens? You've got a name?"

"Yeah, you know, short for J-A-7. What's your team called?"

"I don't think they have a name. They're a little short on that kind of stuff."

"Well, my team hasn't lost a match in two years! I think it might be a school record."

"C'mon, let's go back to the rooms and get ready," Alex said. He turned and headed toward the Jade Pyramid.

Dion spent the entire walk back describing everything he did with his new teammates. How everyone on the team took turns showing him around the planes and all their systems—each pilot quietly informing him that plane they flew was the best out of the four. And how he spent an hour helping them check out the fuel systems on one of the planes.

Alex couldn't help but feel jealous. But he let Dion talk on about it, although wishing the entire time Dion would change the subject.

They arrived back at the pyramid and shot up to their quad. Elka and Maia sat around the table in the common room, eating sandwiches.

Mercure and Panda lay in their usual corner—both of them heavily panting.

"What have you been up to?" Alex asked Mercure.

"We just came back from a refresher class in karate," Mercure said while continuing to pant. *"We've got to get back in shape if we're going to start going to defense classes with you."*

"Looks like you've been struggling with it," Alex said.

"Been a long time," Mercure said, laying his head down on the cool tile floor. *"Class starts next week. You should prepare a little for it."*

Alex shrugged and slumped down into the seat next to Maia. He took a potato chip from the plate in the center of the table and started eating.

"How'd you two beat us back?" he asked.

"We got assigned to a motocross competition team, and we started working on some of the bikes," Elka said, taking a bite of her sandwich.

Alex once again felt a tinge of jealousy when he heard they were all allowed to do something meaningful on their team.

Maia continued for Elka. "Z and Vizier Herabata came over and asked us to speak with them for a few minutes."

Alex sat straight up in his seat and paid intense attention.

"After that, they told us we could leave," Maia said. "Z told us to go and get ready for our next class." She turned and gave her sister a high five. "Oh yeah, we're finally going motocrossing."

Alex popped up out of his chair.

"Did they say anything about your parents?" he asked. It sounded like a demand. Both Elka and Maia were taken back by it.

"A little," Elka answered. She shot Maia a quick look but continued answering Alex. "They asked if anything unusual had happened to us before we came here."

"Me too," Alex interjected. He sat down, on the edge of the seat. "But I couldn't think of anything."

"Well, the only thing we could think of was a man who came to visit our dad just about a month before we moved to Cairo," Elka said.

"The only reason we remembered him was that he had a kind of severe expression on his face," Maia said. "When I looked at him it gave me the same kind of feeling I had when I saw Master Puma for the first time, you know?"

Alex nodded. He knew exactly.

"They wanted to know what the man talked about with our parents," Elka said.

"Once we thought about it a bit, I remembered that was the first time I saw my father studying those Mayan glyphs," Maia said. "Remember? The ones back at the last pyramid?"

"The man helped my parents compare the Mayan glyphs to the ones my dad had been photographing all around Egypt," Elka said, taking another bite of her sandwich.

"Did they find anything?" Alex asked, more subtle this time.

"I don't know," Elka said. "We weren't paying much attention when the man was there. All I know is that as soon as the man left, that's when our parents started talking about moving to Cairo."

"Did you see which glyphs they were interested in?"

"There was a stone carving of a man sitting in a seat," Elka said. "They called him something—I don't remember what though." She looked to Maia for help. Maia looked back to her and took a final swallow of her last sandwich bite.

"Aluxes Man," Maia said. "But I think that was just a nickname they gave him."

Alex dashed off, toward his room. "If our parents were interested in him … I want to know more about this Aluxes guy," he said. He returned a minute later with his goggles on his head.

"I think I saw the guy you're talking about on the wall of that building the other night. I wish I knew how to get this thing to play back what it saw."

"Take that off," Dion said. He held out his hand to Alex. "One of the guys on my flight team showed me how Zeps works." Alex pulled the Zeps straight up off the top of his head and handed them over. Dion placed the goggles down near the edge of the table. "Since they're yours, Alex, you pick up your Z-Con and stand near them. Then think about seeing the video from the Zeps playing out in front of you." Dion pointed the goggles toward the center of the room.

A second after Alex retrieved his Z-Con from his pocket a full-color 3-D image of the Mayan wall projected outward from the Zeps to the center of the room. The image panned from left to right, showing the full length of the wall, just the way Alex had scanned it the other night.

"Right there!" Alex pointed toward the top of the projection. "Carved over the top of the door, there's a guy sitting on a seat of some kind." Alex held his Z-Con out further and concentrated on the projection, trying to make it freeze on the image of the seated man. The panning stopped, and the scene tilted up slightly toward the top of the door. "It's a guy with a big hat and a bunch of glyphs all around him."

Elka moved forward and pointed to the center of the screen.

"That's the guy our father was studying!"

"Did they find anything out about him?" Alex asked.

"I don't think so," Elka answered. She looked over to Maia. "All I remember is they were getting pretty annoyed."

"From what I could tell," Maia interjected. "They didn't find out anything about him from using their Z-Cons. They went to the internet and found a couple of pages on it."

"But how can that that be?" Alex said. "Z-Cons access everything. Any information on the internet should have shown up on their Z-Cons." He moved up close to the image in front of him. "So why didn't this show up on their Z-Cons for them?"

"I don't know," Maia said. "They were getting pretty frustrated. My mom said something about Z hiding stuff from them."

Alex kept concentrating on the image, keeping it stable. But he let his mind wander a bit more.

"What exactly were they trying to find?" he asked Maia.

"They wanted to know who the guy was, what his history was. When they couldn't find out much about it, they wanted to know about the meaning of all the glyphs surrounding him. They were able to use their Z-Cons for that part anyway."

Alex focused hard, back on the image in front of him.

"Okay, let's go do that," he said. "We've got to find out what they learned."

"Why so interested?" Dion asked.

"Z and Vizier Herabata said they lost contact with my parents," Alex said. "They said it was all right, and that sometimes that kind of thing happens. But I don't think so. I just got a bad feeling."

"So, what do you want us to do?" Maia asked.

"Everyone pick a glyph off the image and see what your Z-Con says about it. I'll keep the image steady."

They all took out their Z-Cons and pointed them at different parts of the image.

"That glyph means 'It's finishing,'" Dion said.

"That one means 'sacrificed,'" Elka added.

"That one means 'portal,'" Maia said, quickly swinging her gaze over to Alex

"Portal?" Alex said. He lost most of his concentration on the image. "How'd the Mayans know about portals?"

"I guess 'Aluxes Man' knew something about it," Dion contemplated.

"Elka, try to find out what 'Aluxes Man' means," Alex said.

Elka stared off into space for a few seconds before she had an answer.

"Well, there's nobody called 'Aluxes Man.' The only thing my Z-Con says is that an 'Aluxes' is like some type of Mayan fairy. They float around at night and cause all kinds of mischief if they think they're not being shown respect. It says that that the local people around the Chichen Itza pyramids say they see Aluxes lighting up the whole area at night sometimes." She stopped gazing out in front of her and turned to Alex. "Chichen Itza is the name of the place where we saw the glyphs yesterday, isn't it?"

"Alex!" Dion interrupted. He pointed to the far left of the image. "This glyph says a guy's name. Jawbone Fan."

"What?" Alex asked.

"The Z-Con says this glyph means a name—Jawbone Fan."

"His name is Jawbone Fan?" Alex asked, skeptically.

215

"What can I tell you… that's what it says."

"That is one strange name. What can you find out about him?"

Dion concentrated for a few seconds before retrieving an answer.

"All I find is that his mother's name is Lady Ton Multun."

"And what about her?"

"Nothing."

"There's got to be something," Alex stated.

"Not if Z is hiding it from the Z-Cons," Elka said. She glanced over at Maia and back. "Anyway, that's what my parents thought."

Alex looked over to Mercure, who by this time seemed to have partially recovered from his training session.

"Do you know anything about this?" Alex asked him. "You said you saw a picture of these glyphs on my father's wall sometime in the past."

"About four months ago a lady from the Chinese Embassy came to help Miguel decipher something," Mercure said to him. He got up and trotted over to the image of the glyphs. *"They weren't talking about this though—she only mentioned it on her way out."*

"What were they trying to decipher?" Alex asked.

"I couldn't tell."

"You can't remember?"

"Give me a break Alex. It was up on Miguel's desk. I couldn't see it from where I was standing. You know, the floor."

"Sorry, buddy."

Mercure stepped forward a foot or so toward the image.

"I do remember the lady commenting on the guy sitting in this picture though. When she was leaving, she looked at the poster of him on the wall and said that she always wondered why this guy was banished to the Mayan temple instead of the Chinese one. She said that she always thought it would have been safer for everyone if he was locked away in China."

"Banished?" Alex said. "She said 'banished'?"

Mercure shook his head up and down.

Alex lost all concentration on the image, and as soon as he did, it disappeared.

Elka glanced at Maia, and then over to Dion. Everyone turned toward Alex with a puzzled expression.

It finally dawned on Alex that since nobody could hear Mercure, they all wanted to know what was going on.

"He said that a lady from China told my father that this guy was 'banished' to the Mayan site. She said that she thought he should have been banished to China instead and that everyone would have been safer if he was."

Nobody said anything as they all contemplated what they had just learned.

Alex sat down on the nearest chair and gave it some thought. What could be going on? Was Z putting his parents in jeopardy by keeping information away from them? He didn't know much about what his parents were doing, so maybe that's why none of this made sense. Maybe his parents were all right, and this was just the way things worked. He was getting too paranoid. That was it. He was reading too much into all this. Sunday would come, and he would get to talk to his parents, and he'd find out everything was okay. For sure. Absolutely.

Alex stood up, snatched his goggles off the table, and headed toward his room.

Elka, Maia, and Dion watched Alex leaving. Before he reached the door, Elka jumped up.

"What's going on, Alex?" she demanded.

Alex turned around and faced everyone. With a perplexed expression on his face, he said, "I'm trying to convince myself of something." He paused and dropped his eyes to the floor for a few seconds. When he looked back up, he said, "But I'm not succeeding." He turned around and headed away again. After only two steps he turned back, shaking his head.

"There's something wrong with all this," he said.

After a few more seconds he turned and disappeared into his room.

THIRTEEN

Alex dropped himself onto his bed, leaned forward a bit, and ran both his hands around the back of his neck. After a moment, he looked up and found Mercure sitting quietly in the center of the room.

"Does any of this bother you?" Alex asked him. "You said you've been around a long time … is this normal?"

"When it comes to right down to it, there is no normal. Every time we send out a team to do a job, it's a completely different situation. Each team ends up using all the skills they have to get their jobs done. That's one of the reasons they teach the students here everything they can—about everything they can think of. You never know what skill you might need out in the field."

Mercure got up and walked over to a spot directly in front of Alex.

"Alex, your parents were taught everything they needed to know when they went to school here. They should be fine. You can't spend your time worrying about things that you

have no control over. Let this go for a while. See how things work out."

Alex bobbed his head from side to side and gave Mercure a bit of a smile.

"Okay. I'll wait and see what happens on Sunday. Then I'll find out what Mom and Dad have to say about it."

Mercure trotted over to Feng's perch in the corner of the room, looking back at Alex.

"Until then, you got a flying class to go to, right? Let's see what's up with that."

Mercure turned to face the perch, and a couple of seconds later Feng appeared.

"You have thirty-two minutes before you are scheduled to start your flying class," Feng said. "At that time, report to the center core for transport to the flight facility."

Feng glided over to the closet on Alex's side of the room. He reached in and pulled out a green flight suit. He carried it over to Alex and handed it to him.

"Wear this over your GEM suit. Bring your gloves, hood, and Zeps with you to class."

Feng glided away from Alex, over to his corner post.

"Got an inspirational saying for someone who's feeling down?" Mercure asked Feng as he passed by.

Feng reached his perched and turned around. He gazed up at the ceiling near the center of the room. A look of sincerity washed across his face.

"There is no way to happiness: happiness is the way," he proclaimed. "That is from Buddha." He brought his eyes down from above and crossed his hands out in front of him. "Being unhappy is a choice."

"Very profound," Mercure said. *"Anything else?"*

Feng turned his gaze toward Alex. "I suggest you eat something before leaving." He froze for a second and then disappeared.

"I didn't know Feng can hear you," Alex said to Mercure.

"My thoughts are projected somewhat deeply into the Zero Point Field. That's why you and the rest of our family can hear me. It's one of the little tricks that Nedo gave us dogs. You know, when he was messing around with everything."

Mercure curled up on the floor.

"Qens can access all those thoughts because Z and Vizier Herabata allow them to."

Dion poked his head into the room a few inches.

"You guys done talking?"

"Yeah, sure," Alex said while he started figuring out his flight suit. "Come on—we better start getting ready."

Dion pointed to Alex's suit and said, "Where did you get that?"

"Should be one in your closet. It must have been delivered while we were gone this morning."

Dion reached into the closet next to him and pulled out his flight suit.

"Thank you, Joeks Burlm, Head Fitter."

Alex and Dion laughed a bit and then finished getting ready. They wanted to leave early this time, so on their way out they just shouted goodbye toward Elka's and Maia's room. They left Mercure and Panda curled up in the corner of the common room.

They arrived at the center core just a couple of minutes ahead of schedule. Many students in well-worn overalls

221

milled about the area, preparing to travel to their afternoon classes. Alex and Dion's flight suits made them stand out from the huge crowd, being brand new and much brighter in comparison.

A Qen stood in the center of the core, ready to assist—but by this time of the semester, all the other students essentially ignored him, as they already knew their assigned schedules and no longer needed his help.

Alex marched up to the Qen, with Dion right alongside.

"Alex Vega and Dion Yang," Alex announced.

"To the left, take portal number eight," the Qen casually replied, without glancing at them.

Behind the Qen stood a long blue wall with lines of students extending out perpendicular to it. A circular sign was perched on top of the wall every six feet along its length. Numbers displayed on the signs ranged from number one on the far left to number sixty-four on the right. Alex and Dion walked most of the way to the left until they reached the line that formed in front of the number eight sign. At the front of the line, students took turns jumping into a portal at the wall's base. Although nobody seemed to be in charge, it was all well-choreographed, with a student jumping every three or four seconds. The line was extremely long, but it moved quickly, and Alex and Dion soon found themselves near the front.

"Did your flight team tell you anything about where we're going for this?" Alex asked Dion while taking small steps forward.

"No, they never got around to it," Dion said. "But one guy told me that the initial flight classes go by incredibly fast. They let you sink or swim."

Alex was now next in line. Even though there were only a handful of students remaining behind him, he felt the pressure to keep the line moving, and he didn't hesitate to jump.

A half a minute later, Alex popped out the other end. He immediately got out of the way and fell in line behind a stream of students heading toward a large airplane hangar. A few seconds later Dion came walking up to him from the behind.

The sky in front of Alex was dark and filled with storm clouds rumbling in the distance. Besides the hanger, the only other things to be seen were two long runways that intersected each other. The rest of the vast expanse around him was nothing but sandy dirt. Only a few scrawny bushes grew here and there. In the far distance, a line of tall mountains with snow-covered peaks jutted up from the dark horizon.

"We picked a fine day to go flying, didn't we?" Alex said to Dion.

But before Dion could respond, a voice from behind called over to them.

"I wouldn't worry too much about it," the voice said.

Alex turned toward it. A short woman, dressed in a green flight suit walked past them. She wore a matching green cap and large dark sunglasses that covered most of the top part of her face. The pockets on the legs of her flight suit bulged out from the large amount of equipment she stored in them, giving her a stout, rounded appearance.

"It doesn't rain that long in these parts," she said, stopping about five feet away. She motioned with her right hand. "This way you two." She headed away, toward the far side of the hanger.

Alex and Dion fell out of line and trailed in behind her.

"Look over there," she said, pointing.

The heavy clouds in that section of the sky were dissolving away, and bright sunshine lit up the ground in the distance.

"That's the weather that will be over us in about ten minutes," she added. "Knowing the local weather patterns is vitally important while flying."

She turned the corner, around to the other side of the hanger. Two green ultralight aircraft sat secluded by themselves, about twenty feet apart from each other. An older man dressed in another green flight suit stood over the tail section of the closet one, inspecting it. The woman walked over to him and turned back to Alex and Dion.

"My name is Ms. Brooks," she said. "This is Mr. Amholt." The man nodded to Alex and Dion. "The two of us will be giving you basic flight instruction classes for the next two weeks. After you master the basics, the two of you will go onto more advanced training. At that point, you will start to compete as a team in our weekly competitions, against the other students."

Ms. Brooks headed toward the second plan.

"Alex, follow me," she said, passing him.

Alex gave a quick look at Dion and said, "Good luck." He turned around and hurried to catch up to his instructor.

When they reached the other plane, Ms. Brooks stopped near the cockpit door.

"So, Alex, I presume you remember how to preflight this plane," she said.

"Sure. I'll get the checklist," Alex said. He put his hand on his Z-Con in his pocket and stared off for a second until the checklist displayed in front of him.

"Go ahead. I'll just watch," Ms. Brooks told him.

Alex spent the next five minutes performing the preflight, saying the procedures aloud and stating 'Check' or 'Set' after each step. When he finished, he turned to his instructor for approval.

"Pretty good, Alex. Next time, I want you to concentrate a little more when you're inspecting the engine compartment. Don't just give the wiring and supply tubes a quick look. Trace each one so that you can remember exactly how they're set up. That way you'll be able to tell immediately when something is out of place."

"Got it," Alex replied.

"Go ahead and put on your entire Gem Suit equipment. Then get in. We'll start her up and get going."

Alex put on his hood and goggles, and lastly his gloves. Ms. Brooks had her gloves on, but she didn't bother with her hood and goggles. She just kept them in her hands.

Alex climbed into the cockpit and slid over to the left— the pilot's seat. Ms. Brooks jumped up and sat next to him. After Alex settled in, Ms. Brooks pointed to each instrument on the dashboard and asked Alex to tell her what each was.

"Air Speed Indicator, Artificial Horizon, Altimeter, Gyro Compass, Vertical Speed Indicator, Engine RPM..." Alex responded.

At this point everything seemed very easy for Alex. He had just gone through instruction on the entire cockpit layout in his last flying class and, as promised, everything he learned during the classroom instruction was instantly remembered when needed.

"Okay, get out a start-up procedure checklist and let's get going," Ms. Brooks said, putting her set of headphones on. She pulled the microphone down, close to her lips.

Alex followed suit and buckled up. He used his Z-Con to show a startup procedure. It promptly displayed out in front of him, and he started right in.

"Parking brake set, fuel flow switch on, mixture lever to full rich, carburetor heat off, prime the engine and lock the prime pump, crack the throttle slightly open, master electrical switch on, electric fuel pump on—check fuel pressure, check the area is clear. Call 'Clear the prop!', turn the engine start key."

Alex turned the key, and the entire plane shuttered as the engine turned over several times before catching and then roaring to life. Over the noise, Alex carried out the remainder of the checklist.

"Okay, release the parking brake, give the engine some power and head out that way." Ms. Brooks said over the intercom. "Steer with the pedals at your feet. Keep the ailerons turned into the wind while you taxi." She pointed off to the left. "The winds are light and coming from that direction."

Alex taxied the plane, following the taxiing procedures that popped up in front of his eye. Unexpectedly, the wind direction and speed also popped up next to the checklist in front of him.

Alex taxied the plane from here to there and then back again, following the directions from Ms. Brooks. After a few minutes, they ended up at the end of one of the runways. All the planes with the other students in them headed to the other side of the airport and were using a different runway. That left the runway that Alex was alongside all to himself, except for Dion who was now taxiing about fifty yards behind him.

"Okay, Alex, turn the plane into the wind and perform a 'Run-up' checklist," Ms. Brooks said.

Alex pressed down hard on the left pedal, and the plane turned around. After touching his Z-Con again, the 'Run-up' checklist popped up.

"Parking brake set, throttle to two thousand RPM, engine instruments check, magneto—check operation, carburetor heat—check operation, alternator—check operation. Throttle to idle, check idle cutoff, electric fuel pump on, throttle to one thousand RPM, flight instruments—check and set, flaps—check and set, flight controls free and correct, trim set."

"We've got this runway to ourselves," Ms. Brooks said. "Go ahead and taxi into position and follow the takeoff checklist."

Alex let go of the parking brake, pressed on the right pedal, and the plane turned onto the runway. He moved the plane over to the centerline and pushed the throttle all the way forward. The light plane accelerated quickly. He pushed down on the right rudder pedal slightly, as instructed by the checklist—it kept the plane tracking down the center of the runway. He reached the speed indicated on the checklist, pulled back slightly on the stick, and the plane broke from the ground.

The runway fell away, and Alex glanced out the side. He was in the air! It took a second for him to accept it. He was in the air, and he was the one flying! The plane went up because he told it to. The ground sped past him, and he thought to himself that this was how birds felt every day of their lives. Alex could now go anywhere he wanted, anytime he wanted.

He turned his attention back inside and pushed the nose down slightly, as indicated by the checklist. The plane accelerated even faster. When it reached the speed that the checklist specified, he pulled back on the stick and the plane climb smartly again.

"Now, keep the airspeed that you have now. Pull back to go slower, and push forward to go faster. Get used to the feel of the reactions to your inputs. Remember you use the stick in front of you to control the airspeed, the throttle controls the altitude. Some people think it's the other way around, but you're going to have to start thinking in those terms, got it?"

"Got it."

When they reached two thousand feet, Ms. Brooks tapped on the control stick in front of her.

"Now level out here. Pull the throttle back to two thousand three hundred RPMs and push your stick forward slightly."

Alex performed the procedure flawlessly.

"Very good Alex. Have you've flown before?"

"Just a couple of times on a computer game back home. It's a lot different when you get to do it in real life."

"Okay, let's fly around here for a little while. Get used to the controls. You're the pilot in command. Let me know if you have any trouble."

They flew on for several minutes, with Alex turning here and there. Going up and down, faster and slower.

"Does anybody else know we're all out here doing this?" Alex asked.

"No," Ms. Brooks said. "A long time ago Z placed a gravity and light shield around this facility. Anybody coming to this area in a plane, or on foot for that matter, would unknowingly be diverted around it. Everything would look normal to them, but they would circle around us. No light leaves here, so essentially, we're invisible to the outside world. They can't even detect us from space."

"Are these planes detectable?"

"These planes would be if they were outside of the protection that we have here. But the stuff we fly around in the upper atmosphere and out in space can't be detected at all. That is unless the ships have a hardware problem. Then they can be seen—sometimes. Most of the unexplained UFO sightings that you hear about are just people seeing one of our spacecraft."

She cinched up her seatbelt and scanned the area for other planes.

"Let's make some stall recoveries. Pull the throttle back to idle and start pulling the nose up. When the stall warning sound buzzes, the nose is going to fall out in front of you, and you're going to be looking directly at the ground. To recover, push the throttle up all the way up to full power. Then push the stick all the way forward. That's going to be tough when you're staring straight down at the ground. You'll just have to believe that you got to do it, or you'll stall all the way down and crash. Got it?"

"Got it."

"Go ahead."

Alex pulled back the power and brought the nose up. It didn't take long for the stall warning to blare, and then, as if the plane had been slapped down from above, the nose dropped out and pointed directly at the ground. He pushed the throttles up and, after taking a big gulp, pushed the stick full forward. The plane instantly gained airspeed and the stall warning silenced.

"Now pull back on the stick and get us back to level flight."

Alex brought the nose up and leveled out. All was well again.

"Okay, Alex, let's do some more of that for a while, and then we'll head back for a landing."

Several times Alex stalled the plane and recovered, building up muscle memory so that if it ever happened in real life, he would recover immediately.

After a half hour, they headed back to the airfield.

Ms. Brooks had Alex enter the traffic pattern, giving him explicit instructions on when to turn, and what altitude was required. When they reached the right spot in the traffic pattern, she tapped the stick in front of her again.

"I want you to be in full control of the landing now. Just do what I tell you and let's get this thing on the ground. Preferably in one piece."

Alex nodded.

"Pull the flap lever up and give it one notch of flaps. Time to start descending, so pull the power back to seventeen hundred RPM. Turn to the right now until I tell you. That's it, straighten out. Now give it another notch of flaps. Turn right again and line up with the runway. Put in the last notch of flaps. Use the rudder to keep us tracking on the centerline of the runway."

After looking around the area, Ms. Brooks continued, "Okay, we're close enough now...pull back on the stick and start to level off... pull the throttle back to idle...pull back on the stick...all the way back. Keep it there...keep it there...touchdown! Steer with your feet."

"Very good, Alex! Try to remember what that looked like and how it felt. You do that every time, got it?"

"Got it."

"Now remove the last two notches of flaps and push the throttle full open. Follow the 'Touch and Go' procedures in front of you and let's go around again.

Alex flew the rectangular pattern around the runway and made another three 'Touch and Goes.' On the third take off, while he rotated, Dion entered the traffic pattern directly across from him. The two of them practiced landings and takeoffs for the next hour.

On Alex's last landing Ms. Brooks told him to steer off the runway and taxi over to the far side of the massive hanger. He parked the plane exactly on the spot where he started. Dion taxied up behind him and parked his plane alongside. When the two of them exited their planes, they gave each other a light fist pump—just a light one, after all, they were still wearing their GEM suit gloves.

The instructors dismissed both Alex and Dion for the day.

"Wasn't that great! I still can't believe we were flying," Dion said while walking back to the spot where they arrived at the facility—expecting to follow the crowd returning to The Dome.

"Sure was. This is going to be my favorite class."

When they rounded the corner of the hanger, seven opal students appeared, seemingly out of nowhere. Obviously, they were waiting for Alex and Dion, right where nobody else could see them.

"Hello, Dion," the tallest boy in the crowd said, stepping forward. "We've been trying to have a private conversation with you since you arrived." The rest of the group snickered when he said it.

Dion motioned for Alex to keep going.

"He's got nothing to do with it," Dion told them. But Alex just remained at his side.

"I think I'll stick around for a while," Alex said while glaring at the opal crowd.

"Have it your way," the boy said, turning his attention back to Dion. "If you want to make things right you're going to have to meet us on neutral territory tonight. Behind the Lava Pyramid. Midnight. If you don't show up, we'll figure out something else for you—something I guarantee you'll find to be far more unpleasant. You can bring a teammate for backup if you can find one. Be there. Don't keep us waiting."

The Opal students turned as a unit and left without making another sound.

"Alex, you shouldn't get involved in all this," Dion said after the opal students were out of earshot. "I'll go and face them myself."

"No way. They might go easier on you if you got a witness. Com'on let's head back."

Alex and Dion trailed behind the Opal students, all the way back to the portal. They lined up behind everyone and made the return jump, arriving back at The Dome just where they had departed, near the center core. By this time the core had been converted into a motocross track, and Alex and Dion stopped for a second to watch the dozens of bikes screaming around it.

Two bikes flew over the final jump and split off from the main track. They roared over to Alex and Dion. When the bikes got extremely close, they both turned sideways and slid to a stop a couple of feet in front of them.

The two bikers lifted their helmets off. It was Elka and Maia.

"You guys finished with your class already?" Elka asked.

"We just got back," Alex said. "Looks like you two have been learning a lot."

"Oh yeah…" Elka said, putting her helmet back on.

"This is the most fun I've had in a long time," Maia added.

Elka twisted the bike's throttle, spun the tires, and flung her bike around. She shot away, back toward the race track.

Maia rushed to get her helmet on and the instant she did, she too was off, chasing after Elka.

Laughing, Alex and Dion brushed a few bits of dirt off them and headed back to the Jade Pyramid. The rest of the evening went uneventfully.

At fifteen minutes before midnight, Alex and Dion moved out of their room and into the common area. They walked as quietly as they could, trying to make sure neither Mercure or Panda heard their movement. Alex kept an eye on the two dogs as they crept past them. Mercure's front paws were twitching, so Alex figured he was having a dream. Panda didn't move a muscle.

Alex and Dion both jumped down from the room and scanned the area. Nobody was around. At this time of night, the interior of the pyramid was much dimmer than normal, so they were able to sneak out without any chance of being seen.

They made their way to the rear of the Lava Pyramid, with neither one saying a word the entire way. Before they rounded the last corner, Alex took a final look around to ensure no one had followed them. Everything around The Dome was dark and silent.

They approached the rear of the pyramid and someone far off, near the stream running between the pyramid and the dome wall, shouted over to them.

"You two, over here! Quick!"

Alex and Dion had a fast look at each other. Alex turned back toward the dome wall, and they both cautiously headed in the voice's direction. When they neared the stream, the same seven Opal students they saw at the airfield jumped up from the river bank and surrounded them.

"I see you got someone to come with you," the tall boy said to Dion. "Did you have to pay him something?"

"Why don't you worry about your own business," Alex answered, stepping forward.

"Fine," the boy said, studying Alex for a moment. He swung his gaze over to Dion and then back to Alex. "Let me tell you about my business then. The way we figure it, Dion owes us a few broken bones for what he did to Jago. He can do it on his own, or we can help him with it."

Dion stepped forward, pushing Alex to his rear.

"What do you want me to do?" he asked.

The boy placed his arm around Dion's shoulder. Two other Opal students stepped in behind them. The boy moved Dion away from Alex, over to the edge of the bank of the stream. A concrete wall extended up to them from the stream bed below. It ranged from about twelve feet high right where they stood, to over twenty-five feet high just a little way further along. Alex stepped over to Dion's side to see better. The bottom of the wall buried itself into a flat dirt area that had hundreds of medium-size rocks lying all around it.

"Here's what I propose," the boy said. "You have a choice. We can blindfold your teammate and have him jump off the twelve-foot wall, or we can blindfold you and have you jump off the twenty-five-foot section. Whichever one it is, they're going to have to take off their GEM socks and hood. Now, without GEM socks on, at twelve feet your buddy might only break a couple of bones in his feet against those rocks down there. And here at The Dome, they can fix him up in just a few days. But if you jump from twenty-five feet high without a hood on, you're bound to break something more vital. Something that doesn't heal that fast—you know, like your skull."

He remained silent for a few seconds. "Well? What'll be? You got one minute to decide, or we'll decide for you." The boy walked over to his friends, turned around and waited with his arms crossed in front of him.

Dion still peered over the ledge. Alex tapped him on the back to get his attention, and Dion straightened up. Alex moved in closer to speak to him without being overheard.

"I'll go," Alex said. "Like he said, at worst it'll keep me out for a couple of days."

"No way, Alex. I'm not going to let you take the heat for me."

"What do you want to do, go home to your parents in a box? I'm not going to be missed for just a couple of days. It's a lot better than missing you forever."

Dion looked like he was trying to come up with something to say, but he just remained still.

"I think you'd do the same for me, wouldn't you?" Alex asked him.

Dion stiffened up.

"Yeah," he said. "You know I would."

"Okay, let me do it for you then."

Alex had Dion perplexed, for the time being, so he quickly turned to the opal students.

"I'll jump," Alex shouted over to them.

The tall boy grabbed something out of his pocket and walked over to Alex.

"Right, take off your socks and put this blindfold on," he ordered.

Alex squatted down and removed his shoes and GEM socks. When he stood back up, he placed the blindfold on his head and pulled it down over his eyes.

The tall boy grabbed Alex by both shoulders and guided him forward, toward the wall.

"We've got a long wooden plank on the ground here. Stand up on it."

Alex stepped forward, feeling around with his toes to find the board. He stepped up and steadied himself in the middle of it. He immediately felt the board being raised up by several students. It took all his concentration to keep himself from falling off the board as it moved forward.

"Okay, we're going to stick the plank out over the edge to give you some clearance. We don't want you hitting your head against the wall on the way down do we?" Alex heard some laughter in the background. "Stand still now."

The plank moved forward and stopped.

"Now, step off! And be quick about it!"

Alex inched his way forward, and after a few steps, he felt the end of the plank beneath his toes. He moved his foot forward and down a few inches. He felt nothing.

Plans on what to do next rushed through his head. Maybe he should curl up and try to land on his knees. His GEM suit should protect him from that hit. But of course, depending on how he landed, he could be thrown forward and smash his head against the rocks. Maybe he should try landing on one foot. But was breaking several bones in one foot better than breaking only a couple of bones in two of them? Perhaps he could roll when he landed and have the GEM suit absorb the hit that way—but then he'd have to worry about his head again.

None of the plans provided much hope to him. There wasn't anything left to do but jump and see what happens.

Alex snapped his head to the side when he heard Dion muttering something, but it was so muffled he couldn't make out exactly what he said. He heard a few other students whisper something to each other. Then, absolute silence. All he heard was the water in the stream below him flowing past, and nothing else. No reprieve was coming. There was no use waiting any longer.

Alex stepped off.

He fell a couple of feet and collapsed onto the soft grass. Alex ripped the blindfold off his head to see what was going on. All the Opal students started laughing and hooting. The tall boy came over to Alex and extended his hand to help him up.

"You've got the loyalty and the guts kid," the boy said. Alex grabbed his hand and jumped up off the ground. When the two of them were face to face, the boy said, "That counts for a lot with us."

Alex looked down at the plank and realized that the Opal students had only moved it over to a couple of concrete blocks and placed it down between them. He wasn't anywhere near the edge of the drop-off.

Alex scanned around for Dion. Now he knew why he had heard muffled sounds from him. Dion's hands were tied behind his back, and a rag had been placed in his mouth. The other Opal students were now at work releasing him.

"If you were willing to take the hit for him, I guess he can't be all that bad," the boy said to Alex. He turned to face Dion. "You owe Jago an apology. It was his idea to give you this chance, so the apology better be a good one. Jago's fist is almost healed, and he's gonna be back here in a few days. When he gets back, you find him and get that done. Understand?"

Dion could only nod in agreement, as he still had the rag in his mouth. As soon as he got one of his hands free, he reached up and yanked the rag out.

"You okay, Alex?" he shouted.

"Yeah, sure," Alex answered while Dion ran over to him. "No problems man."

The Opal students turned and left without making another sound.

Alex sat down on the grass and put on his shoes and socks. He walked away with Dion back toward the Jade Pyramid. Neither one of them said anything until they were about halfway back. Alex looked quickly at Dion and then ahead to the path in front of him.

"And this is only the first week," Alex said.

"Think we'll make it to graduation someday?" Dion asked.

"No chance," Alex answered.

They both laughed the rest of the way.

FOURTEEN

The next morning Alex and Dion awoke to the sound of Feng shouting.

"Get up! Both of you!"

They sat up in their beds and watched in confusion as Feng rocketed over to Alex's closet, reached into it, and threw several items of clothing across the room onto Alex's bed.

"You asked me to wake you at eight o'clock," Feng said. "Well, it's eight o'clock, and you'd better get up. I don't have time to wait around for your dawdling." He made his way over to Dion's closet, threw out the same set of clothing onto Dion's bed, and headed for his corner perch. He turned around and said, "Well, get a move on!"

"What is wrong with you?" Alex asked, rubbing the back of his neck.

"What is wrong with me?" Feng responded incredulously. "What is wrong with me? I'll tell you what is wrong with me. I don't get any appreciation around here. So, if you don't care about me, then I don't care about it one way or the other."

"You're putting us on," Dion said.

Feng turned to Dion and then over to Alex. He rolled his eyes and then stared straight out in front of him.

"Have you ever said, 'Thank you, Feng, for that' or 'Good job, Feng!'? No! The answer is 'No'!"

Then in a flash, Feng's face returned to its normal gentle expression.

"This afternoon you'll be taking your first practical sailing class. You'll be provided with all the equipment you need for that class when you arrive at the training facility. Your first classroom instruction this morning is your second History and Use of the Zero Point Field class. It starts in thirty-five minutes at Classroom Facility Number One. Ask the Qen in front if you still need assistance."

Feng's face instantly turned stern again. He froze on his perch, but this time without breaking into the same small smile he had always displayed before. After what could only be described as loud snort, he disappeared.

After a few seconds of stunned silence, Alex looked over to Dion to see if he had a clue. All he saw on Dion's face was a combination of confusion and amusement.

"Every day is certainly different around here," Alex said.

Dion threw off his covers and swung his legs over the edge of the bed.

"Yep," Dion said. "I'm not sure I'll get used to it anytime soon."

They both got dressed, ate a quick breakfast, and headed out to the common room.

In the corner Mercure and Panda ate out of their bowls, while Elka and Maia sat on opposite sides of the center table, sipping tea.

"I'm glad everything worked out for you last night," Elka said.

"How do you know about that?" Dion asked suspiciously. "It just happened a few hours ago—and that was all the way on the other side of The Dome."

Elka nodded over to the dogs in the corner.

"The dogs around here gossip," she said.

Alex slowly turned to Mercure.

Mercure picked his head up from his breakfast, glanced back at Alex for a fleeting moment, and softly walked to the other side of the room to lie down. Panda kept eating, not acting the least bit anxious.

Alex sat in the chair closest to Mercure.

"I thought that between the three different pyramids everything was supposed to be a big secret," Alex said. "Now I find out all the dogs just tell each other everything?"

Mercure picked his head up and said, *"It's not a secret after it happens, right?"* He put his head back down. *"Relax buddy. The whole school knows about it—I'm not giving away any secrets."*

Alex dipped his chin down to Mercure and gave him a frown.

"We've got to have another talk later on."

Mercure didn't respond. He swayed his eyes from one side of the room to the other and settled them back on Alex.

Alex turned his attention to Elka and Maia.

"And what is going on with Feng?" he asked.

Both girls burst out laughing as if they had been waiting for the question all morning. After quite a long time, they both calmed down—a little bit anyway.

"Well…" Elka said, just before getting back to laughing. After another couple of seconds, she was able to continue. "We started programming him again last night, and we found a couple of pre-built personality packages stored in his memory. Probably built by the last group of students in this quad. We installed one of them and…" She started laughing again.

"You saw what we got!" Maia finished for her.

"You should have seen him go last night!" Elka and Maia said together, both laughing even harder now. It took them a few more seconds to compose themselves again.

"He wouldn't calm down!" Elka continued. "And you remember how Kolek told us that the only good way to program him was when he was quiet and not doing anything. Well…" She laughed a bit more. "He's not quiet for very long anymore, that's for sure."

Maia stood up, went over to the window, and sat on the sill. She had settled down a bit more than Elka by this time.

"So, we just told him to leave us for a while," Maia said. "And that we'd try fixing him in the morning. But that wasn't such a smart idea, was it, Elka?"

"No! No, it wasn't!" Elka said leaning forward, almost all the way down to the tabletop. She put her right hand up to her face and giggled into it. "I thought I had joined the army when he woke us up!"

"We'll talk to Kolek this afternoon," Maia said. "Maybe he can give us hints on how to change him back."

"We'd appreciate it," Alex said to both of them.

A few minutes later Elka and Maia finished their tea, and everyone dropped down from their room, heading out to their first class of the day. Halfway there Alex stepped out in front of everyone and turned around, walking backward.

"It's been bugging me how Z can limit a Z-Con's access to the Zero Point Field. I've got a few questions I want to ask this morning. So, when I start asking Mr. Serret a bunch of questions, I need you all to go along with me. Okay?"

"Sure, but what do you expect him to tell you?" Elka ask.

"I don't know. Maybe we can get a hint about why our parents had such a hard time figuring out those glyphs." Alex turned back around. "Maybe he'll give us a clue about why those glyphs are so important."

They arrived at Classroom Facility Number One and went directly to their 'History and Use of the Zero Point Field' class, this time without having to ask directions from the Qen.

They arrived at class ten minutes early and found Mr. Serret already there, waiting for them. He stood in the middle of the room, surrounded by several 3-D images from Earth's history floating all around him. Each image popped up, swirled around him in a big circle and then changed to another event. Scenes from ancient Egypt, including large stones being raised to the top of a pyramid, were mixed in with images from ancient China. The images looked like they were coming in sequence, by year. After a few seconds, images from the building of Rome and London started to circle him. It was at that point Mr. Serret noticed everyone staring at him. All the images instantly disappeared.

"Hello, students! Welcome to day two," he said. "I was just taking a quick tour of history when you came in. Something I like to do when I have a few free moments. So, everyone has their Z-Con's ready? Good. Then let's get to it. Grab a seat up front."

Everyone moved forward and took a seat in one of the chairs arranged in a line at the front of the room. Alex sat down last, and as soon as he did, the room Qen appeared on his pedestal in the corner. He floated over to the group and stood in front of them, becoming perfectly still, with his hands folded in front of him.

"Okay everyone, follow me to today's classroom," Mr. Serret ordered.

Alex closed his eyes, and when he opened them again, he found himself in the new classroom, standing right next to Mr. Serret, with Dion, Elka, and Maia right alongside. The classroom was arranged the same way as the day before when they had taken their first Z-Con class.

"Today I'll be discussing our ancestors' encounters with the people outside their facility—the main one they established in Mt. Olympus," Mr. Serret said.

"Sir, before you continue, could I ask you a question about our Z-Cons?" Alex asked.

"Okay, Alex, go ahead."

"Can Z limit the amount of information that a Z-Con would normally expect to be able to access?"

"Sure," Mr. Serret answered. "That's something that Z has been working on for a couple of thousand years. He feels that the ability to limit a Z-Con's capability will come in handy if we're ever attacked. Making sure that an invading enemy cannot use their Z-Cons to find out all

245

information about what is happening on Earth is an important ability to have. Wouldn't you think, Alex?"

Alex nodded in agreement.

"Actually," Mr. Serret continued, "Z is concentrating on how to turn a Z-Con completely off so it can't do anything at all. In a scenario where we get attacked it would be very helpful if we could destroy all the abilities of an invader's Z-Cons."

"But what about our Z-Cons here at the school? Does Z limit them all?"

"To an extent. You see, you have to use a Z-Con Prime to make a regular Z-Con. It is at the point when it becomes activated that any limitations are incorporated into it by the Z-Con Prime used to create it. It took Z many decades to figure out exactly how to use a Z-Con Prime to make a regular Z-Con, and then how to limit their capabilities. For example, when one is used here at the school, we eliminate its capability to communicate with the outside world."

Alex stepped forward a few inches.

"But why?" he asked.

"The location of this facility is secret. Even an instructor like myself doesn't know exactly where it is. If we were to allow Z-Cons in here to connect with Z-Cons on the outside, then those Z-cons could track the location of any transmissions back to this facility. We put special protocols into effect on Sundays when we allow you to connect to your parent's Z-Cons. Those transmissions can't be traced back here."

"Does Z limit the information that our Z-Cons access?"

"Yes," Mr. Serret said. He stepped a little closer to Alex. "For example, the Z-Cons we create for our students can only access written information that has been already published. That is, only the information that is available to anybody in the world who wants to go look it up, like online or at a library."

"But can he stop a Z-Con from even seeing some of those documents?"

"Sure, but why would he?" Mr. Serret answered suspiciously. Now he made another step forward. "Have you been limited in what you need to know?"

"No. I just wondered," Alex answered innocently. Then he turned serious again. "But I also wondered about the teacher who said his Z-con failed at the sailing facility at the beginning of the term. Do we know how it happened?"

"No, but I'm sure Vizier Herabata and Z will figure it out."

"Just one more question, sir. What does it mean when someone was 'banished'?"

"It's when a Z-Con Prime is used to turn someone into a solid object. In the early days, they used it as the harshest form of punishment. Of course, they only did it to people who committed the most serious crimes. We don't do that kind of thing anymore."

"Can someone use a regular Z-Con to un-banish someone?"

"Yes, but only temporarily, and only while they're fully concentrating on it. After that, the person goes back to the same state they were in originally. It's a very hard thing to do."

Mr. Serret moved even closer to Alex. He put his hand on Alex's shoulder.

"I'm curious as to why you're asking these questions, Alex. Is there something bothering you about your Z-Con?"

Elka stepped forward, next to Mr. Serret.

"No, we all were just talking about it last night," Elka said.

Maia moved up next to her and said, "We disagreed on what we thought our Z-Cons could do."

Mr. Serret looked over to Maia, then back to Alex. He switched his gaze back and forth between the two of them for a couple of seconds more before continuing.

"Very well," he said. "It's time we got back to today's lesson."

A 3-D image of Mount Olympus in Greece appeared in front of him.

"As I was saying, let's investigate our ancestors' first encounters with the local people of Greece."

Everyone spent the rest of the hour going over the subject of the day, but Alex didn't pay much notice. All his attention was on contemplating Mr. Serret's answers to his question. By the end of the hour, he had thought about it long enough and ended up paying at least some attention to the history lecture. When the class ended, he moved on to the daily math, language, and science classes with Elka, Maia and Dion. Then it was time for everyone's first sailing lecture, just down the hall from their science class.

The sailing class was going to be taught by a new teacher, Mr. Wilkinson. He told everyone all about his impressive credentials of having sailed large and small sailing boats all over the world, and how by the time he was done teaching them about sailing, everybody in the class would be able to do the same thing. "If you were so inclined," he added.

The lecture consisted of everyone standing inside a small sailboat sitting on wooden blocks on dry land. Mr. Wilkinson went over the finer points of handling a sailboat, including how to work all the equipment on board. They spent a great deal of time going over the definitions of everything on a sailboat. How the front of the boat was called the bow, the rear was the stern, the right side was called starboard, and the left was called port. They learned how any rope they used to raise a sail was called a halyard and that any rope used to trim the sails was called a sheet—and on and on. There were dozens of details they had to know before they started even to discuss how to sail the boat. Eventually, they did learn what to do to make the boat go forward when the wind was coming from behind them, or from the side, or even from the front.

The last thing they learned was the rules on who gets to keep going straight when two sailboats were on a collision course, and who had to change course so that they wouldn't collide.

That was the longest class Alex had gone through so far. But Alex always liked learning complicated things. Somehow it made the tasks more meaningful to him if they required some amount of thought before he could perform them well.

When the classroom training for the day was over, everyone headed over to the maintenance facility to complete their daily duties.

Alex approached Samuel in the J-A-5 section, who at this time was kneeling under a plane with his head inserted into its left wing through a small access port. Alex had a lot to get off his mind.

"I need to talk to you, Samuel," Alex said.

"Go ahead," Samuel replied, keeping his head inside the wing.

"You need to train me to do something useful with these planes. I don't care what the others are telling you, you've got to give me some training!"

Samuel twisted his body slightly and delicately lowered his head out of the access hole. He looked down at the ground.

"But they were pretty clear," Samuel lamented. "They didn't want me spending any time on that. I've got to get these planes ready for Saturday's competition."

"You can do that better if I help you," Alex said. "Listen, they fly these planes, and that's what they're in charge of. You're in charge of maintenance. It's up to you how to handle it."

Samuel thought about it for a little while.

"You're right," he said. He looked back up at Alex. "It's my responsibility. If I want to train you, then that's my call!"

"Great! What do you want to do first?" Alex asked.

'Well, right now I have to check the insides of all the wings. We've got to see if there are any cracks or corrosion along the aluminum tubes on the inside. Especially at the weak points. These planes get treated pretty hard when they're competing, and if they're going to break, it's going to be somewhere inside the wings."

"How can I tell where the weak points are?" Alex asked.

"Use your Z-Con to call up the plans of the inside of the wings. Any weak points will be highlighted in red. I want you to look at every inch of the tubing and if you see anything strange or out of place, call me over. You start with the plane at the back and work your way up toward me. Go slow. You might as well start memorizing what all the parts look like inside, and exactly where all the weak points are."

"Why?"

"Because during the competitions the rules allow for one maintenance guy to be able to use their Z-Con to fix any of the planes in the air. If someone had a problem with a wing, and if you can picture the exact part in your head, you might be able to use your Z-Con to fix it for them. Then they can go on competing instead of dropping out."

"Cool! I had no idea you could do that on a moving object," Alex said.

"It's hard, but if you keep your eyes directly on the plane that's having the trouble, and at the same time picture in your head what you want to get fixed, you can do it. It's all about how well you can visualize everything."

Alex headed toward the plane at the back of the area, slapping Samuel on the back as he passed him.

They spent the next couple of hours looking over all the wings. Everything seemed to be in place and working well. When the maintenance was over Alex stood by Samuel as they wiped the last remnants of grease from their hands.

"Thanks for that, Samuel," Alex said.

Samuel didn't say anything but gave him a smile and a single nod.

Alex met up with Dion in front of the maintenance building, and they headed over to the core to take the portal jump to the sailing facility. They saw Elka and Maia a short bit ahead of them, and they jogged for a few seconds to catch up.

As soon as they came alongside Elka, she started right in.

"We took a whole engine apart and put it back together today," she said, quickly followed by Maia. "Everyone said we were naturals at it!"

"I adjusted all the flight control cables on two of my team's planes," Dion said. "They said I'd be working on the electric systems next time."

Alex just nodded to each one of them as they let out their stories, and all the time just wearing a big grin on his face. Finally, he felt that he was part of his competition team, just as much as Elk, Maia, and Dion felt a part of theirs.

They reached the core and Alex strolled up to the Qen to get directions to the sailing facility. He told Alex to take portal number five, and Alex led everyone over to the right spot. As soon as Alex got in the line, he saw the back of Bhedi Haley and her sister Jordan standing just a few students ahead of them. Hoping to avoid a confrontation, Alex turned his back to them while he talked to Dion.

"Tell me if she starts coming over," he said.

"Who?" Dion asked.

Alex jerked his head behind him, toward the two girls.

"Oh. Okay, got it," Dion replied.

But the line moved quickly, and Bhedi and her sister jumped through the portal without taking notice of Alex at all.

Alex made it to the front of the line, and he led the way through the portal. As soon as he arrived at the sailing facility, he spun completely around to survey his surroundings. A beautiful light blue sky filled the expanse above him, all the way to the horizon. He stood on an enormous floating metal platform, in the middle of a warm ocean. Soft waves lapped up against all the platform's edges, and in the far distance Alex could just make out the slight shimmering of a transparent dome that enclosed the entire area. Several small sailboats crisscrossed the water in front of him, their sails bringing small dots of color to the vast expanse of deep blue water.

Elka, Maia, and Dion showed up within the next few seconds, and after everyone had gained their bearings, they all went walking toward their right, where the crowd of students flowed. Alex didn't get far before he noticed Bhedi just ahead of him again. This time it didn't take long for Bhedi to notice Alex. The instant she did, she and her sister swung around and headed against the crowd, toward him. Alex stopped in his tracks to avoid walking into her.

"Well, well," Bhedi said loudly as she approached. "Mr. Vega again. Come here to show us how little you know about sailing?" Jordan stood behind Bhedi, keeping watch in the other direction. "I bet you're such a shaky little fellow— you'll be wearing the biggest life preserver they have."

Alex didn't make the slightest move. Not even to acknowledge she was standing in front of him.

The air of indifference he displayed to Bhedi seemed to confuse her. She turned back to her sister, apparently to see if there was anything to worry about. Jordan motioned with her hand, giving Bhedi the all-clear signal. She turned back to Alex.

"You're too afraid to go out without a life vest on, aren't you? Personally, I don't wear the things. Too uncomfortable." She signaled over to Jordan that they were leaving. "Better watch your back out there Vega. Bad things happen to scared little people who don't know what they're doing."

After a couple of seconds, she turned and stormed away, tapping Jordan on the back as she went by her. The two of them merged in with the passing crowd.

"Let's stay away from that one today," Dion said. "What'd you think?"

Elka and Maia nodded. Alex just shrugged his shoulders.

Mr. Wilkinson approached them from the edge of the platform.

"Okay!" he said. "Everyone's here. Good. Normally I wouldn't be teaching your practical class, but unfortunately, your instructor for today's class finds himself unavailable, so I'll do it." Mr. Wilkinson pointed to the other side of the platform, over Alex's shoulder. "Let's head over that way to your boat."

Everyone followed him over to a line of sailboats—all tightly lined up and tied to the platform's edge. Mr. Wilkinson led the way to the sailboat on the far end. He passed the boat and reached into a large wooden box sitting on the platform, handing out life preservers to everyone. He spent the next half hour quizzing Alex and everyone about what they had learned in his classroom that day.

After he seemed satisfied that they had all paid enough attention during his class to understand the workings of the sailboat, he looked up, checking out the weather.

"Excellent! Well, they got the wind set rather light today, so why don't you all take this boat and I'll get in the one next to you. Let's follow each other around for a while."

"What do you mean 'they set the wind'?" Alex asked him.

"Like the other training facilities, this one is enclosed by a dome. That way we can't be detected. It also allows us to set the wind speed and direction. They can make it pretty hairy around here if they want. But not to worry—looks like you've got an excellent day to take out the boat."

He picked up a life preserver for himself, and after he put it on, he turned to Alex and said, "You handle the tiller." He swung to Elka and Maia, and said, "You two handle trimming the jib." And finally, to Dion, "You handle the mainsail."

He headed over to the boat just to the right of them and yelled back, "Now get in and follow me around. Just go where I go and do what I do."

"By ourselves?" Maia asked no one in particular.

"Sure," Dion responded. "Why not? The wind's pretty light. Should be simple."

"Yeah," Alex said with a little uneasiness. "Let's get going." He moved toward the boat and stepped onto it.

Just thinking about himself at the tiller, in command of the boat, caused Alex to shake a bit. He had never actually taken any boat out without his mother or father at the wheel. Certainly, he had never contemplated being in command of anything as complicated as a sailboat, at least without someone more experienced around to keep him out of trouble. But somehow, he convinced himself that it would all be all right in the long run. After all, Mr. Wilkinson wouldn't let them sail off by themselves if he thought they'd get into too much trouble—well at least he probably wouldn't.

It only took a few seconds for everyone to take their assigned positions. Alex watched Mr. Wilkinson raise the mainsail in his boat, and he tried to remember all the steps he needed to take to launch the sailboat. He touched his Z-Con in his pocket, called up the 'launch' checklist, and it displayed out in front of him.

With all the confidence he could muster he gave the command, "Dion, raise the mainsail." He turned to Elka and Maia. "Standby to cast off forward, standby to cast off aft." The two girls moved to the lines that held the sailboat tightly against the platform. Dion pulled hard on a halyard that ran up the mast, raising the mainsail. Once he had it fully raised and tied off, Alex shouted, "Cast off forward, cast off aft!" Elka and Maia let go of their lines. Alex turned back to Dion. "Bring in the mainsail!" Dion pulled hard on the sheet that was attached to the boom, moving it closer to the centerline of the boat. Alex shifted the tiller fully to the right, letting the wind fill the mainsail. They were off!

They increased speed rapidly and fell in line right behind Mr. Wilkinson. After a few minutes of sailing in his wake, Mr. Wilkinson unfurled his jib sail and pulled it in. His boat shot ahead.

Alex knew things were about to get more complicated, but he took a hard gulp and shouted, "Release the jib to the port side!"

Elka and Maia went to the port side of the boat and pulled on the halyard attached to the jib sail. It unrolled from its attachment at the bow, and they pulled on the sheet that was attached to its bottom, pulling the sail close to the boat. The wind skimmed along its length, and it filled with air. The boat leaned over a bit and picked up speed. Dion went to the starboard side of the boat so that his weight would help keep the sails from causing the boat to lean over too much, and as soon as he did, they went even faster.

Mr. Wilkinson gave a big wave and a huge thumbs up. He sailed on for another couple of minutes before changing course ninety degrees in the other direction. He let the mainsail go across to the other side of the boat and brought his jib sail over to the same side. Off he went in the new direction.

Alex followed along giving the orders for Dion, Elka, and Maia to duplicate the maneuver, and it all happened beautifully. The four of them concentrated fully on what they were doing, and all the while with huge grins on their faces.

The back-and-forth course changes went on for the next half hour. Mr. Wilkinson's boat headed toward a red buoy sitting near the edge of the dome, and when he reached it, he threw his tiller hard over, making a complete turn around it. He let out his mainsail and jib, and the two of them filled with the wind again. Alex followed the same procedures and kept his boat directly behind Mr. Wilkinson.

After a few minutes more of sailing, Mr. Wilkinson released both his sails so that the wind wouldn't push him anymore. Alex moved his boat up alongside, and Elka let the jib out as far as she could so they passed by him barely going at a crawl.

"Excellent job!" Mr. Wilkinson shouted over to them. "Well done! Now the four of you keep going back and forth until I return. I'm pulling double duty today, so I need to go to that boat over there for a minute and see how they're doing." He pointed behind him to a sailboat about a quarter-mile away. "I'll be back in a bit!"

He pulled his sails in and took off. Elka and Maia pulled in the jib, and Alex turned the boat back onto their original course. The wind, coming from the starboard side now, had picked up slightly and it pushed the boat over a little harder than before. But by this time Alex felt comfortable handling the boat and it didn't concern him at all. He was having a ball!

Dion tapped Alex on the shoulder and pointed off to a boat coming at them from the front.

"They're heading right at us," he said. "Should we change course?"

Alex sized up the other boat for a few seconds.

"No," he said. "It's not for us to change anything. We're on starboard tack. We've got the right of way."

But the boat kept heading at them, on an intercept course. Alex watched, waiting for them to change direction. Within a minute they were only a few dozen yards away.

Dion tapped him again.

"Isn't that Bhedi at the tiller?" he shouted.

Alex squinted for a few seconds. It was Bhedi. And true to her word, she and the rest of her crew weren't wearing any life jackets. But that wasn't what concerned Alex at the moment. Bhedi was either trying to scare him or was planning to ram him. If she wanted to play chicken, Alex wasn't having any of it. She could have the right of way as far as he was concerned.

Now the boats were only seconds away from colliding.

"Elka…Maia, let go the jib," he shouted. "Dion, release the mainsail!"

Their sails swung away, fluttering in the wind. Alex pushed the tiller hard to the right causing the bow of the boat to rotate left, falling away from the line Bhedi's boat was on. She was going to miss them, but just by a few feet.

At that moment, a gust of wind came slamming in from the front. The bow of Bhedi's boat swung hard to the right, shooting it even further away from Alex's boat. But the gust caught the back of Bhedi's mainsail, causing the boom to shoot across the centerline, striking her hard on the back of her head, and throwing her into the water. Nobody on Bhedi's boat noticed what happened to her and their boat continued sailing away.

Alex threw his tiller all the way to the other side, causing the boat to come to a dead stop. He leaned over the starboard side of the boat looking at the spot where Bhedi had fallen in. Back over his shoulder shouted, "She's not coming up!"

Dion, Elka, and Maia ran over to Alex, causing the whole boat to lean far over, but that didn't stop them from hanging over the edge, trying to catch a glimpse of Bhedi.

Alex grabbed his Z-Con from his pants pocket and slammed down the handle. He pointed it to the spot where he saw Bhedi hit the water. Concentrating on pulling her up, he tried to imagine how it felt the first time he used his Z-Con to pull himself up against the wall, back in his first class. Back then he could feel the pull as he tilted upwards, but now, trying to pull up on Bhedi, nothing—no resistance at all. The top of his Z-Con didn't change to the same reddish color that it had before. It had no color at all. It wasn't working.

"Can anyone swim?" Alex shouted, continuing to scan the area with his Z-Con.

"Not me!" Dion said, backing away.

Elka and Maia looked at each other for a second, turned back to Alex, and shouted, "No, not really."

"There just wasn't any water around where we grew up," Maia said.

Alex tore off his life preserve and crawled over the edge of the boat, hoping it wouldn't lean over any further as he did. He let go and slid into the water. When he popped back up to the surface, he grabbed the side of the boat, holding himself against it.

"Get a rope or something ready!" he yelled, wiping the water away from his eyes.

"I don't know how I'm gonna get her up," he said out loud, mostly to himself.

Alex sucked in a huge breath, threw his head into the water, and dove straight down. At first, the light from above illuminated everything around him, but as he took a couple of strokes further down, everything turned darker. He flailed his hands around, desperately trying to find Bhedi. After several seconds of finding nothing, he took another couple of strokes down, diving deeper. He searched around wildly again, finding nothing. He pulled himself down, hard, one more time. His head slammed into something. It was the back of Bhedi's neck! Desperate now for air, he quickly swung his arm around her middle and pointed his head upward, toward the surface. He kicked as hard as he could with both feet and pulled up through the water with his free arm. But he didn't move an inch! He kicked more, and pulled as hard as he could again, but nothing! The more he tried, the more his lungs burned. He needed a gulp of air. Even a small gulp would do. But the surface remained far above him.

Then it dawned on him. He was actually drifting down, away from the surface, away from the air. It was time to let Bhedi go and save himself. But he couldn't do it. He kicked harder and pulled more.

At the moment he felt himself losing all strength, something from above grabbed his shirt collar and yanked him up. The force almost pulled him away from Bhedi—but he squeezed hard around her middle with both arms, refusing to let go of her. He rushed up, toward the surface, toward the air. It felt like an eternity. They kept moving up bit by bit, and finally, thankfully, the water broke over Alex's face. He sucked in as much air as he could.

Elka was clumsily treading water right next to Alex and holding his arm. Maia leaned over the side of the boat—clasping Elka's other hand. Dion reached out from the boat and grabbed Bhedi by both arms, tearing her away from Alex. In one motion he jerked her up into the boat and let her down easily, onto the deck. As Bhedi lay there, a small amount of water drained out of her mouth. A second later she took a huge, deep breath and started coughing.

Bhedi alternated between coughing and gulping air. She sat up and leaned forward.

Out of nowhere, Mr. Wilkinson jumped onto the deck, landing right next to Bhedi. He checked her over and looked up at Dion.

"Let's get her back to The Dome. We'll use this boat."

Elka by this time had climbed up into the sailboat. Alex was still in the water catching his breath. Mr. Wilkinson leaned over the side of the boat, reached out and pulled Alex over to him by his arm.

"Alex, we're going to take Bhedi back to the platform. I need everyone else to help me with the sails so we can get there fast. Can you handle taking my boat back by yourself?"

"Yeah, get going," Alex said, letting go and treading water. "I'll be fine."

Mr. Wilkinson stood up and looked down at him.

"Use only the mainsail...you'll be okay."

"No problem, I got it!" Alex shouted back. He swam a few feet away from the boat so he would be clear of it.

Mr. Wilkinson ordered Elka and Maia to set the sails while Dion looked after Bhedi. Their boat moved away from Alex, and as soon as it passed him, he swam the short distance over to Mr. Wilkinson's boat. He climbed into it and turned back to watch his friends sailing away. Mr. Wilkinson gave him a wave.

The rest of the crew of Bhedi's boat shouted over to Alex as they steered their boat past him.

"Is she all right?" they yelled over.

"She's okay. They're taking her back to the platform. I'm heading there now."

The crew watched for a little while. The boy standing at the tiller gave Alex a wave and headed his boat away, toward the platform.

It took Alex almost twenty minutes to sail back to the platform where he found Elka, Maia, and Dion waiting for him. He brought the boat alongside the dock, and they all joined in to tie it up.

When Alex stepped off the boat, Elka put a towel around his shoulders.

"Mr. Wilkinson took Bhedi back to The Dome. He said he wanted us all to head back as soon as you returned," she said.

"How'd you manage to lift Bhedi and me up?" Alex asked Elka. "She wouldn't budge an inch for me!"

"Well, when you didn't come up we figured you needed some help, so Maia and I went into the water, and I dove down. Maia held onto my ankles, and she dove down behind me. Dion leaned over the side of the boat and held Maia's ankles."

"When they stopped moving I began pulling up," Dion continued. "But I couldn't get anyone to move. Man, I was devo. So, I leaned back and pulled as hard as I could. And then bang! You all started shooting up. Right at the end, when Maia hit the surface, it was like a rope being cut. When Maia let go of Elka, I went flying back and pulled Maia right into the boat with me."

"It was a good plan," Alex said. "Thanks for that." He dried off his hair with the towel. "I hope she's okay."

"She was fine by the time we got back and docked," Maia said. "You should have heard Mr. Wilkinson giving her hell. He saw the whole thing happen."

A message popped in front of Alex. 'Thanks to each of you…Sorry for all the trouble. - Bhedi'

Elka and Maia turned to each other, and Dion started to say "Hey, I just got a …"

"I think we all just got one," Alex said.

Everyone headed over to the portals without saying another word. One after the other they made the return jump to The Dome. Waiting for them, with his arms crossed in front, was Z.

"You four come with me," he said and walked away.

Everyone followed Z across the facility to a building butted up against the dome wall between the Opal and Lava Pyramids. The three-story structure stood alone, surrounded by a large rock wall. The building was constructed completely out of enormous granite blocks, and its sides sloped outwards, making each level slightly bigger than the one below it. The only entrance to the building was located on its far-right side and guarded by three Qens.

Z passed the Qens without saying a word. The Qens remained motionless as Alex, Elka, Maia, and Dion also passed by them.

Everyone marched up a long, steep staircase located just inside the entrance. At its top was a massive doorway. Alex followed directly behind Z as he went through it.

Alex and the others followed Z across a highly polished stone floor toward a desk sitting near the far wall.

The room's ceiling towered twenty feet above Alex and had several chandeliers hanging down from it, providing a soft light that filled the enormous space. The wall on Alex's left was made from a gigantic piece of glass that provided a panoramic view of the entire training facility. As Alex passed it, he could see all three pyramids in the distance. The right side of the room butted up against the transparent dome wall that enclosed the training facility, providing a magnificent view of the ocean just on the other side of it. In the right corner sat an enormous 3-D hologram of the Earth, minus all the clouds. It looked incredibly real.

Someone sat in a chair that was turned around behind the desk, facing the back wall. That wall had viewing screens showing dozens of pictures of deep space. Each picture periodically changed to show a different a set of distant stars and nebula.

Z approached the desk and pointed to a spot on the floor directly in front of it. Alex and the others stopped there, and Z continued around to the far side of the desk. He started whispering to the person sitting in the chair.

Alex nudged Dion and pointed. Dion nudged Elka, and she nudged Maia. They all stared at a display sitting on a table in the left corner of the room. Propped up against the wall were several maps of various parts of the world. There were close-ups of China, the North Pole, the South Pole, India, and Mexico. Alongside the maps were three pictures of Egyptian hieroglyphs. None of them looked familiar to Alex, but right next to them were four pictures of Mayan hieroglyphs. One of them Alex recognized immediately. It was a close-up of Jawbone Fan.

Z stood back up, and the chair swung around to reveal Vizier Herabata. She had a stern look on her face and was wearing a blue jacket which made her look a bit more intimidating. Z moved back around to the front of the desk, stopping directly in front of Alex.

"Please tell us exactly what happened," he said to Alex. "Don't leave anything out."

Alex proceeded to tell the story, beginning from the moment Bhedi confronted him on the platform. He ended it with the four of them jumping back to The Dome and seeing Z standing there.

"So, your Z-Con didn't help at all," Z said to Alex. "Well that's not surprising. Pulling up with a Z-Con is an extremely difficult thing to do."

"Excuse me sir, but I've been practicing pulling up things with my Z-Con," Alex said. "I've gotten pretty good at it. And it always glows a reddish color when I do it. Today it didn't glow at all. I felt absolutely nothing." When Z and Vizier Herabata didn't respond, he said, "And what about in the beginning of the term, when the sailing instructor tried to save that other student? He said that his Z-Con didn't work either!"

"We're still figuring that out, Alex," Z said to him. "Until then we will be halting all classes at the sailing facility. I'm sure there's some reasonable explanation for what is happening. Some natural phenomena in the area perhaps."

Vizier Herabata stood and moved around the desk, stopping next to Z. She walked down the line and gently shook everyone's hand.

"Thank you for being so brave," she said as she walked. "You are all exactly the kind of students we need training here with us. Thank you. Do any of you need medical attention? Is there anything we can do for you?"

Alex saw his opportunity to find out more information about the Mayan glyphs on display in the corner. But he would have to be subtle about it. He didn't want Z and Vizier Herabata to know that he was extremely interested in the display of maps and glyphs. He would have to use some misdirection.

"Could you tell me about those pictures behind you?" Alex asked Vizier Herabata.

Vizier Herabata turned around to the wall and then back to Alex.

"Certainly, Alex. Those are images that our various bases around the world, as well as on the moon, are transmitting to me. They show the sections of space we are currently scanning, trying to detect any approaching alien ships. We've hardly ever spotted any real threat coming toward us, but we remain vigilant. Several times in our past we have detected ships traversing areas far, far away, but not heading near our direction."

"Oh, I see," said Alex. He moved to the right, over to the hologram of the Earth. "This looks real, does it spin?"

"It does more than that, Alex," Vizier Herabata replied. She walked past him and stood next to the globe. She placed both hands on a small section of Western Europe, somewhere around France. When she pulled her hands apart, that section of the Earth popped up from the globe and enlarged. She performed the same motion to the section again, and it zoomed in even more. After a quick six or seven more enlargements, the section showed a small country road wandering around a green meadow. Alex took a few steps closer to get a good look. He saw several cows roaming around the middle of a large field. One more enlargement motion by Vizier Herabata and Alex could plainly see two people strolling down the side of the road, holding hands.

"With this, we can observe any place on earth and see what is happening in real time," Vizier Herabata announced. She turned back toward Alex. "Very few things catch Z or me by surprise."

Now was the time for Alex to find out more about what truly interested him. He spun around and took several steps toward the corner of the room.

"I see you also look at maps from all over," he said back to her.

"Yes," Vizier Herabata said. "We use them when we plan our investigations about any strange phenomena we detect here on Earth. But most of those investigations turn out to be nothing of interest."

Before Alex could get close enough to the corner to get a good look at the maps, Z stepped in front of him.

"I think this would be a fine time for all of you to head back to your rooms and get a bit of a rest," he said. "You've all had a busy day, haven't you?"

Alex contemplated Z a long time before he answered.

"Yes, sir," he replied, coolly.

Z and Vizier Herabata gave a slight bow to the four of them. Everyone returned the bow, turned around, and headed out of the room. Alex led the way.

Over his shoulder he whispered, "Z is hiding something."

Everyone nodded.

FIFTEEN

Something startled Alex. He blinked his eyes several times, waking up to a bright, quiet room. Dion stood over him.

"Finally!" he said, walking back to his side of the room. He pondered out loud. "How many times do I need to tell you to get up?"

Alex looked around. Something was different, he thought to himself. Why was it that every time he woke up in this room something was different? Where was Feng?

"Feng didn't come if that's what you're wondering," Dion informed him.

"Why?"

"Do I know?" Dion replied, shrugging his shoulders. "We better get a move on, or we'll be late."

They threw on their clothes and went right out to the common room. Nobody was there, not even the dogs. At the same instant, a message popped up in front of both Alex and Dion.

'We took Feng over to Kolek's room. He said he could get Feng back to normal for us. See you in class—Elka'

Another message replaced it.

'The dogs came with us—Maia'

Alex and Dion both shrugged at each other and then headed out for the day's classes.

The next three days turned out to be unremarkable. Alex finally felt he had settled into a rhythm—more like his days had been before arriving at 'The Dome.' Feng had been fixed, that is to say, he was back to his old stuffy self. All the daily classes progressed from subject to subject. Alex's time at the maintenance facility had become more exciting. Samuel had not only started teaching Alex everything he knew about airplanes, but he also met up with Alex after dinner to teach him all the rules and regulations associated with the flying competitions. Since the sailing facility was temporarily closed, Alex and Dion took a flight class every day to fill up the empty time slot. Elka and Maia spent that time in their motocross class.

Saturday arrived, and it wasn't soon enough as far as Alex was concerned. He got up two hours before Feng was set to wake him. The anticipation of participating in a real flight competition had kept him up most of the night. But today, finally, he would get to see it. His J-A-5 team was scheduled to fly at ten o'clock, at the center core.

Alex sat in the common room, reading the rules and regulations for today's competition, paying particular attention to the 'updated' sections. Each Saturday at seven o'clock in the morning a new set of competition rules were released. They contained several updates that changed the standard rules slightly so that the flight teams would have to quickly adapt and improvise any plan they had developed for competition day.

Mercure tilted his head up.

"You're up at seven o'clock on your day off?" he said.

At the moment, Alex was hard at work, studying the rules, and didn't want to pay attention to anything else.

"Umm-hmm..." was all he responded.

Alex wanted to know every regulation by heart. Samuel had drilled it into him over and over again—the judges were sticklers for the exact wording of the rules. Alex didn't want to see his team caught off guard by any of them.

At around seven thirty Elka and Maia strolled into the common room with their teacups in hand and sat down at the center table across from Alex.

"You never get up this early," Elka stated.

"I guess I'm a little anxious," Alex said. "I got the flight competition at ten."

Panda trotted over to Maia for her morning scratch and for a small dog treat that Maia brought out for her each morning.

Alex looked over to Mercure, and when he saw his left eye peer open he asked, "Do you want a treat?"

Mercure shut his eye and said, *So when did you turn crazy?"*

Alex let out a small laugh.

Elka took another sip of her tea.

"What did he say?" she asked.

Alex went back to reading his regulations. "He said no."

"Why did you laugh?" she asked.

Alex looked over at her. "I don't know about the rest of the dogs around here, but Mercure is a sarcastic son of a... dog."

Elka and Maia both gave out a huge laugh.

"So's Panda!" Elka said through her laughing.

"We thought she was the only one!" Maia added.

Alex paced the floor for the next hour and a half and then headed over to the core. It was only nine o'clock, but he had told Samuel he would show up early to help him prep the planes for competition. When Alex arrived, he saw the four Jade planes all lined up, with Samuel looking over one of the engines.

"How's it going?" Alex asked.

"Good!" Samuel said. "Do me a favor. Go preflight the other three planes. I already did it once, but you can never be too careful, okay?"

Alex spent the next half hour meticulously looking over every part of the other three planes, finding nothing out of place.

"I think we're all set," Alex said, walking back to Samuel. He was still hard at work on the same engine. "Something wrong with this one?"

"No. But in the last competition, its engine gave us some problems, so I just wanted to make sure it was in good shape."

Ken and Joey walked up behind Samuel, both of them looking rather miserable.

"Everything okay with the equipment?" Ken asked.

"Sure," Samuel said. He turned toward Joey, and back to Ken. "Why the face? What's going on?"

"Joey got herself disqualified," Ken answered.

Samuel threw his rag on the floor. "Well, we're never going to win with just three planes!" He turned his exasperated gaze to Joey. "What'd you do?"

Joey just walked past Samuel and Alex, heading for a chair in the corner of the pit, refusing to say a word to anyone.

Ken moved in front of Samuel, stopping him from following her. "She was up early this morning, so she used her Z-Con to access the new rules. It was only six thirty, and the rules don't come out till seven, but whoever was holding the rules messed up. Joey's Z-Con showed her the new rules too early. It wasn't really her fault. They should have protected the new rules till seven."

"But they can't disqualify her if someone else messed up and let the rules out ahead of time, right?" Alex asked Samuel. "I mean, it wasn't Joey's fault," he added. When Samuel didn't respond, Alex turned to Ken. "Right?"

"Yeah, they can," Ken told him, dejected. "The standard rules say that no competitor can see the new rules before seven in the morning under penalty of disqualification. It doesn't say anything about the rules being protected till then or anything else. And once the judges make a ruling, it's final."

Alex looked back to Samuel with a look of bewilderment.

"Like I told you before, Alex, they're sticklers when it comes to the rules," Samuel said. He started moving away, stopping after only a couple of steps. He started heading back, with his head still down. "There's no appeal process. She just ain't flying today, and that's all there is to it."

"You're going to have to fly the fourth plane," Ken said to Samuel.

"No way!" Samuel shouted at him. "You've got to have at least one maintenance guy ready to fix any of our planes that run into trouble. And I don't know about you, but I can only do that from the ground."

Alex stepped forward.

"Let me fly the fourth plane."

"Not now, Alex," Ken said, brushing Alex off with a swipe of his hand. "You'll only crash." When Alex didn't move away, Ken explained. "You don't know how all this stuff works. If you crash, you'll lose us all kinds of points. It's better for the plane to stay on the ground."

Alex gave it a few seconds of thought.

"I've been studying the rules. If I just take off, circle, and land at the end, I'll get another hundred points for the team. That's in section three of the rule book. It says you get fifty points for taking off, fifty points for landing safely. I mean, I don't even have to try any of the obstacles. Just take off, and then land at the end. And I've been taking off and landing these planes in my flight class for the last few days without any help. My instructor never had any problems with the way I do it—no problems at all. A hundred points could make the difference."

Two other students in green flight suits came walking up next to Ken. They both had kind of a glazed look about them. Ken just put up both hands toward them as to say 'Yes, she's out.'

"Alex, you haven't met our other pilots yet," Ken said, walking away. "This is Roxanne and Boris."

"We heard the news," Roxanne said to Ken's back. "Hardly worth flying today then."

Ken turned around and put his hands on his hips.

"Alex wants to take off, fly around and get the extra hundred points for it," Ken said. It sounded like a question.

"Couldn't hurt I guess," Roxanne said. She headed away toward Joey.

Boris just made a face and said, "Whatever."

Ken looked off into the distance, pondering. After what seemed like an eternity to Alex, Ken relented.

"Okay, you can fly," Ken said. "But just like you said. Fly around and land. Stay out of everybody's way."

Alex beamed—this was incredible! He was going to fly on his first competition day. Then an idea from nowhere jumped into his thoughts. Yes, of course! Another way to make extra points dawned on him.

"Wait!" Alex said to Ken. "If I'm not going to try any of the obstacles then there's a way I can make a bunch more points!"

"Okay... and just how are you going to do that?" Ken asked suspiciously.

"If I'm not going to be in any danger, then I don't need to wear any GEM equipment," Alex said. "The rules reward you with more points for each piece of GEM equipment you don't wear!"

"How much less equipment?"

"I won't wear any of it! Nothing. Why bother? I'm just taking off and then landing at the end of the competition. People out in the real world take off and land planes all the time, and they don't wear any GEM equipment. Why do I need it?" Alex did some computations in his head.

275

"According to the rules, if I don't wear a hood, goggles, gloves, socks, or my GEM suit, I'll get another hundred points."

"No way! I'm not going to let you do that," Ken said. "Everybody wears at least a GEM suit."

"Yeah, but don't you see…They're all trying to fly through a bunch of obstacles. They might crash, so they've got to worry about it. I don't! I'll simply fly around in a circle and land. You don't need a GEM suit just for that!"

Ken gave it a full couple of minutes of thought. When he didn't decide, Samuel piped in.

"We've got to try it," he implored Ken. "Maybe we can't win, but we could come in second if one of the other teams has some problems." Samuel looked up at the sky and raised both hands. "We've got to try something! I don't want to wear that damn orange vest again!"

"Okay! Okay!" Ken said. "Go get ready, Alex. Give it a shot."

Samuel set Alex up with a flight suit and they headed over to his plane. Alex climbed in, and Samuel drew both shoulder harnesses over Alex's back, strapping him into the pilot seat.

"Now don't take any chances," Samuel said. "Climb to the top of the dome and take out your Z-Con. Connect it to Ken's. You'll be able to talk to any of the pilots and also to me on the ground. But don't take any chances. Just stay up on top. That way none of the other teams can get to you."

"Get to me?" Alex said. "What do you mean? Who's gonna try to get to me?"

"Nobody. Not if you stay all the way up. But everyone else, down in the competition area—they spend a fair amount of time trying to intimidate the pilots on the other teams. You know, cutting them off—that sort of thing. Usually, no one gets hit, but it happens. Anyway, stay up high, and you'll be fine. Ken will tell the judges that you're flying without any GEM's on, so all you got to do is take off with everyone else and then wait until Ken tells you to land."

Alex shook Samuel's hand, started up the engine, and taxied away. He fell in line on the taxiway behind Ken, Roxanne, and Boris. They all turned onto the wide runway together as a team and took off one by one. Ken first, then Roxanne, then Boris. Now it was Alex's turn. He took a deep breath, pushed the throttle up to full power and headed down the runway—the whole time telling himself that this was just like back in his flight class. But the more he said it, the more he knew it wasn't true. There wasn't anyone sitting next to him this time if he made a mistake. Nobody to keep him out of trouble. And all the other planes up there might do something stupid—like try to make him crash. As his plane accelerated, he no longer could think of why he volunteered for this. Maybe he made a mistake. Maybe a big mistake! He could still quit. There was still enough time to bring the plane to a stop.

The plane passed the halfway point of the runway—Alex had reached rotation speed. It was now or never. He pulled back on the stick and lifted off. As soon as he started climbing, all he could think of was how great it felt!

Alex quickly climbed to the very top of the dome and settled into a large circular pattern around the competition ring. The view below him was spectacular. Planes from the

Opal, Lava, and Jade teams followed each other around in a line, all waiting for the competition to start.

Alex pulled out his Z-Con and connected to Ken. A small hologram of Ken sitting in his cockpit appeared on its top.

"Alex, remember!" Ken shouted over the roar of his propeller. "Stay out of the way. And don't say anything. The rest of us will be pretty busy for the next half hour. Got it?"

"Got it!" Alex shouted back.

A loud horn sounded below. The line of planes turned and followed each other to the first obstacle. An enormous scoreboard near the grandstands came to life and displayed the scores. Since every team had successfully launched four planes, they all had two hundred points to start.

The first obstacle was an enormous, long tube that twisted up, down, left, and right. A plane from the Opal team flew into it and after a few seconds came out the other end—upside down! It flipped over, right side up, and flew away. The crowd in the Opal section of the stands erupted into a loud cheer.

When Alex saw that first plane complete the tube maze, he realized that he was nowhere near ready to compete with the rest of these pilots.

The competition moved on, all the planes taking their turn flying through the different obstacles—each time alternating between the three teams. First, an Opal plane had its turn, then a Lava plane, and then one of the Jades. The line kept rotating through until each pilot had their chance. The whole group then moved on to the next obstacle.

Every time an obstacle was finished, the scoreboard showed the Jade team falling further and further behind. Lava went out to a big lead, with Opal in second place.

When half the obstacles were completed, all the planes made a sweeping turn toward a tall wall that popped up near the edge of the competition area. An Opal plane headed directly toward the center of it and at the very last second steeply turned away. The scoreboard showed how many feet the plane had missed the wall by and it awarded points to the Opal team based on how close it got. The first Lava plane performed the same maneuver, and a Jade plane followed. It was Opal's turn again.

Alex turned away for a second to check his heading and altitude. A huge gasp roared up from the crowd below. Alex snapped his gaze back down below him and watched the Opal plane sputtering—falling toward the ground in a wide descending spiral. He could see its tail section had taken a hit against the wall. Just before the plane was about to crash, its nose shot up and its wings leveled out. It hit the ground hard and fractured the left landing gear. But it rolled to a stop relatively intact and, after a few seconds, the pilot climbed out, giving the crowd a small wave. Everyone in the stands erupted into applause.

Now there was a chance for J-A-5! The competition continued with Alex keeping a close eye on the score, watching his teammates close the gap slowly on Opal. Ken kept in constant touch with each one of his teammates.

"Roxanne, the wind is bouncing around the left edge when I went through. Give it some extra right rudder when you hit that first turn."

"Boris, start your run with the nose trimmed all the way up. It'll help you recover from the last dive!"

He coached the team on, getting better scores on each obstacle.

Finally, there was only one obstacle remaining. From what Alex could tell, the planes had to fly through a large circular hoop sitting on a pole, about five hundred feet up. It looked simple enough, but as the first plane approached it, Alex figured out what the challenge was. The hoop was barely big enough for a plane to fit through—it seemed like it had only a couple of inches to spare on each side. One after one, each pilot approached the hoop, and one after one they all turned away at the last second, avoiding a crash. Since each plane only received one attempt, it didn't take long before only two planes remained—the team captains for Opal and Jade.

Opal went first. The white plane lined up on the hoop, but the gusting wind blew it to off the right. Several times the pilot corrected the plane's path, but the wind was too unpredictable. When the plane arrived at the hoop it was so far off, the pilot quit the run and veered off to the left—just like all the other pilots had. Now it remained up to the only remaining pilot—Ken.

Alex took a quick look at the scoreboard. Jade was only a hundred and sixty points behind Opal. Since Opal had lost a plane during the competition, and only had three planes that would be landing, Alex was going to earn Jade division an extra fifty points for landing safely. He was also going to get another hundred points for flying without any GEM equipment. That was going to leave J-A-5 a measly ten points behind Opal at the end. The top of the scoreboard said the last obstacle was worth fifty points.

Making it through the final obstacle and getting those fifty points was the only way Jade could beat Opal for second place. Ken would have to make it!

Alex watched Ken's plane line up on the hoop from a long way out. Ken immediately ran into the same problems as everyone else. He started correcting his path to the left, but each time it was not enough. But even with all the huge corrections to his flight path, he still had a chance to make it. He approached closer and closer, correcting his path over and over again. His run looked good—better than anyone else's. He was going for it!

At the last second his plane veered off. Ken had quit the run. The gusting wind had made it impossible for him.

Alex knew it was over. He pulled his power back and started a descent to the runway. He slowly spiraled down, but when he reached the same height as the last obstacle, he added power to stop his descent. He turned the plane hard to the left and pointed it right at the hoop. He just wanted to know what it looked like from the pilot's point of view—to gain the experience, not to in fact try going through it.

"Alex!" Ken yelled up to him through the Z-Con. "Get that plane back down here! Now!"

Alex was about to veer way and continue his descent when something struck him. If the problem on this obstacle was that the plane was too big for the hole, why not make the plane smaller? Then it would be easy! Anyone could make it through if there was plenty of room to work with. Without thinking much about it, Alex figured out a way to do just that. He could use his Z-Con to fold up the outer tip

281

of one of his wings! Then he would have another couple of feet to spare when he went through the hoop. After he finished, he could use his Z-Con to pull the wing tip back down into place.

A picture of the inside of the wing popped into his head. He had memorized it the other day when he and Samuel inspected the wings on all the planes. He could fold up the wing at one of its weakest spots—right near the inside part of the aileron.

There was no time to lose. Alex grabbed his Z-Con with his right hand and pointed it to the right-wing tip. He kept his left hand on the stick, keeping the plane heading directly at the hoop. He would wait until the very last second to fold the wing tip up.

Alex moved closer to the obstacle. A roar from the crowd bellowed up from the ground. Ken yelled even louder on the Z-Con, but Alex ignored him. He had only one thing to concentrate on now, and that was making it through the hoop!

He was almost on top of it when he pictured the wing tip folding up. He started a vibration in his mind. The right-wing tip slammed up and folded over, almost all the way to top of the remaining wing surface. Alex now had an extra two feet of clearance. He flew the plane right through the center of the hoop! He had made it!

The plane had less lift on the right side now, and it started to roll over to that side. Alex pictured the wing tip being pulled down into place. Once again, he made a mental picture in his head. But nothing happened! Alex concentrated harder but again, nothing. The plane started rolling even more. Alex closed his eyes and let go of every other thought he had and just concentrated on pulling the wing tip over with his Z-Con. Finally, the tip started slowly folding back into place. But after a few seconds, it stopped rotating. It was almost back in line with the rest of the wing but still a little above where it belonged. Alex moved his control stick to the left to correct for it. The plane started flying straight and level again. He was going to make it!

But something new suddenly dawned on him. He would have to use his right hand to keep his Z-Con constantly pointed at the right-wing tip to keep it from folding back up. That meant he would only be able to use his left hand to work all the flight controls to land the plane—and he had to land safely to get the extra points for it!

Alex needed to get the plane to descend. He let go of the stick with his left hand, reached all the way over to the right-hand side of the console, and pulled back slightly on the throttle. The plane started rolling hard over to the right the instant he had let go of the stick. Alex had just enough time to grab the stick again and level the plane back out. That was fine for up here in the air—there was nothing right below him to hit. But it sure could be a problem when he needed to cut the power over the runway to land.

At this point, there was nothing left to do but to try his best. Alex continued down and positioned his plane for a long approach to the runway. All the other planes had landed by now, and all the pilots stood alongside the runway, watching Alex approach.

Ken called up to Alex again, but Alex had to ignore him. He was concentrating too much on keeping his plane from falling out of the sky.

Alex lined up his plane with the runway's center. The wind at the surface was calm. That was going to make things easier. The ground loomed larger and larger as he descended. The plane reached the end of the runway, and as quickly as he could, Alex let go of the stick with his left hand and pulled the throttle all the way back, cutting the engine to idle. The plane rolled violently to the right. Alex reached back, grabbed the stick, and slammed it over hard to the left. The move quickly corrected the rolling and brought the wings back to level—the right-wing tip just barely missing the ground.

Alex pulled back on the stick, bringing the nose up—trying to keep the landing gear just above the runway as the plane lost airspeed. After a few seconds, the gear hit the ground hard and bounced the plane back up into the air. Alex had misjudged the flare. He let the plane settle back down to the runway and pulled back a little more on the stick. The wheels touched down hard again, but just soft enough to keep the plane on the ground. Alex lowered his Z-Con and used the brakes on the foot pedals to slow down.

He taxied over to the parking area and pulled up alongside the other three J-A-5 planes. When he brought the plane to a stop, it looked like the entire Jade Division had run up and surrounded him.

He turned the engine off and heard a roar coming at him from all sides.

"Way to go, Alex!" Samuel shouted as loud as he could over the crowd.

"I told you to come straight back down!" Ken yelled at him, although he was slapping Alex on the shoulder while he said it.

Dion stood a couple of feet away, laughing hysterically. "Are you stupid or just plain crazy!" he yelled.

Smiling broadly, Alex undid his seat belts and climbed out of the cockpit. Elka and Maia squeezed past the crowd, ran up, and high-fived him from both sides.

The crowd suddenly hushed and parted down the middle. Master Kattan and Master Ebo casually walked past everyone and made their way over to Ken.

"We have a protest from the other two teams," Master Kattan stated. "They claim that Alex violated the rules. He modified his plane during the competition."

Alex stepped forward. The two masters turned to him.

"The rules say that the mechanic can use his Z-Con to fix a plane," Alex said calmly.

"But you were a pilot, not a mechanic," Master Ebo said.

"Actually, the rules don't say that the mechanic can't also be a pilot," Alex replied. "It only states that one member of the team can be the mechanic and only they are allowed to use their Z-Cons to fix a plane. I was the only member of the team to use my Z-Con to fix a plane, so I was the mechanic today."

"But you didn't fix your plane, you broke it," Master Kattan said.

Alex shook his head back and forth. "The rules don't say what it means to fix a plane. My plane didn't have the flight characteristics I wanted, so I fixed it by folding the wing tip up. When that wasn't what I needed any more, I fixed it again and folded it back down."

Master Kattan and Master Ebo gave Alex a skeptical look. When Alex didn't offer them any other explanation, the two masters moved away several feet to discuss the events quietly among themselves. The Jade students surrounding Alex buzzed with excitement. After a long few minutes, the two masters headed back from their deliberations. Everyone fell silent. Master Kattan stared at Ken for a few seconds and then announced the verdict.

"We'll allow it."

The entire crowd roared.

SIXTEEN

Sunday morning was finally here. Alex sat alone in the common room, staring out its huge window, con-, templating the view of the facility. He thought it might calm his mind, making the excruciating wait go faster.

In about an hour, Alex would, at last, be speaking to his parents for ten minutes. He could then ask them about Jawbone Fan, and about the mysteries surrounding all the Mayan hieroglyphs. From the moment he woke up, the anticipation of that conversation had made him edgy. The serene view before him did seem to calm his nervousness a little—but not enough.

He jumped out of his chair and paced from one side of the room to the other. Mercure sat in the corner watching, not saying a word. Alex completed several circuits of pacing before stopping in front of him.

"How can you be so calm?" Alex blasted out.

"Who says I'm calm?" Mercure responded coolly. *"Why don't we head down? Let's get on to the line at the Com Room. You want to be in the first group, don't you?"*

"A line? What makes you think they'll be a line?"

"I told you, I've done this before," Mercure said, trotting to the door.

"A line? I didn't even think of that," Alex muttered to himself, following Mercure out.

Sure enough, when they reached the Com Room, they needed to join the back of a short line that had already formed. Alex grabbed his Z-Con from his pants pocket.

"I better pop Elka and Maia and get'em over here."

As soon as he started sending the pop, Elka, Maia, and Dion strolled up behind him.

"We were outside eating," Elka said.

"We thought you could use the sleep Alex, so we left the room and told Feng not to bother you," Dion added.

"Yeah, he told me when I got up," Alex said. He turned to Elka. "You got it all straight? All the questions we discussed?"

"Don't worry," Elka assured him. "Between Maia and me, we won't forget anything."

"I just hope they'll give us some answers," Maia added.

Mercure left, telling Alex he was going outside for awhile. After what seemed like forever, the door to the Com Room swung open. A student at the entrance began letting in enough students to fill the available cubicles. Alex, Elka, Maia, and Dion ran in and sat down next to each other along the near wall. Alex took out his Z-Con and immediately started trying to connect with his father. But nothing happened. He tried picturing the connection in different ways, hoping the problem was just with him being nervous. But no matter how calm he became, no matter how focused he was on the connection, nothing happened.

288

Alex wouldn't give up. He couldn't give up! For several minutes he tried continuously to make the connection. Now he was almost out of time.

Alex ran to the room Qen standing in the corner.

"I can't connect!" he yelled at the Qen as he approached him. "Something's wrong with the security protocols!"

"There is nothing wrong here," the Qen replied coolly. "Other students are connecting without difficulty. The other Z-Con must not be responding to your connection request. Please try again. Remain as calm and still as you can while attempting your connection."

Exasperated, Alex ran back to his cubicle and tried again. After another few minutes, a soft bell rang from overhead, and an announcement blared out: 'Everyone head out! Next group is coming in!' But Alex didn't move. He couldn't.

Elka and Maia came over to him. Elka had her Z-Con hanging down from her hand, barely lifting her feet as she walked. Maia was almost crying.

"We couldn't connect," Elka said, bewildered.

Dion strolled up behind the girls, smiling.

"Did you get through to your parents?" Alex asked him.

"Sure. Why—did you have problems?"

Alex immediately switched from being completely frustrated, to extraordinarily mad. He pounded his fist on the cubicle table, making a loud bang that filled the room.

"Let's go!" he stated to everyone.

The four of them left the pyramid and found a table in the far corner of the terrace. There were no other students around.

289

The second Alex sat down he said, "I'm not waiting another week to see what happens. My dad told me he'd never miss this call, no matter what. Something's wrong. I know it! We've got to find out what's going on, and we're going to have to do it ourselves!"

"Alex, calm down a bit," Elka said nervously. "I agree, but what can we do? I mean we're stuck here, and the answers are all out there."

"We're not stuck here," Alex said. "We can take a portal jump anytime we want."

"To where?" Elka asked.

"Back to the Mayan Temple. Back to Jawbone Fan."

Maia looked over to Elka and back to Alex.

"Right," she said sarcastically.

Alex leaned in toward the center of the table and lowered his voice.

"Think of it. They banished Jawbone for some reason, and whatever that reason was, our parents were interested in it. We can find out from him what's going on, come back, and tell everyone."

"You mean, tell Z and Herabata," Dion interjected.

"No, I mean everyone. Z and Herabata sent our parents out there on a dangerous mission, and it doesn't look like they're helping them very much. If we tell everyone here what's going on, it'll force Z to take some action. Do something...anything!"

Elka and Maia put their heads down and remained very still. Alex wondered what they were doing. Then it dawned on him—they were popping messages back and forth, discussing it. After a couple of minutes, they raised back up.

"Okay, but two things," Maia said. "First, the three of us go together. Whatever trouble we run into, it might take all three of our Z-Cons to get us out of it." Alex nodded his agreement. Maia continued, "Okay, and second… Dion and the dogs stay back here, standing by. If we don't come back right away, they can tell Z and Herabata what's going on and where we went."

"Perfect," Alex replied to them.

"Wait a minute," Dion said. "I'm not staying behind. I'm coming!"

Alex shook his head. "We need you here buddy. Somebody's got to have our back. Anyway, the three of us…we have to go—it's our parents. And who knows what Z and the others are going to do to us when they find out that we left. Whatever it is, it doesn't have to happen to you too." Before Dion could argue about it, Alex turned back to Elka and Maia. "We'll go tonight. It'll have to be late. Real late. Like three o'clock in the morning."

"Why?" Elka asked.

"Because we'll have to bust out of that second pyramid to get over to Jawbone Fan and animate him. We can't have anyone walking around the grounds out there seeing us do it. They'll call the cops or something. And another thing— don't tell the dogs what we're doing. If they find out, they might feel like they have to turn us in."

Everyone agreed, and they spent the next hour planning exactly what to do and then went to sleep.

At three o'clock in the morning, Alex and Dion slid out of their beds and quietly got dressed.

In single file, the two of them slipped out of their room, through the common room, past the dogs, and out the door.

They jumped down into the barely lit interior of the Jade Pyramid. Elka and Maia stood a few feet off to the side, waiting. When they caught Alex's and Dion's attention, they signaled for them to follow along behind as they moved outside.

The Dome was serene. Alex could hear the water moving in the stream flowing around the dome's perimeter in the far-off distance. Alex carried a small green bag with him containing his GEM equipment, a notebook, and a pen. Hanging down over his shoulder were two long coiled up pieces of ropes, each with a metal hook attached to its end. Alex had sneaked them out of the maintenance facility that afternoon. Elka and Maia also carried small bags in their hands. Everyone walked quickly, but quietly to the core, descending the set of stairs that led to the main portal room—the one that linked The Dome to the Mayan temple.

A Qen stood guard at the doorway to the portal system. Elka and Maia handed their bags to Alex to hold while they both raised up their Z-Cons and pointed them at the Qen. A few seconds later the Qen's head dropped down toward his chest. He looked like he was sleeping.

"How'd you do that?" Alex asked.

"We told you we could," Elka replied.

Maia took their bags back from Alex and handed Elka's over to her. She turned to Alex.

"Remember the day we had Koleck help us reprogram Feng back to normal?" Maia asked. Alex nodded. Well, we saw the password he used to access Feng's basic systems. We just used that same access to turn off this Qen's monitoring systems. We'll turn them back on when we get back. He'll never realize anything ever happened."

Alex slung his bag's strap over his right shoulder, walked through the doorway, and stepped over to the central portal. On the way into to The Dome, at each stop, they had to jump through the center portal. He figured that was the one that would take them back one stop to the Kukulcan Pyramid in Mexico.

Alex turned to look at Dion, and Dion gave him a nod.

"I got it covered, Alex," Dion said. "If you don't return in an hour, I'll let everyone know. We'll come get you."

Elka and Maia moved over to Alex.

"Ready?" Alex asked.

Both girls nodded. Maia turned to face Dion.

"See ya," she said.

"For sure... see ya," Dion responded, nervously.

Alex took a step forward and jumped into the portal. The light show only lasted a few seconds. He popped out and landed inside the Kukulcan Pyramid—exactly where he had hoped they would end up. The room was lit from the four corners and had the same color patterns on the walls as before.

Alex moved to the side and waited for Elka and Maia. They arrived seconds later, one right after the other. Alex moved to the hole on the other side of the room.

"Now we have to jump down and take the tunnel over to the El Osario pyramid. I hope they dug out that tunnel collapse." Before he jumped down Alex uncoiled one of the ropes he had brought and set its hook into the ground. He threw the other end of the rope down the hole. "We can use that to help us get back up here when we want to head back to The Dome."

Alex jumped into the darkness. He raised his Z-Con and thought about needing to see. A bright light instantly beamed out the top of his Z-Con, lighting up the tunnel walls, showing that they had been repaired. He shouted up to Elka and Maia that it was good to go. The two of them jumped down, and everyone ran ahead toward the El Osario Pyramid. When Alex reached the end of the tunnel, he looked up to inspect the hole they would have to ascend to get to the interior of the pyramid. He uncoiled the rope he brought with him.

"I'm going to try to pull myself up with my Z-Con. When I get up there, I'll set this rope, and you two can climb it. I'll help pull you up with my Z-Con. Okay?"

Elka and Maia nodded. Alex pointed his Z-Con over his head, and it began pulsating red. He felt it pulling on the ceiling, and he immediately floated up from the floor. He slowly penetrated the hole and quickly disappeared. After a few moments, he reached the top, tilted his Z-Con to the right and let it pull him to the side, away from the hole. He lowered his Z-Con, and he dropped to the floor.

Alex set the hook of the rope into the ground next to the hole and shouted down the Elka and Maia to start climbing. With assistance from Alex's Z-Con, in less than five minutes they were all inside the pyramid.

"Okay then," Alex said. He moved to the wall where the masters had made the breached the last time. "Let's line up here and face the wall. We'll put on our hoods and gloves just in case. Then take out your Z-Cons and when I say 'go' just think about wanting an exit. Don't think of a hole. Just think of an exit, and of wanting to get to the outside. The Z-Con will do the rest. Got it?"

"Got it," Elka and Maia answered together. Everyone put on all their gear, with Elka and Maia putting their goggles on too, just in case.

The three of them lifted their Z-Cons and Alex took a deep breath. He closed his eyes.

"Go!" he said.

A huge rumbling sound immediately started. It grew louder and louder. All the Z-Cons glowed bright red. An instant later, a large hole opened in the wall, and a huge square section of stones flew outwards into the space just outside the pyramid.

Everyone lowered their Z-Cons when the outside became visible through the tunnel.

"It worked!" Maia screamed. She grabbed Elka around the waist, and they both jumped up and down. Elka said to her, "I gotta tell you—I didn't think we could do it."

Alex ran through the opening. "Okay, let's get going."

They reached the outside of the temple and ran past the stack of neatly piled stones. In the distance, on the other side of the pile, was the Mayan building that they had to get to—Akab Dzib, the home of the banished Jawbone Fan. Alex led the way to it. They reached the building, ran past the back of it, around to the front, and into the large indentation that they had huddled in previously.

Alex raised his Z-Con to use as a flashlight again. He moved all around the entranceway, searching. Elka and Maia followed closely behind. Alex came upon the section of the wall that showed Jawbone Fan sitting on a seat with his legs crossed, surrounded by glyphs.

Alex turned around and said, "I'm going to see if I can animate him. I don't know what's going to happen, but if it

295

starts going bad, you two get yourselves back to Dion and bring help, okay?"

Elka and Maia nodded. They both kept on all their GEM equipment.

"Here we go," Alex said while he took off his gloves.

He concentrated on wanting to speak to Jawbone Fan, and about how good he would feel when he received some answers to his questions. The top of his Z-Con glowed a dark blue. Alex raised the Z-Con higher until it practically touched the stone. He focused even harder.

Nothing happened. The stone didn't flicker a bit. Not a single thing changed.

Another idea occurred to Alex. He kept the same thoughts about Jawbone in his head, but this time he reached up to the image and touched his Z-Con to the right side of it. He placed his left palm on the left side of the stone and pushed both his hands apart like he saw Vizier Herabata do on the surface of the 3-D globe the previous day in her office.

The stone tablet expanded out of the wall and grew to fit Alex's outstretched hands. The image of Jawbone did not move, but it twinkled slightly. Alex stepped back and threw his hands even wider apart. The stone expanded again. This time Jawbone's face turned slightly away from the stone and faced Alex.

Alex concentrated as hard as he could on the image of Jawbone, wanting to speak to him and get some answers. One more time he stepped back and threw his arms open as wide as he could.

The stone table expanded to match Alex's outstretched arms, and the image of Jawbone Fan grew to life-size.

Jawbone stood up from his stone seat, and the image's features slowly turned lifelike. Jawbone now looked like a real man wearing a tall hat with feathers coming out of it, but he was still attached to the stone by a shroud of thick gray vapor behind him.

Elka and Maia had by this time moved all the way to the far wall. Alex took a single step back, keeping his Z-Con pointed directly at Jawbone.

"I'm Alex…"

"I know who you are!" boomed Jawbone. "I know everything that is in the Zero Point Field. All about you and your frightened little friends back there."

Jawbone stepped closer to Alex, contemplating him. After a few seconds, he dashed around the side of Alex, but he halted in mid-step. The gray vapor slowly pulled him back to the wall, and after a few seconds he ended up right back in front of Alex again. His face smirked as if to say 'Oh well.' He remained still, contemplating Alex some more.

"You're frightened too, aren't you, young Alex?"

Alex didn't respond. He tried to keep his face from showing it, but frightened was hardly the word that would describe his feelings.

"That's why Z had me banished. He was just like you. A frightened little man. He's afraid of real power—and when men are afraid, they punish."

"Real power?" Alex said. "Z has real power. He has a Z-Con Prime."

"Yes, he does, doesn't he? But he won't use it! No, not like I did. And it's so easy to use. If you have a mind to."

Jawbone turned and faced the stone wall behind him. He ran his hands through the thick vapor, probing it.

"I was a god here," he said back over his shoulder to Alex.

"Everyone around here worshiped me like one anyway. Their Oracle. That's what they called me. I knew everything about everything. Do you understand that little boy? Everything! And that's real power. If you know how to use it."

He turned back to Alex.

"Let's see what else we can learn about the talented Alex Vega…let's see…your parents! Yes!"

"Where are they?" Alex demanded.

"Well not here, if that's what you were hoping for," Jawbone said dismissively.

"Have you seen them?"

"Oh, I've been very busy for the last few weeks. That is to say, busy for someone who's been banished for thousands of years."

He looked around past Alex, toward Elka and Maia.

"Do they speak?" Jawbone asked. When no one responded, he laughed. "As I said, frightened little people."

Alex raised his Z-Con at Jawbone's face.

"I asked you, have you seen my parents!" Alex yelled at him.

"Very good, Alex! You have the power here, so use it! Use it anytime you can!" Jawbone laughed. "Anytime you can, young Alex!" He turned to the vapor, studying it some more.

"Yes, I've been very busy. I've seen many people. First Erebus came to me, then your parents, and now you."

"Who's Erebus?"

"A man who understands real power. Oh, I know, he's a fraud, but he understands power. Even his name—a fraud! Erebus. He thinks that I don't know him? His real name? His real weakness? I tell you that I know everything, and so I know him. He's a fool."

"Is he working with my parents? Does he know where they are?"

Jawbone turned back to Alex again.

"I suppose by now he knows exactly where they are. After all, your parents were chasing after him. They probably caught up to him too. Now that would be funny to see! Your parents up against the power of Erebus!"

"What did you tell them?"

Small pieces of Jawbone's face started turning back to stone.

"You're not concentrating hard enough Alex!" Jawbone yelled. He wiped his hand across his cheeks, feeling the small bumps of rock. "No, it doesn't seem like you have the skill to free me. No, not you. Pity. It would have been so much easier."

"What did you tell my parents?"

"I told them what I'll tell you now. Erebus went to the old portal site. The one they shut down all those years ago."

"Can we get there? What portal?"

"The portal they took the plaque away from, back there in the temple you just mangled."

"Will that one bring us to our parents?"

"It'll take you to where your parents went to find Erebus. After that, who knows? But I'd be careful if I were you,

Alex Vega. Erebus manipulated your parents, and now he's manipulating you."

"How could he be manipulating me?" Alex asked. "I've never even met him."

"Who do you think caused that collapse down in the tunnel last week? Very convenient, wasn't it? It forced you out of those pyramids, and over to discover me in this wall. And he made you lose a little faith in Z's ability to protect you and your parents, didn't he? I'm just giving you a warning, Alex—if you follow after your parents, you better take care."

The gray vapor started retreating into the stone, pulling Jawbone along with it. He reached out his arms toward Alex, but by now Jawbone was too far away to touch him.

"If you ever get Erebus, if you ever kill him, come back here. I'll tell you about other things. Other things you'll need to know. Don't forget me now—young Alex. Don't forget ..."

Jawbone snapped back into the stone and onto his seat. The stone shrunk further and further away from Alex until it was back in its place on the wall.

Alex touched his Z-Con to the stone, placed his left palm on the side of it and pushed both his hands apart again. Nothing happened. He tried several more times to animate Jawbone, but it was useless.

He took a few steps back away from the wall and turned to Elka and Maia,

"We've got to take that portal jump."

"Are you sure?" Elka asked. She turned to Maia and back to Alex. "I mean, our parents might not be there anymore."

"Okay, and if that's true we'll just come back," Alex replied. "But they might be there. We might be their only hope. We've got to find out if they need help."

Maia stepped toward Alex and said, "Let's go." She turned to Elka. "I've got to know what's happened to them."

Elka grabbed Maia's arm. After a few seconds, she relented, "All right, let's go."

They ran back to the interior of the Mayan pyramid and lined up facing the breach in the wall. Pointing all their Z-Cons at the wall, they were able to repair it.

Alex took out his notebook and ripped out a piece of paper and wrote, 'We're taking the unmarked portal to see if we can find our parents.' He placed the note on the landing pad and headed over to Elka and Maia. They were already at the portal, looking down into it.

"Ready?" Alex asked. "This is my idea, so I'll go first. Give me a little bit of time before you follow. If it looks bad, I'll jump back."

Elka and Maia stepped to the side. Alex slung his bag over his shoulder, crossed his arms in front of him, and jumped.

The light show went on for a bit. It was over two minutes before Alex popped out the other side. He found himself in a dark cave, standing on a mildew covered landing pad. Directly in front of him, about twenty feet away, was the cave's small entrance. The entire area around him looked gloomy and dirty. It smelled moldy, and only a tiny bit of light managed to penetrate from the outside, barely allowing Alex to see the walls.

He moved slowly ahead, gently using his foot to feel the ground in front of him before taking each step. He reached the cave's entrance, placed his body up against the side of it, and slowly poked his head out.

Alex peered out into a beautiful, sunny day. Green colored mountains surround the area. Directly in front of him, a well-used dirt trail led steeply down a mountainside to a valley far below. In the middle of the valley sat a small village. Alex took a few steps out away from the entrance and turned around. The cave, hidden in the face of a nearly vertical cliff, extended almost straight up, hundreds of feet over his head.

Alex's head snapped down and over to the cave's entrance when voices emanated from its interior. A few seconds later Elka and Maia slowly emerged, stepping to Alex's side, and gazing around.

"Looks peaceful enough, doesn't it…" Elka stated.

"Let's go down to that village and see what they've got to say," Alex said. He immediately headed for the dirt trail—almost jogging to it.

"Okay, but let's go slow," Maia shouted ahead to Alex, joining in behind him. Alex did slow down, but only a little.

They reached a little more than a couple of hundred feet down the trail when they came upon a tall wooden plank along its right side. The plank was planted in the ground and stood straight up. Beautifully carved Jade statues surrounded the entire bottom of the plank, and fresh vegetables sat in piles along both sides of it. Chinese characters formed several sentences near its top, and in the middle of it was a large painting of what looked like to Alex to be a Z-Con. The center of the painting contained a rectangular piece of real Jade buried into the wood. Intricate white and red painted lines intertwined around each other and darted out from all sides of the Z-Con. They looked like beautifully painted clouds of light smoke. It was obviously a shrine of sorts.

"How could these people know about Z-Cons?" Elka asked, examining the picture.

"I don't know. Let's get going," Alex said. He headed down the trail, but much slower this time. At one point the trail dropped down extremely steep, about twenty feet. To get past it, everyone had to turn around and climbed down on their hands and knees. There were already footholds dug into some parts of the hillside from the many times it had been climbed and descended by other people. They reached the bottom and dusted themselves off.

After several more minutes of hiking, they all approached the first outlying house, still a couple of miles away from the village.

A boy sat on its porch with his feet folded in front of him and his hands resting on his knees—looking like he was meditating. He didn't move at all as Alex, Elka, and Maia approached and surrounded him. Maia reached down and touched him on the arm.

The boy sprang up as if startled out of a dream. He turned to the right, and then to the left, studying each one of them. His look of shock turned into joy.

"You've come! He told me you would soon come!" The boy grabbed each one of them on the shoulders saying, "You came for your parents, correct?"

"Who?" Alex shouted at him. "Who said we would come?"

"I welcome you. Please call me Zhang. I'm here to take you to the others.'

"What are you talking about?" Alex demanded. "Are our parents here?"

"Four others came here before, so maybe."

"Where are we?" Alex demanded.

"Hotan Prefecture," Zhang answered, with a look of puzzlement.

Alex shook his head slightly and said, "Where?"

"China. The Xinjiang Region," Zhang said. "Many years ago, your people acquired their Jade from here. All the good Jade is gone now. They don't come back for the Jade anymore." He pointed at the village below them. "Come, I'll take you to the others." He hurried away, toward the side of the house.

Everyone followed behind him, giving quizzical looks to each other. Zhang ran up to a mound covered by a red tarp. He grabbed the tarp near its bottom edge and threw it off to the side, revealing two motorcycles. Elka and Maia kneeled alongside the last one in line, studying it. Zhang grabbed the handlebars of the one nearest to him, turned it around, and pushed it toward the front of the house. Alex followed along with him while Elka and Maia remained behind looking over the other bike.

Alex noticed Zhang continuously looking at the Z-Con hanging from his belt. It made him feel very uneasy.

"How do you know about Z-Cons?" Alex asked.

"The people here worship it. Not those Z-Cons. The other one. The one that is alive."

Alex realized he was speaking about a Z-Con Prime. The one that looked like the Z-Con pictured in the shrine, further up the trail.

"Is that Z-Con here?"

"No," Zhang said. "It was stolen. Many years ago. It angered the people greatly. They think that someday it will be returned. The one who returns it to the people will earn the warrior's sword. He will be a hero forever."

Alex stopped when he heard Zhang say that. Zhang turned back to face Alex.

"Oh, do not be concerned," Zhang said. "You will all get a very warm welcome when the people see that you know about Z-Cons. They will be very happy to talk to you. I will see to it. I will talk to them about you."

Elka came around the side of the house, pushing the other motorcycle.

Zhang looked at Elka and asked, "Are you okay to ride it?"

"You bet!" she responded.

Elka climbed on the motorcycle, turned the key, pulled out the choke, and jumped down hard on the kick starter. It roared to life. Maia jumped on behind her.

Zhang started his motorcycle and Alex climbed onto the back of it.

"It is not far," Zhang said to everyone over the engine's rumble. "Slowly! The trail is not good in many places."

Zhang rode off, closely followed by Elka. They navigated the winding, bumpy trail, constantly veering around the washed-out areas. After only a few minutes, they approached the outskirts of the village. Around the last turn, a huge crowd filled the roadway, spilling over to the left and right sides of it. There was well over a hundred people, mostly sitting on motorcycles—waiting. Zhang stopped about fifty feet in front of the crowd and shut off the engine.

He climbed off the bike and headed away, turning back to Alex as he walked.

"I will speak to them," he said. "Wait here. All is well. Do not worry."

Elka shut off her motorcycle and stepped off, immediately followed by Maia. Alex climbed off the back of Zhang's bike and moved over to them.

"They all look pretty angry," Elka said. "Are we sure we should be here."

"Zhang said he would get us a warm reception," Alex said still feeling a bit uneasy.

Zhang reached the crowd and spoke for a few seconds. The entire crowd roared. The roar grew louder and louder, developing into a rhythmic chant. After a few seconds, Zhang stepped forward from the crowd holding a large golden sword out in front of him. He turned back to the crowd, raised the sword to the sky, and swiftly turned back around toward Alex. He raised his other arm into the air, and the shouting stopped. He gave out a cry, and the entire crowd immediately started their motorcycles. All of them launched ahead.

Alex, Elka, and Maia instinctively took a step back. The crowd would be on top of them in seconds—and there was nothing they could do about it.

Then, instantly, a translucent membrane slammed down from the sky, directly in the path of the oncoming horde. The front line of motorcycles crashed into it and bounced off, throwing their drivers into the air.

Elka yelled at Alex, "Did you do that?"

"No!" Alex shouted back. He turned to look at Maia.

"It wasn't me!" she said.

"They want our Z-Cons!" Alex shouted.

Elka ran to her motorcycle, climbed on, and jumped down on the starter. The engine started up. Maia dashed to the motorcycle by Alex's side.

"Get on!" she yelled.

Maia kicked the motorcycle engine to life, and Alex jumped on behind her. She twisted the throttle open, spun the bike around, and followed Elka up the trail away from the crowd. The two bikes gained speed, severely bouncing over the ruts and washouts in the roadway.

"Hang on—it's going to get worse!" Maia yelled back to Alex, twisting the throttle open more.

Alex turned around and saw five motorcycles giving chase about a hundred feet back. Another pack of motorcycles followed a few hundred feet behind them.

The two bikes rocketed past Zhang's house with the chasing group of motorcycles gaining slightly on them.

"We got that hill coming up on the trail!" Maia yelled.

"Can we make it?" Alex asked.

"With one person on a bike, sure! With two on it—I don't know!"

In less than a minute they approached the hill. From Alex's viewpoint, it looked like a vertical wall, twenty feet high. The only way to the top was to go straight up.

"Lean forward as much as you can!" Maia shouted.

Maia turned the throttle wide open, and the motorcycle zoomed off, gaining speed as they got close to the base of the hill. She quickly shifted her weight from side to side trying to keep the bike upright as they bounced harder and harder off the ruts.

In seconds they reached the wall, and the motorcycle started the near vertical climb. As the bike slowed, Maia jumped up and down on her seat. Each time her weight slammed down on the bike, the wheels dug in harder, shooting the bike further ahead. In less than four seconds they cleared the hilltop and launched five feet in the air. When they hit the ground, Maia fell off to the side, with Alex slamming down right alongside her. The bike veered off to the right, bouncing twice before toppling over, its engine dying. A second later Elka shot over the top and landed her bike smoothly, sliding to a stop.

Alex got to his feet and helped Maia up.

"You okay?" he asked.

"Thank God for GEM suits," Maia said, laughing.

Maia ran over to her motorcycle, stood it up, and tried to start it. The engine kept turning over but wouldn't catch. Elka slowly putted over to them from the edge of the hilltop.

"A few of their bikes fell over when they tried getting up here," Elka said. "They're climbing by hand now. It's not going to be very long."

"Should we run?" Maia asked her.

"No, jump on!" Elka said.

Maia climbed on behind Elka, and Alex squeezed in behind Maia. Elka started away, working hard to keep the bike upright as the wheels dug deeply into the loose dirt.

In a few minutes, they reached the cave entrance. Alex jumped off and looked behind. Several men were running up the trail in a full sprint, chasing after them. They would be at the cave in less than a minute.

Alex turned around and said, "Let's go. We'll jump back to the Mayan Temple and figure it all out later."

Everyone headed into the cave. Alex lit the interior with his Z-Con. They reached the portal and Elka jumped through immediately. A few seconds later Maia followed her. Alex looked back at the cave entrance before leaving. The men had just arrived—all of them remained outside the cave entrance, watching. Alex took aim at the portal hole, tucked his Z-Con up near his chest and jumped.

It was another long light show, but Alex finally popped out the other end.

He landed on a slightly raised, icy platform right alongside Elka and Maia—they were both hugging each other against an intense freezing wind. Cold air bit into Alex's face and ice crystals instantly formed in his nose as he breathed in. Brightly lit snow covered the entire landscape around the landing platform. About two hundred feet to the right, a small jet sat by itself on an ice-covered runway.

Elka raised her head away from Maia and yelled over the howling wind to Alex. "Where are we? Where's the Mayan Temple?"

"I don't know!" Alex shouted back. He turned around and found himself facing an enormous building—its large metal door directly in front of him. Alex ran up and tried to open it, but the knob wouldn't turn. He banged his fist against the door three times, hard. He fell to the floor, curling himself into a ball from the freezing air, not under-standing why the GEM suit wasn't keeping him warm. He reached up and started banging again, even harder this time.

A few seconds later the door cracked open.

SEVENTEEN

The gray, frozen door slowly swung open, and Alex yelled back to Elka and Maia, "Over here!"

Elka and Maia released their grip on each other and ran through the entrance, quickly followed by Alex. They all stopped a few feet inside the door and huddled together. A Qen slammed the door shut behind them. He slid over to the back of Alex and yanked him away from Elka and Maia, flinging him to the side.

Alex spun away and thought about trying to use his Z-Con to disable the Qen. But in his confusion, he needed to find out more about what was going on, so, for the time being, he decided to wait and see.

The Qen folded his arms across his chest.

"Erebus is expecting all of you in the King's Hall," the Qen said. "Move down that hallway. Quickly." When nobody moved, the Qen glided in front of them and said, "You will all move along, or I will place you back outside until you are ready to follow my instructions."

Alex reluctantly moved ahead. Elka and Maia kept a firm hold on each other and slowly fell in line behind Alex. The Qen glided along, just to their rear, as if herding them.

About fifty feet down the long, bright corridor, they came to a stop in front of a set of tall doors. To the left and right of them, other smaller hallways headed away to the rest of the building.

The Qen waved his hands, and the twin doors swung inwards. Alex, still in the lead, stared into a massive, tall room with brilliant white walls and floors. Rows of black stone seats lined both sides of a wide aisle that led down its center. The Qen moved ahead of Alex, and everyone cautiously followed him down the aisle. They stopped in front of a huge throne sitting on top of a wide pedestal, three feet off the floor. The marble throne was pure white, matching all the surrounding walls and floors.

A man dressed in a bright orange robe strolled out from the right side of the room. The robe he wore was impressive—having long gold trim hanging down from all its edges. The man himself was short and overweight, with thinning brown hair and dull gray eyes.

Halfway out into the hall, the man broke into a dance and twirled around several times as he moved on. Alex heard him humming a song to himself. The man reached the base of the pedestal and tap-danced his way up it, toward the throne. He reached the top, twirled around, and plopped down into the wide stone seat. He pulled a Z-Con Prime out of his pocket. Red vapors emanated from all sides of the green and white stone.

"Now, now… Don't try anything foolish," the man said to everyone below him. He pointed toward the Qen.

"That's my Qen, Diakonos. He's rather special. My own design of course." The man flicked his finger at him.

Diakonos grabbed Elka, spun her around and pulled the Z-Con off her belt. He instantly moved to Maia and did the same thing, next jumping over to Alex. Alex reached into his pocket, pulled out his Z-Con, but before he could raise it up, Diakonos disappeared and materialized again directly behind him. He reached around Alex and snatched the Z-Con out of his hand.

Diakonos glided up the pedestal and deposited all three Z-Cons at the man's feet.

The man opened his arms wide, and his magnificent robe draped down from them. "I am Erebus. I can't tell you how enormously happy you've all made me! So, welcome. Welcome, all of you!"

"Where are we?" Alex demanded.

"You are at my facility in Antarctica," Erebus said. "I found this beautiful spot right here on the coastline about ten years ago. Oh, but don't worry, Alex. No one will disturb us…I've made it quite hidden."

"Where are our parents?" Alex shouted at him.

"Of course! The question of the ages! You've been asking everybody that exact thing, haven't you, Alex? Well, I thought you might be asking me about that, so let me show you." He nodded at Diakonos, and the Qen moved toward a large white curtain on the far side of the throne. From behind it, he pushed out a cart holding four very straight and stiff bodies with a shimmering membrane around them piled on top of each other—two of the bodies were Elka and Maia's parents. The other two were Alex's.

As soon as Alex saw his mother's and father's face he couldn't believe it to be true—it just couldn't be. Alex ran for the cart. Diakonos jumped in front of him, blocking his way. When Alex tried to dash around him, Diakonos seized him by his arms, holding him like a vice.

Elka and Maia raced forward, toward the cart. Erebus pointed his Z-Con Prime in their direction, and a purplish film encircled the two, stopping them instantly. Elka pressed hard against the membrane with her hand, but she couldn't break through.

Erebus bent forward and laughed, shaking his head wildly as he did.

"Oh, you should see your faces!" he said. "Not to worry, not to worry, your parents aren't dead. No, no, far from it." He casually pointed toward the cart with his Z-Con. "No, your parents are just in a time bubble."

He sat back up in his chair. "You see Z-Con Primes control space and time. Those two fools, Z and Herabata, never spent much effort trying to figure out the time component of the Zero Point Field." Erebus stood up, dropped his arms, and tapped his Z-Con into his chest. "But I've spent all my efforts figuring out the time component. And I've succeeded. Your parents over there are spending all their existence in one instant of time. Never going forward or going backward for that matter. They're completely unaware of what's going on around them. And they'll stay that way forever if I desire it."

Erebus flicked his finger at Diakonos, and the Qen pushed Alex all the way over to him. Erebus flicked his finger again, and the Qen disappeared. He leaned forward and whispered down to Alex.

"Would you like to restore your parent's lives, Alex?" Erebus asked.

Of course, he would, Alex thought. But what did he have that someone with a Z-Con Prime could possibly need? Alex was sure he wouldn't like the answer.

"How?" Alex responded.

Erebus outstretched his hands and shouted, "Join me!"

"Doing what?" Alex asked.

"Why, taking over of course!"

"Taking over what?"

"Everything!" Erebus jumped down from the throne and onto to the ground in front of Alex. "Take your place amongst my followers, and I'll let your parents go."

Alex took a quick look around at the empty hall. "You don't seem to have any followers at the moment."

"No," Erebus said. "And up to now, I didn't want any." He grabbed Alex by his shoulders. "But you'll be the first of my followers! You see, thanks to you I can now destroy Z and Herabata. And after I do that...who in their right mind wouldn't follow me? When I have Z and Herabata's Z-Con Primes, no one can stop me from doing whatever I want. People from all over the world will come, flocking around to please me. And wherever I go, I'll rule."

Erebus let go of Alex and stepped even closer to him.

"People were made to be ruled, Alex. All this strife in the world. It's got to stop. Everyone will be happier once I'm in charge." Erebus stepped to the side and walked past Alex, toward Elka and Maia. "And with my Z-Con Prime, I'll live forever. Think of it! I can make it so that you live forever too—if you join me now." He stopped in front of the two girls. "Elka and Maia, I haven't forgotten you. The both of you are also welcome."

"Why us?" Elka asked through the purplish haze. When Erebus didn't respond immediately, both she and Maia leaned a little further back.

"Just consider it a reward and be happy about it," Erebus coolly replied. He went back to his throne, picked up the three Z-Cons from the base of it, and began inspecting them.

"Alex, you'll soon give me the prize I need to destroy Z and Herabata. You see, for years I've known where Z has been hiding out. In that huge hole in the Himalayan mountains. That was easy to find. So many people coming in and out of it all the time. No, it was finding Herabata—finding the training facility. That's what I needed from you."

"I don't know where it is," Alex said defiantly. "And I wouldn't tell you if I did."

"Oh, you certainly will tell me, Alex," Erebus said. "Don't worry about that. It took too much time planning this whole thing for me to let you screw it up now. Here, let me show you what I've done."

Erebus threw the three Z-Cons back to the floor and pointed to Elka and Maia.

"You two stay here," Erebus said. "Alex, you come with me."

Alex instantly found himself in front of his house in his old neighborhood, standing right next to Erebus. He realized that Erebus was using the Zero Point Field to inject the scene into his head—just like giving him a training class.

"It was a brilliant plan, Alex," Erebus said. "You see, what I needed to do was find someone young and foolish who that idiot Z would just rush off to the training facility.

315

And that's when I found you. You've got quite a good connection to The Field, Alex. It made it easy to focus in on you. Oh, I've been planning your trip to The Dome for several months now. The first thing I did was send the orbs to destroy your home."

Alex watched his entire family run out of the house, past him and down the street—just as it happened the previous week. A moment later, four orbs appeared overhead, and the house blew up. The explosion went right through Alex and Erebus without any effect on them.

"Of course, I allowed Z to find out that the orbs were coming so he could get you out of there in time. By the way, nice job on the orbs, Alex. I thought they were going to blow you up. I'm so glad I didn't have to find someone else to replace you."

The scene changed, and Alex now stood next to Erebus in front of the home of Jawbone Fan.

"The next thing I knew, Z sent you through the portals to The Dome, just as I had hoped. Jawbone had already told me that the portal ran right through this little Mayan town of his, so watching for you wasn't very hard to do. I collapsed the tunnel between the two pyramids to give you a chance to come out here and discover Jawbone."

"I know you used Jawbone to help arrange of all this," Alex said.

"Oh yes, I sure did. And Jawbone did everything I wanted him to do."

"And now you're going to release Jawbone and let him roam around on the Earth?" Alex asked.

"Oh, for goodness sake, no! He expects me to of course. But why on Earth would I release him? All he would be is a problem to me. No, he can remain exactly where he is."

"I guess he told you where The Dome is."

"Not at all, Alex. He doesn't know where it is any more than you do. Outside of Z and Herabata, nobody knows where it is. No, if I wanted to find The Dome I had to get you into it, and then back out. Back to me, that is. And that wasn't easy to arrange, believe me. But I did!" He turned around, tilted his face up to the sky, and shouted, "I can hardly believe it, but I did it!"

He turned back around. His eyes were wide open, and he grinned right at Alex for a few seconds before composing himself.

"Where was I? Oh, yes, you see I couldn't take the portal jump myself to Herabata's training facility. Only people that Z gives permission to can travel that last portal jump to The Dome. But I knew that Z would naturally send your parents to find out who sent those orbs. So, I dropped some clues along a trail to lure your parents here to Jawbone, and then Jawbone sent them through the portal, and eventually to me. Then all I had to do was make sure it looked like your parents needed your help, and that Jawbone had all the answers to your questions."

The scene changed again, and Alex now stood next to Erebus floating above a sailboat in the middle of the water. Below them, Dion had just pulled Bhedi out of the water onto the deck.

Erebus pointed to the boat below and said, "And I see you certainly lost all faith in Z's abilities to protect your

317

parents when he couldn't even keep his little sailing facility safe."

A horrifying thought jumped into Alex's mind.

"That was you?" Alex shouted. "You held Bhedi under the water?"

"Of course," Erebus said matter-of-factly. "Once I knew where the sailing facility was, it became easy to breach. Although I do have to admit, it did take me a few years of searching my globe to find it."

Erebus turned away from the sailboat and looked at Alex. His face broke out into a proud smile.

"And then the three of you headed out to find your parents, just as I hoped you would." Erebus's face slowly turned serious again before he continued. "When you animated Jawbone, he told you to jump through the unmarked portal, just as I instructed him to."

Once more the scene changed, and Alex stood off to the side of the trail in China were the two motorcycles came to a halt in front of the mob.

"That dim-wit, Zhang, was supposed to just turn you around and have you jump right to me at the South Pole. But it looks like he made a better deal with the elders of that village. I guess they figured they could use you three against me somehow. Soon I'll repay the little traitor for that."

Then all the motorcycles sprang to life and headed toward Alex, Elka, and Maia. The membrane slammed down in front of them.

"I had to do something to save you from the mob. But unfortunately, I could only hold the membrane for a few moments." Erebus brought his Z-Con Prime out in front of him. "After all, this all happened on the other side of the

318

world from where I was, and I'm still learning how to use this thing."

"But how did you know we were in trouble?" Alex asked.

Erebus held his Z-Con a bit higher. A large 3-D hologram of the Earth appeared floating a few feet out in front of him.

"I used my globe," he said, pointing to the hologram. "I was told that Herabata has one of these in her office," he said. "Once I found out that she had one, well I just had to make one for myself." He spun the globe with his palm. "And since I knew exactly where you were in China, with this I could watch every move you made." He flicked his finger, and the globe disappeared.

"But why would the elders of the village possibly want Zhang to bring the three of us to them instead of you?" Alex asked.

"The people around this part of China had been worshiping this Z-Con Prime for a couple of thousand years. Never letting any outsiders in to mess with it. But one day, about fifty years ago, I stumbled in. You see I'm a geologist by trade and I was paying a visit to the area checking out the ancient Jade deposits. I saw all the shrines and temples dedicated to the Z-Con Prime they had. When I saw it, I recognized its powers right away."

Erebus walked down the dirt path a few feet, contemplating what he just said. He swung around and quickly walked back to Alex. "I'm not sure how I knew. But I did know it was powerful! I knew that I had to do whatever it took to get my hands on it. The villagers were praying to it—wasting it. With me, it was going to be useful again."

319

"But there aren't supposed to be any Z-Con Primes left," Alex said. "How did the village get one?"

Erebus walked away again, gazing around at the vast mountains surrounding them.

"From the beginning, Z realized that the Jade from this part of China was perfect for making Z-Cons," he said. "So, he set-up some Jade mines throughout the area. One day he sent his wife to inspect the operations. She was at the bottom of one of the deep mines when an earthquake hit. The entire mine collapsed right on top of her—over a thousand feet down. Z and Herabata assumed the Z-Con Prime was destroyed, so they let it be buried there for what they thought would be forever. The Jade in these mines had just about run out anyway. Z closed the whole operation down."

Erebus turned back and pointed over to the village.

"But the local villagers—well, they knew the Z-Con was something special. They had seen it being used to help with the construction of the mines. So, they and their descendants spent a couple of hundred years digging mine shafts down to find the lost Z-Con. And once they found it, the entire village worshipped it for over a thousand years—keeping it a secret." Erebus smiled. "That is until I came along and took it from them."

Erebus flicked his finger. Alex found himself back in the hall, standing where he just had left.

Erebus stepped up to his throne and sat down.

"For the last fifty years, I've been figuring out how this Z-Con works. I eventually used it to build my little home here, away from meddlesome eyes. But then I discovered there were two other Z-Con Primes. I realized that if I started using this one too much, the other primes would detect it. Z and Herabata could easily team up against me and take mine away. So, you see I'm going to have to destroy those other two Z-Con Primes first. And Z and Herabata of course."

"But they're both trying to protect the Earth!" Alex protested. "They need their Z-Con Primes to do it."

Erebus jumped up and headed toward Alex.

"Absolute fools!" he screamed. "They've been planning and training to defend the Earth for over four thousand years, and nothing much has ever happened. And nothing ever will. There's nobody out there who cares one way or the other about this little pebble in space!"

Erebus reached Alex and studied his face. After a few seconds, he turned away.

"In any case, it's all over now," Erebus said, more calmly. "You brought me the Z-Cons. Soon I'll know where The Dome is, and I'll destroy it. Then I'll take out the mountain in the Himalayas and Z right along with it. Nothing can interfere with me after that."

Dion poked his head out from behind a curtain on the left side of the room. Alex was stunned. How did he manage to get here? There was no time to think about it—Alex had to give Dion a chance to get to Erebus. He would have to stall to give Dion some time.

"But why do you need my Z-Con?" Alex asked. He took a few steps to the right and a little forward. "You already have a Z-Con Prime."

"Oh, not for its powers Alex. For its knowledge." Erebus stepped away from Alex. "Z-Cons have memories of where they've been. You see, Herabata doesn't allow Z-Cons to leave the protection of her training facilities—except for the

Z-Cons that the handful of the masters have. Masters know how to protect their Z-Cons in certain ways. But your Z-Con, well, once it connects to my Z-Con Prime, it's going to tell me exactly where The Dome is."

Alex stepped forward, and Erebus stepped back. That was as much as Alex could do. Dion would have to try it now.

"So, all I need from you, Alex, is to make a connection from your Z-Con to mine. Then my Z-Con will calculate where your Z-Con has been. Simple. Right?"

"No," Alex said defiantly. "Not simple. I'm not helping you!"

Erebus turned toward Elka and Maia.

"I'll tell you what. If you don't help me, and I mean right now, I'll start freezing your little friends into time bubbles." Erebus pointed his Z-Con at the girls. "Well? What do you say, Alex? Perhaps I should freeze one of them just to show you I mean business."

"No!" Alex yelled. There wasn't any more time. He shot Dion a quick look.

Erebus snapped his head back to Alex, and yelled, "Then go pick up your Z-Con and connect it to mine. Right now! I won't wait anymore."

Dion ran out from behind the curtain and headed right for Erebus's back. But without even turning around, Erebus calmly raised his Z-Con prime and Dion immediately halted. A purple membrane surrounded him, freezing him in place.

"Sorry, Dion," Erebus said, laughing. He walked over to him. "I've been just messing with you." He reached through the membrane and withdrew Dion's Z-Con from his hand.

He threw it on top of the other three Z-Cons near the base of the throne.

"You see, a Z-Con Prime can tell when any other Z-Con is approaching, so I knew the very instant you landed here from the portal jump. I've been just waiting for you to show yourself." He faced Alex again. "Pity, I had hoped it would be Z coming to save you, Alex. Or at least Herabata. But I guess Dion just had to play hero. Well, now I have another Z-Con to use."

Erebus turned his attention back to Elka and Maia. "One final time, Alex, connect to my Z-Con or watch your friends get put into time bubbles."

Alex had to try something—anything! He'd have to attack Erebus right now while he still had a chance, no matter how small the odds. He walked to the base of the throne and reached down to pick up his Z-Con. As soon as he had it in his hand, he lunged at Erebus. A membrane instantly formed between the two of them. Alex slammed into it and bounced off, falling to the floor.

"That was foolish, Alex. Do you think a little boy like you could ever surprise me?"

Erebus raised his Z-Con toward Elka.

"Goodbye, Elka," Erebus said. His eyes closed, and the top of his Z-Con began turning blue.

A blur shot past Alex, flying off the ground, toward Erebus's back. Alex couldn't believe what he saw. It was Mercure!

Mercure flipped over in the air and kicked his rear feet into the top of Erebus's right shoulder. Both of them crashed to the ground. Erebus rolled over and raised his Z-Con. Mercure jumped at it, his mouth wide open. But before he could reach it, a red beam of light shot out from the top of the Z-Con and slammed into Mercure's stomach. He flew backward, all the way to the wall behind the throne.

"Stupid dog!" Erebus screamed. He stood up, switched the Z-Con to his left hand and raised it at Mercure. The top started turning blue again.

Another blur came charging in from the left. This time it was Panda! She streaked in and bit down on Erebus's left arm, hard! Erebus screamed in agony and dropped the Z-Con. He ran away a few steps before falling to his knees, grabbing the wound. The membranes in front of Alex, Dion, Elka, and Maia instantly disappeared.

Erebus gathered himself up from the floor and charged back toward his Z-Con. Alex and Dion both lunged forward and tackled Erebus before he could reach it. Mercure and Panda circled, both of them growling, slowly closing in for another attack.

Diakonos suddenly materialized next to Erebus. He reached down, touched the top of Erebus's head, and they both disappeared.

Alex picked up the Z-Con Prime and sprung up off the floor. He gave a quick scan around to see if there was anyone else in the area to contend with. As far as he could tell they were alone, for the time being anyway.

"Hurry, get your Z-Cons," Alex said. "We better get out of here before they come back."

Elka and Maia had already picked up their Z-Cons and were also looking around for threats.

Dion made his way to the base of the throne and picked up his Z-Con. He grabbed Alex's Z-Con and tossed it over to him.

"Everyone, get behind that cart and push it out with us," Alex said.

"Where are we going?" Elka asked, stepping behind the cart holding their parent's stiff bodies.

"To that jet outside," Alex said.

Alex went over to Mercure, kneeled down next to him, and scratched him behind the ears.

"You all right buddy?"

"Well, that was sure something I never did before!"

"We better get going," Alex said. He and Mercure stood up and headed toward the doors on the other side of the huge hall. He glanced behind him and watched the others starting to push the cart ahead. "I'm not sure how much it'll help, but I'll go first with the Z-Con Prime," he said to everyone. "Maybe they'll be afraid of it and leave us alone."

Dion, Elka, and Maia followed Alex, with Mercure and Panda trotting along both sides of them, scanning around for any signs of trouble.

They headed out of the hall and down the long corridor, toward the door to the outside. Amazingly to Alex, nothing tried to stop them. He reached the door, cracked it open, and took a short look around.

"All right, as quick as we can," he shouted. "We've got to get inside that jet before we start freezing out there. Ready?'

Alex ran out in front. With three people pushing, the cart holding their parent's bodies went right through the frozen snow without much problem.

Halfway to the jet, Alex stopped and dropped to the ground.

The Z-Con Prime he was holding began glowing bright red—getting hotter and hotter in his hand. Before Alex could figure out what was going on, he had to drop it before it completely burned his hand. The Z-Con hit the snow and melted right through it, instantly sinking out of sight.

Alex stuck his hand in the snow to stop the burning pain and at the same time signaled for everyone else to keep moving ahead to the jet. The group continued past him, but Mercure stopped by his side.

"Can you keep going, Alex?"

"Yeah, it's not bad," Alex said. He picked his hand out of the snow. "Let's go."

Alex and Mercure ran ahead, catching up with everyone just as they reached the plane. Dion reached up and pulled the handle to release the door, and a small staircase unfolded to the ground. Alex, Mercure, and Panda immediately ran up inside the jet.

"Start handing everyone up to me," Alex shouted down. He drew his Z-Con out of his pocket.

One by one, Elka, Maia, and Dion picked up the stiff bodies of their parents and started handing them up toward Alex. Alex used his Z-Con to pull each one up into the jet. He landed them on the floor and slid them back to the aisle behind him, both dogs sniffing away at them as he did. After all four parents were on board, Alex headed for the cockpit.

He climbed into the left seat and scanned the instrument panel. Dion came forward and jumped into the right seat. He turned to Alex with a look of bewilderment on his face.

"I don't know what most of this stuff is," Dion said.

"We know what the important stuff is, so let's just go with that for now," Alex replied.

Dion pointed toward the window on Alex's left side "Well, we better go fast!" he said.

Alex turned and looked out the window. He saw Erebus standing next to the hole that the red-hot Z-Con Prime had created in the snow.

Erebus stood perfectly still, clutching his left arm up close to his chest, staring at the jet.

Diakonos dug furiously in the hole next to him, using his hands like shovels. Huge chunks of snow and ice flew twenty feet in the air as he chased after the sinking Z-Con Prime.

EIGHTEEN

Alex held out his Z-Con and thought about wanting a start-up checklist for the small jet. The list instantly appeared in front of him. He thought about wanting the checklist to indicate the area of the instrument panel that each step on the checklist pertained to, so he wouldn't have to search for it himself. There was an amazing number of switches and dials, and Alex certainly knew he didn't have any time to figure out where everything was.

One by one Alex followed the checklist's steps.

'Aux Power Unit—ON, Thrust to Idle, Fuel Flow—ON, Left and Right Ignition Switches—ON, Left Engine Start Button—ON.' The left engine wined up to power. Alex continued quickly through the steps until he reached the last item on the list. 'Parking Brake—OFF.'

The instant he released the brake, the checklist disappeared. Alex jammed the throttles forward and taxied the jet toward the end of the runway. The runway itself was nothing more than extremely hard packed snow. Alex figured that if Erebus created it and landed the jet on it, then he could certainly use it to take off from. In any case, there was nothing left to do but try. After all, who knew how long it would be before Diakonos would catch up to Erebus's Z-Con Prime.

The jet reached the end of the runway and Alex performed the last steps.

'Elevator Trim to TAKEOFF, Flaps—8 DEGREES, Pitot Heat—ON'.

"Hold on," he yelled back to Elka and Maia. "We're going!"

The takeoff checklist appeared before him. He took a huge gulp and looked over at Dion—maybe for a bit of support, but then again maybe to be told to stop. It sure wouldn't take much for someone to talk Alex out of it. After all, as far as he was concerned, this had to be the most ridiculous idea he ever had.

Dion just looked over at Alex, shrugged his shoulders and said, "Go for it."

Alex read off the last items on the takeoff list. 'Thrust to 40% then to FULL, Breaks—RELEASE'. The jet lurched forward and quickly increased its speed. The landing gear pounded up and down against the dense snow, bouncing the jet around as it did. The final items on the checklist appeared before Alex in red. 'Rotate at 130 KNOTS, Pitch—10 DEGREES UP'.

Alex looked at the airspeed indicator. When it said 130, he pulled back on the steering column, and the jet shot into the air. The few remaining steps appeared. 'RETRACT LANDING GEAR- Check Gear Lights, Set Cruise at 434 KNOTS'. When the list disappeared, Alex couldn't believe it. He was flying a plane that wanted to go five hundred miles per hour.

Dion reached over and bumped Alex's shoulder with his fist. Alex nodded and looked straight ahead.

Alex kept the wings level and the jet heading up, directly away from the runway. Within minutes Erebus's facility in Antarctica fell out of sight.

The sky above was light blue with hardly a cloud in sight. At least they've got good weather to work with, Alex thought. But where were should they go? He had no idea. Alex had to find someplace to land, but there was nothing but freezing blue water below him, and the only land that he knew about was directly behind him, toward Erebus. He couldn't think of where to head.

A flashing indicator on the dashboard said, "LR CAB PRESS FAIL." Alex brought up his Z-Con and asked for an explanation.

"It's a warning that the plane is not pressurized," he said to Dion. "We'll have to stay low so we can keep breathing up here." He took hold of the steering column. "I'll level out at ten thousand feet," Alex said, moving the steering column to make the change.

"I'm going to change our heading a few degrees. I don't want Erebus to be able to figure out where we're headed. I hope he can't use his Z-Con to mess with us if he can't visualize exactly where we are."

"How could he tell where we are?" Dion asked.

"He's got a 3-D globe, just like Vizier Herabata's. He could be searching the area right now, looking for us."

After he altered course and everything in the jet quieted down some, Alex's mind started racing. He was sure there were things he should be doing, but his mind had gone wild. Only questions consumed him, but no answers. Where should he head? Would the plane stay in the air without problems much longer? Would his parents be okay inside their time bubbles if they left the vicinity of Erebus? Would they all be dead soon because of the decisions Alex had made? No, he thought, this was a horrible mistake, and they would all end up paying the price for it. If only he had stayed on the ground. If only he had figured out something else instead of this insane plan.

Dion hit him in the arm. "Are you all right?" Alex heard him, felt him, but ignored him. Dion hit him again, hard this time. "Alex, are you okay?"

It was like a switch being thrown. Alex's mind cleared.

"Yeah. Okay. I'm Okay." Alex said. "Any ideas what we should do?"

"No," Dion said. "Just keep flying I guess. We're bound to see some land soon, shouldn't we?" He stared at Alex, apparently looking for some sign of hope.

"I don't know," was the best Alex could come up with. He gave it a few seconds more thought. "If we were on the coast of Antarctica and we're heading north, then we would have to find the tip of South America or even Africa, but I don't have any idea if we're heading for either one of them."

Elka and Maia popped their heads into the cockpit. "What's up?" Maia asked. He pointed to the instrument panel.

"Get your Z-Cons and see if you can figure out all this stuff," Alex said. "Dion, see if you can figure out the navigation system. Elka and Maia, try to find out if there is anything else I should be doing to keep this thing flying. I'm going to look into the radios and landing procedures, just in case we come by some land."

A few moments after they started their searches, Alex was looking at landing procedures when they disappeared from his view.

"Something happened," he shouted out. "I can't access anything with my Z-Con."

"Me neither," Dion said in shock. "Mine just stopped working."

Elka and Maia started shaking their Z-Cons, moving them all around to see if it helped. They shook their heads at Alex.

"Maybe Erebus found his Z-Con Prime," Alex said. "He might have a way to shut ours off."

"Quick," Alex said behind him to Elka and Maia. "See if you can find any manuals around here. Anything that would tell us how to fly this thing."

Elka and Maia went to work, first looking in every nook and cranny in the cockpit, then back in the main cabin, but soon returning.

"We can't find anything," Elka said. She sounded scared.

"Well…we'll just have to keep going," Alex said, but he couldn't find a way to make it sound reassuring.

Things turned quiet in the cockpit as everybody began digesting the events of the last couple of hours. It seemed almost unreal to Alex that he would be sitting here, in the cockpit of a jet, trying to figure out a way that everyone would survive the flight. But now that he had time to think, something else jolted his brain. He turned to Dion.

"And just how did you manage to end up saving us back there?" he asked with a certain degree of astonishment.

Dion turned to Mercure and Panda for a couple of seconds before turning back to Alex to answer.

"Well, when none of you came back in an hour like you said you were going to, I went to go get Vizier Herabata. I ran into Mercure and Panda sitting right outside the portal room. I guess we didn't fool them much when we tried to sneak out last night. Anyway, they ran past me into the room and jumped through the center portal, so I just followed along."

Elka laughed and scratched Panda on the top of her head.

"And that sounded like a good plan to you?" she asked.

While Panda spoke with Elka and Maia, Mercure moved forward and put his paws up on the center console.

"Look, Alex, our job is to take care of you. You know, keep you out of trouble. We were hoping we could just jump to wherever you were and bring you back before anybody at the school noticed that you were gone. I didn't know the three of you would be traveling all over the world actually searching for trouble."

"But we kept it a secret," Alex said. "How did you know what we were all up to?"

"Please..." Mercure said sarcastically. He headed back to the cabin. *"As if I couldn't figure out what you were up to."* He passed by Panda, and they both gave a small yelp to each other. Alex thought maybe they were laughing.

When Mercure left, Dion continued, "Anyway, we saw your note on the floor in the Mayan pyramid, and we followed you through the portal jump to try and catch up. When we landed in China, there was a big crowd of really angry people standing outside the cave. They saw us arrive, but they wouldn't come into the cave. All of them just stood outside screaming at us in Chinese. I tried to ask if they knew where you were, but they didn't seem to be in a mood to talk. They just kept screaming 'return the stone' over and over. Any idea what that meant?"

"Yeah, I'll tell you about it later," Alex said.

"Well, I thought at that point it was time to go get some help, so we took the portal jump back out of there. We landed on the ice sheet in front of Erebus's building. The door wasn't locked, so we went inside, and when we saw what was going on, well after that…I kind of made it up on the spur of the moment."

No one spoke much after that. The jet flew on for almost another hour and a half. There just wasn't much for anybody to do. Elka and Maia went back to the cabin and started talking to their parents, telling them about everything that happened so far. Alex supposed they hoped their parents were able to hear them—maybe giving them a small amount of comfort. He made a few attempts to get something on the instrument panel to tell him about where they were, but every time he pushed a button or turned a knob he worried that he might make things worse.

Dion took some stabs at the radio. He turned the dial on one of the panels to 121.5. That was the emergency frequency they had learned about in class. Dion called over and over on it, but nobody responded. Not a lot of people near the South Pole Alex figured.

Alex turned his head to the left when he saw a black airplane materialized out of nowhere, right alongside the jet—just slightly ahead of it. It was the most unusual plane

Alex had ever seen. It didn't seem to have much of a wing on it, and the shape looked more circular than the long tube you might expect on a normal plane.

"Dion, look!"

The plane slowed down slightly and settled back to a position just outside Alex's left window. It was close enough for Alex to see the pilot. He wore a rather large helmet with a dark green visor pulled down in front of it. His flight suit was somewhat lumpy and completely black. He held up a Z-Con and pointed to it. The pilot must have wanted Alex to make a connection.

Alex held up his Z-Con to the window, shook his head, and dropped it to the floor. That seemed to baffle the pilot somewhat. After a few seconds, the pilot held up his fingers. First one finger, then two, then four. He did it again. Dion tapped Alex on the shoulder.

"I think he means to tune the radio to 124," Dion said.

"Let's give it a try," Alex said, scrambling to put on his radio headset.

Dion pushed a few buttons on the radio panel and said, "That should do it. Give it a try."

Alex pushed the radio button on the control column.

"Can you hear me?" he said.

"Roger, Alex. This is Flight Leader Johansen. I can't tell you how glad we are to find you. Z sent about fifty of us out here looking for you. I'll let the others know you've been found. What's the status of your plane?"

"I don't know much. We've been flying okay for about an hour and a half. All I've been doing is trying to hold altitude and the heading. We haven't been able to figure out much on the instrument panel. And our Z-Cons stopped working. We're not sure why."

"That's okay, Alex. You're heading toward the tip of South America. Turn now to a heading of 287."

Alex made the slight turn and said, "Okay, the heading is now 287."

"Great," Johansen said. "Now tell me how much fuel you have remaining. There should be four fuel indicators. Read the one that says Fuel Total."

"Okay, it says 10.2."

"No, Alex, it looks like you're reading one of the wing tip tanks. Those tanks are labeled Right and Left. Read the one that says Fuel Total."

"That's the one I'm reading. Now it says 10.1."

The radio fell silent.

"Is it that bad?" Alex asked.

"Well…actually…you're about twenty minutes from the nearest runway, and you have only a few minutes worth of fuel left. It looks like you're going to have to ditch it in the water. Standby."

"We can't! Our parents are on the plane. They're unconscious. If we land in the water, they'll all drown."

"Copy that, Alex. Standby. I'm getting in touch with Z."

Another plane materialized off the right side of the plane, just outside of Dion's window. This plane was much bigger. It looked like it had enough room in the cockpit for two or three pilots, but there was only one pilot in it.

After a couple of minutes, Johansen came back on the radio.

"Alex, I spoke with Z. He is going to see if he can get one of the school's masters to make a portal jump to the inside of the plane on your right side."

"Can someone do that?" Alex asked.

"I'm not sure," Johansen said. "I don't think anyone's ever tried to make a portal jump onto a moving plane before. It might not work."

"What if it doesn't? What would happen to the master?"

"Let's not worry about that right now, Alex. Your engines are going to flame out any minute. When they do, follow me down. I'll descend at an angle that will keep you in the air for the longest amount of time possible, okay?"

"Yeah, okay. But what about our parents? If the plane breaks up into the water and starts sinking, we won't be able to …"

The left engine flamed out. Almost immediately after that, the right engine quit. The nose of the plane started dropping, so Alex pulled back on the column to raise it back up.

"Alex, I want you to move the control column up and down to keep the plane descending at the same angle I am."

Alex looked out the left window, eyeing Johansen's plane, trying to keep the plane in the same formation with it. Minutes passed as the jet slowly lost altitude.

Dion turned toward his side window and without turning back to Alex said, "It looks like there's someone popping in and out of the other plane's cockpit! He keeps appearing and disappearing."

Alex didn't dare look away from his window. It was all he could do to keep the jet flying alongside Johansen.

"Can you see who it is?" Alex asked.

"It looks like Master Puma," Dion said incredulously. "I think he just made it!"

"Alex, this is Johansen. The other aircraft is going to fly directly on top of you. Whatever you do, do not pull up or slow your rate of descent—you'll end up crashing into them. Master Puma is going to use his Z-Con to pull up on your plane. Once he does, you let go of the controls, and he'll level you out."

"Okay, but can he lift a whole plane? Is that even possible?

"If anyone can do it, it's going to be him. To tell you the truth, he's the only one I know who would have even tried that portal jump."

Alex felt the jet lurch upwards and vibrate widely.

"Alex, let go of the controls!" Johansen said.

Alex let go, and the shaking halted.

"Okay, great!" Alex shouted. He punched Dion in the arm and turned toward the rear of the jet. He yelled back at everybody. "Master Puma's got a hold of us with his Z-Con. He's going to keep us in the air." When he turned back to the cockpit, reality hit him again. What could they do next? How are they going to get this thing on the ground?

He keyed up the mike, and after thinking about it for a few seconds said, "What do we do now?"

"Alex, we're turning you toward an old landing field that we used a long time ago near the tip of South America," Johansen responded. "You'll have to try landing there. It's not in very good shape, but it's got a long runway. Without any thrust reversers, you're going to need every foot of it. Z just released the protection dome covering it, so you should see it on the horizon in a little bit."

"Okay, I'm looking," Alex replied. He and Dion scanned through the windshield for the next several minutes, trying to spot land.

Elka and Maia came back to the front. Mercure and Panda squeezed up against them.

"Can we do anything?" Elka asked.

"I'm not sure how this landing is going to go," Alex told them. "You two will have to be ready to get our parents out of here as fast as you can if things go wrong. Make sure the dogs stay right with you."

He looked at Mercure and Panda. "You keep them safe back there, okay?" Both dogs nodded, backed away, and headed toward the rear. Alex turned back to Elka and Maia. "We all better get strapped in now," he said. Elka moved forward and hugged Alex. Maia did the same to Dion. A moment later, they both headed back to the cabin.

A few minutes later Alex spotted a gray runway pointing out from the southern tip of an island they were approaching. He keyed up the radio.

"I got the runway in sight. Now what?"

"I'll tell you step-by-step," Johansen said, "Follow my instructions, and you'll be fine. Standby." After several more seconds, Johansen came back on the air. "Alex, Master Puma's going to let go of you now. You've got enough altitude to get to the runway and circle it once before you land. Just do what I tell you to do, okay?"

"Okay, we're ready," Alex said with as much confidence as he could muster.

A few seconds later, the plane bounced up and down a couple of times, and the nose started dropping again. Alex pulled back on the column to control the descent, following

339

Johansen's lead. The jet's nose pointed right at the center of the abandoned airfield.

Without warning, four glowing orbs appeared about a half mile out in front of the jet. Flight Leader Johansen started immediately barking orders.

"Flight One Seven Five, take out those four orbs in front of me. Two Eight Niner, handle the ones materializing over the airfield center. Alex, stay with me no matter what got it?"

"Got it, but I'm not sure…"

"Just stay focused and keep right alongside me."

Alex kept his gaze out the left window, keeping the jet aligned with the fighter. Johansen kept his plane steadily descending. Four other fighters materialized and zoomed in and out of Alex's view as they chased after the orbs.

The fighters shot blue beams of light at the orbs, instantly vaporizing them as they struck.

Someone called out to Johansen, "Flight leader, four more popped up directly over you."

Johansen threw his plane into a dive. Alex followed along, making his stomach float up into his throat. Johansen turned to the left and then to the right. Alex tried his best to keep up with him, but the jet wouldn't change course nearly as fast as Johansen's. Two fighters dropped down from above and passed Alex's window in a blur. Johansen's plane came back to level, and Alex followed right along although feeling a bit shaky.

"Okay, Alex, you're going to be over the runway in just a few seconds," Johansen yelled. "No time to circle it. I've got you pointing right at the runway centerline now. Drop your landing gear and set the flaps all the way down."

Alex pushed down the gear lever and felt the wheels slam into place. He moved the flap lever down to the last notch.

"Alex, I don't know how hard that runway is going to bounce you around, but it is imperative that you stop before you reach the end. There's a fifty-foot drop off into the ocean just past it. Keep this angle until you have to flare. I'm moving out below you to keep the way clear."

"Gotcha!"

Alex now switched his gaze to the front windshield, doing his best to keep the jet on course for the runway directly in front of him. He was just seconds away from landing.

From high above and in directly front of him, a single orb came plummeting down toward the jet—and Alex couldn't do a thing about it. He was just too low—there was absolutely no room to maneuver. He had to keep the jet heading toward the end of the runway if he was going to have any chance of landing on it. The orb turned slightly and headed directly for the jet's windshield. Alex and Dion turned their heads to the side just as it was going to collide.

Johansen's plane shot up from below and absorbed the orb's full impact, right into his plane's belly. His plane veered away toward the right, spinning wildly—out of Alex's path. Alex looked forward again—the runway was right there! He pulled back on the steering column, leveling the jet out five feet above the ground. The jet quickly lost the airspeed it needed to keep itself in the air, and it dropped toward the concrete. Alex gave one last pull on the column to soften the blow, but they hit hard.

The impact bounced the jet back into the air a few feet before it slammed back down again. Two more times the jet slammed into the concrete and bounced back up, but on the next hit the main wheels absorbed the blow and the jet screamed down the centerline of the runway. Alex pressed down on both brake pedals, but it only had a small effect. The jet started hitting potholes in the concrete. The landing gear pounded in and out of them, each time causing different sides of the jet to fly up off the ground and crash back down again. It took everything Alex had to keep the jet on the runway.

A horrifying sight came into view. The runway end was coming up quickly, and the jet had hardly started to slow down. Alex pointed downward, toward Dion's feet.

"You're going to have to help me turn this thing," he shouted over the noise and vibration. "When I tell you, press down on the right pedal. Hard! Okay?"

"Got it," Dion yelled back to him.

The airspeed indicator finally started showing the jet decreasing in speed. But now they were only a few seconds from the end of the runway, and the cliff just past it.

"Push!" Alex yelled at the top of his voice.

Alex and Dion both bore down on the foot pedals, and the jet veered off the runway to the right. It hit the grass strip that lined the side of the runway, and the jet's tail section spun halfway around. The plane now headed straight backward—still toward the cliff!

"Dion, change to the left pedal!" Alex yelled as he also switched.

The jet rotated around in the other direction and rocketed back onto the runway—this time sliding sideways down the centerline. Just as it approached the runway end, the right landing gear dug into a deep pothole—jolting the jet to complete stop and lifting the left wing four feet off the ground before slamming back down.

Instantly, there was complete silence. Alex and Dion sat motionless, staring out the front windshield.

After a few seconds, Dion took a deep breath, undid his seat belts, lifted his armrest, and started slowly rising out of his seat.

"Good landing," he said to Alex with a big smile on his face. He gave him a light bump on the arm and said, "Maybe we should get the hell out of here."

Alex could only nod his agreement. Feeling a bit numb, he followed Dion out of the cockpit to the front of the cabin where Elka, Maia, and the two dogs had gathered near the door. Maia was struggling to open it.

"Help me—it's stuck," Maia said. Elka and Dion joined in to help her and after several hard tugs on the handle the door popped open, releasing the staircase to the ground.

Everyone descended the stairs and gathered at the base of it. An enormous gust of wind slammed down on them from above as a huge plane hovered past, landing about thirty feet away. It was the plane that Master Puma had portal jumped onto. Its engines wound down, and the area fell silent again. A door at the rear of the plane opened downward to the ground, forming a ramp. Several men and women dressed in dark flight suits ran out and headed over to the jet. A few of them pushed medical gurneys. Several others carried medical kits.

They reached the staircase, and Alex shouted at them, "Our parents are inside!"

Alex led them up the stairs, down the aisle, and to the frozen bodies on the floor.

"A guy used a Z-Con Prime to put them in a time bubble," Alex told them. "Can you get them out of it?"

"A time bubble?" one of the team said. "I've seen these at our research facility. But they could only form them around really small objects, and for only a couple of milliseconds."

"Yeah…okay…but can you get them out of it?" Alex asked.

"I'm sure we can," another one on the team said looking up at Alex. "Frankly, it's harder to keep the time bubble stable than it is to collapse it. But I think it's going to be best to take them back just the way they are—then release them from it in the lab. Okay?"

"Okay," Alex said. "Just hurry."

"You should head back down to your friends and give us some room. We'll get them right out."

Alex turned and walked away, but he stopped after a couple of steps and turned back around.

"What happened to Johansen?" he asked the medics. When they all turned to him with a quizzical look, he added, "You know, the plane that took the hit from the orb."

The medics turned back to the parents. One of them said, "Haven't heard anything about him, sorry."

Alex headed out of the jet again and descended the stairs. He heard several other planes landing nearby. Elka, Maia, and Dion stood at the foot of the stairs, waiting for news.

"They said they could help," Alex said to everyone. "They're taking them back to a lab, and they'll release them from the time bubbles when they get there."

Elka and Maia put their arms around each other's shoulders. "That's good news—we were so worried," Elka said smiling. Maia nodded her head several times.

Master Puma descended the ramp at the rear of his plane. He walked over to Alex, Dion, Elka, and Maia, limping on his right foot the whole way. When he reached the jet, he stood stiffly in front of everyone for a few seconds. There was a small tear coming out of his right eye, as if from pain. But then a wide smile washed across his face.

"Are you all okay?" he asked.

Elka and Maia dashed over to him and squeezed in on him from the left side—Alex and Dion took his right. After a few seconds, Master Puma put his left arm around the girls and painfully raised his right arm, placing it on top of Alex's and Dion's shoulders. Alex backed away and moved in front of him, looking him over.

"Thanks for saving us," Alex said. "Are you all right? Did you get hurt?"

Elka, Maia, and Dion stepped back to inspect him.

"Will you be okay?" Maia asked. "What happened to your leg?"

"You don't need to be concerned about that," Master Puma said. "I'll be fine. That portal jump kept slamming me into the wall of the cockpit. But Z will fix me back up." He nodded reassuringly. "He always does."

Elka and Maia moved in on either side of him, helping him to sit down on the staircase of the jet.

Someone tapped Alex on his back, and he spun around. A man in a dark flight suit stood there, lifting his helmet's visor and extending his right hand.

"I'm Flight Leader Johansen," he said.

Alex grabbed his hand, hardly being able to contain himself. "You're all right? I mean...I can't believe it...I thought the orb destroyed you!"

Johansen removed his helmet and put it under his arm.

"No, those orbs aren't much of a match for our shields," he said. "It was your jet we were worried about."

Dion stepped over and shook his hand. All Dion could muster was, "Thanks."

Johansen let go of Dion and took a step back to take a good look at the two of them. After a few seconds, he said, "So what do you think? Maybe a few more lessons before you try that again?"

"How about we never try that again," Alex said.

"Oh, you'll be surprised how much of this kind of stuff you'll run into after you graduate," Johansen said. "Let's just say you should wait until then and have something a little more substantial to fly around in."

"Yes, sir," Alex and Dion said, almost at the same time.

Johansen gave a slight salute and said, "Good luck. Best be getting on that transport plane. They'll be taking everyone back to the Himalayan facility—then they can get your parents fixed up." He took a few steps backward, turned, and headed back to his fighter plane.

By this time both Elka and Maia had moved off, helping Master Puma over to the ramp of the transport plane. The medics had loaded the four parents onto gurneys, and they were heading back to the plane as well. Mercure and Panda followed right alongside them. Alex and Dion followed everyone else up the plane's ramp, and they sat down on a long bench that lined the interior wall of the plane. They both watched all the medics monitoring the parents.

"They'll get them out," Dion said.

A few seconds later, Alex slowly nodded his head.

The plane took off vertically and headed away. Through a window behind him, Alex watched the small jet on the end of the runway grow smaller and smaller. Elka and Maia eventually came over and sat down next to him and Dion, everyone now intently watching their parents.

Elka and Maia looked over at Alex and Dion. Elka placed her hand on top of Alex's shoulder and turned back to watch her parents again.

"We can't believe it either," she said to no one in particular.

The plane went faster and faster, and higher and higher. At one point, Alex could see the curvature of the Earth out the window.

It took less than twenty minutes for the transport plane to reach Z's facility in the Himalayans, entering it through a huge tunnel carved out of the snow-covered mountainside. As soon as the transport touched down, the medics whisked their parents off into the bowels of the vast and busy hanger. Mercure and Panda ran down the ramp right after them, needing to sprint to keep up with the gurneys. Alex also tried to go after them, but to his great surprise, he found Master Kattan standing at the base of the ramp blocking his way. Dion, Elka, and Maia came up behind Alex and gathered with him in front of the master.

"Let them go," Master Kattan said, with his two hands in the air. "They're in good hands. Don't worry—we'll be meeting up with them soon. In the meantime, I want you all to come with me."

They all fell in line behind Master Kattan and followed him through a maze of large hangers, each one filled with many types of strange looking aircraft. The hangers seemed to go on and on into the mountainside.

They arrived at the portal room—the same portal room that Alex and everyone had used previously on their first trip to the training facility. Alex's mind was in somewhat of a fog just thinking about the condition that his parents were in, and he didn't pay much attention to the portal jumps that Master Kattan now led them through. They went through the Egyptian pyramids, the Mayan pyramids, and finally to the portal receiving room at The Dome. Master Kattan led them through another long series of tunnels, eventually coming up to the base of the main staircase in Vizier Herabata's residence.

The group

made the long climb up the stairs, with Alex bringing up the rear. At the top, Master Kattan stood in front of the entrance to Herabata's office.

"Take a seat here."

Everyone quietly sat down on the long wooden bench that ran off to the side of the doorway. Master Kattan continued into the office alone, shutting the thick door behind him.

Alex and his teammates waited outside without saying much of anything to each other. They all seemed a bit happier to have a little more peace and quiet – at least for a while longer anyway. Alex was anxiously contemplating the enormous trouble they were all about to face.

The group sat there quietly for well over an hour.

Master Kattan finally appeared at the door and signaled for everyone to enter. He remained outside and shut the door behind them.

Alex tagged along with everyone else, down the long center aisle, and soon found himself standing with his friends in front of Vizier Herabata's desk, confronted by her and Z. Up to this point, Alex had not been paying much attention to what was going on around him, but as soon as Z started speaking, his mind seemed to clear up. He figured that Z and Herabata would now be telling him how he would no longer be welcome at the school and that he had to go home as soon as his parents were well enough to take him away.

"First, I want you to tell us what happened and why you left The Dome last night," Z said. "Start from the very beginning. Alex—go ahead."

Alex took a deep breath and started in on the story. He spent the next thirty minutes detailing everything that happened to them over the last couple of days—particularly the events of the last few hours. When he finished, Z walked behind Herabata's desk and spent a few minutes whispering back and forth with her. At some points, they seemed to be incredibly angry. Eventually, they finished, and Z walked back around the desk and stood in front of Alex before addressing everyone.

Alex felt that this was it. Now that they would be expelling him, this would be the only chance he would get to ask questions and get some answers—and perhaps get a chance to tell Z and Herabata about the outrage he felt for the two of them letting his parents end up in the condition he found them in.

Z folded his arms in front of his chest.

"Neither Vizier Herabata or I can find a way to condone what you did…" Z said with an intense tone of disapproval. He scanned everyone's faces for a couple of seconds. "But because of your actions we now know what has been causing the anomalies we've been noticing in the Zero Point Field over the last few years. Coupled with the fact that you rescued your parents from an incredibly horrifying state, Vizier Herabata and I wish to extend to you our extreme gratitude and thanks."

Alex was stunned.

Z stepped forward a couple of feet before continuing.

"Your efforts, although certainly outside of what is considered to be the rules of this training facility, have significantly secured the safety of our community and the world in general. Now that we know about Erebus and his acquisition of our Z-Con Prime, we can start to track him down and eliminate the threat he represents to us."

Z looked at Alex directly.

"You have some questions, Alex?" he asked.

Alex, still feeling quite taken back by Z's reaction to their journey, could only think of the one question that had been bothering him for the last few hours.

"How did Erebus fool our parents into walking into a trap?" Alex asked. "I mean, they were trying to track him down, right? Wouldn't they be looking out for something like that?"

"Your parents didn't know that Erebus had a Z-Con Prime, Alex," Z said. "A regular Z-Con is limited on what it can do, but a Z-Con Prime has many powers. Erebus used his to influence how The Field acted on your parent's thoughts and how they would react when confronted by him. The Field has many ways it can influence us, Alex."

Z strolled behind the desk again, stood next to Vizier Herabata, and continued.

"For instance, don't you think it quite remarkable that all four of you chose Jade stones for your Z-Cons? Did the Zero Point Field influence you to do that? That single choice allowed all of you to be assigned to one section in the Jade Division and together figure out that your parents were in trouble—and then decide what you could do to help them. If you had selected different colored stones, you would have all ended up in different divisions and probably would have never gotten together to do that."

Alex nodded. Since he had Z and Vizier Herabata's attention, he figured now would be a good time to ask about something that had been puzzling him for days.

"I was climbing up one of the pyramids in Mexico, the first time we were heading here," Alex said. "A white light shot out of the top of the pyramid while I was struggling on the rocks, and all of a sudden I jumped up right to where I wanted to be." Dion, Elka, and Maia shot a quizzical look at each other. Alex moved forward a step. "I didn't use a Z-Con or anything. I can't figure it out."

Vizier Herabata raised her chin a few inches and gently stroked it with her right hand.

"You could have made that happen by using the huge volume of rock inside the pyramid as a kind of make-shift Z-

Con," she said. "Very good, Alex, not many students your age would be able to do that. You always seem to impress. Do you have any other questions?"

Dion stepped forward.

"I have one," he said. "How did you know to send all those planes out to rescue us?"

Z stepped forward and stood next to Vizier Herabata.

"When Erebus used his Z-Con Prime to reach out and deactivate all your Z-Cons, we detected the enormous change in the Zero Point Field on Vizier Herabata's globe," Z said. He pointed to the 3-D globe in the corner of the room. "We could tell that it was your Z-Cons he de-activated, and we saw the general area of the world where it happened. That's when we went out looking for you. Up to now, Erebus must have been very careful about not using all the powers of his Z-Con Prime in such a forceful way, or we would have detected him sooner."

Master Kattan returned to the entrance and signaled Z and Herabata for attention.

"We're ready," he said across the room.

Z and Vizier Herabata walked out past Alex, Elka, Maia, and Dion. Herabata gave a slight tap on everyone's shoulders as she passed.

"Follow us," Z ordered.

The entire group headed out of the office, down the staircase and outside the building. They walked across The Dome to the center core and took a staircase down toward the assembly room below it—the same room where Alex and the others had received their Z-Cons when they first arrived.

The group walked into a side room and there, in the far corner, were Mercure, Panda, and all four of their parents. Alex, Maia, and Elka raced over and grabbed each of their parents around the middle. Mercure and Panda ran around, barking their excitement, and periodically jumping up on someone's shoulders.

Alex pulled away from his parents and then lunged back to his mother, hugging her as hard as he could.

"Alex, they told us what you all did," Janet said to him as the hugging continued. When they finally broke apart, she said, "That was a terrible idea, Alex, I hope you know that!" she scolded him. When the smile would not leave Alex's face, she said, "But I'm sure glad you found us."

Alex couldn't say a word—he just turned to his father and gave him the same hard hug.

As the two of them held each other Miguel said, "Alex, they told us that if you want to follow us home tonight, you can. We're going to Mexico City to get back with your little sister. You know, Alex...you weren't supposed to be here until next semester anyway. It might be for the best."

Alex released his hold on Miguel and stared at him for a few seconds before composing himself enough to answer.

"Well...I think I better stay here, Dad. You know— finish out the semester. I'm already on a flight team and well..." He looked over to Elka and Maia hugging their parents. Then he looked over at Dion kneeling against the wall playing with the still excited Mercure and Panda. He turned back to his mother and father, and said, "I just think I should stay." After a few seconds, the two of them smiled and nodded their approval.

Master Kattan came up behind the group.

"Everything's ready," he announced. He pointed to Alex, Elka, Maia, and Dion. "The four of you please come with me."

Alex gave one last quick hug to his mother and father, and joined everyone in line behind Master Kattan, somewhat concerned that once again he had no idea what to expect. They all moved across the auditorium stage, looking out past the spotlights into the crowd. The entire school had once again assembled. Z and Vizier Herabata stood next to each other in the center of the stage.

"Line up here to my right," Master Kattan told them. With a little juggling, they stood next to each other in a straight line.

Vizier Herabata took out her Z-Con Prime and raised it in her right hand.

"Everyone, please rise," she said softly.

The entire student body stood as one.

"As you all know by now, we are here for a special changing of colors," she said.

All the students in the crowd raised their right hand, revealing their arm bracelets. Each one held their Z-Cons out in front of them.

Vizier Herabata turned to Alex, Dion, Elka, and Maia.

"Please raise your right arms," she said to them.

Alex raised his arm along with his three friends. Almost immediately a warm feeling engulfed the area around his bracelet.

Vizier Herabata walked down the line. She touched her Z-Con Prime to Elka's bracelet, and it slowly turned from white to yellow. She moved on to Maia, and then to Dion, both of their bracelets turning the same yellow color. She continued to Alex, and when her Z-Con touched his bracelet, it instantly turned orange. Vizier Herabata stopped a brief second in front of him and smiled before continuing, stopping just on the other side of him.

She turned back to the crowd and said, "Our congratulations and thanks to these brave students."

The entire crowd roared in applause. It went on and on, with no sign of slowing.

A strong feeling came over Alex as he stood there with his arm in the air, his parents watching him from the side of the stage, and his three friends next to him. A broad smile burst across his face.

The Earth Defense Operations School was exactly where he belonged.

Epilogue

The end of the semester came far too quickly as far as Alex was concerned. But on the plus side, he was now an excellent pilot, sailor, and the self-defense classes he took with Mercure were the most fun he ever had with his dog.

Alex, Elka, Maia, and Dion did well in their competitions and had an exciting time during the semester. But it was certainly time for a break and the entire school had a month off before beginning the next semester.

Alex met up with his mother and father in Mexico City, and the family spent the month there at his aunt's house. Alex felt wonderful being back with his sister Aura, and the two of them spent a great deal of time exploring the city together, with Mercure keeping them out of too much trouble.

On the final night of his months' vacation Alex climbed into bed, and as usual, Mercure curled up on the floor next to him. As Alex dozed off, it dawned on him that even though he thought he would miss having his Z-Con with him when he left The Dome, it turned out that he didn't miss it that much at all and had a great time without it. Nevertheless, he looked forward to getting back to the training facility, and to a new set of classes.

At a few minutes past midnight, Mercure woke up, trotted down the stairs, and headed out the back door of the house. He came to a stop in front of a small hole in the middle of the backyard. A minute later, Carl Bellon launched out of the hole and quickly turned, just in time to brace himself against Mercure's large paws. After a few seconds of stumbling around with Mercure on his shoulders, Bellon enthusiastically scratched both sides of his neck.

"Mercure! How ya doing?"

Bellon stiffened his back and looked around.

"Tough times tonight, old fella. We have to talk to Miguel right away!"

Mercure dropped to the ground and hung his head.

"Not again…"

We hope you've enjoyed

'Alex Vega and the Oracle of Mayans.'

Please share your thoughts about this book with your friends! Word-of-mouth is vital for us to let everyone know about the exciting world of Alex Vega. If you enjoyed the book, please leave a review on Amazon (5 stars means you loved it), even if it's just a sentence or two. That's how other readers will know that *Alex Vega and the Oracle of Mayans* is a great story. Your reviews are very much appreciated. To leave a review, go to :

Amazon.com

Then type in - *Alex Vega and the Oracle of the Mayans* – scroll down till you see the little box that says: **Write a Review** (to the right of the line of Stars)**.** Click on it, and the review section will pop up. Make sure you highlight the stars on top, then write your review.

If you leave a review and would like to become a member of our Advance Team, send the name that you left your Amazon review under to:

AlexVegaSeries@gmail.com.

You'll receive emails whenever there is a sneak preview of the next book, free short stories, or news on any contests and specials that we offer - less than one email a month, promise!

For more information on Alex and his friends, join us at these sites Our Website contains a Blog that has interesting information on the characters and other facts:

Website – www.AlexVegaSeries.com

Facebook- https://www.facebook.com/AlexVegaSeries

Twitter – https://twitter.com/alexvegaseries

Made in the USA
Lexington, KY
20 February 2019